About the author

Nathan Dylan Goodwin was born and raised in Hastings, East Sussex. Schooled in the town, he then completed a Bachelor of Arts degree in Radio, Film and Television Studies, followed by a Master of Arts degree in Creative Writing at Canterbury Christ Church University. A member of the Society of Authors, he has completed a number of successful local history books about Hastings, as well as several works of fiction, including the acclaimed Forensic Genealogist series. His other interests include theatre, reading, photography, running, skiing, travelling and, of course, genealogy. He is a qualified teacher, member of the Guild of One-Name Studies and the Society of Genealogists, as well as being a member of the Sussex Family History Group, the Norfolk Family History Society, the Kent Family History Society and the Hastings and Rother Family History Society. He lives in Kent with his husband, son and dog.

CU00253896

By the same author

The Sterling Affair
by
Nathan Dylan Goodwin

For Rhiannon, Gavin,
Lily, Leo & Max

Abstract

'Thousands of government papers detailing some of the most controversial episodes in 20th-century British history have vanished after civil servants removed them from the country's National Archives and then reported them as lost... Almost 1,000 files, each thought to contain dozens of papers, are affected. In most instances the entire file is said to have been mislaid after being removed from public view at the archives and taken back to Whitehall.'

The Guardian online, 26th December 2017

Prologue

The fact that they had finally come for him was of no great surprise to Maurice Duggan; that it had taken so long and had arrived with so little fanfare was the only aspect to cause him any real wonder. He was ninety-two years of age and had thought of this moment on many occasions throughout his life. In his visions of how this moment would play out he was a much younger man with more vitality and fight in him. His anticipation that it would likely come in the dead of night with the violent arrival of several ruthless heavies had not been borne out. The man standing before him —short, trim and well-dressed—in the hallway of his small fourth-floor flat displayed all the outward characteristics of a rather timorous salesman. In some strange way, despite knowing how this would end for him, Maurice was somewhat disappointed by his adversary.

'Maurice—this is the name you go by, now, yes?'

Maurice said nothing but stared at the man.

'We know what you have been working on and we'd like to see it, please,' the man said softly, placing his hands into his trouser pockets.

Maurice frowned, trying to discern for whom the man worked from his accent. He knew that he had no choice but to hand over the document on which he had been working for many years now. He nodded and turned to move into the lounge, but the man reached out and grabbed his arm.

'Don't try anything,' he warned.

'I'm ninety-two. What on earth do you think I'm going to do?' Maurice asked.

'I was told you weren't to be trusted.'

Maurice emitted a short brittle laugh. 'I'll take that as a compliment.' He eyed the man carefully for a few seconds, wondering if he had detected something in his pronunciation of the word *weren't*, then turned and made his way into the lounge with the man close on his heels.

The room was tiny and contained little furniture. Beside the Juliet balcony stood an old formica table, upon which was situated a 1950s Imperial typewriter. Maurice shuffled over to a large stack of paper beside the typewriter—twenty-five years of work. He picked it up carefully and handed it to the man.

'Is this the only copy?' he demanded.

Maurice nodded.

'Of course, I will search the place…after,' the man replied with a smile, taking a cursory flick through the typed pages. 'You've put a lot of work into it, yes?'

'I've put everything into it,' Maurice answered truthfully.

'You know, it is a shame you had to do that,' the man said. 'You know…at your age. You could have just gone peacefully in your sleep.'

'And instead?' Maurice asked.

The man curled his lower lip and raised his free hand into the air, as if it were the first time that he had considered the question. Or, perhaps there *would* be an element of choice.

Maurice looked around the room, his eyes coming to rest on the balcony door. He looked again at the man, who, he knew, had intuited his thoughts. Maurice walked slowly towards the door, pulled it open and drew in a long breath. He looked out over the village of Ardingly, as flickers of his past ran through his mind.

Placing his hands on the warm metal rail, Maurice Duggan leant forwards, as if to get a better view of the tarmac carpark below. He continued to lean until his slippers began to lift from the carpet and gravity took over.

Chapter One

Morton Farrier was puzzled. Having conducted a routine check of all of the different genealogy websites hosting his DNA, he was surprised to discover that a new cousin match had appeared by the name of Vanessa Briggs.

'Nine hundred and two,' Morton remarked to himself, sipping a coffee at the kitchen table, staring at his laptop.

'What?' Juliette, his wife, asked, as she entered the room wearing her police officer uniform.

'Oh,' Morton replied, looking up and realising that he had just spoken aloud. 'I've got a new DNA match.'

'Right,' she said, standing still and placing her hands on her hips. 'And?'

'Well, she's matching me at nine hundred and two centiMorgans,' he clarified.

Juliette stared at him. 'I've literally no idea what that means.'

'It means that, according to Ancestry, this'—he looked back down at the screen—'Vanessa Briggs is my first-to-second cousin.'

'And you've never heard of her, I presume?'

'Nope, no idea,' he answered. Given the research, which he had already conducted into his family tree, Vanessa Briggs was definitely somebody of whom he should already be well aware. Rather typically, as so many seem wont to do, she had added no genealogical or geographical information to her Ancestry profile, which might have helped Morton to establish how they were related. Beyond her name, all that he knew was that she appeared in her profile picture to be around the age of forty.

'Well, as interesting as all that is, I need to get Grace ready for nursery before D-Day starts,' she said, looking at her watch.

'D-Day?' Morton queried.

'Desk Duty,' she said, sighing as she left the room. 'Grace Matilda Farrier! Time to get ready for nursery!'

'I'm sure it'll be fine,' Morton called after her, swiftly returning his focus to the Vanessa Briggs conundrum. He clicked on her name and viewed their shared matches. Immediately, he observed that they had six DNA matches in common, all on his mother's side of the family,

4

which confused Morton even further. Opening a new tab on his internet browser, he went to the DNA Painter website, selected the *Shared cM tool* and entered 902 centiMorgans into the filter box. The search results then presented him with all the potential ways in which he *could* be related to Vanessa Briggs. Two of the options, that she was his great-grandmother or great-granddaughter could immediately be discounted, leaving just five possibilities: that she was his great-aunt, half-aunt, first cousin, half-niece or great-niece. Although his family tree was somewhat complicated, he did know enough to discount the possibility of Vanessa Briggs's being his first cousin, half-niece or great-niece. There were just two options left: that she was his great-aunt or half-aunt.

As he was beginning to examine his family tree more closely, Morton's mobile phone beeped with the arrival of a text message. It was from his friend, Jens, texting from his hot chocolate shop, Knoops, down the road on Rye High Street.

Morton, there was an old lady just here who was desperate to find you. She wanted your address, but I didn't give it to her. She wouldn't wait or leave a message, insisting she saw you personally. Jens.

Odd, Morton thought, turning back to his computer, just as Juliette strode into the room holding Grace's hand.

'Bye, Daddy,' Grace said, stretching her arms up towards him.

'Oh, goodbye my little one,' he said, picking her up with feigned straining. 'You're almost too heavy to lift! My goodness, you're growing so fast. Two and a half years old and already Daddy can't pick you up!'

Grace giggled. 'Yes, pick up!'

'Alright, one last try,' Morton said, heaving her up onto his lap with exaggerated effort. 'There we are. You have a good day at nursery and Daddy will collect you at the end, okay?'

'Okay, Daddy.'

Juliette leant over and kissed Morton on the lips. 'Bye.'

'I won't try and pick *you* up,' he said with a smile. 'You've *definitely* grown.'

'Not funny,' she said. 'See you tonight. Wish me luck.'

'Good luck for D-Day,' he responded.

Juliette and Grace went out of the front door and the house fell into that strange quietness, where he found himself simultaneously yearning for the bustle and chaos of their return and embracing the stillness that allowed him to focus on his work as a genealogist. He just had a concluding report left to write for the case on which he was currently working and then he had a few days free that would be perfect to follow-up on this new DNA match of his. The timing was impeccable.

'Great-aunt or half-aunt?' he asked himself, as he pulled up his family tree on Ancestry, instead of opening the report that he needed to write. Great-aunt was without doubt the most likely match, meaning that she would be a sibling of one of his maternal grandparents, Alfred Farrier or Anna Schmidt. Morton had worked on Alfred's siblings extensively but had done very little on Anna's side of the family, and the potential of having found a sister of his German grandmother filled him with a keen eagerness to make contact.

From beside him on the kitchen table, his mobile phone beeped again. This time, it was from his brother, Jeremy: *Stalker alert! Old woman just came into the shop desperate to find you. Shooed her away. Is Juliette home to protect you?! x.*

Morton frowned and re-read the message. Then he re-read Jens's message. Both of them had used the word *desperate*. He replied to Jeremy, who was evidently at work in his new shop on the High Street: Granny's Scones.

Did she leave her name? What does she look like? x, Morton sent in reply.

Jeremy is typing…, his mobile informed him. So, he waited.

No name. She looks like an old woman x.

Helpful, Morton replied.

He sighed, put his mobile down and resumed his careful review of what he knew about his Schmidt family tree. He knew the names of Anna's parents but had, until today, no knowledge of any of her siblings. Vanessa Briggs. Not the most Germanic-sounding person that he had ever come across, he thought, clicking on her name again and scrolling down to *Ethnicity Estimates.*

'Oh,' he said. The ethnicity estimate for him for Germanic Europe was twenty-six percent, which fitted accurately with his ancestry, while the estimate for Vanessa Briggs for Germanic Europe was zero percent.

Clearly, the next step was to message her, but, owing to the very low response rate which he had experienced over the years, he wasn't confident of a reply. Still, he always had to give it a try.

Dear Vanessa, he typed, already fully anticipating the usual lack of response, *I see that we have a high DNA match through my maternal line. As far as I can tell, you are my great-aunt or half-aunt. Do the names Farrier or Schmidt (my maternal grandparents) appear in your family at all? Do let me know either way — you can contact me by email at TheForensicGenealogist@hotmail.com in case you can't use this service to reply. Looking forward to hearing from you, Kind regards, Morton Farrier.*

Sent.

Now he needed to wait, possibly for all of eternity.

In Morton's estimation, the probability of her not replying was sufficiently high to make him proceed immediately to the next step: to identify which of his maternal grandparents was related to Vanessa. He returned to the six matches that he shared with Vanessa but did not recognise any of their names, since they all fell into the fourth-to-sixth-cousin bracket, meaning that their common ancestor could be as far back as a great-great-great-grandparent, or even beyond. Which of his thirty-two great-great-great-grandparents he had in common with each of these matches was the convoluted question that needed answering.

He sighed, realising that he would need to build a skeleton family tree for each of those matches and work on them until he had identified the common ancestor. The chances of him achieving it today, before it was time to collect Grace from nursery, was nil. If he worked on it solidly for the next few days, though, then he might just achieve it before his next genealogical investigation began.

'Here we go,' he muttered, trying to figure out where to start. Three of the DNA matches had no linked trees at all and were, therefore, the least helpful at this stage. Two of the matches had private family trees and Morton messaged them politely to request access to their locked trees, explaining his motivation. Just one of the matches, a Pamela Sweetman, had an unlinked tree on her account. According to Ancestry, he shared forty-one centiMorgans of DNA with Pamela, who had last logged in to Ancestry in 2016. Pamela's unlinked family tree contained just her name, along with those of her mother and father. It was very little to go on, but it was enough for Morton to begin constructing a skeleton tree.

Needing a large roll of paper from his office at the top of the house, Morton stood from the table and headed out into the hallway. Just as he passed the front door, the knocker sounded loudly, making him jump. He pulled the door open with a hint of annoyance at the disruption, then inwardly groaned when he saw an old lady standing on the cobbled street outside. She had to be *the* old lady who was, for some reason, so desperate to track him down. Great, someone in the town had given her his address. Marvellous.

'Morton Farrier?' she questioned, eyeing him suspiciously, as though it had been *he* who had knocked on *her* door, rather than the other way around.

He nodded, just as it occurred to him that he could equally have lied and said that Morton didn't live here anymore, or that he had gone out for the entire day. 'Yes, that's right,' he confirmed reluctantly.

'I read about you in the papers,' she said, as though she were accusing him of something.

'Sorry,' he felt compelled to say.

'Oh, nothing to apologise for. It was that smuggling man that tried to kill his uncle... What was his name? Phil Garrow, that was it. He deserved that prison sentence, I should say.'

'Yes, he did,' Morton agreed, trying not to show his rising impatience. Was that what she had come to tell him? He doubted it, somehow. 'Can I help you at all?'

The old woman clearly took that to be sufficient invitation, smiled and took a step up towards the house. 'Thank you so much, that would be simply wonderful.'

'Erm...' Morton said, finding himself backing inside his own house, as the old woman shuffled up the steps and entered his hallway.

'It won't take long,' she said breathlessly.

'Can I ask what this is pertaining to?' he asked.

'Genealogy,' she mouthed, as though she had uttered something shocking or improper. 'Where would you like me?'

Outside of my house, he fought with himself not to say. 'In the kitchen, I suppose,' he actually said, showing her the way.

'Lovely place,' she commented, glancing around the room, before turning to face him with a frown. 'Two front doors, though? Seems a bit excessive. For a good moment, I didn't know which one to knock on.'

'Yes, that can be a problem,' Morton agreed, though not really wanting to alter the entire history and nature of his home, named *The House with Two Front Doors*, just to please casual passers-by who couldn't determine which of the two doors to make use of. 'Please, take a seat.'

The woman sat down with a large outbreath and looked up at Morton expectantly.

He smiled politely, then said, 'Normally I take cases based on an initial email or contact through my website,' he ventured, '*not* through personal visits...'

The woman waved a hand dismissively, removed a handkerchief from her sleeve and began to dab her brow. 'Oh, I've no idea what the internet and emails even *are*. My neighbour tried to explain once, but it was all foreign to me. Too complicated. Something about the line, a spider's web and the Philippines… That's really all I can remember, now.'

'Hmm,' Morton said, taking her in fully while she went on. She was a large-set woman with a full face, which made it difficult to gauge how old she was. If he were to have taken a guess, he would have thought her to be in her eighties. She had rouged cheeks, neatly permed white hair and gave off a general odour of lavender.

Opening her brown leather handbag, she pulled out an envelope and handed it to Morton. 'Here.'

Morton took it and withdrew the contents, presuming that he was to read it in order to make sense of why this old woman was roaming the streets of Rye, searching for him. In his hands he held three pieces of paper, the top-most sheet being a letter headed with the address of the West Sussex Coroner, which he began to read:

2ⁿᵈ July 2019.
Dear Miss Duggan,
Form 2, Notice of Discontinuance.
The investigation into the death of Maurice DUGGAN has been discontinued under section 4 of the Coroners and Justice Act 2009.
The Investigation was discontinued for the following reason(s): Cause of death was suicide. Please bear in mind that you are now required to contact the Register Office to register the death as soon as possible if you have not done so already.
Signature: Penelope Schofield
HM Senior Coroner

Morton briefly studied the name of the deceased, Maurice Duggan, wondering if he ought to have heard of him, because he hadn't. He placed the letter to the bottom of the stack in his hands and looked at the second document: Maurice Duggan's death certificate, which stated that he had been found dead at Priory Flats, College Road, Ardingly, West Sussex on the 3ʳᵈ April 2019. The informant of the death was his sister, Miss Clarissa Duggan. Morton glanced at the old lady sitting at his kitchen table, presuming her to be the said sister. The final document was a letter from Frank Dawson Solicitors, also addressed to Clarissa:

Dear Miss Duggan,

I am pleased to confirm that we have now completed the administration of your late brother's estate. Enclosed are the final estate accounts for your retention. You will see that after the payment of the interim distribution, there is a balance of £89,692.92. Enclosed is a cheque in your favour for this amount.

This concludes matters but obviously, if you have any queries at all, please do not hesitate to let me know.

Yours sincerely,

Frank Dawson

Morton put the letter to the back of the pile, then looked at the old lady. 'Am I right in assuming that you are Miss Clarissa Duggan?'

The old woman smiled and nodded enthusiastically, as though he had just passed some kind of a test. 'Correct!'

'And…your brother, Maurice, took his own life and you've inherited his estate?' he continued vaguely, not having an inkling where this was all leading.

'*In*correct,' Clarissa announced. 'My brother, Maurice Duggan, died in 1944.'

'Oh,' Morton said, entirely confused. He raised the three documents in his hand and asked, 'So, who's this man, then?'

Clarissa Duggan threw her hands up in the air. 'That's what I want you to find out.'

Chapter Two

'I don't understand,' Morton said. 'Was this not *you*, who informed of Maurice's death and who was in receipt of almost ninety thousand pounds from his estate?'

Clarissa looked down at the table and nodded. Morton realised from her body language and facial expression that there was something that she couldn't quite bring herself to say. After a moment's thinking, he guessed that what she was struggling to articulate was that she had actually acted fraudulently.

'I…I was so confused when the police turned up at my house and said that my brother had died and, well, I know it's not an excuse but I'm on medication which affects my memory and…and, well for the few moments that they were in my house, I thought I believed them. They were the *police* telling me that Maurice had died. A few days went by and the feeling that I should contact them and tell them the truth faded. After all, I hadn't *actually* told a lie, I just hadn't corrected them. Then I got a phone call from the coroner's office saying that I needed to get an interim death certificate for my brother whilst they were investigating the circumstances of his death. And I went to tell the woman on the phone everything, but she just said that that wasn't a matter for her and to tell it all to the police. So, there I was. I found myself registering his death and using the death certificate to close his bank accounts. And that's when…' She suddenly burst into tears and reached for the handkerchief wedged in her sleeve.

'That's when you found out that he had eighty-nine thousand pounds,' Morton finished, none-too-tactfully.

'Oh, don't!' she sobbed. 'The solicitor told me this chap had left no will and with no other family I would be the only beneficiary…'

'So, what's changed?' he asked.

'I haven't slept a wink since they sent me that cheque,' she answered. 'I've not even been and banked it, look.' She rummaged in her handbag and then threw the cheque down on the table. 'I just couldn't bear to.'

'Am I right in saying,' Morton began, 'that you want me to find out who this man *really* was in order to give the money to his real family?'

Clarissa nodded and muttered something unintelligible through her tears.

'Right,' Morton said, trying to weigh up the ethics of this potential case. Would he be aiding and abetting a crime, or would the reverse actually be true; would he be helping to prevent a crime from taking place by solving it? Whichever way he looked at it, he had to admit that it intrigued him.

'Will you do it?' she asked. 'Please!'

'Let me get a paper and pen and take some more notes from you and then I'll decide. Would you like a cup of tea, while we discuss it?' he asked.

'Oh, I thought you'd never ask. Spitting feathers, here! Yes, please. White and one sugar.'

Morton placed the three documents on the table and turned to make their drinks.

'You've no idea how relieved I feel just to have told someone,' she said. 'You'll not share it with anyone, will you? Only I'm certain I'll be sent off to prison and, well, I've got my cats to think about. And...' She began to cry again.

'Well, I don't really feel it's my place *to* tell anyone,' Morton said earnestly. 'Besides which, you're trying to do the right thing now.'

'Oh, I'm desperate to,' she sobbed.

Morton made a cup of tea for her and a large coffee for himself, then went upstairs to the top floor of the house to fetch his notepad and pen. As he went to leave the room, he remembered that he had been on his way up here to collect a roll of paper for his research into Vanessa Briggs, which would have to be pushed to the backburner for a while if he took on Clarissa's case. He grabbed the roll of paper and took it downstairs with him, still not having made up his mind either way.

He found Clarissa drinking her tea and looking much calmer than she had a few moments before. He took a chair opposite her and turned to a clean page in his notebook. 'Right,' he said, not entirely certain as to where to begin, 'I think, first of all, tell me a bit about your brother: are you *absolutely* certain that he had already died? This man who died in April this year—is it at all possible that he could actually have *been* your brother?'

Clarissa shook her head firmly. 'No chance. He definitely died long, long ago. For some horrific reason or other, my parents thought it a good idea to have his body on display at home. I was just a little girl, and for three days I had to walk past his open coffin—right before Christmas it was, too. I've not fully enjoyed Christmas since.'

'I'm sorry to push this point,' Morton pressed, 'but did you actually *see* his body?'

'Yes, and I can still see him now, as clear as day in my mind. Awful, just awful.'

'Sorry,' Morton said. 'And what had happened to him?'

Clarissa took a long breath in, then answered, 'He drowned. We lived in Ardingly, West Sussex, ironically not far from where this imposter...this impersonator of my brother died. He was messing about with his two best friends at Westwood Lake, which had frozen over in that bleak winter of 1944, and he fell through the ice. Just like that. His friends tried to save him, but it was all too late.'

'How terrible,' Morton said. 'How old were you at the time?'

'Just shy of my tenth birthday,' she replied.

'And how old was Maurice?'

'Seventeen. No age at all, is it?'

'No,' Morton answered, doing his best to ward off intrusive ideas of anything similarly dreadful ever happening to his Grace. 'Did you have any other siblings?'

'No, it was only me left...and I was just old enough to understand what was happening as our little family crumbled all around me. My mother had what would now be termed as clinical depression and was parcelled off to her sister's for long periods at a time, while I was sent off to boarding school, just like Maurice had been. While we were away my father frittered all his money, ruined his businesses and took the Duggans from a well-to-do, lower-upper-class family from good stock to...well, something much farther removed from that, let's say.'

Hence the alluring appeal of almost ninety thousand pounds, Morton thought.

'I just really don't understand why somebody would want to go around pretending to be my poor brother,' Clarissa said, taking a sip of her tea before continuing. 'I mean, why not just make somebody up, if your intention is to become somebody else? Pull a name out of thin air, for heavens' sake. This chap was in possession of my brother's birth certificate and all sorts, you know. It's shocking the lengths he seems to have gone to.'

'The Day of the Jackal loophole,' Morton started to explain. 'Back then it was much easier to be a dead double—to take on an existing identity—than it was to fabricate a whole new one, especially if that person had died young. Anyone could walk into a register office and, knowing some basic details of a person who had already died, could get

13

a legal copy of that person's birth certificate. With their official birth certificate, they could marry, get a passport, open a bank account—'

'—*Become* that person,' Clarissa interjected.

'Exactly,' Morton agreed, looking down at his notepad. 'So, what do you know about this man who died in April pretending to be Maurice?'

'Next to nothing. He jumped from his balcony, but why, the police weren't able to establish. According to the police there were no suicide notes left behind and he'd not been depressed or showing any signs that he might take his own life, but similarly there was no sign of foul play, either.'

'Right,' Morton said, jotting the new information on his notepad.

'And how, may I ask, will you find out who this imposter was?' Clarissa asked.

Morton blew out a puff of air. Now, *there* was a question. '*If* it's possible, then the way forwards will likely be backwards.'

Clarissa laughed. 'I'm not sure what that means, but as long as *you* do, that's the main thing.'

'It means I'll need to start from his death and work backwards chronologically and hope, somewhere along the line, there's a link back to who he really was before. Tell me, did you receive any of his property?'

'Yes, unfortunately,' she groaned. 'My dining room is choc-a-bloc with this chap's junk. I've got a house-clearance firm coming to take it all away in a few days' time.'

'I'd like to see it before it goes, if I may,' Morton said.

'By all means—take anything you think is relevant. I'd be quite glad to be shot of it, truth be told.'

Morton looked down at the informant's residence on Maurice Duggan's death certificate. 'Are you still living at this address in Horsham? May I come by tomorrow?'

Clarissa nodded. 'So, you'll do this for me, then, will you? Find out who this chap was and help me make any sense of it?'

'I'll decide tomorrow,' Morton answered noncommittally, as he gazed at his laptop, still tantalisingly displaying his DNA matches onscreen. 'You do know that my rates are quite high? I'll give you a copy of my terms of business, then you can also decide based on that.'

Clarissa waved her hand in the air. 'After what I read about you in the papers, I'm certain that I want you to do it. I've got some savings,' she said, glancing quickly to the cheque on the table.

'Right, well,' Morton said, trying to wrap-up proceedings, 'If I come to your house around eleven tomorrow and we'll take it from there, then, yes? Is that okay?'

'Wonderful,' she said, standing up and drinking the last dregs of her tea, then, extended her hand forward to shake his hand: 'See you tomorrow.'

Morton shook Clarissa's hand and then showed her out. 'Goodbye,' he said, closing the door with a sigh. He hurried back into the kitchen and saw that she had left the three documents and the cheque on the table. Scooping them up quickly, he rushed to the front door and stepped outside onto Mermaid Street. No sign of her. He turned back in to the house and took another cursory look at the papers. The case had certainly piqued his interest, but if he did decide to take it on, then for quite a while there would be little time to work out how on earth Vanessa Briggs fitted into his family tree.

He looked up at the kitchen clock: still another few hours before he needed to collect Grace from nursery. Time to begin constructing Pamela Sweetman's family. But first, he needed another coffee.

As he waited for the machine to grind the beans, he looked at his mobile and noticed that he'd had a further two text messages from his brother, Jeremy.

Old stalker woman has your address! Your neighbour Mandy overheard her asking in The Apothecary if they knew where you lived and she told her x.

Thanks, Mandy, Morton thought, as he scrolled down to the next message, sent fifteen minutes later.

Presume old stalker woman found and killed you. Too busy in the shop to come and help. Sorry x.

Morton smiled and wrote a message in reply: *Still alive. Old stalker woman came to the house wanting me to find out who a man was who had jumped off a building in April pretending to be her brother who had drowned in 1944 x.*

Normal day, then x, came Jeremy's immediate reply.

Morton set his mobile down on the table, pulled open the roll of paper and wrote *Pamela* at the bottom. Then he added her parents' names, David Sillifant and Brenda Puleston directly above hers. That was all the information that he had to go on. Opening Ancestry, he ran a marriage search for Pamela, assuming Sweetman to be her married name. At this juncture, he needed to be as accurate as possible but without applying the usual Genealogical Proof Standard of requiring documented evidence of his findings; the discovery of the common ancestor would be sufficient endorsement of his research in getting to

15

that point. Of the several results presented, the top one was highly likely to be correct: Pamela Sillifant had married Robin Sweetman in the Penzance registration district of Cornwall in 1979.

Switching to the birth indexes, Morton ran a search for the birth of Pamela Sillifant with the mother's maiden name of Puleston. One result in 1958, also in the Penzance registration district. He copied the details to his roll of paper, then located David and Brenda's marriage in 1953. Next, he found the reference to David's birth in 1936, giving his mother's maiden name as Valentine. Typing David's name and birthdate into the 1939 Register, he was able to locate him as a three-year-old child, living in Newlyn, a small town outside of Penzance. The register provided his precise date of birth, and the names and dates of birth of his parents, Frederick and Gwen Sillifant, which Morton added to the top of the growing skeleton tree. Returning to the marriage indexes, he ran a search to confirm the marriage of Frederick Sillifant to Gwen Valentine, which he discovered had occurred in 1930.

He looked at the tree in front of him. So far, he had only identified Pamela Sweetman's paternal grandparents. He still needed to pursue all lines a further three generations back, and then repeat it for the maternal Puleston line. Only then *might* Morton discover the connection which linked him to Vanessa Briggs.

Three coffees and two hours later, Morton had traced just one branch, the Sillifants, back the required five generations beyond Pamela Sweetman when it came time to collect Grace from nursery.

'Shall we do some drawing together?' Morton asked Grace, when they returned home.

'Yeah!' Grace exclaimed, jumping up and down.

He looked at her happy face and kissed her lightly on the forehead. She had inherited his chestnut brown eyes and hair, but most people remarked that she most resembled Juliette, which Morton didn't think was necessarily a bad thing. Today, she was wearing a dark-blue dress which was now bespattered with the grubby evidence of her day at nursery: paint splodges, dried plasticine, glitter, lunch and snacks, and a dubious-looking snail-trail on her sleeve.

'Super,' Morton said, ushering her into the kitchen and sitting her up to the table. 'I'll just get your colouring pencils.'

'Thank you, Daddy,' Grace said, clapping enthusiastically.

Morton collected her tin of pencils, sat beside her and unravelled the long roll of paper, upon which he had been previously working.

'What that?' Grace asked.

'A family tree,' Morton said.

Grace giggled. 'Not tree! *This* tree,' she said, grabbing a pencil and proceeding to scribble something with no resemblance to an actual tree.

'That's beautiful, Grace. You draw me some trees on this side of the paper,' Morton said, 'And Daddy will draw *his* trees on this side of the paper.'

'Okay.'

Morton grinned contentedly as his daughter sat beside him creating a veritable forest of green squiggles, while he pursued the link to his mysterious new relative, Vanessa Briggs.

'Really?' Juliette said, when she returned home some time later. She stood behind Grace and Morton, kissing them in turn. 'Wow, what an...*interesting* picture.'

'Grace tree,' Grace said, proudly pointing to her woodland, then, jabbing her pencil towards Morton's tree, she added, 'Daddy tree.'

Juliette looked at Morton through narrowed eyes. 'Really?' she repeated.

'What?' Morton asked innocently. 'I'm training her up to be my assistant.'

'That's *never* going to happen,' Juliette said. 'Far too dangerous a career.'

'How was D-Day?' Morton asked.

Juliette groaned, sitting opposite them at the table. 'Well, they're not called restricted duties for nothing. I've been sitting at a desk all day long taking telephone enquiries and missing person statements. Fun, fun, fun.'

Morton reached across the table and placed his hand on hers. 'It's not forever.'

'No, thank God,' she agreed.

'Dinner?' he said.

'Yes, if that's an offer. No, if that's a request,' she answered.

The following morning, at precisely eleven o'clock, Morton drew his red Mini to a stop outside of Fig Cottage on Trafalgar Road in Horsham, West Sussex. The white pebble-dashed house, wrapped with the autumnal remnants of a deep-red Virginia creeper, held the quaint charm of a traditional country cottage.

Morton switched off the engine, picked up his bag from the passenger seat and walked down the pea-beach drive towards the house. Before he had reached the front door, it yawned open.

'Good morning!' Clarissa greeted dramatically. 'Do come in!'

The interior was just as he had imagined it might look; dimly lit with low beamed ceilings.

'Can I get you a drink before you start?' Clarissa asked, closing the front door behind him. 'I noticed you have one of those fancy coffee machines at your house, which I don't have, I'm afraid; but I do have instant, or there's tea.'

Morton smiled. 'Instant's great, thank you.'

'Shall I show you to the junk room?' she asked with a titter.

'Yes, please,' he said, following her through a good-sized lounge containing some beautiful antique furniture. Fixed to the walls, under the subtle yellow glow of brass picture lights, were several landscape watercolours.

'It's in here,' she said, stepping through a door at the rear of the lounge. She lowered her voice unnecessarily, as though she might offend somebody nearby, and added, 'It's all a load of rubbish.'

The room was rammed with clutter, which clashed starkly with Clarissa's high-quality pieces: two white formica bedside tables stacked precariously on a worn armchair; a lopsided wardrobe with archaic decorative mirrors on the doors; an old typewriter; a chest of drawers with some of the handles missing; an old-fashioned ottoman; an upended single bed and mattress against which leant a small portable-style television set. And, in front of it all were several tea chests revealing an abundance of dated kitchen apparel, food, two lamps and a bin. To one side of the door were around ten mismatched boxes, which had evidently been purloined from a supermarket.

'Are all the drawers and cupboards completely empty?' Morton asked, gesturing towards the wardrobe and bedside tables.

'Yes, I checked them all, but you're more than welcome to look for yourself,' Clarissa said. 'I'll go and get that coffee on.'

'Great,' Morton replied, slightly losing his enthusiasm at the sight of it all and the clearly rushed and haphazard way in which it had all been boxed up. 'Where to begin?' he asked himself, not having the first clue for what he was actually searching. Something—anything—with a trace of Maurice Duggan's previous existence, he supposed.

He took in a deep breath, knelt down and picked the nearest box to him and pulled it open. Books. He withdrew them one at a time, checking for any inscriptions before briefly fanning through the pages, to ensure that there were no letters or photographs hidden inside. Some of the authors he didn't recognise, but others he did: John le Carré and Frederick Forsyth seemed favourites. A well-thumbed copy of a book on memoir-writing caught his attention. Only one book in the entire box contained anything additional: in the very front of Ian Fleming's *Live and Let Die* was a slip of paper headed with the words WILLESDEN LIBRARY and below it were several date stamps, the last being 7th July 1974. Morton put the book to one side, then continued with the next box, which was a large one containing Maurice Duggan's clothing.

'Lovely,' Morton commented, removing several pairs of rather off-white underpants by the absolute tip of his thumb and forefinger.

'They suit you,' Clarissa said, arriving with his coffee. 'You're very welcome to keep them, if they'd fit.'

He turned to her with a frown, not able to discern from her face whether she was joking or not. 'I've got plenty, thank you,' he said flatly.

'Anything of help or use, yet?' she asked, placing the coffee down beside him and leaning on the doorframe.

'No, not really,' he answered, checking the pockets of an old pair of trousers. Though, why he felt the compulsion to do it, he couldn't be sure, he just felt the need to be extra vigilant. After all, this man had been pretty good at deception for a good many years, it seemed.

The bottom of the box became visible after Morton had taken out every vest, shirt, cardigan, pair of trousers, socks and a squashed Homburg hat; none of it had revealed anything about the man who had once worn them.

Still under Clarissa's gaze, he next chose a small box containing just one item, which he carefully withdrew: an old radio set. It was a standard 1950s Marconi radio with a speaker in the top half and two dials either side of a bandwidth display below. He returned it to the box and placed it to one side.

Morton was able to search the next box quickly, as it contained a range of washing and bathroom products, two towels and a flannel.

'I'm going to give all that to my neighbour Stan,' Clarissa said.

A biting cramp began to take hold in Morton's left calf muscle, and he stood up with a sigh. As he sipped his coffee, he eyed the remaining two boxes.

'Not much of use, is there?' she said, sensing and sharing his disappointment.

Morton shook his head. 'I don't think so, no.' He took another mouthful of drink, then knelt down and opened the penultimate box.

'That was all from his bedside table,' Clarissa explained, as Morton peered inside at a tube of Denture Grip, a box of tissues and a pair of black-rimmed glasses.

'So, he had false teeth and wore glasses,' Morton noted, placing the glasses down on the *Live and Let Die* book. Lying at the very bottom of the box was what appeared to be the back of a small wooden-framed photograph, which Morton lifted out gently. He turned it over and was surprised to see a black-and-white photo of a rather beautiful woman in a wedding dress, clutching a bouquet of flowers, smiling out at him. It was a close-up, with very little background detail to identify except what might have been the entrance to a church just behind her. In the bottom corner were the handwritten words *To my husband, with love, Ellen x*.

'Last box, I think,' Clarissa commented pointlessly. 'And a riveting one at that.'

Morton lifted open the cardboard flaps and peered inside. Four empty bottles of pink gin and half-a-dozen used typewriter ink ribbons. Maurice had evidently been a prolific drinker and writer, Morton thought, glancing at the old machine.

He stood up and grimaced, looking from Clarissa to all the stuff around the room. Compared to the numerous cases, where Morton had had cause to rifle through a deceased person's affairs in this way, he felt that something was really not quite right: it felt too sterile, as though his belongings had had his personality whitewashed and expunged from them. 'And this is really *all* of it?' he asked, facing Clarissa.

'Absolutely,' she insisted. 'And that's plenty enough, thank you, as it is.'

'There's literally nothing of *him* in here, though, is there?' Morton said, as much to himself as to Clarissa. He tried to view the contents of his own house like this, disconnectedly and dispassionately; every box would be littered with evidence of who he was, his family and a profusion of their individual personalities.

Morton bent down and picked up the copy of *Live and Let Die*, the glasses and the photograph of Ellen. 'May I take these three items, please?' It seemed a peculiar question to be asking of her, given the

20

dishonest way in which she had come by the property, but he felt compelled to ask it, nonetheless.

'By all means. And are you absolutely sure you don't want the underpants, too?' she asked, still not revealing whether she was joking or not.

'No…thank you.'

'Am I right to take this as meaning that you'll help me to find out who this other chap was, then?' she asked hopefully.

'Yes,' Morton replied. 'I can't make any promises, though. As you can see, he left precious little to go on.'

'Oh, wonderful!' Clarissa said, throwing her arms around him and kissing him on the cheek.

'One more thing… I wondered if you would have a photograph of your brother, which I could borrow, at all?' he asked.

'Yes! One moment,' she said, turning on her heels and heading to a cabinet across the room. 'Here we are.' She handed a small black-and-white headshot to him. 'He must have been—oh, now then—fifteen or sixteen when that was taken.'

'Thank you,' Morton said, looking at the image. He was a handsome, confident-looking boy, who, in that single picture, seemed to exude an astuteness beyond his years. Morton placed the photograph inside the paperback and then remembered the cheque which she had left in his possession. 'Right. I'll get back to you when I have something to report,' he said, making his way into the lounge, rummaging in his back pocket as he walked. 'You left this among the papers at my house.' He stretched out his arm and Clarissa took the cheque from him.

'Right. Yes. I also just wanted to say… Don't take *too* long, please.'

'I'll do my best. Goodbye.'

Morton walked out to his Mini. He placed the three items on the passenger seat beside him, started the engine but didn't go anywhere for a moment. He stared at the glasses, the photo of Ellen and the library book. Of the three, the photograph offered the only real glimpse into the man's past. Morton had no idea why he had taken the glasses; they somehow helped him to imagine Maurice as a real living person. He picked them up, placed them on his nose and noticed…well, nothing. No perceivable difference, he thought. Picking up the book, he flipped to a random page and began to read alternately through and around the lenses, finding that the glasses had no prescription in them and were simply cosmetic, apparently one further part of this imposter's costume and subterfuge.

He removed the glasses and placed them down beside him. The only conclusion he could reasonably draw, given the lack of anything personal among the possessions, was that the person in question had deliberately chosen to live this basic and desolate existence in order to obscure his true past. If that was *not* the case, then another alternative explanation, the only one which Morton could imagine currently, was that somebody had erased his past from his flat for him after his death.

Both possibilities left Morton with one nagging question: why?

Chapter Three

It had been a perfect flight so far; the skies had been clear for his ninety-minute journey across the English Channel. Now, though, he was flying directly towards an ominous gathering of heavy rain clouds. A typical welcome back to England. He was flying solo in a Cessna 150 under his newly assumed identity of Maurice Duggan. All documentation and references to his former life had been discarded somewhere over the channel.

Maurice grimaced from the unfamiliar sensations brought about by the new clothing which his switch in character had necessitated. He removed his Homburg hat, placing it down on the suitcase on the vacant seat to his right, then loosened the cravat from around his neck. His new look was complemented by a thick camel-hair coat, black-rimmed glasses and a pair of red suede shoes.

Heathrow Airport came into view and Maurice straightened in his seat. He had always been surprised at how at night an airport stood out so starkly by its darkness and, tonight, Heathrow was no exception: a black hole amidst a galaxy of streetlights. It had been a long while since he had landed a plane at night and even longer since attempting it without the aid of landing lights. He was forty-seven years old and the audaciousness of the antics of his youth, when such folly had been unremarkably commonplace, now felt as though they had all happened to somebody else. In a way, they had.

He knew that, between the hours of half past eleven at night and five o'clock in the morning, little went on at the airport and that, unless by some unfortunate stroke of bad luck, the tower controllers should not be looking out of their windows. Even so, with his navigation-, beacon-, and landing-lights off, he'd be very hard to see. Maurice had already switched off his transponder. Though not quite invisible, he was now just an anonymous blip on the radar screen. His hope was that if he were noticed on the scope, they would believe him to be heading to Denham Airfield, ten miles north, and outside of Heathrow's airspace.

He took a breath. It was time to get this plane down and get on with his plan. He turned down the cockpit lighting to improve his night vision and turned the control yoke to line up the aircraft with the runway. A straight-in approach was not standard, but time was of the essence. When he judged he was about a mile away from the airport he turned on the carburettor heat and pulled the throttle to 1500 RPM, waited a moment, then pressed the switch to extend the flaps to thirty degrees.

He felt the Cessna slow down and pitch forward as the big flaps bit into the air. It then settled to seventy miles-per-hour and Maurice made a further adjustment to his positioning, as he descended towards the tarmac.

Just to the left of the runway he saw the Visual Approach Slope Indicator—a pair of angled lights denoting his height. Both were showing white, meaning that he was coming in too high. He pulled the throttle back a little further, then waited until the top light filtered to red. *Red over white, you're alright,* he thought, remembering his old instructor's mnemonic phrase. He was now gliding in at the right approach angle.

As the runway threshold disappeared under the nose of the plane, he pulled the throttle to idle, then pulled back slightly on the yoke, reducing the speed to sixty miles-per-hour. By now the cloud had entirely obscured the moon and he would be landing blind.

He held the nose up, as the plane approached the tarmac, and held his breath.

Touchdown was seconds away.

The Cessna bumped the runway once, then bounced a few feet into the air. Maurice braced himself as the plane jolted down again, repeating the same action.

He held the plane steady and finally, the wheels remained in contact with the tarmac. He pressed down hard on the two brake pedals and the speed of the plane quickly reduced to a crawl.

He'd done it. He was back.

'Damn it,' he muttered. A Rover police car, with its lights flashing, was heading straight towards him, as he followed the blue taxiway illuminations away from the runway.

He continued slowly, then pulled into the first available bay and switched off the engine, suddenly aware of the eerie stillness surrounding him. He could just have landed in the middle of a desert for all the lack of any signs of activity.

The police car came to a dramatic stop in front of the Cessna, as if to prevent his escape, and two officers hastily jumped out, placing their helmets on their heads, as they dashed towards the plane.

Maurice calmly placed his Homburg on his head, opened the door and greeted the policemen. 'I'm not lost, officers—I'm just not where I wish to be.' He snorted. 'This really isn't the free lane at Denham Airfield, now, is it?'

'No, sir, it is not,' one of the policemen replied. 'You've landed at Heathrow Airport in the early hours of the morning with your transponder switched off and no landing lights.'

'Ah, yes, it did seem a tad dark,' Maurice said with a smile. 'You see my alternator failed earlier in the flight and, as I am bound to do as per established procedure, I turned off all non-essential circuits to save battery power. I was so focused on landing I must've forgotten to turn them back on.'

The two officers glanced at one another but Maurice could tell that they had not believed his story.

'Whatever the reasons, the facts stand, I'm afraid,' one of them responded. 'I'm arresting you under the Air Navigation Order of 1972 for failing to file a flight plan with the appropriate Air Traffic Control unit and for failing to obtain Air Traffic Control clearance based on a flight plan from the appropriate Air Traffic Control unit.'

'Bugger,' Maurice said, just as the first fat droplet of rain bounced from his hat.

Maurice Duggan cut an arresting figure as he strode down Kilburn High Road in North-West London. Hunched under his black ebony-handled umbrella, with his Homburg tilted downwards, he passed along the wet pavement, clutching his suitcase. He was oblivious to the stares and gazes which his attire was attracting from the people cowering under the rain-soaked awnings of the shops that he passed. With barely a glance up to check his location, he drew to a stop at a plain blue wooden door, situated between the Superdrug and Our Price shops. He took a key from his coat pocket and unlocked the door. Pushing against a resistant tide of junk mail, he stepped inside a dark hallway and collapsed his umbrella. He removed his hat, quietly closed the front door and then turned. In front of him was a narrow staircase with thread-bare carpet.

With one foot on the bottom step, Maurice paused, angling his head slightly and training his ear to filter out the traffic noise and the hum of activity from the shops on either side.

Nothing.

He took another step up and stopped to listen.

Nothing.

A low thud from somewhere nearby made him whip around defensively. But the sound had emanated from outside—not inside, as he had feared.

Maurice took a few more stairs, treading at the outer edges of each step so as to avoid unnecessary noise, then waited and listened.

Still nothing save for the rain-amplified noise from the road's traffic rolling by.

He climbed further still, not making a sound, until he reached the top floor. He found himself in an enclosed hallway. Directly in front of him was a tiny kitchenette and to his right were two closed doors.

Maurice placed his suitcase down onto the lino and leant his umbrella against the garish orange wallpaper. He moved slowly across the landing, but when the floor groaned beneath his weight, revealing his presence to any who heard it, he rushed towards the first door and thrust it open. It flew back and crashed noisily into whatever was behind it. Maurice leapt into the small room, quickly ascertaining that apart from a small wall-mounted cupboard, avocado-coloured toilet, sink and bath set, it was empty.

He edged slowly back into the hallway, cursing himself that the all-valuable element of surprise was now lost; anybody in the next room, which he had deduced must be the lounge-bedroom, would unequivocally know that he was here.

Maurice wiped his glasses with the back of his sleeve and drew in a long breath. He could tell from his breathlessness and clumsiness that it had been several years since he had needed to use these self-preservation skills.

Keeping as far off to the side as he could, Maurice stretched his hand across to the handle and, with a quick action, turned it and thrust open the door.

Nothing.

With moist, clenched fists he moved swiftly towards the open doorway and hurriedly entered the room. Empty. Completely empty. He strode over to the grey net curtains and glanced down at the busy road, before fully taking in the room. Black spots of damp festered where the external wall intersected with the ceiling, curling and repelling the hideous flowery wallpaper. It was, like the rest of the flat: small, dirty, unhealthy and outdated. But it would suffice.

Maurice finally lowered his guard and began to breathe normally.

There was a lot to do and soon the inclement weather was going to pull in the darkness. He needed to work quickly, but thoroughly. He tried flicking on the light switch, but nothing happened.

He returned to the landing, picked up his suitcase, carried it into the lounge-bedroom and put it down onto the bare floorboards. He placed a key into the two small brass locks and swung the case open wide. Visible inside were a few items of clothing and a washbag. Maurice fumbled beneath the top layer and withdrew a large bottle of pink gin. With a smile, he removed the cap and took a long glug. The bite of the alcohol instantly calmed him. After another long drink, he searched beneath the façade of clothing again, removing a paperback-sized leather case, which he opened to reveal an array of small metal tools. Taking off his Homburg and jacket and placing them on his suitcase, Maurice stood up and carefully scanned the room: two single electricity sockets; one light switch; and the bare light fitting dangling from the centre of the ceiling. Additionally, he would need to search and check the skirting board, dado rail and the underside of the windowsill.

He carried the leather case to the plug socket closest to him and, selecting the correct screwdriver, began to remove the socket from the wall. Inside he saw everything that he had expected to see and nothing untoward. Still, he probed around with the end of his screwdriver, checking the wiring. Once satisfied, Maurice replaced the façade, took another swig of pink gin and tackled the second socket. That had also not been tampered with. He found the same with the light switch and fitting. Next, he ran his fingers carefully along the entire length of the dado rail and around the complete window frame.

Maurice sighed, drank more pink gin and was content that the room contained no listening devices of any kind. But the light was fading fast and he still needed to check the rest of the flat.

The hallway was easy and took just a few minutes to check. The bathroom was more problematic, requiring a check of the wall-mounted heater, cabinet, the removal of the bath side-panel and an examination of the copper pipework feeding the bath and sink.

He had just managed to finish his final checks of the bathroom, when the low levels of light prevented him from continuing. Maurice stood in the hallway, holding the half-empty bottle of pink gin, staring suspiciously at the kitchenette. He faced two choices: one, feed some fifty pence pieces into the electricity meter, which would allow him to complete his sweep of the flat but, given that there were no curtains up yet, would render him and his activities visible to anyone caring to watch from outside; or two, wait until daylight tomorrow morning to finish, leaving the possibility of a bug hidden somewhere in the kitchenette, listening to his every move overnight.

Really, there was no option. He couldn't risk being seen from outside, so it would have to wait until the morning. If he said nothing and moved little, then what could they hear anyway? Hours of heavy snoring behind a closed door, the shuffling of bare feet, as he moved across the flat, and maybe the sound of him urinating in the early hours.

Returning to the lounge-bedroom, Maurice closed the door and took a long drink of the gin. He held the bottle up to the window to gauge its level and, with the subdued light from the streetlamps and passing cars below the flat, could see that there were just a couple of inches left: certainly not enough to bother saving. He tipped the bottle back and glugged down the gin until it was all gone.

He looked at his watch: 4:16 in the afternoon. He was hungry but couldn't be bothered to go out and then return only to have to repeat all his checks. Once finally set up the next morning, he would always know if anyone had been in. Sleep, he decided, was what he should do now. He removed his shoes and loosened his tie. Taking a knitted cardigan from his suitcase, Maurice rolled it up and placed it on the dirty floor as a pillow, then lay down on the bare boards with his coat pulled over the top of him.

Maurice woke with the sunrise at eight minutes past seven. He was freezing cold, his throat felt scorched and his back ached from the hard floor. Chilled air rose from his dry lips. Beside his head his eyes met the cause of the throbbing in his brain: the empty bottle of gin. With a struggle, he managed to prop himself up onto his elbows.

His thoughts began to spool through the tasks that lay in front of him.

The first job to complete was his sweep for potential listening devices in the flat.

With a low groan he stood up, staggering slightly as his thigh muscles buckled under him. He opened the door, peering cautiously into the hallway, before carrying his leather tool case into the kitchenette. It was a basic area, which, owing to its size, couldn't really be described as a room, just a sink, cooker and a few cupboards above and below a short run of worktop.

28

First, Maurice carefully took apart the plug sockets and light switch, checking that the wiring had not been tampered with or that no devices had been concealed inside. When he was certain that they were clear, he methodically searched every inch of the cupboards and the thin window frame.

The flat, he finally concluded, had *not* been interfered with. They were, therefore, likely unaware of his arrival back in England, which is exactly what Maurice had wanted: anonymity under which he could conduct his investigation.

He drank for a long time from the fast-running cold tap, then took a handful of loose change from his trouser pocket and dropped four fifty-pence pieces into the electricity meter on the wall in the kitchenette. The flat came to life with a buzz with all the lights flickering on and the heater in the bathroom starting up a rhythmical clicking, as its elements began to warm.

Maurice switched off all the lights, then entered the bathroom and stood in front of the mirror, enjoying the warmth radiating from the twin orange heater bars mounted above him. He looked a wreck. He might easily have been mistaken for someone in his late fifties. Heavy dark circles sagged under his eyes and lines furrowed his brow. He tried smiling, but it only made matters worse.

'Maurice Duggan,' he muttered, looking beyond the mirror and into his past. He wondered, as he had done so many times in recent years, how his life had taken such violent twists and turns to bring him to this point. The answer, as it always did, eluded him. 'Maurice,' he said again, returning to the face staring back at him.

He realised then that although he was deeply cold, the top of his head was being seared by the intensity of the overhead heater and he pulled the cord to switch it off. The heater responded by clacking noisily as the bright orange lights faded.

Maurice ran his fingers through his thick blonde hair, trying to make it resemble some kind of a style but failing. He straightened his tie, cocked one eyebrow and tried smiling again: he looked as jaded and worn-out as he felt.

Returning to the lounge-bedroom, he placed his Homburg onto his head, pulled on his coat and shoes, and was just about to head out when he spotted, peeping from amongst the clothes in his suitcase, the top of his second bottle of pink gin. He bent down, pulled it from the case, unscrewed the cap and, without removing his mouth between swallows, took several long glugs.

29

He put the bottle down and walked from the room, closing the door behind him. He descended the staircase and pulled open the front door. Yesterday's bad weather had abated, and despite the early hour, Kilburn High Road was already bustling with activity, as the run of shops on either side of the street began to open for business. A red London bus pulled up at the stop opposite the flat, causing a pause in the flow of cars behind it.

Maurice shut the door and strode a short way down the road, before crossing over to Willesden Lane. His destination was just a few short minutes' walk, but instead of heading directly there, he took a turning down St Julian's Road, increasing his pace to a gentle jog. The road was entirely residential, comprising a long run of tall, four-storey Victorian terraced houses. Maurice reached a parked brown Ford Cortina and stopped, bending down to pretend to tie his shoelace. Using the car's wing-mirror, he spotted the woman walking down the street in his direction. He had caught a glimpse of her at the bus stop when he had left the flat and was now certain that she was following him. She was young, possibly in her early twenties, with flared jeans, a blue coat and a wide-brimmed white hat. Not exactly the typical guise of the Watchers, but then perhaps things had changed in that domain over the intervening years: God knows they had needed to modernise and adapt. She was getting closer and Maurice could see that she was gazing at him.

He stood up and made a pantomime performance of checking his pockets for something and failing to find it. 'Oh, bloody hell,' he lamented with a theatrical sigh. The woman reached him just as he spoke and he nodded to her, before beginning to retrace his steps, checking his pockets as he walked for good measure. Without a glance behind him, he retreated back to Willesden Lane, wondering if he had imagined that she had been following him. If she had been trailing him, then certainly there would be more Watchers positioned around the area. He fought the urge to run and instead fell back on his past training. He crossed the street and headed up Streatley Road, smiling pleasantly to two elderly ladies, who were walking towards him.

'Good morning,' he greeted.

'Morning,' the women said in unison.

He turned his upper body, ostensibly to say, 'Lovely day, isn't it?' to the ladies, but in reality, to check whether there was anybody behind him. There wasn't. Not that he could see at any rate. Maurice increased his pace, making a quick turn at the end of the road, then pausing to pretend to check his laces once more beside a Hillman saloon. Behind him, the road was empty. Maurice was as certain as he could be that he was not being followed.

Walking with a pace, he turned down Plympton Road, ending up at the junction of Willesden Lane. Waiting at the roadside longer than was necessary in order to allow the passing of a Ford Corsair, he risked a backward glance. Nobody in sight in any direction. If they were watching him, then they were doing a damned good job of it.

With his hands slung casually in his pockets, he continued to walk down the road until he reached his destination: Paddington Old Cemetery. The entrance was marked by two brick pillars topped with egg-shaped stone vases and a pair of white gothic-style gatehouses mirrored on either side of the path. Maurice took the footpath which arced around the oval top of the cemetery. To his left were long stretches of lawn, interrupted by a haphazard arrangement of monuments and memorials to the dead: grey angels; weather-beaten tombs; pristine obelisks of white marble; the grand mausoleums dedicated to the rich and noteworthy; lichen-covered headstones, scarcely half-a-century old and already illegible; and amongst them all lay the silent majority in unmarked graves.

People like Ellen.

Maurice reached her grave. He knew that it was hers because he had buried her there and could never have forgotten it, but it was just an empty space of flat grass between two low-kerbed graves, appearing as a cut-through path to the graves behind. It was markedly different from the last time that he had been there, over sixteen years ago on the day of her funeral, when the soil had been piled up in thick clods beneath the bouquets and wreaths pronouncing universal sorrow and incomprehension at the tragedy.

'Ellen,' he said softly, removing his hat, crouching down and placing one hand onto the dew-damp grass. He hated that there was not a headstone, as though it somehow diminished and lessened the importance of the person below the ground. He resolved to rectify the situation and added it to his mental list of tasks. He couldn't have done it before now. He had necessarily fled the country directly after her funeral and the Watchers would almost certainly have been monitoring communications with the cemetery in these intervening years.

'I'm back,' Maurice whispered to the ground. 'I'm back to find out who did this to you, Ellen, and I won't rest until everyone knows the truth. One day *everything* will be revealed.'

A wash of long-stifled emotion rose suddenly inside him, taking him quite by surprise. He stood up as the feeling broke. 'I've missed you,' he stammered.

Maurice's tears coursed down his cheeks and fell from his chin to the ground, being instantly absorbed into the soil above his wife's body.

He stood there for a long time. He stood there until the emotion had subsided. He stood there until the shroud around his thoughts had lifted. Then, he said goodbye to her, placed his Homburg back on his head and strode from the cemetery.

Making his way back to Kilburn High Road, Maurice joined a short queue at the first bus stop that he reached. Although he had a specific destination in mind, and one which he wished to get to as quickly as possible, he hopped up onto the back of the first bus to arrive, irrespective of its route or ultimate destination. As he held on to the metal rail at the back of the bus, he found himself smiling for the first time in a long while. In spite of the circumstances and the reason for his being there, it felt somehow self-affirming to be back.

A few miles along the route, the bus pulled over and an elderly woman, holding the hand of a young boy, boarded, squeezing past Maurice at the rear.

Just as the bus began to pull away, Maurice leapt from the back steps onto the pavement. He turned to make sure that nobody had followed. They hadn't.

'Excuse me,' he asked a smart gentleman in a pin-stripe suit and long cream coat. 'Where might I find the nearest tube station?'

'Kilburn Park. Turn down there and you can't miss it,' the man replied, pointing to a road spurring off to the right.

Maurice thanked him and followed his instructions to the tube. He descended to the platforms, standing with his back against the white-tiled wall whilst carefully studying the assembled crowd. As the tube pulled into the station with a blast of warm air, Maurice jogged to the far end of the train, boarding the last carriage, before quickly jumping back out as the doors closed and the train pulled noisily away, leaving him standing on a deserted platform.

People steadily joined him in waiting for the next train, but none of them drew his attention. He was alert but calm, so certain was he that he could not have been followed to this point. When the train arrived, he stepped inside and took a seat for the seven stops to Oxford Circus, where he changed for the Central line for three stops to Lancaster Gate.

Here, in the affluence of the squares and mews adjoining Hyde Park, Maurice felt at home. He momentarily closed his eyes and took in a long draw of air and smiled, before meandering the short distance to Hyde Park Square.

He entered the corner of the square, which comprised grand four-storey Georgian townhouses built around a rectangular communal garden. He slowed his pace, taking in the house numbers as he went. Here, the commotion of London was reduced to a barely audible background hum. Blackbirds were singing happily from somewhere in the mixed-shrub hedge, designed, Maurice observed, in tandem with the spiked black railings to protect the rich and famous who might use the private gardens which their exclusive homes overlooked. A fat ginger and white cat slowly sauntered across the road, seemingly reflecting the sedate pace of life among these elite streets of north London.

Outside of number thirteen, Maurice stopped; the person, whom he had come to see, lived here in the basement. He pushed open the black metal gate and descended the stone staircase to a glossy red front door. He pressed the doorbell, removed his hat and tried to smile.

The door opened quickly, but just a sliver and not enough for Maurice to be able to tell who might be on the other side of it.

'No press, darling,' a female voice purred.

'I'm not press!' Maurice rushed to say, but the door had already closed. He bent down, lifted up the brass letterbox flap and looked inside. He could just make out the short slender figure of the woman, who had answered the door, sauntering away. 'Wait!' he called through the gap. 'I'm not press. I've come for some information about my wife, Ellen.'

The woman stopped and turned, and Maurice could see that she was the very person with whom he had wanted to speak: Mariella Novotny. Without any hint of urgency, she walked back over to the door and pulled it wide open. She was in her early forties, stunningly beautiful with thick, painted eyebrows and black shoulder-length hair, cut with a perfectly straight fringe. She was wearing a white scanty negligee which left little to Maurice's imagination with regard to what may be beneath.

'Ellen?' Mariella said, staring at him. 'The girl who killed herself after my Christmas party?'

Maurice nodded.

'Yes, it rather put the dampeners on all my parties after that,' she said. 'Damned inconsiderate of her, I should say.' Mariella looked down at the fingernails of her left hand, waiting, Maurice presumed, for him to take her provocative bait and respond angrily in Ellen's defence, thus providing ample cause for her to slam the door in his face.

'I can well imagine,' he replied with a dry smile, playing her at her own game.

She looked up with what appeared to be a mixture of uncertainty and scrutiny. 'What is it that you want?'

'Just a few moments of your time,' Maurice said earnestly. 'I just want to know what really happened that night; to fit the pieces together. Only, I don't actually believe that Ellen killed herself.'

Mariella seemed surprised, arching one eyebrow and saying, 'Oh, is that so?'

'Yes, it is.'

Mariella pursed her lips, seeming to weigh up the decision of whether or not to admit him. She took a long breath in and stared at him some more. 'It's unusual for a gentleman caller to have my time *gratis*, so you'd best make it quick and very much to the point.' She stood to one side and beckoned him in.

'Thank you,' he said, entering a spacious hallway with high ceilings and well-appointed with striking antique pieces.

'Come through to the drawing room,' she said, walking in the recognisable, stylised gait of a fashion model.

As he followed her diminutive figure down the corridor, Maurice peered into the open doors which they passed. The rooms were unexpectedly large and in each was an assortment of types of elegant and tasteful furniture. He followed her through an open door to the left, entering a lavish room which spanned the entire width of the house. On the walls, modern works of art somehow managed to sit tastefully alongside traditional paintings in oil and watercolour. Persian rugs were placed attractively on the polished dark-wood floor and positioned around a grand stone fireplace were an assortment of chairs and a pair of *chaises longues*.

Mariella turned around and pointed to one of the chairs. 'Sit.' It was more an instruction than an invitation, which he duly obeyed.

Maurice perched himself down and watched, as Mariella took her hair in her left hand and removed it, revealing a slicked-back blonde bob beneath where the black wig had been. He gave no reaction, believing it to be all part of this woman's need for provocative performance and drive to seek attention. He knew that he needed to tread very carefully in order to procure the information that he required. Obsequiousness, he was sure, would be the key. It was time to exhume his former charm, the attribute for which he used to be most well-known.

'Drink?' she asked.

'Yes, please,' he answered.

'Of course, you want to drink; that wasn't the question,' she said.

'Pink gin,' he replied. 'Triple, no tonic.'

Mariella smiled. 'Yes!' She flounced over to a drinks cabinet and poured two large glasses. 'Pink gin! To your dead wife,' she said, raising her glass to his.

He chinked her glass, bit his tongue and downed the entire measure.

Mariella smiled again. 'Naughty.' She copied him and sank the lot in one go. 'So,' she began, refilling their drinks as she spoke, 'you're here to find out why your poor wife slit her wrists a couple of hours after attending one of my parties? What terrible thing must have happened to her here? Is that it?'

Maurice shook his head and took the proffered chaser. 'No, I don't think she killed herself at all: *that's* the problem.'

Mariella curled her lower lip in mockery. 'Let me guess: you're religious and can't cope with the idea of her taking her own life?' She raised the back of her hand to her forehead and acted overwrought. 'My wife won't go to heaven!'

'No, it's just not something she would have done.'

'Maybe she hated you,' Mariella suggested.

'Maybe she did,' Maurice agreed.

'I don't know why you're here,' she snapped, finishing her second gin and turning to refill it afresh.

'I was led to understand that you kept detailed diaries of your parties. Who came, what they wore, what they ate, who ended up with whom.'

Mariella laughed an ugly, exaggerated laugh. 'Darling, darling! Really? My parties were attended by the worst, most depraved in all of high society; the most degenerate and debauched of people used to come here. The *last* thing that I could do, darling, would be to hand over a list of these MPs, diplomats, film stars and members of the royal family. Darling, really! Besides'—she took a long swig of her drink—

'the diaries, which once existed, and, yes, which detailed my guestlists of immoral attendees, the little clothing that they wore, and their particular proclivities, were all stolen. Every last one of them, gone.'

Maurice took a glance around the room. It would certainly be a prime target for a burglary and, with rumours of at least one party here per week, a lot of people would have witnessed the kinds of treasures which had been on offer here. 'Well, you've done a fine job in replacing your things.'

Mariella laughed. 'Oh, no, it wasn't *that* sort of a theft.'

'I don't understand,' Maurice said. 'I wasn't aware of there being different categories of burglary.' He smiled playfully, hoping that his tactic of subservient humouring was working on her.

Mariella finished the last of her drink, tossed her hands into the air and, whether by design or accident, released the glass from her grip, sending it straight to the hard floor, where it shattered into hundreds of tiny pieces.

Maurice jumped up.

She pushed him back down forcefully and said, 'Leave it, I want it there as a reminder of the fun we're having.'

Maurice smiled and watched, as she lowered her big toe down onto one of the shards of glass until it pierced her skin, releasing a small trickle of blood.

'So, what kind of burglary was it, then?' he asked, trying to refocus her from revealing any more of her darker pursuits.

Mariella removed her toe from the glass, sat beside him and said, 'One where they only take my diaries and journals and nothing else,' she revealed with an odd laugh.

'Really? *Nothing* else?'

Mariella shook her head. 'They could have taken cash, jewellery, paintings, furniture, but instead they chose *diaries*.'

'And what did the police say?'

'They said that I must have disturbed them before they could get to the valuable things, which is, of course, darling, complete and utter nonsense.'

'You think that they took the one thing that they came for?' he surmised.

'Of course I do.'

'And who do you think stole them?'

Mariella laughed raucously. 'Did you not hear my guestlists? It could have been anyone! Literally. I've no idea and don't really care, to be honest. I just hope they enjoy reading them as much as I enjoyed writing them.'

'When did this happen?'

'The early hours of 18th December 1957,' she said.

'Four days after Ellen's death?'

Mariella shrugged.

The link between the two events seemed inconsequential to her, as though she had never given the matter any thought before now. To Maurice, it was a substantial revelation, although he didn't yet know what, if anything, connected the two.

'Do you recall writing about Ellen and what happened to her after she left here?' he asked.

'Of course, I did,' Mariella said, topping up their glasses, then sitting back down beside him. 'She was a funny little creature and not at all my usual type of guest.'

'In what way?'

'Well, she was just very *ordinary* and plain and not at all the type of girl to come to my parties. I don't even recall how she got an invite, come to think of it, actually.'

'What about Ellen's friend, Doris?' Maurice asked, the alcohol beginning to fray the edges of his thoughts.

'Doris, darling? I'm *quite* sure that I know nobody by that ghastly name and very certain that they wouldn't be attending one of *my* parties,' she answered. '*Doris.*' She shuddered and sank some more gin, as she moved her hand higher up his thigh.

Despite the mulishness of his thinking, this was new startling information for Maurice. Ellen's best friend, Doris, the woman who had found Ellen's lifeless body and who had phoned for an ambulance, had always stated that they had gone to the party together, left together and that the whole thing had been Doris's idea. He looked down at her hand, now uncertain of how to play the situation. He still had more questions but, if he remained here, then he would need to deal, one way or another, with this woman's advances. 'Do you have a lavatory?' he asked, standing up.

'No,' she replied. 'We're terribly primitive in the borough of Kensington and Chelsea. Lavatories have yet to catch on.'

He smiled, picked up the half-finished bottle of gin, and said, 'I should like another glass…'

'Second door on the right,' she said with a dramatic sigh.

In the decadent bathroom, Maurice splashed his face with cold water, then drank from the tap for quite a time. He looked in the mirror at his glassy eyes. His cognitive function was beginning to wane and he could only hold back Mariella's attentions for a short while longer, he thought. He needed to find out more, and quickly.

He returned to the drawing room to find Mariella holding two full glasses of gin, her negligee having slipped down over one shoulder.

'Cheers, darling,' she said, handing him a glass.

'Cheers,' he responded, sitting back down beside her. 'So, do you remember when Ellen left the party, or who she left with?'

'No idea, I don't recall seeing her leave. One thing *is* certain: she wasn't here in the morning, but then you knew that already, darling. She was on the mortuary slab by then.'

Her words stabbed Maurice, but he refused to show it; if he became angry with her, he would discover nothing more. 'And what did she do while she was at the party? Who did she talk to?' he pushed.

Mariella imbibed still more and stared at him. 'Darling, if I asked you the same question, could you answer it? The antics of a boring, dowdy stranger at a party sixteen years ago?'

Maurice drank more in an attempt to appear on the same page but really to curb his frustration. 'But what did she *do* here?'

Mariella shrugged. 'Nothing from what I can remember. As I said, she was dull.'

Maurice had heard enough. He downed the last of his drink and stood to leave. 'Thank you for your time, Mariella. And for the gin.'

She appeared shocked. 'But you're leaving, darling?'

'I've got a lot to do,' he said. 'Goodbye.'

'Wait!' she said, hurrying over to a bureau beside the bay window and retrieving something from inside. 'Here. My phone number, in case you ever get widow melancholia, or need to share a few pink gins with someone… You know…'

He pocketed the card, thanked her once more and left the flat. Outside, the fresh air combined with the effects of the alcohol, instantly impairing his thoughts, distorting his vision and upsetting his sense of balance. He reached out to steady himself against the railings outside of number thirteen. Most of all, though, he wanted to retain everything that she had just told him: Ellen didn't attend the party with her friend, Doris, and four days after her death, Mariella Novotny's diaries and journals were stolen.

He began to walk back towards Hyde Park, rehearsing over and over again what he had just discovered. Even in his inebriated state, two things clearly did not make sense: Ellen would not have killed herself and burglars don't steal diaries.

Chapter Four

Maurice slumped down on the bed with a great sigh. His new furniture had just been delivered by MFI and this was the first time in almost a week that he had lain on a proper bed. The two men had also delivered a white formica wardrobe, two bedside tables, a chest of drawers and an armchair. It wasn't much but it would do for now. Besides, he didn't want too many belongings: the more he possessed, the greater the opportunity they had to plant listening devices. The moment that the men from MFI had left, Maurice had diligently checked every part of the new furniture for such things. He had found none.

And now, after so many nights of sleeping on the hard floor, Maurice was tired. He rolled over onto his side, enveloped by the soft mattress. Sleep began to lure him in, and he curled up into the foetal position, as his eyes began to close. As they did so, he caught sight of the photo frame on his bedside table. Ellen.

He sat up with a jolt. Now was not the time to sleep, especially since he had finally tracked down the new address of Ellen's friend, Doris. Maurice, seized by this sudden new motivation, swung his feet down into his shoes, stood up straight and stretched. In the kitchenette he buttered a piece of Co-op brown bread, folded it in half and devoured it in three mouthfuls which he washed down with a good swallow from a new bottle of pink gin. Picking up his hat and coat, Maurice left the flat and began an elaborate and complex route across the city, jumping on and off random buses and catching the tube to and fro between the same stations three times.

He reached Doris's house in Streatham two hours later in the certain knowledge that he could not have been followed.

The house was a small, brick-built, terraced property, replicated exactly on both sides of the road. Dreary and lifeless, Maurice thought, as he knocked on the door and waited.

'Oh, my goodness me!' Doris declared, as she opened the door, drying her hands urgently on her apron as she did so. 'What—'

'Don't say my name,' Maurice warned.

'What?' Doris asked.

'Don't say my name,' he repeated.

Doris raised her eyebrows. 'Come in.'

It took Maurice a moment for his eyes to adjust to the dimly lit lounge which he had entered. There was a smell, which he couldn't place, lingering in the air. Onions, or something similarly unpleasant.

'Am I allowed to ask *how* you are? Or is that forbidden, too?' she asked, her arms folded across her chest.

'I'm fine, thank you.'

'Where have you been, for Pete's sake?' she demanded. 'Nobody's seen hide nor hair of you since Ellen's funeral.'

'It doesn't matter where,' he replied. 'Just away.'

'And now you're back,' she commented.

'Yes,' he confirmed, noting the hint of condemnation in her voice.

'Well, are you stopping? Do you want a cup of tea?'

'Yes, please,' he answered.

'You'd best sit down, then,' she said.

He sat on one of the two worn settees and waited. From the adjacent kitchen came the sounds of the kettle boiling and Doris's preparing the teacups.

'How long have you lived here?' he called out, taking stock of the room. The walls were decorated in a dark paper with a repeating pattern of varying shades of orange circles and the more Maurice stared at it, the more it hurt his eyes. The rest of the furniture was of the current modern style: cheap, curved and wooden.

'Oh, about a year now,' Doris shouted back over the kettle's final crescendo.

'Nice place,' he lied.

'Yeah, thanks, we love it here,' Doris said, appearing moments later, carrying two cups of tea. 'You don't take sugar, do you?'

'No.'

Doris handed him one of the cups, sat down opposite him and removed a packet of Players cigarettes and Swan Vesta matches from a pouch at the front of her apron. She withdrew a cigarette and lit it, then offered him the packet.

'No, thanks.'

Doris took a long drag on the cigarette, then blew the smoke in his direction. 'So... No name. No asking where you've been. What *am* I allowed to say?'

'What happened on the night of Ellen's death,' Maurice answered, blowing back against the smoke.

41

Doris rolled her eyes. 'I went through all of this at the time. What, you think sixteen years later some new detail will have popped into my head that hadn't occurred to me the day after?'

'Humour me. Remind me.'

Doris puffed on her cigarette, then said in a robotic, perfunctory voice, 'It was all my idea. Me and Ellen got ready at my house, then we took a bus to the party. We stayed for a few drinks, had a dance and a laugh, then took a taxi back to mine. I went to bed, leaving her downstairs listening to music. In the morning I came down to find her dead.'

Maurice nodded, picked up his cup and sipped the tea. He met her veiled nervous gaze, as she drew in a long drag on the cigarette. 'Okay, let me just speak plainly for a moment, Doris. I know you're lying. I know that you didn't go to the party with Ellen. In fact, you didn't go to the party at all. I accept that this is the version that you told the police, and, whatever you tell me next, I won't be passing on to them or asking them to look again into the circumstances surrounding Ellen's death.' He paused, watching, as tears began to well in Doris's eyes. 'I know that she didn't commit suicide and I've come back to find out who did this to her and why. I'm not interested at all in the official version of events—really, I'm not. I don't care, either, whether you lied or not, but I do want you to tell me the truth now. If, however, I don't get the truth from you, I *will* go to the police and provide them with several witnesses, who will attest that you were *not* at the party that night.' He took another mouthful of tea, then sat back in his chair.

'It won't bring her back, you know,' Doris stammered. 'Whatever I do or don't say, she'll still be gone.'

'I'm well aware of that.'

'She made me say it,' Doris said, sobbing and trying to purse her curling lips around the cigarette. 'She made me promise that, whatever happened, I must stick to that story.'

'Even to keep the truth from me...sixteen years later?' Maurice exclaimed.

'*Especially* from you,' Doris spluttered, bursting fully into tears.

Her words struck Maurice, wounding him far more deeply than Mariella's crass and deliberately spiteful remarks. He could see that Doris had meant what she had said, that Ellen had told her to keep her secret, even from him. Maurice displayed no outward sign of the injury that he felt keenly inside.

'She came to my house to get ready—make-up and a nice dress— then went alone to the party. I didn't see her at all after that,' Doris admitted through her tears. 'I woke up in the morning, came downstairs and there she was, stone cold with her wrists slit, in my old grandmother's armchair. No note. No explanation. Nothing. I phoned the ambulance but obviously there was nothing to be done for her.'

'So, you've no indication at all of what time she might have arrived at your house?'

Doris shook her head. 'None at all. I went to bed around eleven o'clock, fell almost straight to sleep and woke just before seven.'

'And what did she tell you she was doing that night?' Maurice asked.

'Just that she was going to a party in Hyde Park Square.'

He could see that she was withholding something. Keeping an even temperament to his voice, he asked, 'Why did she want to go to the party?'

His question had hit on something. Doris squirmed in her seat, clearly not wishing to answer.

'A man?' he suggested.

A vehement shake of the head was Doris's response.

He had no other plausible explanation to propose. 'What, then?'

'Work,' Doris muttered.

'Work?' he challenged. 'Ellen hadn't worked since we got married.' A dark image fell into his mind, that perhaps she had been seeking dubious employment with one of Mariella's sleazy associates. No, he simply wouldn't believe it; not Ellen.

'She'd worked something out, apparently,' Doris finally revealed, 'from the previous year and needed to go to the party to speak with some woman or other to confirm it.'

Maurice was baffled. 'Worked *what* out from the previous year?'

'Oh…I can't remember,' Doris said, welling up again. 'It was all just such a long time ago, you know.'

'Think,' Maurice instructed.

'Something from her days working as a Watcher for MI5,' Doris said, shaking her head uncertainly. 'A double-agent inside MI6.'

'A double-agent?' he repeated. 'Who?'

Doris huffed. 'I'm pretty sure the person was called Jericho. It's stuck with me ever since because…well, it's not a real name, is it?'

'What about Jericho?' Maurice pushed.

'She thought she'd found out who Jericho was and needed to go to that party to confirm it,' Doris blurted. 'Someone was there she needed to speak to.'

'Who?'

Doris shrugged. 'I truly can't remember. A woman, I seem to think, but I could be wrong.'

Maurice believed her, yet the story still made no sense to him. Ellen had worked as a Watcher for MI5, spending her time trailing Soviets, suspected of spying around London, in order to build up a network of their British contacts. But she had left her job just a few days before their marriage on the 8ᵗʰ February 1957—ten months prior to this party. Quite what she had been doing investigating a potential double-agent inside MI6 was beyond him. 'So, Ellen was back working for MI5?'

'I don't know. I don't think so, no. I think she'd just worked out who this Jericho character might have been, that's all.'

'And who was he or she?'

'She didn't tell me. She just said that I couldn't tell anybody ever, not even my Richard. And I didn't...until now.'

'Is there anything else—anything at all—that you can tell me about that night?' he asked. 'Anything that might help me find out what went on?'

Doris shook her head. 'No, I don't think so. As much as I feel so terribly guilty for having broken my word to her, it does feel an enormous relief to finally tell someone. Honestly, you can't know what it's like to... I never thought she'd taken her own life; it just wasn't something Ellen would do. I suppose I was being selfish, too. If something untoward *had* happened to her, then the same might have happened to me if I ever told the truth. Sorry.'

'We've all done things we regret,' Maurice said, finishing his tea and unable to stop wishing that it were something stronger.

'But the alternative to her taking her own life is equally as impossible to imagine. Why would someone do that to her?' Doris asked.

'I think you've already answered your own question as to why: because she knew something that someone else didn't want her to reveal.'

'Oh, how awful,' Doris said.

'Yes, it is. I'm going to go now. Thank you, Doris.'

'I hope you find out what happened to her,' she said quietly, seeing him to the front door. 'Goodbye.'

'Bye…and take care,' he replied, stepping out into the street.

Maurice strode quickly from the property, not caring in which direction he was headed. His mind was swimming with the new information about what had happened to Ellen that night. He hated himself now for fleeing the country the day after her funeral. But then, what choice had he had? None.

He had taken a convoluted route home and, in light of what he had just learned, Maurice once again spent some time meticulously searching the flat for listening devices, or the signs that somebody might have been in during his absence this morning. Ultimately, again he concluded that they had not and felt himself begin to calm a little inside. On his way home, he had stopped off at an independent electronics shop at the far end of Kilburn High Road and had purchased two items: a brand-new Phillips stereo record player and a second-hand FT 200 Yaesu transmitter receiver. He carefully removed the latter from the box and smiled at the device, as though it were an old friend. It was black and the size of a large shoebox. On the front were a series of dials and knobs, and a narrow glass window with a numbered gauge behind it. Maurice plugged it into the mains, then plugged a microphone into the front jack point. He was almost ready. Just one thing left to do to get the machine working.

He entered the kitchenette, approached the small window and picked up the pair of binoculars which he had purchased yesterday from Woolworths. The kitchenette was not an ideal place from which to look out: it was cramped with the sink fixed directly below the window. But it was the only room in the flat with a rear-facing view, so Maurice was forced to prop himself up with his elbows resting on the edge of the basin in order to peer through the net curtain with the binoculars. Running as far as he could see in either direction was a line of three-storey terraced houses with tiny back yards. Maurice carefully rotated the eyepieces, bringing the house directly opposite into sharp detail. It was bare brick with white sash windows, thankfully none of which were netted. It took him little time at all to work out the function of each of the six back rooms; in his mind he was able to picture the inside of the house as plainly as when one looks at a child's open dollhouse. The retro-fitted pipework and obscure-glazed window of the middle-left room told him that it was the bathroom. A similar

45

range of pipework in the bottom-right window, plus the ability to see a cooker and refrigerator there, revealed it to be the kitchen. The bottom-left room, which Maurice believed served as a dining room, contained a table and at least four chairs. In his time living here, he had yet to see a light or any sign of life in the top-left room, giving him the impression that it was perhaps an empty box room or a seldom-used guest room. The top-right and middle-right rooms were bedrooms. They were the first rooms to be illuminated of a morning and the last where light was extinguished at night.

Maurice meticulously checked each room of this particular house to ensure that nobody would see what he was about to do.

Satisfied that the house was either empty, or that the occupants were at the front of the property, Maurice placed the antenna wire between his teeth, slid open the small window and hauled himself awkwardly up into the sink. He shuffled backwards onto the windowsill, briefly glancing to the concrete yard three floors beneath him. Raising his hands up above him, he felt the edge of the gutter. Thankfully, it was made of iron. Maurice gripped it tightly and lifted his bottom from the sill. It was holding.

Slowly raising himself to a standing position, with his feet precariously in the sink, he pulled himself upright and found that he was still a good few feet from the base of the two chimney stacks. He had no choice but to climb out and up onto the tiled roof.

His heart began to pound in his chest, as he hauled his own bodyweight up onto the roof, hearing an unhappy and unwelcome groan from the Victorian guttering. If it were to decide to give up under him, then he would most certainly fall to his death.

He pulled himself up until finally he was on his knees with his feet resting in the gutter. He took a breath, then reached out for the closest chimney stack, his fingertips still a few inches shy of the crumbling brickwork. Given the steep upward angle of the roof, he would not be able to inch his way closer on hands and knees: to attach the antenna to the chimney, he would need to stand up having nothing with which to steady himself, step towards the stack, trust the tiles and hope for the best.

Slowly, Maurice raised one knee, pitching his bodyweight forwards so as to try to avoid falling backwards off the roof. It was painfully slow progress and he began to fear who might be watching from the other houses behind him. It was reckless to attempt such a dangerous thing in the middle of the day, he realised now. Any number of people could be watching or, worse still, have called the police. He cursed himself through his clenched teeth for not having done it at first light tomorrow instead: 'Stupid. Stupid.'

With his hands placed on the tiles in front of him, Maurice arched his back and drew himself into a position resembling some hunchbacked old crone. Feeling himself beginning to falter, he needed to move quickly. He lunged forwards and grabbed at the chimney stack, fortuitously catching hold of a misaligned brick edge and managing to steady himself before pulling closer still.

He took the antenna wire from his mouth and sucked in a big lungful of air, feeling as though he had been unable to breathe for the past few minutes.

Maurice worked quickly, tying the wire between the two chimney stacks and then coiling the lengthy remainder in the guttering directly above the kitchen window. It was ready. Now he just needed to get back inside the flat.

With the chimney stacks to the side of him, Maurice flattened himself to the roof, then allowed gravity to slide him down the tiles slowly. His feet met the guttering and he came to the reassuring halt and hold that he had hoped to achieve.

Once again, he moved onto his knees, which enabled him to reach for the guttering below him. He gripped tightly and began to dangle himself over the edge, his feet searching the void below for the kitchen windowsill before he could transfer any more weight to his lower half.

Panic began to rise inside Maurice, as he heard the guttering moaning under the now full weight of his suspended body, which was threatening to flail. It began to shift slightly away from the wall. He needed to move quickly but steadily.

Fumbling with the tip of his right foot only, he felt for the windowsill below him.

With a sudden jolting crack, the guttering came away from one of its fastenings. Maurice yelped slightly from the shock but still clinging on, as he dropped a good few inches.

Both feet found the windowsill, and, with one rocking pivot motion, he released his hands from the guttering as his feet carried him inside the kitchen. His bottom landed with a thump on the window ledge and his balance was slightly favouring the outside, as he began to tip backwards.

Reaching out with both hands, he grabbed at the sides of the window casement, managing to gain a grip and stop himself from falling at the last moment.

With his heart about to rupture through his chest, Maurice stood up in the sink and reached outside for the antenna wire, pulling it inside the kitchen. Taking a moment to catch his breath, he jumped down to the floor with a soft thud. He'd done it. By the skin of his teeth. Just.

For a few moments, with his hands resting on his knees, he simply breathed and allowed his heart rate to return to normal. Then, he connected the antenna wire to the tuning device which matched the wire to the FT 200, receiving a metallic hissing sound from the speaker in response.

Maurice gently moved the frequency dial to seven megahertz on the high frequency band, which would pick up radio signals emanating from Europe. With a further infinitesimal turning of the dial, a voice crystallised over the airwaves. Maurice had no idea of the identity of the two people speaking, nor anything about the conversation which they were having, yet still he smiled.

'Right,' one of the men said, in pidgin English, 'I'm going QRT.'

'Cheerio for now.'

'Goodbye.'

The airwaves were silent for a moment, then the second person to speak said, 'CQ 40 metres. Golf foxtrot two niner eight hotel. Anybody there?'

Maurice was tempted. Very tempted. The idea of striking up a conversation with a stranger somewhere in Europe was utterly compelling. But he had no licence yet and, after the fiasco of landing at Heathrow, the last thing he needed was to be hauled up for transmitting without one. No, he would content himself—for now at least—with just listening.

Then he did something that he hadn't done for many years: he nudged the frequency to fourteen megahertz and listened. Nothing at all. He turned the dial slowly, hoping to hear something, but the only sound was that of a tinny cackle echoing its way over from Egypt. It wasn't really a surprise that the bandwidth was empty: since Egypt had lost Gaza to Israel in 1967, amateur radio by civilians had been forbidden.

Just a decade prior to that, he had been out there in Egypt and the airwaves had been humming with activity. But they would have been, he remembered, given the political situation out there at the time.

Memories slowly unfurled into Maurice's mind until they became unbearable, leading directly, as they always did, to Ellen's death. He opened a cupboard, took out a bottle of gin and took a long drink. Another of his problems. Another of his solutions.

A certain time later—he had no real idea of how long—he had returned the past to the back of his mind.

He picked up the binoculars, training them on the house directly behind. Carefully checking each room, he caught sight of a female figure, lying on a single bed, close to the window in the middle-right bedroom. She had long mousey hair, was wearing mustard-coloured cords and a patterned white shirt, and was holding a paperback above her head, obscuring her face from his view.

Not the right room, then, Maurice thought, shifting the focus to the top-right bedroom. In that room, he could see no signs of movement at all and lowered the binoculars, planning to look again later in the afternoon. Just as he did so, he caught sight of the girl moving in the middle-right bedroom. He re-trained the binoculars on her, just as she left the room, tossing her book down onto the bed.

Maurice lowered the binoculars, looking with the naked eye at the back of the house, waiting for her to emerge in a different room.

Moments later, the back door opened, and she appeared.

Maurice focussed the binoculars on her and laughed.

She was a *he*. And *he* was in the process of lighting a cigarette. He leant one foot back on the wall behind him, seeming to look up in Maurice's direction, making him falter for a moment, until he reassured himself that it was impossible for the boy to see him through the net curtains.

Maurice watched the boy's every timorous movement, taking in every detail of his face. He appeared to be around the age of sixteen or seventeen. He had dark brown eyes and a face thinned by the framing of his long hair which Maurice considered he might be using as a veil to his introversion, as if not being able to see those around him would create a reciprocal invisibility. It was the band of acne, which bridged the boy's nose and cheeks, that Maurice presumed to be the cause of the timidity.

The boy finished smoking his cigarette, carefully extinguishing the stub on the wall behind him, placing the butt back into the packet and popping a chewing gum into his mouth.

The boy disappeared inside the house, not reappearing at any of the rear windows, making Maurice wish that he could just open the back of

49

the house and see right through into the front. Perhaps, though, the boy had gone out.

He waited a while longer, then abandoned his surveillance. Behind him on the worktop was another bottle of gin. Maurice picked it up. Empty. He really could do with a drink right now. Putting on his coat and hat, he headed down the stairs and out of the flat, where he paused for a moment. The off-licence was quite a walk away, whereas the Black Lion pub was just a short distance on the street corner. It would cost more but it would be quicker.

A smell of stale beer struck Maurice, as he stepped inside the pub. Two beetroot-faced men sitting up at the bar turned to look in his direction. Maurice nodded, removed his hat and approached the bar.

'What can I get you, love?' a short round woman with wide circular glasses asked.

'Pink gin—double. No tonic.' He remembered himself, '...please.'

The barmaid nodded and turned to face the various optics fixed to the mirrored wall right behind her with the wrong type of glass in her hand.

Maurice looked around at the grimy place. The décor appeared not to have been updated since the war: brown walls and a stained carpet so worn as to conceal any idea of its original pattern and colouration. Right now, though, he just wanted a drink. In fact, he wanted several. *Needed* several. He didn't care.

'Here you go,' the barmaid announced, placing the drink onto the bar top. 'Sixty pence, please, love.' He handed over a one-pound note, took the change and carried the drink over to an empty booth, where he sat on a sticky, ripped leather seat. Delightful place, he thought, gazing around him.

Maurice raised the glass to his lips, barely resisting the urge to down the drink in one manoeuvre, and instead took a short sip. Immediately, he relaxed with a long exhalation. He raised his legs and placed his feet onto the seat opposite, as his thoughts turned to what he had just learned from Ellen's close friend, Doris.

He tried to wade through the memory-fog which had closed in around him following Ellen's death, attempting to recall if she had behaved any differently, had acted out of character or dropped any hint that she had returned to the employ of MI5, but there was nothing. From his recollection, the weeks leading up to her death had been completely normal, but maybe that had just been his mind's way of coping with the situation then and ever since.

Maurice took another restrained sip, replaying his conversation with Doris over and over in his mind. She'd said that Ellen had needed to meet someone—a woman, she thought—who would have been at the party. He racked his brains for a female who would move in the intersecting circles of Mariella Novotny's exclusive socialite parties and also the murky world of the intelligence services. One name alone came to mind and the more that Maurice thought about her, the more that it made sense. He downed the last of his pink gin, then rushed over to the bar.

'You having another?' the barmaid asked.

'Do you have a payphone in here?' he demanded.

'Over there,' she said, pointing to the far side of the pub.

Maurice hurried over to the black Bakelite phone, inserted a ten-pence piece, and then dialled Doris's home phone. She answered after some moments.

'Doris, it's me again. The woman. The one who Ellen was going to meet... Was she called Flora Sterling?' Maurice asked.

There was a brief moment of quietness from the other end of the phone, then Doris said, 'Yes...yes. I do think that could have been it.'

Maurice placed the receiver down, his mind elsewhere, already racing through the implications of what he had just heard. Perhaps she had been mistaken, though. There's one way to find out, he thought, feeling in his pocket and retrieving a small card. He placed another ten pence into the phone and dialled the number. It rang for some time and then she answered in a typically theatrical way: 'Yes, darling?'

'Mariella, it's me. Ellen's husband.'

'Oh,' she replied emotionlessly.

'I've another quick question about the night of the party: was Flora Sterling there?'

'Yes, she was, darling.'

Maurice clutched the receiver to his ear, his hand starting to quiver. 'And did you see her talking to Ellen at all?'

Mariella laughed raucously. 'Darling, if there's one thing that I can say about Flora Sterling, it's that she would talk to anyone and *everyone*. The men wanted her, and the women wanted to be her.'

'Do you know where I can find her?' Maurice asked, feeling suddenly tight-chested.

'She *vanished*. Like many of the boys and girls who frequented my gatherings, she stopped coming.'

'Do you know anyone who might know where she is now?'

51

He heard Mariella draw a quick breath in through her nose. 'No, sorry, darling. After the Profumo Affair I went from society elite to discarded leper. I've not heard anything of Flora Sterling for years. Will you be coming here—'

Maurice returned the receiver to the cradle.

'Flora Sterling,' he whispered, as a surge of long-buried feelings were reawakened.

Chapter Five

Morton sat back in his chair and looked at his investigation wall; it was the only part of his study not to be filled with floor-to-ceiling bookshelves and which he kept deliberately empty in order to affix the ongoing research from his genealogical investigations. Today, it was entirely covered with long rolls of paper, each one a different inverted pyramid with Pamela Sweetman's name at the bottom. So far, Morton had identified the line through to six of Pamela's great-great-great-grandparents; none of them, however, yet related to either his Farrier or his Schmidt line.

He stood up and examined the sheets of paper in closer detail, wondering if perhaps he had made a mistake somewhere. It was certainly possible. He convinced himself, though, that he still had another twenty-six lines to pursue before that conclusion could be drawn.

Returning to his desk, Morton logged in to his Ancestry account and clicked on Vanessa Briggs's profile.

Last signed in: Today.

Today. She'd signed in today. Brilliant, except that she hadn't responded to his message.

Thinking that he had nothing to lose, Morton clicked to message her again: *Dear Vanessa. Not sure if you got my last message? We're closely related and wonder if we can work out how we're connected? I believe our relationship is via my grandparents, Alfred Farrier and Anna Schmidt. Do these names appear in your family at all? Looking forward to hearing from you. Kind regards, Morton Farrier.*

Sent.

He stared at the blank roll of paper on his desk and sighed. As much as he wanted to continue working on Pamela Sweetman's pedigrees, Morton needed to make a start on finding out who this Maurice Duggan imposter really had been. Before he headed out to begin his research, he wanted to examine the photograph of the lady, labelled Ellen, which was on his desk below the paperback and pair of glasses.

He had already done the most obvious thing and tried to search for a possible marriage between Maurice Duggan and a woman with the Christian name of Ellen. However, not one marriage had occurred with those exact criteria between 1940 and 1980.

Turning the small wooden frame over, he saw that it had been sealed professionally with brown tape many years ago and, although he didn't like to damage the frame, needed to see the back of the print, if he stood any chance of finding more clues as to who the woman could be on the front. As carefully as he could, Morton lifted a corner of the tape and began gently to draw it along the seam of the frame until the backing board was entirely exposed. He smiled as he lifted it off, glimpsing, as he did so, the photographer's logo. In lieu of an actual description of the person in the picture, it was the next best thing to find, since his analysis of the image itself had proven difficult and any firm ideas of date, location or her identity had so far eluded him.

The words *Daniel Price Photography* were emblazoned on the back, arching over a silhouette of a vintage camera. Below it was written *99 Camden High Street*. It wasn't much to go on, but it was a start. Perhaps *Daniel Price Photography* would still be in business and have kept their records of past customers. Unlikely, but possible.

Google provided no help in identifying the years in which *Daniel Price Photography* had been in business. The fact that it wasn't coming up in his searches, though, strongly indicated that it was not still a going concern. A thorough analysis of the photograph was in order, but for the moment it was time to go to West Sussex Record Office to begin his active research into the Duggan Case.

The archive was situated in a mustard-coloured brick building close to Chichester city centre. Morton parked his Mini in the car park opposite and entered through the blue double-doors. He was familiar with the archive, although he hadn't been back here for some time.

'Good morning,' a smiling lady greeted from behind a semi-circular desk, directly in front of him, as he entered the lobby.

'Morning,' Morton responded.

'Are you wishing to use the search room today and do you have a CARN card?' she asked.

'Yes. And yes,' he replied, fishing his County Archives Research Network card from his wallet.

'Marvellous, if you could just sign in here, that would be great,' the receptionist said, sliding a book with yellow paper sideways across the desk.

Morton scribbled down his name, postcode, reason for his visit and CARN card number, then asked, 'Could I have a locker, too, please?'

'Yes, that's a one-pound deposit, please.'

Morton handed over the money in exchange for a locker key, thanked the lady and then crossed to the cloakroom area, where, once he had removed his laptop, notepad and pencil, he stowed his bag and coat. He returned to the lobby, where the receptionist buzzed him into the search room. The door closed automatically behind him and Morton instantly became aware of the change in atmosphere to the familiar one of quiet, intense busyness. The room was T-shaped: to the left of him was a long help desk, beneath which were dozens of microfilm boxes. Several archivists busied themselves behind the desk, coming and going with documents and using the computers there. To Morton's right were several banks of computers and microfilm readers. Guides, books, reference materials and large adjoined desks were found in the perpendicular section at the far end of the room, which was where he was now headed.

Only three of the tables were occupied by researchers, so Morton placed his things down at a table at the far end and then approached the help desk.

'Hi,' Morton said to the middle-aged lady working there. She was thin with long, curly blonde hair, wearing black jeans and a black top.

'Hello,' she said, with a bright smile. 'How can I help?'

'Electoral registers for Ardingly, please,' he said.

'Okay. Which time period are we talking about?' the archivist asked.

'Erm…the most recent,' Morton faltered, 'working backwards until I'm not sure when…'

She smiled, despite his vagueness. 'Right, well, because of a shifting boundary line, the first ones we hold for Ardingly are 1975 and the most recent are 2014.'

'That's fine,' Morton said.

The archivist handed over a small slip of paper and told him what to do. 'Fill this in with your name, CARN number and today's date, and then, here'—she pointed at *Manuscript Catalogue Reference*—'just write 'Ardingly electoral registers' and the dates that you're interested in. Then place the paper in this box, here and we'll deliver them to you.'

'Perfect,' Morton said. 'Thank you very much.'

'Oh, you're very welcome.'

Morton walked over to his table and completed the document request slip, then carried it over to the help desk, placing it in the small Perspex box, there. 'Sorry… Two more things if I may,' he said to the archivist, who was busy tapping away at a computer keyboard.

She looked up with a smile. 'Of course, go ahead.'

'Am I right in saying that the electoral registers you hold here are the ones which the public can't opt out of?' he asked.

'That's right,' she confirmed. 'If somebody was living in—where was it again, sorry? Oh, yes, Ardingly—then they would be present in the registers.'

'Brilliant.'

'And the second thing?' she asked with a grin.

'A DIY Photography Request Form, please,' he said.

'No problem,' she answered, producing an orange form. 'So, you just need to write down the references for each document you photograph, and one thing I must say is that I'm afraid you can't photograph electoral registers from the last ten years for privacy reasons.'

'That's okay,' Morton replied, completing the form.

'Eleven pounds, then,' she said, snipping off the corner of the paper for some reason unknown to Morton.

He paid by credit card, then took the orange form over to his desk and waited. While he did so, he reviewed his notes on the Duggan Case thus far, which largely made very little sense. He hoped today to be able to pin down the year in which the man posing as Maurice Duggan had appeared in Ardingly. He also wanted to look up details of the real Maurice Duggan's life and death, to see if any clues could be found there. Beyond that, he had no idea how he might uncover the real man's identity.

'Wow, that was quick,' Morton said, when, ten minutes after handing in the request slip, a trolley laden with books was wheeled to his desk.

'We aim to please,' a young man said with a sideways wink.

'Thank you.'

Morton crouched down beside the trolley and examined the green hardbacked volumes. He selected the most recent with *MID SUSSEX DISTRICT REGISTER OF ELECTORS 2013 / 2014*, typed in gold lettering on the spine, and sat down with it at his table.

The first page told him that the register was arranged alphabetically by street name across the entire district. Morton checked in his notepad for the location of Maurice's last address, where he had committed suicide six months prior: Priory Flats, College Road, Ardingly.

Morton found the page reference for College Road and began to carefully search the property names. He located Priory Flats with little difficulty and ran his finger down the list of occupants until he found him:

DUGGAN, Maurice - 18 Priory Flats

He was the sole occupant of the flat, as were all of the others also living in the building, making Morton wonder if Priory Flats was some kind of sheltered accommodation for the elderly. He made a note of his findings, then took a surreptitious glance around him. Nobody was looking in his direction, so he took a sneaky photograph of the entry. Placing the volume back on the trolley, he took the register for 2011 / 2012 and found Maurice living alone at the same address. He photographed the page, then proceeded to the previous book: 2009 / 2010. Same result.

Morton worked his way backwards through the early 2000s to the 1990s, diligently photographing each record. As other occupants of Priory Flats came and went over the years, the man, living his life under the stolen identity of Maurice Duggan, remained living alone at number 18. Each year was the same through the 1980s until he reached 1978 / 1979 when Morton found a different occupier, residing at number 18:

LAWSON, Gene – 18 Priory Flats

He carefully checked the rest of the building, but there was no sign of Maurice. But just because he hadn't been residing at Priory Flats, it didn't mean that he would not have been living elsewhere in Ardingly, he reasoned. Morton had no choice but to begin a meticulous search of the entire village. Within fifteen minutes he had concluded there to have been no sign of Maurice Duggan in Ardingly. He now had one nebulous new fact: the man had arrived in the village at some point in the late 1970s. But where he had come from and what his real identity was, Morton still had no better understanding.

He had other avenues which he wished to pursue, but for now he wanted to turn his attention to the real Maurice Duggan. For some reason, a tiny part of him urged him to substantiate Clarissa Duggan's story. Perhaps it was because he had been duped by past clients. Whatever the reason, Morton wanted to firmly establish for himself that the boy really had died in 1944.

Standing up from his desk with a stretch, Morton pushed the trolley of electoral registers back over to the help desk. 'I've finished with these, now,' he said to the blonde archivist.

'Great. Any joy?' she enquired.

Morton thought for a second. They had served their purpose of telling him when Maurice had arrived in Ardingly. 'Yes, helpful, thank you.'

'Super,' she replied.

Morton thanked her again, drifted over to the shelves and then took down the folder which provided an index to the archive holdings of parish registers and bishop's transcripts. He thumbed his way through the first few pages until he reached Ardingly, then sighed.

1884 – 1910 PAR 231/2/2/3 BAPTISMS
1837 – 1937 PAR 231/1/3/2 MARRIAGES
1937 – 1953 PAR 231/1/3/3 MARRIAGES

No baptisms for 1927 and no burials at all. Great.

Morton carried the folder over to the help desk, approaching the closest archivist—a man in his fifties with thinning hair and a pair of glasses perched on the end of his nose. He looked up and smiled, sliding the glasses closer to his eyes.

'Hi,' Morton began. 'I think I already know the answer, but I'm after Ardingly baptisms post-1910 and Ardingly burials for 1944.' Morton turned the folder and waited while the archivist scrutinised the ledger.

'We don't hold them, I'm afraid,' he confirmed. 'It means they're still at the church and have never been deposited with us.'

'Thought as much,' Morton said. 'Okay, thank you.'

He replaced the file and returned to his desk, considering his options. He could contact the church and request to see the registers, or he could simply order Maurice's birth and death certificates. He decided to do both, wanting to be absolutely certain that his man had existed and had died in 1944.

On his mobile phone, he ran a Google search for Ardingly Church. Second to a Wikipedia entry, the church had its own website, to which Morton clicked through and, under the *Contact Us* tab, he found the email address of The Reverend John H Crutchley. Morton clicked the link and composed a quick message: *Dear Sir, I am researching a family tree and wonder if it might be possible to view the baptism and burial registers you hold for around 1925-1945? I believed that the records were held at West Sussex Record Office but have been told that they are still with the church. It should only take a few minutes. Kind regards, Morton Farrier.*

He sent the email, then paused to consider his next steps. Both of the deaths of Maurice Duggan were suitably tragic to have made the local newspapers, he thought, heading back over to the help desk, certain that he must be getting on their nerves with his persistent questions.

A young lady, with short dark hair, glasses and a red floral dress, stood from the desk with an armful of papers, but when she spotted him heading towards her, smiled pleasantly and placed the papers down. 'Are you okay there?' she asked.

'Sorry,' Morton said, 'Newspapers. Six months ago, and 1944. Please.'

'Which newspapers were you after, exactly?' she asked.

'In which paper would a death in Ardingly village be most likely to appear?' he countered.

'Probably the *Mid Sussex Times*,' she replied. 'We don't have any newspapers at all for the last six months, though, I'm afraid. For the *Mid Sussex Times*, your best bet is Haywards Heath Library. For editions in 1944, the paper has been digitised as part of our First World War and Second World War project. Follow me and I'll show you.'

Morton thanked her, as he followed her over to the run of half-a-dozen computer terminals.

'Right,' she muttered, wiggling the mouse to bring the computer back to life. 'All the digitised papers are in here,' she said, double-clicking a yellow folder icon, named *Local History Sources*, followed by *1914 to 1945 Newspapers*. 'These are all the titles, and then you click into each one and browse to the date you're after. Once the newspaper is up on-screen, you can use the search function to look for keywords or just scroll through one page at a time. Okay?'

'Yes, very helpful, thanks,' Morton said.

'Give me a shout, if you need any more help,' she said, heading back towards whatever she had been going to do before he had interrupted her.

Morton watched her go, as he took a seat at the computer, unsettled by the warm friendliness of the staff here. Not a Deidre Latimer to be found.

He looked down the list of available newspapers—*Bognor Regis Observer, Chichester Observer, East Grinstead Observer, Horsham Times,*

Worthing Gazette—and clicked to open the *Mid Sussex Times*. He was presented with a further selection of folders, dated for the years of the two world wars. He clicked 1944 and a PDF opened with the entire year's newspapers. Then he scrolled quickly through to the edition for 21st December, when Maurice Duggan had died for the first time.

Sandwiched between a story about political plans for post-war Britain and public information advice from the Ministry of Agriculture about making pig swill safe, was the story for which he was searching. Morton zoomed into the story and read purposefully.

DUGGAN BOY DROWNED WHEN ICE GAVE WAY
Maurice Duggan, the son of renowned local businessman, Gerald Duggan of Knowles, Ardingly, was drowned on Saturday afternoon when the ice gave way on which he had been playing at Westwood Lake. This tragedy was attended by a deed of great pluck and heroism by a 17-year-old boy, named Hubert John Spencer from 2 Street Lane, Ardingly. He was nearby and plunged into the icy water to Maurice's rescue. He succeeded in getting Maurice onto his back and, holding him with one hand, swam to the edge of the lake. Hubert continued his heroic endeavours to get Maurice out of the water but he suddenly slipped out of his grasp and disappeared under the ice. Hubert, himself well-nigh exhausted by the cold and his strenuous efforts, managed to scramble out. Another of the boys' friends, William Gilmour sent for P.C. Foster, and after attempting to reach the hole in the ice, ran half a mile to fetch a ladder. Sub-Divisional Inspector Martin and other officers made efforts to get to the boy. They procured a boat which they launched, quickly finding Maurice Duggan's body. Attempts to revive him were made whilst still in the boat and continued when he was on the bank. A resuscitator was also used until the arrival of Dr Rooney, who pronounced life extinct. At the inquest of Wednesday, Mr J. Baily-Gibson, Deputy Coroner recorded a verdict of "Death by misadventure."

Morton took a breath, saddened by the tragic account of the boy's death. He realised, then, that in his mind he had been treating the genuine Maurice Duggan, as though he hadn't been a real person at all; an actual boy, who had died under dreadful circumstances at a young age. And, for the first time, too, he felt resentment towards the man, who had stolen his identity several years later.

Morton photographed the newspaper article, then ran a confirmatory check for any other references to the Duggan family in 1944, but there were none. He returned to his desk and opened his notebook to see what his next steps might be. Between Maurice's death in December 1944 and his supposed resurrection in the same village in 1979, there was so far no trace. All he had from this period was the *Live and Let Die* library book and the photograph of Ellen. On his mobile phone, he looked back at the photograph which he had taken of the inside of the book cover, showing that it had last been taken out from Willesden Library on 7th July 1974. Had Maurice been the one to remove the book and never return it? He opened Google on his laptop, ran a search for the library phone number and called them. A female voice answered almost immediately.

'Hello,' Morton said in a low voice, not wishing to irk the otherwise very pleasant staff in the archive. 'I've come by a library book of yours from 1974 and—'

'—want to return it but without paying the fees? I know,' the woman guessed with a quite reprimanding tone.

'Er, no,' Morton defended. 'As I said, I've come by the book and—'

'How did you *come by it*?' she demanded.

'Among the possessions of a dead friend,' he said bluntly, hoping that that would put an end to her telling-off.

It worked. 'Oh,' she said. 'So, what do you want to know, then?'

Morton swallowed down his irritation and said politely, 'I wondered if it might be possible to find out the name or address of the person who had last taken it out in 1974.'

The woman laughed. 'No chance. Our systems don't go back that far and, even if they did, privacy laws would prevent me from divulging that kind of information. GDPR and all that. Besides which, surely *your friend* would have been the last person to sign it out?'

Morton ended the call with a huff. That was going nowhere.

'I'm really sorry, but you can't make phone calls in here,' the blonde archivist said, pulling an apologetic face.

'Sorry,' Morton said. 'I won't do it again.'

She smiled appreciatively and walked off. Even when they were telling you off, they were nice, Morton thought. Deidre Latimer needed to come here for some customer service training.

Assuming that Maurice *had* been the last person to take out the book, then it was reasonable to think that he had lived somewhere within that London borough. Would electoral registers provide the answer? Without an address, it would mean a search of the entire area. Morton asked Google, *How many people live in Willesden?* and received the answer of 329,102. A search such as that would take days and, being

61

based on several assumptions, was not one upon which he was about to embark. Next, Morton typed *Maurice Duggan* into the search box, then spent several minutes fine-tooth-combing the results. Nothing obvious. Adding the word *Willesden* brought Facebook and LinkedIn profiles to the fore. Beyond that, Google seemed to have trouble establishing any link between the three words.

Logging in to his Findmypast account, Morton clicked on the *Newspapers & Periodicals* tab and, before entering Maurice's name into the keyword search, applied the *1970-1979 British newspapers* filter. *Your search returned 1 article.*

The record related to an article in the *Harrow Observer,* dated 22nd March 1974. The small headline, *Heathrow Charges* was highlighted in blue, whilst Maurice's name was highlighted in green. It looked promising, Morton thought, as he clicked to read the full article.

HEATHROW CHARGES

Maurice Duggan, 47, was fined a combined £225, when he pleaded guilty to two offences at Uxbridge Magistrates' Court yesterday. Police said that Duggan had landed his Cessna 150 aircraft at Heathrow Airport in the early hours of 19th February this year without filing a flight plan and failing to obtain clearance from Air Traffic Control.

The story was brief, yet interesting. Was it the same man? His age certainly matched with the real birth year of 1927 but there was little else to prove or disprove that they had been the same person. Morton took a screenshot of the entry and noted the details on his pad.

Whilst he was pondering the newspaper article, his laptop pinged with the arrival of an email. It was a message from the vicar of St Peter's Church, Ardingly, the Reverend Crutchley: *Hi Morton, I'm more than happy to help. Would meeting with me tomorrow morning, at say 10am in the church be good for you? Best wishes, John.*

Morton typed a reply that tomorrow morning would be perfect, then clicked send.

Next, he ordered Maurice's birth and 1944 death certificates. It was then that he noticed the time: 4.24pm. The archive would be closing in twenty minutes and he had a two-hour drive home. It was time to leave, but he wanted to check one last thing on his laptop. He was sure that, at some point in the past, he had seen some pilot records on the Ancestry website and logged in to check. After playing with keywords on the Card Catalogue search page, he found what he was looking for: *Great Britain Royal Aero Club Aviator's Certificates 1910-1950.*

Morton typed Maurice's name into the search box and hit enter. *Your search for Maurice Duggan returned zero good matches.* He removed the Christian name. *Your search for Duggan returned zero good matches.* He re-entered the Christian name and removed the surname. 299 results. Morton scanned down the list of names, but no one appeared any more likely than the rest to have offered any clues.

It was time to stop for the day and head home.

'Hello, my darling girl!' Morton exclaimed as he entered the front door, to be greeted by an excited Grace. He scooped her up into his arms and kissed her. 'What have you been doing today, then?'

'Nursery playing,' she answered.

'Nursery playing? Wow,' Morton said, then lowered his voice. 'Is Mummy super happy after her day at work?'

'No,' Grace said.

'I heard that,' Juliette called from the kitchen. 'And I'm perfectly happy, thank you very much.'

Morton pulled a face and carried Grace into the kitchen. Juliette was sitting at the table with a cup of tea, reading a magazine. 'Good afternoon, Constable Farrier,' he said, leaning down and kissing her on the lips. 'So, it was better today, then?'

'Well, I was allowed out of the station, so that was something.'

'Were you?' he asked, unable to conceal the concern in his voice.

'Don't worry. Unmarked car. Plain-clothes stuff,' she replied.

'So, basically CID?'

'No, just gathering CCTV from some shops after a hit-and-run yesterday. Not usually the most exciting of jobs, but after being stuck behind a desk, it was bliss.'

'Hit and run!' Grace said, slapping Morton hard on the leg and hurrying from the room, giggling.

'Whoops,' Juliette said. 'We're going to get a phone call from nursery tomorrow, complaining that Grace is going around hitting and running.'

Morton laughed, moving behind Juliette and placing his hands onto her shoulders. 'Fancy a wander down to the playpark?' he suggested, gently massaging her neck.

Juliette's head sank forward and she mumbled something incomprehensible, evidently enjoying her massage.

Grace returned with a cheeky smile on her face.

'No more hit and run,' Morton warned.

Grace scowled, sidled up to Juliette. 'No hit and run Mummy.'

'No.'

Grace prodded Juliette's tummy. 'No hit and run baby.'

'No, definitely not hit and run baby,' Morton agreed.

He should be in bed. He should be asleep. It was gone midnight and the house was silent. Juliette and Grace had gone to bed hours ago, and Morton was now sitting alone in his study working by the light of his laptop and desk lamp. He had eliminated a further two lines from Pamela Sweetman's tree and a third had proven so difficult that he had set it to one side.

He sighed, stretched and yawned. *Really*, he needed to go to bed.

Just a little more research, he told himself, knowing that in the morning he would be back on the Duggan Case with no time to work out how Vanessa Briggs was related to him.

Another sigh. Another yawn. Back to the pedigree chart. Back to Pamela Sweetman's great-great-grandfather on her maternal Puleston line, a man born in 1859 by the name of Benjamin Perl. Morton had already found him on the 1861 census, living with his parents, Eliza and Jack Perl.

Morton typed Jack Perl's name into the marriage search index on FreeBMD, in order to ascertain his wife's maiden name.

There was just one marriage, in the March quarter of 1857 and in the correct registration district. He clicked the entry to see the potential names of John's spouse. Eliza was there, with a very familiar surname.

'Wow,' Morton said, asking his tired brain to work out the implications of this surprising revelation.

He had found how Pamela Sweetman was related to him and how Vanessa Briggs was also related to him, therefore.

Chapter Six

'I don't get it,' Juliette said dismissively, taking a bite of her bagel and turning around to watch Grace pull a stack of saucepans from the kitchen cupboard, sending them crashing down onto the stone floor around her. 'Grace! You've got your *own* kitchen over there. Why don't you play with that?'

'No,' Grace replied, banging two of their best pans together with glee.

'God, how are we ever going to cope with *two* of these creatures?' Juliette mumbled. 'We really need to get those child-lock things fixed to the cupboard doors.'

'I'll do it later,' Morton said. He sipped his coffee, then steered the subject back to his discovery late last night. 'So, Pamela Sweetman is my fourth cousin.'

'But I thought it was Vanessa somebody you were interested in? Who's Pamela? Grace! Oh, my giddy aunt…' Juliette said, jumping up and putting the saucepans back into the cupboard. 'Come and play with *your* kitchen. Look.' Juliette strutted over to the other side of the room, to the toy cooker and placed a miniature packet of tea into a miniature saucepan onto the miniature hob. 'Yummy!' She turned to Morton and muttered, 'What has happened to us?'

Grace finally relented and tottered over to Juliette. 'My kitchen.'

'Yes, exactly.' Juliette sighed and focussed back on Morton. 'Pamela. Fourth cousin. Is this somebody we need to invite to gatherings? Is she coming for Christmas?'

Morton laughed. 'No, she was the person I was using to triangulate how I was related to Vanessa Briggs.'

'Right. And how *are* you related to Vanessa Briggs?'

'Through the…*Farrier* side,' he said with dramatic emphasis.

'Right,' she responded flatly.

Evidently his revelation had not been quite as exciting to Juliette as it had been to him at two o'clock in the morning. 'So, then I needed to work out which of the Farrier men was Vanessa Briggs's biological father. The most likely date-wise was my grandfather, Alfred Farrier, and so I used the *What are the Odds?* tool on the DNA Painter website and…'

'And what *are* the odds?' she interrupted, trying to move him along with this long reveal.

'Five thousand eight hundred and thirty-three.'

'Morton,' Juliette began, 'you know when Grace picks up her guitar and sings, and it's complete and utter gibberish nonsense that comes out of her mouth?'

'Yes.'

'I understand *that* more than I'm understanding what you're telling me, right now. Is your grandfather, Alfred Farrier, Vanessa Briggs's dad, or not?'

'Yes.'

Grace wobbled over, carrying a small plate upon which was a plastic tomato, banana and tin of tuna. 'Baby food,' she informed Juliette, handing her the meal.

'Oh, thanks, Grace,' Juliette said, pretending to tuck in.

'No!' Grace shrieked. 'Baby food.' She took the plate from Juliette and pressed the plastic tin of tuna into her stomach.

Juliette rolled her eyes and selected Morton's thread of conversation again. 'So, remind me. Your grandmother died in childbirth with Aunty Margaret in the late 50s. So, this Vanessa woman is the product of another relationship of your grandfather's after that time? That it?'

'Correct.'

'And why is this such a big deal? Am I missing something here?'

It was a fair point. Why did the discovery feel so significant to him? 'Maybe because she was clearly kept a secret from our family. Aunty Margaret has a half-sister out there somewhere that she's got no idea exists.'

'Are you going to tell her?'

Morton shrugged. It was one of those ethical-dilemma moments which he constantly had to navigate in the line of his forensic genealogy work. 'Not right now, no. I need to find out more, first.'

'And how are you going to do that? You said Vanessa wasn't answering your messages.'

Morton shrugged. 'There's no sign of her birth in the indexes, so Briggs could be her married name. I don't know… I need more time on it.'

'Well,' Juliette said, standing up and draining the last of her tea. 'We'll leave you to it…because Miss Grace Matilda Farrier has swimming lessons in forty-five minutes. Come on! Let's go and get ready.'

'Yeah. And I need to go and get ready to meet the vicar of Ardingly.'

'Not the vicar of Dibley, then? What fun. Enjoy,' Juliette said. 'Come on, Grace. We're going swimming.'

'Swimming!' Grace yelled, as Juliette carried her from the room.

Morton found a perfect parking space for his Mini; just a short walk away from Priory Flats and directly outside the Ardingly Café. He slung his bag over his shoulder, locked the car and hurried from the chill wind into the small but bustling café.

'A large latte to take away, please,' Morton ordered at the counter.

'Anything else for you?' the waitress asked, as she made the drink. 'We've got some gluten-free pineapple cake or lemon drizzle cake, all freshly baked this morning.'

'I'd better not,' Morton answered, aware of how much cake he had been eating since his adoptive brother, Jeremy, had set up the scone shop troublesomely close to his house. Every time he passed the shop, another weird and wonderful daily special would be foisted upon him.

'That's two pound forty, then, please,' the waitress said, placing a take-away cup down on the counter.

Morton paid for the drink, thanked her and left the café. He glanced up at the ominous-looking, dark clouds in the distance. Winter was on its way.

He crossed the street to College Road, one of the main thoroughfares through the small Sussex village. The area was semi-rural, with a motley mixture of house-types, varying in architectural style and size. He had already located Priory Flats on Google Street View, so knew that it was just a short distance away.

Morton walked quickly, clutching his coffee for warmth. The flats soon came into view, standing rather incongruously against almost every other building in the village. Lacking any kind of elegance, the four-storey building was simply a pebble-dashed, up-ended oblong standing in a square of tarmacked carpark. It was the kind of monstrosity thrown up by councils in the 1950s in response to the acute post-war housing shortage.

He sipped his latte, then pulled out his mobile phone to take a photograph of the building. The interloper posing as Maurice Duggan had ended his life by jumping from one of those windows, Morton thought, gazing at the upper floor.

67

Taking another sip of his drink, he approached the front door and tried the handle. Locked. Beside the door was a silver intercom panel with small buttons alongside each flat number. Morton was half-tempted to press one of them but decided against it, reasoning that there was probably little to be gained from actually going inside.

He decided to take a walk around the side of the building, stopping to photograph it from various angles, wondering which flat had belonged to Maurice. At the rear, Morton believed that he had found the answer, when he spotted a small section of tape tied to a drainpipe, now flapping frantically in the wind. He pulled it taut. *POLICE LINE DO NOT CROSS*, read the blue letters over a white background.

Morton looked at the window directly above him, wondering if that was where Maurice had jumped from. His mind drew his eyes to the ground, as if he might see some tell-tale indentation.

'Terrible business, that,' a male voice said, startling Morton. He turned to see an elderly man unloading a sack of manure from the boot of a tiny old Nissan Micra.

'Yes,' Morton agreed, hoping that they were talking about the same thing.

The man was short, elderly, missing most of his front teeth and was dressed in scruffy old clothing.

'Did you know him?' Morton asked.

'Maurice?' the man said, before answering the question. 'Yeah. Well, you know...'

'Hmm,' Morton said.

'You a relative, are you?'

'Sort of,' Morton replied.

'Coming to lay flowers at the spot. That's a thing nowadays, isn't it?' the man said.

'Was this something you'd expected?' Morton asked, with a nodded gesture to the window above.

The man shrugged. 'Didn't know him well enough to know. Besides, mentalness is all the rage now, isn't it?'

'Erm...' Morton said. 'Well, it is talked about more, now, yes.'

'Yes,' the man agreed. 'Quite the fashion.'

'Was anybody living here close to him, would you say?' Morton asked, keen to change the line of conversation.

Another shrug. 'Kept hisself to hisself did old Maurice. He spent most of his time at his typewriter.'

'Oh, right,' Morton said. 'Do you know what he was typing?'

The old man shook his head. 'Never allowed in his flat and he wasn't the type to talk about what he was up to. Kept hisself to hisself. Mind you, he did make an appearance at last year's residents' Christmas party, which was very unlike him. I think Winnie Alderman from number fifteen had a thing for him and she persuaded him to go.'

'Residents' party?' Morton queried.

'Well, you know. A gathering. Egg sandwiches, twiglets—not me, coz they hurt me gums—that sort of thing.'

'I don't suppose anybody would have photographed it, would they?' Morton asked, hopefully.

The old man blew out his cheeks. 'Maybe Winnie did, she likes to take photos, but none of them are much cop,' he said with a laugh. 'I can ask her, if you like.'

Morton glanced at his watch. Fifteen minutes until his meeting with the vicar of St Peters. 'I've got an appointment right now. Could I pop back afterwards, do you think?'

The old man grimaced and nodded simultaneously, which Morton took to be an affirmation. 'Thanks. Which number do you live at?'

'Sixteen.'

'Okay, great. I shouldn't be more than an hour. Thank you,' Morton said, turning back towards the front of the building and the main road.

He walked quickly, partly to counter the chill seeping into his bones and partly so that he arrived on time for his appointment. He reached the Mini, climbed in and was immediately grateful for the warmth from the inside of the car. Finishing the last mouthful of his coffee, Morton started the engine and drove along Street Lane towards the church.

As he drove, he mulled over what the old man had just said about Maurice keeping himself to himself. Suddenly, Morton spotted something to his left and, having quickly checked that the road was clear behind him, slammed on the brakes, then reversed a few metres backwards.

Knowles, read the wooden house-sign affixed to the fence panel. Maurice Duggan's house in 1944.

With five minutes to spare and knowing that the church was just a short distance away, Morton pulled the Mini over to the side of the road and stepped from the car. Behind the wooden gate was a pea-beach drive and a large stone house, mostly concealed behind a sizable yew tree. He could see little of the actual house but was able to determine that it was substantial, which fitted with Clarissa Duggan's story about the family's having wealth once upon a time. Morton took a photograph of the entrance, then retreated back to his car and continued the last short stretch to the church.

The square tower of St Peter's rose from behind a low privet hedge on a quiet, little-used junction between Church Lane and Street Lane. Morton parked his car directly opposite the fourteenth-century stone church, crossed the street and walked through the lychgate. Following a brick path, which wound around the left side of the church through the ancient burial ground, he found himself at the wooden porch entrance at precisely ten o'clock.

He pushed open the thick-set door and stepped inside the church. Like many from this period, it was decorated in the Gothic style, with hood-moulded, stained-glass windows, the most impressive being that which was situated high above the altar. As Morton studied the window, there was movement in his peripheral vision. He turned with a smile to see a tall man wearing a black suit, blue shirt and a white dog-collar. He had glasses and a warm welcoming smile. 'Morton Farrier?' he greeted, extending his hand forwards. 'John Crutchley.'

Morton shook his hand. 'Thank you for meeting me. I much appreciate it.'

'No problem at all. We get quite a few visitors from around the world, searching for their relatives; usually from America and Canada. It was the baptism and burial register you were after, wasn't it?' the rector asked.

'Yes, that's right. Baptisms for around 1927 and burials for 1944,' Morton confirmed.

'Okay, well, they're just over here,' he said, crossing behind the several rows of wooden pews which ran the length of the nave towards the altar. In the side aisle, the rector removed a maroon cloth, revealing a long metal trunk. 'The parish chest,' he declared with a grin.

'Wow,' Morton said, impressed at the wonderful old chest, the only modern part of which were two shiny metal padlocks that the vicar set about unlocking. Having removed the padlocks, he swung open the lid of the ornate trunk.

Morton peered inside at the collection of ledgers and other intriguing documents, watching as the rector leant over and, after a little delving, retrieved two thin books, which he passed to Morton. 'There you go.'

'Thanks,' he said, taking the ledgers and placing them down on the nearest pew. Originally white with two brass clasps on the side, they were now covered in brown mottling and one of the clasps had been broken at some point. *REGISTER OF BAPTISMS NOVEMBER 1910 – APRIL 1964*, the top-most book read in gold lettering below the royal coat of arms of the United Kingdom.

Morton opened the book and turned the pages until he reached 1925, where he began a methodical search down the list of surnames. The parish was small and so it took him just a few seconds to find Maurice's name.

Date: 8th July 1927
Child's Christian name: Maurice
Parents' Names: Gerald and Marie Duggan
Abode: Ardingly
Quality, Trade or Profession: Gentleman

'That's him,' Morton said, more for the vicar's benefit than for his own. 'Do you mind if I take a photograph of it?'

'By all means, go ahead.'

Morton took a picture of the whole page and then a close-up of Maurice's specific entry. He closed the book, then opened the burial register which ran from 1886 to 1969. Morton opened the ledger and flicked through to the year 1944, which occupied just two pages of the register. Maurice Duggan was the final entry for that year.

Name: Maurice Duggan
Abode: Knowles, Ardingly
When buried: 24th December 1944
Age: 17 years

The poor boy had been buried the day before Christmas. Morton suddenly felt guilty for his mistrustfulness of Clarissa Duggan, who had told him just how horrific it had been for her to see her brother's dead body on display prior to the burial.

'He drowned in Westwood Lake,' Morton told the vicar, pointing to the burial entry.

'Oh, how dreadful,' he commented. 'That's just a couple of fields away from here.'

'Is it easy to get to?' Morton asked, photographing the page.

'Not from this side of things, no. Back in 1944 you probably could have walked there from here in five minutes. Now it's fenced off—it's part of Wakehurst Place, you see—so you'll have to go in through their property and walk down to it. Nice little spot.'

'Thank you,' Morton said, folding down the two brass clasps, as best he could, and passing the registers back to the vicar. 'Thanks for allowing me to see these at such short notice. I really do appreciate it.'

'You're very welcome. Have a good day,' the rector said.

Morton shook his hand, thanked him again and left the church. He followed the brick path back to the lychgate and started to cross the road, when he spotted a separate burial ground on the opposite side of the road behind a pair of low wooden gates. He still had plenty of time to get back to Priory Flats, and so walked over to the gates and entered the cemetery. It was relatively small, rectangular in size and, judging by the modern graves, still in use. As Morton began to wander along the grass path, he estimated there to have been around two hundred gravestones.

He looked at his watch. If he were quick, he could just about undertake a cursory check of the legible graves. His hope was that because the Duggans had been wealthy, there would be some kind of a memorial to Maurice.

Morton ambled along the grass path, checking two rows of graves, as he walked. He paused occasionally to check the more indecipherable stones, wondering why he was so keen to pursue Maurice's original incarnation. Certainly, finding his baptism, burial and headstone was of no consequence to his investigation into the fraudulent Maurice, yet something was driving a meticulousness in him to explore every part of the original boy's short life, too.

The answer to his question came just as he spotted the grave. It was a simple cross of stone which time had aged prematurely; it was now a jaded dark grey colour, covered in orange lichen blotches and losing the battle against a deep green ivy which reached insidiously up from the square base. At the bottom, in diminishing clarity, letters gave Maurice's name, carved above his birth and death dates.

The cause of his thoroughness, Morton realised, was because of something that Clarissa had said. It was roughly along the lines of its being ironic that the man impersonating her brother had died in the same village as her actual brother. It wasn't ironic or a coincidence, Morton believed, staring at the grave. The man had chosen the name deliberately, maybe even having walked this very spot in search of a suitable identity to assume. But it was audacious, he reasoned. What if people still lived in the village, who remembered the real Maurice Duggan from thirty years before? Something didn't feel right.

Morton carefully lifted the tendrils of ivy from the stone, snapping them at the base, then took a photograph of the grave before heading back to his car.

He sat for a few seconds with the engine running, gazing at the cemetery gates, pondering the case. It was certainly an odd one.

With a deep inward breath, Morton turned the Mini around and headed back into the centre of the village, where he took a vacant parking space beside Priory Flats.

He stepped from the car and crossed to the front door, pressing the button for flat sixteen.

'Yes?' a gruff voice, which Morton recognised, answered.

'Hi,' Morton said cheerfully, 'it's me, from earlier.'

The man said nothing more, but the door handle vibrated in his hand, as the buzzer signalled the release of the locking mechanism. 'Thanks,' Morton said, unsure of whether he was even listening any longer. Inside was a cold concrete vestibule with two doors and an elevator. Above one of the doors was a crude handwritten sign, which read, *Flats 1, 2, 3, 4*. Above the other door was written, *Stairs to flats 5-18*. The same person had evidently felt the need to write *Lift* above the battered silver doors to the self-evident elevator.

Morton didn't quite trust the look of the lift and, preferring to get a feel for the inside of the building, opted to take the stairs. He made his way up to the top floor, finding himself on a short corridor, from which fed the four front doors for flats fifteen, sixteen, seventeen and eighteen. Maurice had lived in the last flat of the building. If his intention was to keep 'hisself to hisself', as the chap from number sixteen had previously suggested, then this was the place to live. Yet Morton could still not reconcile the fact that this imposter had returned to a small village where his namesake had died just thirty years before.

'Are you coming in or not?' the man said, stepping from number sixteen.

'Yes, sorry,' Morton said. 'Daydreaming.' He entered the flat and the man closed the door behind him. The place was tiny, enhancing an unpleasant smell of urine which hit Morton, as he was ushered into the lounge-diner.

A lady with flushed cheeks, grey hair, and who appeared to be in her eighties, stood from one of the two armchairs and headed towards him with a smile.

'This is Winnie,' the man introduced.

'Hello,' she said pleasantly. 'Derek said you were related to Maurice. I *am* sorry.'

Morton smiled awkwardly, hoping not to be drawn on the specifics of his relationship with Maurice. 'You were a friend of his?' he asked her.

Winnie raised her eyebrows. 'Well, you know what he was like. Friend is probably a stretch of the word. I do miss him, you know, and'—she lowered her voice and leant in closer —'there's a miserable old woman taken over his flat now. Never smiles. Never says hello.'

Derek laughed. 'Well, nor did Maurice most of the time.'

'But he did go to your Christmas parties?' Morton asked.

'Party,' Winnie corrected. 'Just the one! I've been on at him to come for years and last year was the first one where he finally relented. Probably just to shut me up, I wouldn't doubt.'

'And Derek, here, thought that you might have a picture of him?' Morton quizzed.

'I do!' Winnie declared, triumphantly producing a six-by-four photograph.

'Great,' Morton said, studying the image. The composition was perhaps the worst that he had ever seen. It was taken on a strange angle, with a large thumb or finger across the top quarter and was pretty-well out of focus. The image was of four people, two with their backs to the camera, sitting around a table, wearing colourful hats which appeared to have come from crackers. 'Is this him?' Morton guessed, pointing to the man sitting beside Winnie on the other side of the table.

'Yes!' she said proudly, seemingly unaware of how terrible the photograph was. 'Not an ugly chap, was he?' she giggled.

It was hard to tell. Morton held the photo closer to his face. The man had a full head of white hair, dark eyes and, yes, he supposed for a ninety-two-year-old man he had retained the good looks of his middle years. And he was wearing the pair of glasses which were now sitting on Morton's study desk.

'Did you think it strange that he took his own life?' Morton asked Winnie.

'Well, yes,' she said. 'For heaven's sake, he probably only had a couple of years left in him! Why would he do that? Besides which, I'm *convinced*'—she placed a hand on her chest—'that there was somebody else in his flat that morning with him.'

74

'*Winnie*,' Derek said in a warning tone.

'What? I *do* believe it,' she insisted, training her focus on Morton. '*Somebody* entered the building and walked past the door of my flat. A few minutes later, they left again.'

'So you said to the police,' Derek interjected, rolling his eyes at Morton and shaking his head. 'And what did they say?'

Winnie, undeterred, inhaled impatiently. 'That nobody was buzzed in and nobody reported having visitors.'

'Exactly,' Derek said. 'Maybe it was Spiderman.'

'Curious,' Morton said.

'Suicide. That's what the police said,' Derek confirmed.

Winnie shrugged and mumbled, 'I knows what I knows.'

'Did he ever talk to you about his life?' Morton probed.

Winnie and Derek shook their heads in unison.

'It was something you just knew not to ask about,' Winnie said. 'That's why I was so interested to come and meet you: you're the only family member that ever came here. How are you related to him, exactly?'

'He was my great uncle,' Morton said, judging that a small lie was better than the truth under the circumstances. Evidently it had satisfied Winnie, who offered a sympathetic smile. 'Do you mind if I take a picture of this?' he asked, indicating the photograph.

'Oh, keep it. I've got another one,' she said. 'I had two done and tried to give one to Maurice, but he didn't want it.' She laughed, but Morton could see that this rejection had evidently hurt her.

'Thank you,' he said. 'Right, I'll leave you to it. Oh, one quick question: have you lived in the village long?'

'Born here,' Winnie answered.

'Do you, by any chance, recall a young lad falling through the ice on Westwood Lake in 1944?' Morton asked. 'He drowned.'

'Yes. Now you say it, I do. Golly,' Winnie said, folding her arms. 'Now you're bringing back old memories.'

'Do you remember his name?'

'Yes, it was…' Winnie faltered, as the penny dropped in her mind. 'Mau…Maurice Duggan. But…'

'Maurice Duggan?' Derek checked. 'Funny coincidence.'

'Yes, it is rather,' Morton said. 'Anyway, must be off. Lovely to meet you both and thanks for the photo.' Morton left the flat, as Winnie and Derek debated the chances of there having been two Maurice Duggans, who had both lived in Ardingly thirty years apart.

Morton got into his car and took another look at the photograph of Maurice, before telling his SatNav to take him the short distance out of the village to Wakehurst Place.

At the entrance to the property, Morton took the proffered leaflet from a man in a high-vis jacket and parked his car. Wakehurst, according to the pamphlet, consisted of 500 acres of ornamental gardens, woods, nature reserves and an Elizabethan mansion. Today, however, was not the time for a leisurely exploration of the property: he had work to do.

Opening the Maps app on his mobile phone, Morton splayed his fingers to zoom in and located Westwood Lake. It was a good thirty-minute walk away from the car park and it had just started to spit with rain. Was it really necessary to see the lake in which Maurice Duggan had drowned? Would it help him to solve the case? No and no, he reasoned. Yet, still he found himself getting out of the car, pulling his coat tight and making his way down a footpath which, the map promised, would eventually lead to Westwood Lake.

He walked past several visitors, some of whom were rapturously studying and photographing the range of unique tree species apparently on display around the estate. He wandered past tree-carvings and giant mushroom sculptures, as the path wound, seemingly directionless in its myriad deviations, down through the woodland, leaving Morton certain that he was taking twice as long to get to the lake than was necessary.

He was breathless by the time he reached the lake. He really did need to stop eating scones and get fit, he told himself.

The lake, shaped like a thick-heeled boot, was much larger than he had imagined. The path on which he was standing ran directly beside the water's edge to a dense line of trees on the other side. It was here, in the deep winter of 1944, that Maurice Duggan, playing around with two other young people from the village, had plummeted through the ice and drowned in the freezing water below.

Today, the lake betrayed nothing of its past. It was now a place of quietness and tranquillity.

Morton looked around him but there was not another soul here. He took a photograph, then continued walking beside the water at a much slower pace, trying to envisage how it would have been on that cold day in December 1944. He imagined that Maurice and his friends would have approached the lake from the far side, at its closest point to the village.

76

Morton photographed the lake from a variety of angles. Now satisfied with the investigation into the real Maurice Duggan's short life, it was time to focus on establishing the identity of the imposter.

He walked quickly back to his car and set the SatNav for Haywards Heath Library.

The automatic doors of the Library and Registration Service building opened, and Morton stepped inside. In front of him was a long run of bookshelves, above which was a direction sign: right for *Biography, Fiction, Large Print* and *Teen Area*; left for *Borrow, Return & Renew, Children's Library, Computers, Help Desk, Local Studies, Non-Fiction* and *Reference*. He turned left and found the help desk.

'Hi,' he said to the young lady, who was manning the desk. 'I'm looking for copies of the *Mid Sussex Times* for July this year, please.'

'Okay, follow me,' she said, leading him to a local studies area to the rear of the library. 'Take a seat and I'll bring them out.'

Morton sat down and took out his notepad and pencil. The inquest into the death of the man posing as Maurice Duggan had occurred on 2nd July 2019. Morton was hoping that it might have made the local papers and that some extra detail might have been gleaned by police investigating his death. He remembered what Winnie had said, that she was convinced that somebody had walked past her flat door around the time of the supposed suicide.

'*Mid Sussex Times* for July,' the young lady said, returning with a brown packet which she placed down on the desk in front of him. 'When you're done, just leave them here and I'll put them away.'

'Thank you,' Morton said, emptying out the four editions.

His search was over quickly: the inquest had made the front page of the first newspaper of the month. Morton photographed the page, then read the article which was written below a photograph of the block of flats.

Man, 92, died after falling from balcony

A pensioner died after falling from the fourth-floor balcony of a block of flats, an inquest heard. Maurice Duggan, 92, was found dead in the car park of Priory Flats, Ardingly on 3rd April this year. An inquest into his death was held last Thursday and Dr Amy Earl, who carried out the post-mortem examination, said that Mr Duggan's injuries were consistent with a fall from a height. A witness to the tragedy said that he saw Mr Duggan deliberately lifting himself onto his balcony railing before falling to his death. Investigating officers found no evidence of suspicious circumstances. Dr Hannah Reeves, his GP, said that Mr Duggan had suffered from paranoia in the past and believed that people were watching him all of the time. Coroner Penelope Schofield concluded the inquest with a verdict of suicide.

No mention of Winnie's mysterious visitor, Morton thought, wondering if perhaps she had imagined it; or maybe it had been Derek loitering outside her flat but who now wouldn't admit it.

Opening up the photographs on his mobile, Morton selected the ones taken this morning of Priory Flats, where he zoomed in to each, searching for any signs of CCTV cameras, but there were none. Presumably this was an avenue already explored by the police, anyway.

He came out of the photos app and noticed that he had six email notifications. He sighed and opened his mail. Five of them were instantly deletable but the sixth caught his attention: a response from Vanessa Briggs. At last. *Hi Morton. Sorry for the delay. Owing to BM work sieving higher matches at GEDmatch priority. Will be in touch, Vanessa.*

Morton re-read the message several times, trying to make sense of it. *BM?* The obvious acronym in a genealogical context was birth mother, but that didn't help clarify the email at all. Had Vanessa meant that she had higher matches owing to her birth mother's work? Or, owing to her birth mother, she was working to sieve through higher DNA matches? *Higher matches at GEDmatch* he took to mean that Vanessa had matched with other people more closely than she had matched to him on the GEDmatch website. Morton hadn't visited the GEDmatch website since a debacle back in May over privacy rules. He now returned to the website and logged in. As with all the other DNA kits, which Morton managed, beside his name was the word POLICE with a red cross through it. Morton clicked the word and then ticked the radio button beside *Public, with Law Enforcement access.* Done. Law enforcement were now granted permission to access his DNA data.

He was about to log out from the site but thought that he would quickly check his own matches. Vanessa Briggs was there, now his second closest match. But above her, with a startling 2,220 centiMorgans of shared DNA, was another new match, listed under the name LZ025 with the email address of lazarus84101@gmail.com.

Morton was stunned.

Scrambling quickly to the DNA painter website, Morton entered the astoundingly high figure of 2,220 centiMorgans into the Shared cM Project tool.

Three options were returned: Lazarus was either Morton's grandparent, grandchild or half-sibling.

He was bewildered. What the hell was going on?

Chapter Seven

Maurice Duggan left Uxbridge Magistrates' Court in a rage. He gritted his teeth, put his Homburg on his head and walked briskly away from the damnable building.

'Two hundred and twenty-five pounds!' he exclaimed to the world, receiving curious glances from a man and woman entering the court. 'I ask you.'

The Magistrate had fined him—harshly in his opinion—for landing at Heathrow without a flight plan or clearance from Air Traffic Control. The problem wasn't the money, though. The problem was the exposure that his name's being in the local paper might generate. It wasn't actually *his* name, of course, but it wouldn't take much for one of the cleverer sorts at MI5 or MI6 to join the dots together. He would need to be extra vigilant from now on.

He craved a drink. His furious pace slowed, as he wrestled with his own mind about whether to stop off at a pub. Before he convinced himself with the usual placations of its being only one drink and its not taking long, he stood firm in his conviction: he had work to do, which required him to be sober and clear-headed. It was all for her—for Ellen—and her name and her image in his mind were enough to quell the yearning for alcohol.

He slowed his walk, breathing the warm afternoon's spring air through his nose until his heart rate normalised and the fog of anger, shadowing his thoughts, had dissipated. He continued along the busy thoroughfare of Harefield Road, stopping at the first bus stop that he met.

Maurice placed his hands inside his camel-hair coat pocket and felt for the small leather pouch, as he surreptitiously turned to survey those around him. The street was busy with cars and pedestrians, but most were transient, paying him no heed. The ones to watch were the ones taking a longer-than-normal interest in him, or who were loitering. Two people caught his attention. A young man with long unkempt hair in scruffy clothes was leaning against the bus stop, chewing gum and overtly staring at Maurice. If he were a Watcher, then he was showing outrageous indiscretion which could very well be a double bluff. Then there was a man, further along the road, who fitted the profile of a

Watcher from the 1950s perfectly: long overcoat, trilby hat, idling on the street corner. Maurice held him in his peripheral vision. He had a copy of the *Daily Express* open, covering the lower half of his face, standing outside of a public toilet, apparently reading. Again, very conspicuous.

A red bus approached and grumbled to a stop. The door opened and the youth chewing the gum glanced at Maurice, then boarded.

Maurice was in two minds. He looked across the street at the man in the trilby, who had been staring at him but who hastily looked down at his paper when their eyes locked.

'You getting in, mate?' the driver called out.

Maurice nodded and stepped onboard.

'Where to?'

'Where are you going?' Maurice countered.

'Harefield,' the driver answered.

Totally the wrong direction. 'There, please,' Maurice answered, throwing some loose change down onto the tray.

Maurice took his ticket and deliberately chose a seat on that side of the bus, which would offer him the best view of the man in the trilby. There was no sign of the gum-smacking youth, having evidently taken a seat upstairs.

The bus lurched forwards and, as it did so, the man in the trilby lowered his newspaper, met Maurice's gaze and held it until he was out of sight.

As the bus travelled onwards, Maurice mulled over the possible implications of what had just happened. It was possible that the man had simply been puffing his chest in a confrontational display of his masculinity; Maurice had certainly met a fair few of those in his time. It was also possible that the complete opposite was true; that the look had been intended to convey lubricious intentions. Or, as Maurice had feared, perhaps the man had indeed been a Watcher. And, if that were the case, then he needed to tread very carefully, if he wanted to procure the answers which he so desperately sought.

The bus came to a halt and, just as Maurice prepared to step off and change direction back towards central London, the youth from before hurried down the stairs and leapt from the bus without a second glance back.

Maurice exhaled and sat down. He took two more stops, then alighted alone from the bus, not having the faintest clue where he was. Up ahead was a busy junction and he made his way towards it. On one corner was the Kings Arms pub, and the temptation for a drink, stronger than before, edged into his thoughts. Ellen, he reminded himself. Ellen. He brought her image clearly to mind, diverted his gaze from the pub and managed to cross the street.

'Excuse me,' Maurice said to a young mother, who was heading past him, holding a little girl's hand. 'Where's the nearest train station or tube?'

The woman scowled, as she thought. 'That would be down in Ruislip. You'd need to get a bus there, really. It's miles away.'

'How far to walk?'

The woman pulled another face. 'At least an hour. It's basically almost all the way down Breakspear Road over there,' she said, pointing behind him.

'Thanks,' he muttered. He looked at his watch. He had plenty of time and the walk might help to clear his head.

He strode purposefully, trying to think of nothing at all. He was certain that he was not being followed and so, upon arrival at Ruislip Manor tube station an hour and twenty-five minutes later, stepped aboard the first train on the Metropolitan line to Baker Street. Switching to the Circle line, he arrived at Bayswater fifty minutes later, just as dusk was creeping in. By the time he had made the walk to Gloucester Square, it would be completely dark, which is exactly what he needed.

The ten-minute walk came within spitting distance of Hyde Park Square and Maurice briefly considered calling in on Mariella Novotny but knew that she would only ply him with gin and undoubtedly render her advances much more open and explicit. No, he told himself, as he entered Gloucester Square.

Maurice bent down and pretended to tie his laces, as he studied the house opposite him, number forty-seven, which was near-identical in architectural style to the imposing houses on nearby Hyde Park Square. The first-floor flat was in darkness, as he had expected it to be at this time of the day. The only light coming from the house shone from a window on the top floor. He stood, checked that nobody was around, then made his way to the portico entrance. The front door was locked. Maurice examined the intercom beside the door. The surnames of each of the occupants of the four flats was written in illuminated rectangular boxes beside a small button. *HIGGINS* was the occupant of the top-floor flat, according to the intercom.

Clearing his throat, Maurice pressed the buzzer for the HIGGINS apartment.

'Hello?' a well-to-do female voice answered.

Maurice, changing the pitch of his voice and making himself sound far more well-spoken than he was, said, 'Mrs Higgins. GK—George Kennedy Young—here. I've only gone and forgotten the house key, haven't I? You couldn't—'

Before he had finished his request, the door buzzed open and he could hear Mrs Higgins chuckling in the intercom.

He called back his gratitude, as he stepped into the hallway. A light automatically switched on, illuminating the grand entrance, with its high ceiling and ornate cornicing.

Maurice headed up the carpeted stairs to the first floor and lightly tapped on the door. No response. He bent down and studied the lock: a single-lever mortice held it shut. He had expected more, frankly. Retrieving the leather pouch from his coat pocket, he unbuckled it, revealing a selection of miniature tools, each stowed in individual sleeves.

Maurice selected an L-shaped metal tool which he inserted into the lock, applying an upward pressure until he had gained tension on the bolt. Holding this tool carefully in place in his right hand, he took another from the leather wallet. This was similar-looking but with a perpendicular handle at the other end. He placed this inside the lock, just below the point of the other tool. In just a few seconds, he had located the single lever and felt a gentle release. Turning the handle in his left hand, he could feel the bolt sliding out from the lock. It was picked.

Maurice quickly pocketed the pouch and turned the door handle. Cautiously, he stepped into the dark hallway, closed the door and listened. The only sounds seemed to be emanating from Mrs Higgins upstairs and the not-too-distant thrum of London life. He stood, patiently waiting for his eyes to draw an adjustment from the streetlamps which were filtering light in through the window at the other end of the corridor. His memory of the flat's internal layout returned with a burgeoning internal vision. The hallway was long, stretching out in front of him. All six doors along its length were shut.

Keeping to the right-edge, Maurice trod slowly down the carpeted corridor towards the far end. There, he pressed his ear to the door and listened. Nothing. He quietly got down onto his knees and looked through the quarter-inch gap between the door and the plush carpet.

The room was in darkness. More importantly, there was nobody standing on the other side. Maurice turned the handle. It was, as he had remembered, the lounge. Being at the back of the building, there was substantially less light in here, and Maurice could only make out vague dark shapes in the blackness of the room. He couldn't risk using the torch which he had on him, and he indubitably couldn't risk switching on the lights, so he made his way carefully across the room to one of the armchairs, sat himself down and waited.

A muted bang roused him and it took a moment for Maurice to get his bearings. He cursed himself for having fallen asleep. The room was still shrouded in darkness and he could have been sleeping for seconds or hours. What time was it? He couldn't chance checking. His thoughts caught up with him and he recalled what had woken him: some noise or other. Had it been outside? Or inside the building? Hang on. Or even inside the flat itself?

He leant forwards and strained to listen.

Suddenly, the door flew open and the lights went on, momentarily stunning him.

'Don't move,' a voice instructed.

Maurice blinked through the discomfort from the light, as the figure of George Kennedy Young—or GK, as he was known—formed in front of him. He was aiming a Smith and Wesson handgun at him.

'Care to explain yourself?' GK said, almost light-heartedly.

'Old habits, ay, GK?' Maurice replied, with a nod to the handgun.

Maintaining his trained aim on Maurice, GK stepped into the room. 'What are you doing here?'

'I came to see you,' Maurice replied with fake cheeriness. He stood up and mouthed the silent words, 'Operation Sawdust.'

'Good of you to drop by,' GK replied. His agreeable words clashed with his hostile, bitter facial expression.

Of course, Maurice knew it to be a false-façade, counter-surveillance technique which would allow GK to speak more freely.

'Drink, old chap?' GK asked, still unsmiling. He had now at least lowered his gun. 'Gin man, are you not?'

'That's right,' Maurice said, playing along. 'All thanks to you.'

'And music: what are you into?' GK queried, as he went to a drinks cabinet and poured out two drinks.

'Oh, you know me. Anything you like,' Maurice replied with false jollity.

GK laughed through a wooden smile and handed the drink to him. 'Cheers, old man. Wonderful to see you again.'

Their glasses chinked and both men sipped their drinks.

'Music,' GK said, heading over to a sound system below the window. GK tugged the curtains shut, then began to choose a suitable record to play.

He was flustered, Maurice observed with fixated interest. The gun-toting swagger had all been an act. GK was rattled, and that could only be a good thing.

Maurice smiled at his choice of music: *The Triumphal March* from Aida. A huge orchestral number, perfect for masking sensitive topics of discussion from potential eavesdroppers.

'So, how have you been?' GK asked, stepping across the room to an antique bureau which he silently opened, removing a notepad and pen.

'Oh, jolly well, thank you,' Maurice replied. There was no need to warn GK not to use his former identity and he knew that he needn't worry about questions arising as to where he had been. 'And your good self?'

'Much the same. I'm in merchant banking now—much more suitable for a sixty-three-year-old, wouldn't you say?' He sat down beside Maurice and wrote *What are you doing here?* on the notepad.

Need info on Operation Sawdust, Maurice wrote, as he said, 'A very rewarding job, I should think.'

Op Sawdust files gone. Whitewash. Why now? GK scribbled. 'It has its own challenges. To be honest, I'm looking now to retirement.'

Ellen was murdered. Something to do with Sawdust mole - Jericho. 'Will you stay here, or head off to sunnier climes?' Maurice asked.

Files gone. Jericho gone, GK wrote, opening his palms, as if there were nothing more to say on the subject. 'I expect I'll tour the Med at a leisurely pace, then settle back here for my golden years.'

Maurice laughed and scrawled, *Need to meet and talk freely.* 'Well, thanks for the drink old chap.'

GK glowered and, after a moment's pause, wrote, *Tomorrow. 1pm. Italian Gardens, Hyde Park.* 'Lovely of you to stop by.'

'Cheerio,' Maurice said, drinking the last of his gin and shaking GK by the hand. 'I'll see myself out.'

'Goodbye,' GK said, quietly pulling the sheet of paper away from the pad.

Maurice saw him wandering towards the kitchen, no doubt to destroy the evidence of their conversation.

He left the flat and headed out under the amber streetlights of Gloucester Square, beelining to the nearest pub. He was glad that he had resisted the temptation of drinking before going to see GK; their written exchange was etched firmly into his memory. *Operation Sawdust files gone. Whitewash.* What did that mean? Somebody had stolen the files? Somebody had destroyed the files? A whitewash implied an instruction from high-up. If the files *were* gone and Flora Sterling *was* out of the picture, then where could he look next for answers? He had no idea, but right now he couldn't concentrate; he had lost the mental battle over his alcoholism. He saw the pub in the distance and, with that, saw his evening dissolving into oblivion.

Chapter Eight

22nd March 1974, London

Like most days, Maurice woke with an excruciating, searing pain behind his eyes, as he opened them to see Ellen's face looking back at him: always smiling, never changing, never aging. It was no coincidence that her face was the first thing that he saw each morning. It was the only antidote strong enough to combat the daily battle with self-poisoning; a battle which he knew that he was gradually losing.

He then followed the same routine, as he did every day: exert an inordinate amount of effort to get himself out of bed; drink a gallon of water from the cold tap in the kitchen; rummage in the cupboards for something edible; take pills to counter his headache; bathe; ready himself for the day; and fight against himself not to open another bottle of gin.

Today, however, more than any other day, he needed to try to remain sober.

Maurice descended the stairs of his flat with almost three hours to spare until the meeting with GK in Hyde Park. He had factored in ample time for an elaborate and deviated route to get there: it was vital that he not be followed.

He opened his front door and stepped out onto the busy pavement. The instant warmth from the sun on his face seeped deep into the workings of his mind and attenuated some of his anxiety. He began to walk down the street, but quickly stopped in his tracks, doing a double take in the shop window of Our Price. Standing behind the counter, chatting to a customer, was the boy with the long hair, who lived in the house behind him.

Without thinking ahead, Maurice opened the shop door and entered the music shop.

The boy looked up, met his gaze, smiled and nodded briefly, then continued with the man presently in front of him.

Maurice, feeling strangely off-guard, glanced around at the shelves of records and tapes.

'Can I help you with anything?' the boy asked Maurice, as his previous customer left them alone in the shop.

'Erm…' Maurice stammered.

The boy grinned, strolled over towards him and clapped his hands together. 'What are you into?'

Maurice studied his face. Perhaps he had been incorrect in his judgement that the boy was painfully shy, possibly because of his acute case of acne; he was coming across as anything but introverted. 'George Harrison.'

The boy smiled. 'Good answer! I like it. Well, his albums are all over here'—the boy side-stepped a few paces and pointed into the racks—'and I'll bet you haven't got *this* one.' He selected a record and handed it to Maurice. *The Concert for Bangladesh.*

'A live triple album,' the boy enthused.

'Are you just trying to get me to spend a lot of money?' Maurice asked with a wry smile.

The boy threw open his arms. 'Well... I can play it for you, if you like.'

'No, it's fine. I've got to rush. I'll take your recommendation.'

'You won't regret it,' the boy said, carrying the record over to the till.

Maurice followed him and handed over the cash. 'Thanks, Christopher,' he said, picking up the carrier bag containing the record. 'I'll let you know how I get on.'

'You're welcome. Enjoy!'

Maurice walked away from the counter and pulled open the shop door.

'Hey! How do you know my name?' the boy called after him.

Maurice paused, the open door in his hand. He turned and said, 'Name badge,' as he walked away.

'But I'm not wearing one!' the boy shouted after him.

His route to Hyde Park seemed to take in half of central London. He took buses, tubes and even a taxi, so important was it that he not be followed to this meeting.

The Italian Gardens were built around four identical octagonal ponds, each replete with its own central fountain and variety of water plants.

Maurice was standing behind a line of plane trees, casually observing the gardens from a safe distance. He looked at his watch: 12.57pm. So far, there was no sign of GK, but that was to be expected. Maurice knew that he would arrive at 1pm precisely and likely not hang about much afterwards.

At the end of the park, Maurice observed the fine buildings of Kensington Palace and briefly recalled attending an Ambassador's Ball there in 1956. A key night in his life, which started an unstoppable trajectory that had led him directly to this point.

Maurice turned his back on the buildings and ambled slowly, as though out on a Sunday afternoon stroll without a particular place to be.

At 12.59pm Maurice spun around, increasing his pace in the direction of the gardens. Taking a glance to his right, he caught sight of the back of a man who fitted GK's profile, heading to the exact spot, where Maurice had assumed that they would meet: in the very centre of the gardens with a clean three-sixty view all around.

At 1pm Maurice was striding between two of the ponds towards the figure, who was seemingly observing an ornate stone statue. It was GK, Maurice confirmed, as he drew within a few paces of the man.

'What the hell do you think you're doing, breaking into my flat like that?' GK blasted, spinning around, his face awash with anger. 'And what's that? Some kind of signal to someone?' he asked, nodding down to the Our Price carrier bag, then looking across the park, as if expecting to see somebody watching them.

Maurice couldn't help but laugh. 'It's a George Harrison album that I don't have. Who do you think I would be signalling to, for God's sake?'

GK shrugged, grabbed the bag and threw it into the closest pond.

Maurice watched the red and white carrier floating on the water's surface. He was angry but biting his tongue.

'Listen,' GK said, 'I'm not in the business anymore and what I told you yesterday was the truth: everything incriminating to do with Operation Sawdust has gone.'

'Gone where?' Maurice pushed.

'How the hell should I know?' he spat in return.

'Because you were the Deputy Director of MI6,' Maurice replied.

'*Was.*'

'You must still have contacts and be able to find out what happened to those files,' Maurice pressed.

'Why the sudden interest in Sawdust, anyway?'

'Will you sit down, for just a few minutes and let me explain?' Maurice asked, indicating the bench nearby.

'Five minutes,' GK agreed, sitting down beside him.

'Ellen was murdered in December 1957 after she discovered the identity of Jericho.'

'And?' GK stammered.

'And, I want to know who killed her,' he replied, trying not to lose his patience.

GK exhaled noisily and met Maurice's eyes for the first time. 'Look, I've *no idea* how your wife could have revealed Jericho's identity, when MI5 and MI6 had failed to do so. She wasn't even working for intelligence services anymore, so how she came by any material, which would allow her to identify Jericho, is beyond me. And, as I have repeatedly said, *the files simply no longer exist.* Operation Sawdust doesn't exist.'

'And I'll ask again,' Maurice said. 'What happened to the files?'

GK looked around them and lowered his voice. 'The Cabinet Secretary, Norman Brook was ordered to remove all sensitive papers to do with Sawdust,' GK revealed. 'And that's just what he did and now they're gone. So, *were* there something in the files that *might* have helped you, it is now lost.'

Maurice was exasperated. He knew categorically that Operation Sawdust had failed because of a double agent, named Jericho. But why destroy the evidence of the operation's very existence? A myriad of operations had been launched by the secret services over the years, which had ended in failure; it was part and parcel of their very existence. He posed that question.

GK responded, 'You've heard of the Profumo Affair, yes? And you've heard of the Cambridge Spy Ring? And the Portland Spy Ring?'

Maurice nodded. Of course he had. Everyone had. Huge scandals which caused embarrassment to the British establishment.

'What do you know about the Sterling Affair?'

Maurice thought for a second, confident that he had never heard of it in such terms, although not doubting that the Sterling Affair must be an eponymous reference to Flora of that name. 'I don't believe I know anything of it.'

'Exactly,' GK said with a malevolent smile. Clearly GK felt that a point well made, but which somehow remained elusive to Maurice.

'I don't follow.'

'You don't know anything about it, and nor does anyone else. And the reason that the world is in blissful ignorance of its existence is because it has been whitewashed from history. The Sawdust files are gone. Jericho is gone and, the linchpin of it all, Flora Sterling has left the country. The public, Fleet Street, our detractors, are all wonderfully unaware of this scandal.'

'Where's Flora gone?' Maurice asked. 'It's really imperative that I see her. She was among the last to have spoken to Ellen and might know what happened to her.'

GK grinned. 'You'd best get yourself off to Mother Russia, then, dear boy.'

'Russia?'

'That's where she was last suspected of residing, yes.'

'Why wasn't she prevented from leaving the country?' Maurice asked.

'For the reasons that I've just set out: to avoid further scandal. You know just as well as I do, the kinds of incendiary damage contained in those files.'

Maurice sighed. 'So, that's it? Flora's gone. The files on Sawdust are gone and there's nobody else who will tell me what happened to my wife...'

GK turned to face him. 'There's maybe one person, who might know.'

'Who?'

'A Russian defector, Nikita Sokolov. He was Flora's handler at the time.'

'And where will I find him?' Maurice asked.

GK studied his face, weighing the decision. 'I'm only telling you this because of our past, okay?'

Maurice nodded.

'Enjoying English beer and Kentish oysters, and getting some sea air for his emphysema, was the last I heard. But he could be dead now, for all I know.'

'Can you be more specific, GK? It's important. What name does he go by, now?'

GK drew in a long breath. 'That's all I know of his new identity. Goodbye.' He stood and added, 'If ever I see you in my flat uninvited again, I *will* shoot you. Do you understand?'

Maurice nodded. He watched GK march away, then stepped into the knee-deep water and retrieved his Our Price carrier bag.

One of the worst hangovers, which Maurice had ever suffered, occurred yesterday, leaving him with scant recollection of the night that had preceded it. And, having spent the day being severely ill, he could still conjure up only very little memory of what had actually taken place. One thing, though, had stuck: he remembered asking the same question over and over to everyone whom he had encountered that night. That question had been asked again and again: 'where do you go for the best Kentish oysters by the sea?'

And the answers had been fairly unanimous in their agreement, settling him on Whitstable on the north coast of Kent.

And so, here he was, standing on Whitstable High Street in torrential rain. The town was, unsurprisingly on a day such as this, deserted by nearly all pedestrian traffic.

Maurice pulled up his coat collar, lowered his Homburg and strode aimlessly along the road. He stopped outside of a shop, Wheelers Oyster Bar, then stepped inside. The shop was small and its every table was empty.

'Nice day out,' a young man with bare tattooed arms greeted with a grin. He was leaning on the counter, his head in his hands. 'What can I do for ya?'

'Slightly odd question,' Maurice ventured. 'But…I'm looking for an old friend of mine, who lives in Whitstable. Baltic accent, wheezy, enjoys beer and oysters…'

The man laughed. 'Christ, what a description! Don't think so, no. What's his name?'

'Erm,' Maurice stammered. 'That's part of the problem. He changed it and I don't know to what.'

Maurice's answer was apparently hilarious. 'You've got ya work cut out there, mate!'

'Yes, I suppose I do rather,' Maurice agreed, leaving the shop and heading back out into the rain. The idea of coming down to Whitstable and tracking down Flora's former handler had seemed like a simple enough notion. After all, there couldn't be too many Russians with breathing problems and a penchant for beer and oysters in the small town. He just needed to find him.

A local bus stopped a few yards in front of him and an elderly lady alighted. Maurice was half-tempted to get onboard and just go wherever it took him. Instead, he dashed over and said to the driver: 'Sorry. Where does one go for good local oysters and a good beer?'

The driver, without a moment's thought or hesitation, replied, 'Old Neptune on Marine Terrace. You can't go wrong over there.' He pointed behind him: 'Left at Terry's Lane, right on Neptune Gap, and then you can't miss it.'

Maurice thanked him and hurried along the wet pavements past the empty shops, until he reached the terminus of the High Street and, of the three roads before him, took Terry's Lane on the left. The street consisted of small, brick cottages and, owing to the inclement weather, was entirely empty. Maurice was grateful to find the streets largely abandoned but feared that he would find the pub also devoid of life. Would an old man with breathing troubles really venture out in damp weather like this? The more Maurice thought about it, the more he doubted it and questioned this whole enterprise.

Just as the driver had instructed, Maurice turned down Marine Terrace, a narrow road which spurred out as if heading directly to the sea. On his left was a grassy wasteland and, on his right, over a low concrete wall, was a stony beach.

Maurice paused for a moment, watching as ten-feet-high waves pounded the wooden groins which punctuated the north Kent shoreline as far as he could see. Today was really not the best day to try to track down Flora Sterling's handler, but he had come this far and was here now.

He continued along the road with his head down until he reached The Old Neptune pub, a white weather-boarded building, which stood forlorn and alone on the beach corner where Marine Terrace turned ninety degrees to run parallel with the sea.

Maurice pushed open the door and entered. The familiar waft of warm but stale air enveloped him, as he closed the door on the stormy day. Wheezy Russian or no wheezy Russian, the dark interior of this pub was going to be where Maurice passed the next few hours of his life.

As he had feared, the place was empty. A plump redhead behind the bar nodded at him. 'Alright?' she said. 'You lost or something?'

'Nope,' Maurice answered. 'I'd like a drink, please. Gin. Double.'

The barmaid raised her eyebrows, then turned to make the drink. 'You ain't lost, no?' she repeated.

'No. Do only lost people come here, then?' Maurice asked.

The barmaid shrugged. 'On a day like today; yeah, pretty much.'

'That's a shame. I'm looking for someone; an old friend of mine. He's Russian and he's got emphysema.'

The barmaid set his drink down and smiled. 'Oh, Ivan, you mean? Tonic, ice and a slice?'

'No, thanks. Neat. Wheezy, likes beer and oysters?' Maurice said.

93

'And vodka,' she added. 'And making up stories about being a spy, and all.'

'Really?'

She nodded and laughed. 'He gets paralytic, stands on the tables and makes up all kinds of crap. And that's when I know it's time to start serving him free triple measures of Whitstable Special.'

'Wow. What's in that?' That sounded right up *his* street, he thought.

'Pure tap water,' she said with another laugh. 'He's always so drunk he doesn't notice. Then we turn down the lights, tell him we're closing and turf him out. He sound like he might be your friend?'

Maurice nodded and smiled. 'That's Ivan. Do you think he'll be in today, or do you perhaps know where he lives?'

'He's in now,' the barmaid said, tilting her head to the left. 'In the other bar, polishing off his fifth double vodka. You're not going to get much sense out of him, I'm afraid.'

Even though finding Flora's handler was the purpose of his visit, Maurice was surprised to hear that the man, for whom he was searching, was sitting in the adjacent room. That Ivan was already blind drunk was even better, potentially saving him several hours and several pounds in loosening his tongue.

Maurice picked up his drink, walked around the bar and into a room, larger but equally as dark, with a series of tables, all of which, except for one, were empty. Just one overweight man sat alone, staring out of the window towards the sea.

'Comrade!' Maurice exclaimed, as he approached his table, as if greeting an old friend.

In no great hurry to see who was speaking to him, Ivan slowly turned, his glassy eyes struggling to get a fix on Maurice. Short, shallow breaths puffed from the old man's nose. His heavy eyelids hung loosely over cold grey eyes. His salt-and-pepper hair, balding in the centre, was cropped short, reflecting the length of his facial stubble.

'You don't remember me, do you?' Maurice said, in mock annoyance. 'Come on! I met you at the bar at the Czechoslovakian Ambassador's Ball. Maurice… Maurice Duggan!'

A deep guttural grumble rose from Ivan's chest and he began to laugh. 'Yes. Yes! Of course, I remember you, comrade!' The laughter continued as Ivan stood awkwardly from his chair and then shook his hand. His laughter, revealing a black tooth in the upper front of his mouth, steadily ebbed away. 'What do you do here?'

Maurice sipped his drink, trying to judge how best to play the situation. 'My asthma,' he lied, hitting his chest with a clenched fist. 'The doctors said I should get some sea air.'

Ivan grinned and pointed to the window. 'You want sea air; you get sea air.' A husky laugh mutated rapidly into a heaving coughing fit. The Russian spluttered with intermittent barks of random words in his native tongue, which Maurice took to be expletives. He took the final dregs of his drink, steadied his breathing, then said through a smile, 'I also need sea air.'

'You also need another drink,' Maurice said, eyeing the empty glass. 'Vodka?'

'Double,' he answered. 'And don't let her give the Whitstable Special; it is urgh!'

Maurice went to the bar and returned with two drinks.

'*Nostrovia*,' Maurice said, raising his glass.

'*Na Zdorovie*,' Ivan replied, meeting Maurice's glass with his.

'Do you still see anyone from the old days?' Maurice asked, feeling the arriving edge of impairment from the gin.

Ivan shook his head. 'No. I change name. I change job. Nobody knows me here.'

Maurice raised his eyebrows in feigned surprise. 'You defected to the West. Well done.' He reached over and shook Ivan's meaty hand.

Ivan shrugged, as though it had been an obvious choice to have made.

Maurice watched Ivan's glassy eyes rolling around in his head and found him in the perfect state of inebriation to ask his questions. 'Do you ever see anything of Flora Sterling anymore?'

Ivan laughed so hard that his dewlap danced on his tatty shirt collar. 'She is somewhere in Odessa. So no, I see her not at all!' He laughed again and Maurice felt compelled to join in.

'So, you don't have any contact with her any longer?' he pushed.

The Russian's laughter increased until it turned into the gut-wrenching cough, turning his face the colour of a tomato. There was a brief enough pause in his coughing fit for Ivan to reach for his vodka and drain the glass. 'I see or hear nothing from Flora since party at Christmas time fifteen or sixteen years ago.'

'Mariella Novotny's party?' Maurice asked.

'You know it. The one where the woman supposed to kill herself,' Ivan said, mimicking slitting his wrists.

'Didn't she kill herself, then?' Maurice said.

Ivan shook his head and shrugged again. 'Ask too many questions, this what happens.' He turned to face Maurice. 'Trust me, comrade. Keep quiet and live by the sea. Beer, vodka, oysters… This is all you need.' He closed his eyes. 'Beer, vodka…and whatever else…'

'So, this woman was asking questions at the party and then what happened?' Maurice said, prodding Ivan in the leg.

Ivan opened his eyes. 'What?'

Maurice repeated himself, speaking slowly and carefully, knowing that he was on the verge of finding out the truth about what happened that night.

Ivan stared at him, then answered. 'Flora find out about it and the problem go away.'

A cold vice gripped Maurice's heart and it took a moment to compose himself to speak. 'Dealt with it? How?'

'The usual way. Drugged woman and slit her wrist, make it look like she kill herself.'

Maurice picked up his drink with a shaking hand and tipped it back until every drop was gone. He fought back against the tears which were beginning to well in his eyes.

Flora Sterling had killed his beloved wife, Ellen. It couldn't be.

'You cry?' Ivan said, laughing hoarsely. 'You cry!'

The rage inside Maurice rose suddenly.

Chapter Nine

A thick green volume with a red spine, and the words UXBRIDGE MAGISTRATES COURT 1974 in gold lettering, was sitting on the desk in front of Morton, as yet unopened. He was seated at a table in the Archive Study Area of the London Metropolitan Archives, checking the emails on his mobile phone for the second time in five minutes. Still nothing.

After discovering a bewilderingly close DNA match yesterday, Morton had sent an instant email to Lazarus84101@gmail.com, politely asking who on earth they were and how they were related to him, but he had so far not had a response.

He pondered the ominous name again: Lazarus. He was a man from the Bible, whom, according to Google, Jesus had resurrected four days after his death. Was there something to be read into that name? At GEDmatch the facility to recreate the DNA of a deceased, untested ancestor, using multiple tested family members, bore this same name. However, if such a Frankenstein kit had been created by somebody, it should not be visible in his match list. And then there were the numbers. Were they just random? Or were there—he considered in his sardonic way—84,100 other people by the name of Lazarus, all wanting that same email address? When Morton had run a Google search for those same digits, the results list was dominated by its being the zip code for downtown Salt Lake City.

Once he had made the discovery, he had double-checked his research to make sure that he had been correct, and, sure enough, Lazarus could only be Morton's grandparent or half-sibling. Lazarus's DNA had been uploaded on the 17th August 2019. Only one of Morton's biological grandparents was still alive: Velda, his father Jack's mother. Not only was she suffering from advanced dementia and highly unlikely to have taken the DNA test, but further investigation on the GEDmatch website revealed Lazarus's gender to be male. Morton had considered that it could have been his actual half-brother, George Jacklin, simply using a slightly strange or quirky email address. He was quite an odd person, after all. But, a little further research into the people who had matched both his and Lazarus's kits, found them all to emanate from his maternal side, leaving only one option which both terrified and excited him: that his biological mother, whom he had always known as Aunty Margaret, had had *another* illegitimate child that hitherto she had kept secret.

His head actually ached from the numerous circles of possibilities, whose conundrums he could never prevent himself from trying and failing to break, when such things happened. He needed a resolution. Talking to Juliette would probably have helped. But she had been working late last night, and the brief window of time, in which they had both been present together at home this morning, had been dominated by the clear-up operation following Grace's having smashed a large bottle of olive oil on the kitchen floor; the blame for which had been squarely placed at Morton's feet for having still yet to fix child-locks to the kitchen cupboard doors.

Then there was Vanessa Briggs. She had also not replied to his email asking what she had meant by *Owing to BM work sieving higher matches at GEDmatch priority*. He still couldn't quite get his head around the coincidence of two highly significant DNA matches having occurred within days of each other. He had never been one to believe in coincidences, thus it was through the lens of deep suspicion that he viewed the discovery of a new half-sibling and a new half-aunt in the space of a week. Something was going on, but he couldn't yet figure out what it might be.

Morton sighed and checked his emails again.

Nothing.

Concentrate, he scolded himself, pocketing his mobile and turning to the task for which he had come here.

He opened the Magistrates' Court book at the first page and began to look down at the variety of offences which had been presented before the court.

John Henry Dowden, 22, of Park Street, West Drayton. Within the Middlesex commission did dishonestly receive a quantity of assorted tools knowing or believing the same to be stolen goods, contrary to section 22 Theft Act, 1968. Fined £20.
Glyn Jenkins, 20, of Station Road, Ruislip. At Blunts Avenue West Drayton did take a Hillman Imp saloon motor car index GMP 863B for his own use without having the consent of the owner or other lawful authority, contrary to section 12 (1) Theft Act, 1968. Remanded to 23rd September. Bail £50.
Dominic McFadden, 34, of Stonefield Road, South Ruislip. At Church Road, Hayes assaulted Clive Donner, a constable of the Metropolitan Police in the execution of his duty, contrary to section 51 (1) Police Act, 1964. Remanded 3rd October. Bail £100.

Morton read through several interesting accounts of theft, assault, bringing drugs into the country, failing to pay maintenance orders, and one account of attempted murder, before he had understood enough to be able to discern quickly the matter in hand in each case and was then able to flick through to 21st March 1974, the date upon which Maurice Duggan had been sentenced. He found the case sandwiched between a man convicted of failing to provide a specimen of breath after an RTA, and another man convicted of deserting his wife and failing to support their children.

Maurice Duggan, 47 of Kilburn High Road. At Heathrow Airport being the commander of an aircraft bearing the registration letter G-ARFH did fail to cause a flight plan to be communicated to the appropriate air traffic control unit before flying the said aircraft within the controlled airspace of the said airport in contravention of rules 22 and 28 (1) of the schedule to the Rules of the air and air traffic control regs, 1972. Guilty. Fined £200. Costs £25.

Well, that was a legal mouthful, Morton thought, as he finished reading. The entry had provided him, though, with one more piece of information than the sum of which he had already gleaned from the newspaper article on the case: Maurice Duggan's abode. That was a crucial piece of evidence in a case such as this.

Morton photographed the entry, wondering if this man was indeed the same Maurice Duggan who had assumed the identity of a boy, drowned in 1944. His gut feeling was that they were indeed one and the same person. Time and research, he hoped, would tell.

He checked his emails once again. Nothing. Why was nobody as bothered as was he, by such an exceptionally close familial connection? He'd potentially turned up a new half-aunt and new half-sibling in the space of a few days, yet nobody else seemed remotely concerned or interested.

Morton opened his laptop and, having established that Kilburn High Road fell under the borough of Brent, accessed the London Metropolitan Archives website. He typed in his History Card number, then ran a search for electoral registers for Brent, pleased to find that they were held in this very building. He placed an order for each register for the years 1970 to 1980, the year after which Maurice had first appeared in the village of Ardingly. If this was indeed the same man, then he should not appear in the 1980 electoral register for Brent.

Morton carried the Magistrates' Court file back to the collections desk.

'Finished?' asked the stout man.

'Yes, thank you. That's all for the moment,' Morton said, collecting his laptop and notebook, and heading out of the Archive Study Area. He made his way down to the Visitor Lounge, where he opened his locker and pulled out the black-and-white photograph of Ellen. He turned it over to double-check the name of the photographer: Daniel Price of 99 Camden High Street. Having already established that the business was not currently in operation, Morton had undertaken a detailed analysis of the picture itself. Of the year it had been taken, he could not be completely certain. The photo had the characteristics of a gelatin silver print, which had been the most common method of photography until colour had been introduced in the 1960s. Ellen's style of dress he had dated to the mid-to-late 50s, but it was the posy of flowers held in her hands which had been the most useful part. From the monochrome bouquet, he had managed to identify two species of British wildflower, wood sorrel and sweet violet, which only flowered in early spring. His best estimate was that Ellen had married in one of the early months in the mid-to-late nineteen-fifties. He hoped that the street directories would help further narrow his search.

He returned the picture of Ellen to his locker, closed it up, and headed back to the Information Area, hoping to find that the street directories for Camden were on the open shelves. He wandered through the library area, keeping his eyes open for the tell-tale-red hardbacked series of *Kelly's Directories*, but couldn't spot them.

'Can I help you?' a young woman asked, evidently discerning perplexity on his face.

'I'm looking for street directories for Camden around the mid-to-late nineteen-fifties,' he explained.

'They're kept in the strong-room, I'm afraid, and will need ordering up to the Archive Study Area,' she said, pointing to the adjacent room, where he had just been looking at the Magistrates' records.

'Right,' Morton replied. 'Thank you.' He walked over to the nearest vacant table, opened his laptop and ordered street directories for Greater London 1954-1962.

At the bottom of his laptop screen he noticed a small red circle with a white number one attached to his mail app.

Opening his emails, he was elated to see that it was from Vanessa Briggs. At last.

Morton, where do you live? I'm in Westerham, Kent. Might be better to meet and discuss? Vanessa

Morton smiled, as he tapped out an immediate reply: *Hi Vanessa! Yes, I'd be delighted to meet! I'm in Rye, so not far away! I can be fairly flexible – name a time and place, and I'll be there. Looking forward to it! Morton.*

He re-read the message and deleted all the exclamation marks, fearing that he sounded slightly deranged. He pondered for a moment whether, or not, he should tell her anything of his findings so far, but quickly convinced himself that it would be much better to explain everything face-to-face. The last thing that he wanted to do was to frighten her away. He hit the send button and hoped that she would reply quickly.

There was still nothing from the Lazarus person.

Morton looked at the digital display on the wall; the electoral registers, which he had ordered, should by now be ready for collection. With his laptop under his arm and his notepad in his hand, he entered the Archive Study Area again and approached the collections desk.

'Hi,' Morton began, sliding his History Card across the desk. 'Can I have the electoral register for Brent 1974, please?'

'Certainly,' a young lady with long grey hair replied. She turned to face the run of black open shelving behind her, taking a moment to locate his documents: a pile of thin blue books. '1974?'

'That's right,' he confirmed.

She handed him the book, and he headed over to a nearby desk. On the cover of the first book was typed *REGISTER OF ELECTORS 1974 CONSTITUENCY OF BRENT EAST,* which Morton copied onto his notepad. He quickly established that the register was arranged in alphabetical order by road. He soon found Kilburn High Road and began to run his finger down the list of occupants. The road was a long one, spanning several pages, but Morton found Maurice quickly on the second page.

Kilburn High Road, N.W.6
Duggan, Maurice   83a

He now had Maurice's precise address and the fact that, officially at least, he had been living alone. He copied down the information, closed the register, returned it to the desk and took the volume for the following year. There he found Maurice living in the same house, still alone.

Much to the increasing annoyance of the archivist, Morton worked his way quickly through the years of electoral registers, with nothing changing until he reached 1980. Just as he had anticipated, Maurice was absent at the address and a new person, Leon Fink, was listed as the sole occupant of the flat. Morton was now convinced that the Maurice Duggan, who had been arrested and charged for failing to record a flight plan at Heathrow in 1974, had been the same man who had moved to Ardingly in 1979, and who had died at Priory Flats earlier this year. The timeline of Maurice's life was gradually expanding.

Finally, Morton requested the electoral registers for 1970-1973 but could find no trace of Maurice, leaving him with a new potential hypothesis: one in which he had arrived in the UK on the 19th February 1974, landing at Heathrow Airport. But where had he been? And under what name had he been living? He flipped backwards in his notepad to the information gleaned from the article in the *Harrow Observer*. Maurice had flown to Heathrow in a Cessna 150. Morton ran a search for the flight range on such an aircraft: approximately 350 miles. What did that mean in terms of the possible points of origin? He brought up a map of Heathrow on his computer, then slowly zoomed out, watching as more of England, then the United Kingdom and finally Europe appeared.

After a few minutes of searching, Morton had deduced that Maurice had to have flown in from somewhere either within the United Kingdom or else beyond in Northern Europe. A good number of major and minor airports in France, Belgium, the Netherlands and Germany were well within reach. He studied the map of potential countries, containing dozens of small airfields, wondering how on earth he could further narrow down his search. Perhaps, though, from where Maurice had flown in was irrelevant. If he could just find Ellen's marriage, then, in turn, that would reveal Maurice's former identity, which was the whole point of this case.

Morton asked if the street directories had been brought up from the strong room yet. The mildly uninterested lady with grey hair stood up and folded her arms. 'Any one in particular?' she asked.

'Surprise me,' he answered with a hopeful smile.

She stared blankly at him, saying nothing.

'1954,' he revised, starting at the beginning of his selection range.

The archivist turned around to face the shelving behind her and took the first volume from the pile.

'Thank you,' Morton said cheerily.

At his desk, he opened the *Kelly's Directory* and saw that it was arranged according to London borough, and then alphabetically by service- or shop-type. He located the thick section for Camden and thumbed through to *Photographers*. There were four, but Daniel Price was not one of them. What he did notice, however, was that a different photographer, one *W. Squires* was operating from 99 Camden High Street. Evidently, Daniel Price had taken over the premises at some point after 1954.

Having made a note of his search, Morton closed the book and exchanged it for the following year, finding exactly the same result: no sign of Daniel, yet.

Much to the exasperation of the archivist, who was clearly disgruntled at the frequency of his exchanging of records and must have expected him to read the thing cover-to-cover, Morton took the 1956 edition back to his desk. Bingo. Daniel Price was listed as the photographer at 99 Camden High Street.

Morton copied down the information, then hurriedly exchanged the directory for 1957. Daniel Price was still noted as in business for this year, also.

By 1958, however, the place had once again changed hands and *Say Cheese*, despite their puerile name, remained at the address until at least 1962.

Morton was now looking at a two-year window during which Ellen could have married. Making an educated guess that she had chosen a photographer from the district in which she had lived at the time of her marriage, Morton opened up the FreeBMD website, typed in the name *Ellen* with no surname, selected the district of Hampstead, which included Camden, from March 1956 to December 1957 and then hit the *count* button.

39 records match your query.

Thirty-nine potential marriages, where he knew nothing more to help him deduce the correct one, was slightly too unwieldy a number. And that was without taking into account the question of whether Ellen might have been a shortened version of her name and not the official one appearing in the records. Focusing just on those marriages which had occurred in the months of January, February and March in 1956 and 1957, based on his assessment of Ellen's floral corsage, he whittled the list down to just six within this registration district.

Morton sighed. He could place an order for those six marriage certificates and leave now, or he could save the money—and more importantly, the time—and try to search the parish registers which were held there for the Hampstead registration district, right now. He looked at the time: 4.27pm. Tonight was late opening hours, meaning that he had another three hours there, if he wanted. He withdrew his mobile and sent a text message to Juliette: *Sorry, going to be late home. Lots to do at LMA – open late tonight. Give Graciekins a kiss from me xx.*

Whilst he had his phone out, he checked his emails again. Another from Vanessa Briggs.

This Friday? 11am? Got no transport. Can you come to me? Vanessa.

Morton replied that Friday—two days away—would be great and that he would happily go to her. His mind began to enter into another unbreakable, ruminating thought-cycle about the situation, but he managed to bring himself out of it quickly. If he was going to miss putting Grace to bed and probably miss dinner, too, then he needed to make the most of his time there.

On his laptop, he ran a search for Camden parish registers. Some were available on microfilm and some were the original registers which needed to be ordered up from the strong room. He glanced over at the collection desk. The miserable grey-haired lady was still on duty; she'd be delighted to see him back up there again, of that he was certain.

Morton meticulously worked his way through all the parish registers for the period in question, placing an order for the original marriage registers for eight churches. He copied down the details of a further six which were on microfilm. Of course, if the marriage had occurred in a Register Office, or at certain of the non-conformist churches, then the registers would not be in this building.

From inside his pocket, Morton's mobile vibrated. He withdrew it to see a reply from Juliette: *Graciekins?!? In case you'd forgotten, she was named after my g. grandmother, a courageous suffragette, who went to prison for her beliefs, if you don't mind... Doubting Mrs Pankhurst ever called her Graciekins. I'll keep you some dinner by xx.*

Morton grinned, then exited the Archive Study Area.

'Goodbye!' the young grey-haired lady called, a little too gleefully for his liking.

'I'll be back in a while!' he responded, making his way towards the run of microfilm readers in the Information Area. Almost all of the twenty or so machines were vacant, so Morton chose the one closest to the filing cabinets containing the microfilms. He switched it on, went to the cabinets with his notebook and searched for the first microfilm: *X099/009, Saint Mary the Virgin Church 1945–1968.* He found the boxed film and carried it over to the machine, where he quickly loaded it up and buzzed through to early 1956 and checked each of the two marriages per page for the months of January, February and March. Finding no sight of any one of the six Ellens, he moved on to 1957. Nothing. No sign of them. So, he fast-rewound the film, boxed it back up and returned it to the cabinet, now looking for the second reference: *X096/228, Saint Peter, Belsize Park 1944–1961*. He repeated his checks for the early months of the year but found no trace. The third reference number, *X095/611* pertained to *Saint Saviour's Church 1947-1975*. Morton was just beginning to question the validity of such a broad search, based on a good deal of educated speculation, when he came upon one of the marriages: Ellen Ingram to Alexander Emmett.

Morton was pleased to have found at least one of the six marriages. He made a brief note on his pad, photographed the entry, then completed the search before rewinding the film and moving on to the next.

He worked for a further fifty minutes on the remaining three parishes, finding another of the six marriages: Ellen Tobin to Thomas Swift.

Morton emitted a satisfied sigh, as he switched off the microfilm reader and made his way back inside the Archive Study Area. Even if he couldn't track down any of the remaining four marriages, the two, which he had just located, would give him plenty to start with, tomorrow.

'Marriage registers?' the grey-haired woman asked flatly.

He looked around the room and could see that there were only two other researchers left besides him. 'Yes, give me any of them, please.'

'St George, Bloomsbury,' she announced, passing him the thin black register.

Morton thanked her and carried it over to the nearest desk. He flicked through to January 1956 and almost immediately found another of the marriages: Ellen Murphy to Patrick McGarty. Three Ellens down; three Ellens to go. He photographed the marriage detail and then exchanged the register for that of Christ Church, Holborn. The parish was evidently a large one and this volume took the longest of them all, thus far. But, with his search of it complete, there was no sign of the other two elusive Ellens.

Morton was beginning to flag. He still had six more registers through which to wade, all with under an hour to go. Juliette hadn't helped matters by messaging him a photograph of her with her feet up on the sofa and a glass of non-alcoholic wine in her hand. He yawned and half-heartedly wandered over to the returns desk, where he set one register down, the assistant now automatically and wordlessly handing him the next in his diminishing pile.

He reached the early summer of 1957 without sign of another of the Ellens.

'We'll be closing in half an hour,' the grey-haired lady informed him, swapping the checked register for that of St Mary the Virgin, Primrose Hill.

'Oh, hopefully I'll get through the rest in time. How many are left?'

'Four,' she said, giving him the first smile of the day.

'Thanks,' he said, taking the proffered book. He realised, then, that he was the last researcher left in the room. He needed to work quickly, if he was going to get through the remaining registers before being literally thrown out. He could really do with a coffee right now. A large one, highly caffeinated. He wondered if the loss of time that it would take to get one from the vending machine in the Visitor Lounge might be compensated for by the surge of energy that it would provide him. He thought better of it.

With the end in sight, Morton worked swiftly, and, in the final marriage register, which was handed to him five minutes before closure, he found his fourth and final Ellen. Ellen Hobbs had married Arthur Edward Smart in March 1957.

He handed the register back with a smile, packed up his things and left the building ready to go home.

It was gone ten o'clock when Morton finally stumbled into his house. He found a full glass of red wine on the kitchen table, beneath which was a fluorescent pink Post-it note: *Sorry, had to go to bed – early start. Dinner in the microwave. Hope you got everything done. Netflix & chill tomorrow night?! xx.*

He took a large mouthful of the wine and felt his muscles accepting that their work for the day was almost over. Inside the microwave he found a plate of spaghetti Bolognese, which he set to reheat whilst he looked at the small pile of post on the table.

The microwave pinged with the announcement that his dinner was ready. He carried it to the table, sat down, sipped the wine and pulled out his mobile phone. Five emails, his notifications declared. As usual, three were instantly deletable. One was from Vanessa Briggs, providing Morton with her home address.

106

The last was from Lazarus.

Chapter Ten

'Here we go,' Jeremy said, carefully setting a plate and large latte down in front of Morton. 'Tell me what you think.'

'Oh, God,' Morton moaned, viewing the scene in front of him with deep suspicion. 'Dare I ask'—he leant forwards for a closer inspection—'what the flavour of the day is?'

'Taste it and see,' Jeremy replied enthusiastically. Morton eyed *him* with deep suspicion. He'd never seen Jeremy so happy than since he and his husband, Guy, had opened up Granny's Scones on Rye High Street. It still felt a sudden shift in his mind from annoying younger adopted brother, to active-duty soldier, then to *this*. 'Try it!'

Morton huffed, sliced the scone in two and spread a thick layer of butter on both sides, wondering what culinary delight the grey lumps, over which the knife was passing, might transpire to be. He took a small cautious nibble. Not bad. Took a bigger bite. Enjoyed it. He nodded his approval. 'Don't ask me what flavour I think it is, but yes, I like it.'

'Pear and gorgonzola,' Jeremy revealed, with a flamboyant upturning of his hands.

Morton frowned. Two flavours that *definitely* should never be mixed. Still, they worked somehow. 'Okay, I concede. It's nice.'

Jeremy grinned. 'So, how are things with you? Any news?'

Morton took in a long breath, whilst he sifted his thoughts for that which he felt that he could tell Jeremy. He didn't feel as though the story of Vanessa Briggs made any kind of sense to *him*, so trying to explain it to Jeremy was pretty pointless. He would tell him after he had met with Vanessa the following day. The next most obvious thing pressing into his thoughts was the email that he had received last night from Lazarus, but there was no way on earth that he was about to tell him about *that* major bombshell. He would have to eventually; but not yet.

'Nothing? Really?' Jeremy said, misinterpreting his silence as a struggle to find anything exciting to say, when the complete reverse was actually the case. 'When's the next scan?'

'What scan?' Morton asked.

Jeremy rolled his eyes. 'The baby! Your baby, Morton!'

'Oh, yes,' Morton mumbled, embarrassed that, with all that had been going on lately, Juliette's pregnancy had actually slipped his mind.

He couldn't even bring to mind when the next scan would be. 'Er…think it's next week sometime.'

'Bet you can't wait to find out what you're having,' Jeremy enthused.

'Yes. No.' He wasn't sure what the correct answer should be. 'I am excited, yes.'

'Are you going to tell everyone? Make a big announcement? You could have a gender-reveal party! Have it here!'

Morton tried not to betray his feelings. The image in his mind of this shop filled with family and friends nibbling on obscure-flavoured scones—perhaps Marmite, lemon and milk chocolate—as he and Juliette made some fantastical gesture—maybe releasing a blue or pink balloon into the crowd—was wholly horrific. 'Well, that's something to think about,' he said.

'Do,' Jeremy encouraged, as a customer entered the shop. 'Better go. Shout if you want another scone.'

'Or coffee,' Morton replied, which was a far more likely need, given the mountain of work that he had to get through. His priority today was to eliminate some, or all of the four Ellen marriages that he had discovered yesterday. If he could build skeleton family trees for each of them, taking their husbands' lives beyond 1974, then they were almost certainly *not* the correct couple.

From his bag, Morton took four sheets of plain A3 white paper and wrote the names of each couple in the centre, along with the dates and places of their marriages. He worked out their approximate years of birth from their presented ages on the certificates and added these to the document. Ellen Hobbs and Arthur Edward Smart immediately looked the least likely; it was a second marriage for both of them and they had been born in the 1890s. Morton ran a death search for Arthur Edward Smart and found a probable death for him in 1966. *Highly unlikely*, Morton scribbled at the top of the piece of paper, folding it into his bag and eliminating it from his enquiries at this point.

Next, he worked on Ellen Murphy and Patrick McGarty: they had been born in the 1920s and so he fitted the approximate age of Maurice Duggan. Morton found three children born to the couple in quick succession after the marriage. A gap in the family, appearing in online genealogical records, caused Morton to wonder if he had found the right people; but then, using modern electoral registers on Findmypast, he located Ellen and Patrick living in an adjacent house to one of their sons well into the 2000s. Patrick's death had occurred in

2006; thus, he could not have been Maurice Duggan. *Unlikely*, Morton annotated on the paper, before putting it into his bag.

The sheet now in front of him pertained to Ellen Ingram and Alexander Emmett, who had married on the 8th February 1957 in St Saviour's Church. Morton ran a search for children born to the couple and found just one: Christopher, born in the September quarter of 1957. A six-month pregnancy, Morton noted wryly. He located Alexander and Ellen living in Lancaster Gate on the *London Electoral Registers 1832-1965* on Ancestry—solely for the year of 1957—and then they were no longer recorded at that address; nor indeed elsewhere within this record set.

Morton sipped his latte, as he ran a death search, first for Alexander—nothing conclusive or obvious—then for Ellen. He found a death in 1957, where the age matched that which had been stated on the marriage certificate. There was a strong chance, Morton felt, that this death matched with Ellen Ingram, who had married and given birth just months prior. Perhaps she had died from childbirth complications. As a short-cut to finding some information about her death, Morton looked on the BillionGraves and FindAGrave websites, but found nothing. He then searched the DeceasedOnline website and smiled, as what appeared to be Ellen's burial in Paddington Cemetery appeared at the top of the search results. After paying £2, an original scan of the register appeared full-screen on his laptop.

Name of person buried: Ellen Emmett
Age: 30 years
Place where death occurred: Harrow Road, Kensal Green
Date of death: 14th December 1957
Date of burial: 20th December 1957
Number of grave: D
Section: 24 J
Remarks: headstone added 18th September 1974

Morton re-read the remarks. A headstone had been added in September 1974. Why the delay of 17 years? Interesting. He drank more of his latte as his working theory of Maurice Duggan's arrival in February 1974 expanded now to include his finally getting around to adding a memorial to his wife's grave. Kensal Green, Paddington Cemetery and Kilburn were all a stone's throw from each other. Was he stretching his imagination too far to link all these events together?

Certainly, for the moment he was finding nothing to *disprove* that this man, Alexander Emmett could have been the imposter, Maurice Duggan.

Morton returned to the picture which he had taken the day before of Alexander and Ellen's marriage certificate, studying the details from this new possible perspective. Alexander was thirty years of age, which matched exactly to Maurice Duggan's date of birth of 1927. He had stated that he was single, a journalist and living at 46a Lancaster Gate, London, and that he was the son of Geoffrey Owen Emmett (deceased), a Colonial Administrator. Ellen Ingram, also stating that she was single, was resident at the time of marriage at 18b Harrington Square, Camden, which, Morton supposed, was why they had married in that area. Her occupation was stated to be a civil servant in Leconfield House and her father was listed as Charles Ingram (deceased). The final piece of information from the certificate was that the couple had married by licence.

Watching disconnectedly as Jeremy chatted with a customer, Morton sat back, drank more coffee and finished the scone, all the while trying to assemble the pieces of the story into something resembling a working narrative. He was still a very long way from being certain that Alexander Emmett and Maurice Duggan were one and the same person. There had to be an irrefutable document available somewhere that would conclusively link the two men. He looked down at the piece of paper before him, beginning to think through some of the records that might help him, when he saw Ellen and Alexander's son's name: Christopher. *He* could very easily provide the irrefutable evidence which Morton sought.

Morton ran a marriage search for Christopher: several possible; none certain. He checked the modern electoral registers. The criteria of searching for any address for a Christopher Emmett, from his eighteenth birthday in 1975 until 2008, pulled up 104 results. He sighed, called over to Jeremy for another latte, then began to wade his way through the tide of results. As he worked his way down the list, he made notes on the piece of paper of any who struck him as being potentials.

'I'm telling Juliette… You've gone over your caffeine allowance for the day,' Jeremy jested, putting the latte down on the table. He'd also brought another unrequested scone with him, Morton observed.

He smirked. 'Thanks, but I need it.'

111

'What you working on?' Jeremy asked, craning his neck around to see his laptop.

Morton exhaled. 'Don't ask.' Just as with Vanessa Briggs, just as with Lazarus, it was much too complicated to try to explain.

'Fair enough,' Jeremy answered. 'I'll leave you to it.'

'Thanks for the coffee…and scone,' he said, slicing and buttering it.

He ate, drank and carried on his way down the list of addresses for the 104 Christopher Emmetts. Typically, it wasn't until the final page that he clicked on a result which jumped off the screen at him. Living with Christopher Emmett at 56 Kingsgate Place, Kilburn in 1981 was a Sophie Emmett and a Sarah Ingram.

Morton knew that he was on to something when he ran a Google Map search for that address, finding that it ran parallel to Kilburn High Road. In fact, it appeared to Morton as though 56 Kingsgate Place actually backed *directly* on to 83 Kilburn High Road, where Maurice Duggan had taken up residency in 1974. Coincidence? He thought not.

Next, Morton cross-referenced Ellen Ingram's birth with the marriage of her father, Charles, and found that Sarah Ingram was Ellen's mother.

Morton's hypothesis had now been supplemented with the idea that perhaps Ellen's mother, Sarah Ingram, had raised Christopher at Kingsgate Place. Was Sophie Christopher's wife, or a sister, whom Morton had failed to pick up in the birth registers?

The marriage indexes confirmed that Sophie was Christopher's wife. Two children had followed the marriage, and it was the combination of this family group, who were all friends with each other on Facebook, which allowed Morton to send a direct message to Christopher Emmett. He kept the message short and slightly vague, telling him that he was researching the Emmett family tree and asking Christopher if he had any information on Alexander or his father, Geoffrey.

Morton swallowed the remnants of his latte, which had turned cold, and looked at all of his scribblings on the paper in front of him. He was ninety-nine-percent-certain that Alexander Emmett and Maurice Duggan were one and the same person. But he couldn't stop himself from returning to the fundamental question of *why* Alexander had needed to assume someone else's identity. Had Ellen's death had something to do with it? Had Alexander left the country at some point after the 14ᵗʰ December 1957, then flown back in February 1974 under a new identity? Didn't the newspaper report into his arrival at

112

Heathrow say that it had been 'in the early hours'? Flying in under the cover of darkness, without having filed a flight plan, implied that Maurice's former self had had something to hide. Perhaps he had *killed* his wife and fled the country?

Morton backtracked over his thoughts. *Flown back...* He had checked the *Great Britain Royal Aero Club Aviator's Certificates* for Maurice Duggan and drawn a blank, but perhaps a pilot's licence might have been recorded under the name of Alexander Emmett.

He pulled the Ancestry archive collection up onscreen once again and typed in Alexander's name. *One result.*

Alexander Emmett, born 7 Dec 1927, Port Said, Egypt. A button to the side offered an option: *View Record.*

Morton clicked to view the original scan and an off-white typed index card appeared in front of him, with Alexander's name and address confirmed at the top.

EMMETT, Alexander
46a Lancaster Gate, London

Born: 7th December 1927
at: Port Said, Egypt
Nationality: British
Rank, Regiment, Profession: Journalist
Certificate taken on: Miles Hawker Trainer
at: London Aeroplane Club
Date: 3rd August 1948

The exact date of birth did not match Maurice Duggan's, just the year, but when Morton clicked the next image in the file, which was the reverse of the index card, he felt sure that he had found the correct person. A headshot of a smiling, open-mouthed suave young man, wearing a shirt, tie and blazer, stared out at him. There was more than a passing resemblance, Morton thought, to the man in the blurred image taken at the Priory Flats Christmas party last year. Moreover, and crucially, he bore no resemblance at all to the photograph of the real Maurice Duggan, leant to him by Clarissa.

Morton hurriedly scrolled back in his mobile phone's camera roll to find the party picture. He found it and zoomed in to Maurice Duggan's face. The nose, hairline and ears he considered to be identical, but the overall quality of the party photo was too unsatisfactory for Morton to draw a firm conclusion. So, he resolved to send a copy of it to Maurice's former neighbour, Winnie Alderman, for her opinion as to whether it was indeed the man posing as Maurice.

He scrolled through his pictures and stopped at the photo of Ellen in her wedding dress, remembering that he had initially been unable to identify the nondescript building behind her because he hadn't known the place of her marriage. But now he did.

He typed Saint Saviour's Church into a Google image search and saw immediately from the selection of results, both old and modern, that the photograph of Ellen in her wedding dress had been taken outside this church.

Morton sat back with a smug smile on his face. In a pleasingly short time, he had identified Maurice Duggan's previous identity. But a lot of questions still remained.

'More secret coffee?' Jeremy called to him.

Morton shook his head. 'Think that's me done for the day. Thanks, though.' He didn't have long now until he needed to get home, wanting to make sure that he had a decent amount of time to spend with Juliette and Grace. He also needed to find a subtle way to get out of Juliette the date and time of the twenty-week scan, without her suspecting that he'd forgotten.

Before he packed up for the day, Morton ordered Ellen's death certificate on the priority service, then used his last few minutes of worktime to conduct some open searches in the various genealogy websites for Alexander Emmett. The global records presented ranged from family trees, census returns, sacramental documents, naturalisations, wills, land papers and birth, marriage and death indexes, but nothing, Morton felt, pertained to the Alexander Emmett whom he was investigating. Adding the birth year of 1927 and the place of Port Said did little to change the results.

Seeing that Alexander's father, Geoffrey Owen Emmett was a Colonial Administrator, which Morton guessed had been in Egypt, he turned to the *Discovery* section of the British National Archives website, typed in Alexander's name and looked eagerly at the single result.

Secret Service Reserves
Cabinet Office: Cabinet Secretary's Miscellaneous papers. Organisation and funding of British Intelligence.
Date: 17 January 1957 – 08 December 1958
Reference: CAB 301/118

The tantalising reference contained no further detail; it was only available to view at the National Archives. The document may have referred to an entirely different Alexander Emmett or contained an innocuous link, owing to his father's work in the Colonial Office, but seeing the words, *Secret Service*, somehow offered Morton a satisfying explanation for the complexities and subterfuge of the case so far. A low-level excitement bubbled inside him about the next phase of his research. Now, though, it was time to head home.

'Thanks, Jeremy,' Morton said, heading towards the shop front. 'What's on the menu for tomorrow's scone of the day?'

'Red chilli, apple and white chocolate,' Jeremy replied with a smile.

Morton answered with a guttural grunt: 'Don't think I'll be in. See you.'

Jeremy laughed and called after him, 'You'll be missing out!'

'Hmm,' Morton mumbled, making his way out of the door and along the busy High Street. As he walked, he mulled over the Duggan Case, very pleased with how his research was progressing. *If*, and it was a giant *if*, Alexander Emmett had been involved with the Secret Intelligence Services, then Morton's job was about to get harder. Much harder.

The moment he crossed the threshold of his house, his thoughts about the case evaporated.

Grace rushed up to him and grabbed his legs. 'Daddy! Play amals!'

'Play animals?' he asked, bending down and kissing her.

'Yes!' she said, reaching for his hand and pulling him into the lounge.

'Hi,' Juliette called from the kitchen.

'Hi,' he called back. 'Just playing amals, will come and see you at some point during the evening.'

Juliette laughed. 'How was your day?'

'Err… I'll tell you later,' he said, squatting down on the floor beside Grace. He took a leopard from among the menagerie of plastic animals scattered around the lounge floor and began prancing it around the carpet, whilst attempting his best impression of a vicious feline.

'What doing, Daddy?' Grace asked.

'I'm being a leopard,' he responded, enunciating the word leopard in the hope that she might remember it. 'Daddy's a *leopard*.'

'No,' Grace said, taking the cat from his hand and scowling disapprovingly. 'No.'

'Okay,' he said, selecting an elephant and making it waddle across the carpet. 'Elephant,' he said on repeat.

'Effluent,' Grace copied.

'No, el-e-ph-a-n-t,' he corrected.

'My effluent,' she insisted, taking the toy from his hand.

'Do you want to play animals by yourself, Grace?' Morton asked.

'Yes. Bye, Daddy.'

'Bye, then,' he said, standing and leaving Grace attempting to balance a sheep on the back of the elephant. 'Sheep effluent,' she said, as he left the lounge.

'She's playing with effluent,' he told Juliette, who was sitting at the kitchen table, drinking tea. He leant down and kissed her on the lips. 'Good day?'

She thought for a moment and then nodded. 'Yeah, I think so. Grace and I went down to the playpark. Had a play. Came back. More play and then she had a nap. More play. Snacks. Attempt at potty training. Snacks. Play… Think that's about it. Very strenuous.'

'Sounds fun. I've been in Granny's Scones all day, working. Gorgonzola and pear,' he said, anticipating her next question.

She grimaced.

'Sounds awful but tasted nice. And Jeremy came up with the idea of a gender-reveal party there,' Morton said, trying to wheedle out the date of the scan, without Juliette's realising. 'Can you imagine anything more horrific?'

Juliette grimaced. 'Well, that's not going to happen. We'll just keep that to ourselves, won't we?'

Morton nodded. 'I'm happy either way. Not with a party, I mean, but with people knowing. Maybe see how we feel afterwards?'

'Okay.'

'Not long now…' he added hopefully.

'Nope,' she agreed, stroking the small bump, then looking up at Morton. 'You don't know when the scan date is, do you?'

She could read him like a book. He thought back over what he had just said, looking for what could possibly have given it away but could think of nothing. Female intuition? Years of working for the police?

Juliette picked up her mobile and waved it vaguely in his direction. 'Jeremy texted me to ask when it was, as you hadn't a clue.'

Morton pouted.

'Tuesday, nine o'clock,' she said, rolling her eyes.

Morton pulled out his mobile and added it to his calendar. Forgetting once seemed to have escaped corporal punishment, but if it happened again, or worse still, if he double-booked, then his life wouldn't be worth living. 'I'll make dinner and put Grace to bed, and then I want to talk to you about a minor bombshell in my family tree.'

'Sounds worrying,' she said.

'Worse,' he answered. 'Very, very much worse.'

Juliette emitted a sound that suggested interest in what he had to tell her. She would certainly be fascinated by the genealogical revelation which he had to make, but the identity of Lazarus, he was fairly convinced, would not be met with such welcome enthusiasm.

Morton put Grace to bed at eight o'clock and then padded quietly down to the kitchen.

'Sorry, but do you mind if I have a wine?' he asked her.

Juliette mock-snarled. 'What happened to us both not drinking for the pregnancy? That didn't last long.'

'It's a fair point,' Morton conceded, pouring himself a large glass of red anyway. 'I'll do better for the next baby.'

'Excuse me? I presume you're carrying it, then?'

Morton laughed. 'What do you want to drink?'

Juliette turned her nose up. 'Something exotic... Water, please.'

Morton made her a drink and then sat down opposite her at the kitchen table. He took a necessary amount of his wine, fired up his laptop and then said, 'Where to start?'

Juliette shrugged. 'From a point I'll understand.'

'Right, so you remember Vanessa Briggs came up as a really strong DNA match?' he began.

'Yes,' Juliette confirmed with a nod. 'Nine hundred and two centimetres,' she added, clearly proud of the recollection.

'Centi*Morgans*,' he corrected, 'But yes...'

'And she's your half-aunt, daughter of a relationship your grandfather had at some point after his wife died in childbirth with your Aunty Margaret?' Juliette checked.

'Yes, exactly that.' Morton drew in a long breath. 'Well, after that, *another* DNA match came up at 2,220 centiMorgans.'

Even Juliette, with her limited experience of genealogy gasped at the figure. 'That's high.'

'Yes, it is. It was uploaded by someone using the email address of lazarus84101@gmail.com and who could be related to me in one of only three ways: my grandparent, my grandchild or my half-sibling, and be a male on my maternal side.'

Another gasp from Juliette. 'That's a weird coincidence, isn't it?'

'Hmm,' Morton said.

'So, who's Lazarus?' she asked. 'Half-brother?'

Morton shook his head.

'What, then?' she asked.

He turned his laptop so that they both had a view of the email which he had open on screen from Lazarus. They read it silently together.

Dear Morton,

Well, this is difficult. We don't usually respond to the Lazarus email address, but because of our past connection I feel I owe you an explanation.

A couple of years back I started my own company, Venator, based in Salt Lake City and my small team and I specialise in solving cold cases using investigative genetic genealogy. We've cracked a good number of murder and rape cases, but one has eluded us recently: the murder of Candee-Lee Gaddy from Reno, Nevada. She was a prostitute, killed one night in 1980. As is our standard procedure, we uploaded her killer's DNA to GEDmatch. The kit number for her murderer is LZ025: a guy I'm afraid you're related to, pretty closely. I'm guessing you know who this person might be.

I'm sorry that our first communication in a lot of years has to be this, really I am.

With fond regards,

Maddie

Madison Scott Barnhart
Venator
#5 Floor
Kearns Building
136 Main Street
Salt Lake City
UT 84101

Morton stared at Juliette, who was staring at the screen openmouthed, and wondered which part of the email had been so startling to her. He waited.

'A murder...cold-case...' she eventually said, '...1980? So, that must be'—she was working through the list of potential relationships—'your grandfather?'

118

Morton nodded. There was literally nobody else who it could have been. Alfred Farrier, his own grandfather, had killed a woman in Reno in 1980, apparently.

'Wow,' Juliette breathed. 'That's incredible. So… Vanessa Briggs?'

'Give me your professional opinion, given what I've just told you,' he challenged, gulping his wine gone.

Juliette thought for a moment. 'That her mother was a prostitute?' she ventured. 'Which might be why you can't find a birth reference, because she would have been adopted or fostered? Which also explains what your Aunty Margaret told you in an email before, about her dad being absent from home a lot of the time in the 1970s?'

It was the same horrendous conclusion which Morton had himself reached.

'And Maddie?' she said.

Morton thought that he detected a slight rise in her voice at the end of her ambiguous, two-word sentence. This was the part, where he had most feared her reaction. 'Yes,' he said, also vaguely.

Juliette raised her eyebrows. 'Have you replied?'

'Not yet,' he answered. 'I've no idea what to say. Clearly, I need to inform her that, yes, I know exactly who the killer is.'

'Why haven't you, then?'

Morton stood, reached for the wine bottle and topped up his glass. 'Alfred died when I was twelve, so I remember him quite well. He was a bit grumpy at times and lost his temper with everyone a lot, but I just can't think him capable of murder. By emailing Maddie back and giving his name, I feel as though I'm acting as judge and jury with no evidence in front of me.'

'You've got DNA evidence, which, as you're well aware, is irrefutable,' Juliette countered.

'Totally,' he agreed. 'But what if there was a mix up or I'm somehow misinterpreting something? I've literally no recollection of him going on holiday anywhere, never mind Reno. I just want something…else, I suppose.'

'Then look for it, before telling her,' Juliette said.

There it was again: a minor inflection on the word 'her'. Morton and Maddie had once been in a relationship together and even though Maddie had long been out of the picture before Juliette had come along, she didn't quite trust that Morton had fully gotten over her. This was because of the way in which Maddie had just upped and left one day, returning to her home in America with little explanation. He was, of course, entirely over her and felt nothing more than shock and surprise, when he had received her email. Besides which, judging by the shifting of her maiden name, Scott, to the middle and the addition of the surname, Barnhart, it strongly suggested that she had also since married.

'Have you looked to see if the murder is online anywhere?' she asked.

Morton shook his head. 'I've done nothing other than fret about it.'

Juliette pushed the laptop towards him.

He opened a web browser and logged in to Newspapers.com. He typed *Candee-Lee Gaddy* and *Reno* into the search box. The top result was for the *Reno Evening Gazette*, dated Monday 22nd December 1980.

Woman found murdered in Reno is identified

A woman found murdered in Governors Bowl Park in Reno Saturday afternoon has been identified as Candee-Lee Gaddy, 23, whose last known address was in K Street, police said last night. Relatives of the woman were notified yesterday after identification was established from fingerprints taken at Saint Mary's Regional Medical Center. Deputy Coroner Lin Anderson said that an autopsy performed at the hospital revealed that Ms. Gaddy had died from multiple stab wounds. Last night, police were trying to establish when Ms. Gaddy was last seen before she was killed. They said they would try to find witnesses from the East Fourth Street bars where she had reportedly worked. Homicide Detective Henry Gale said two young boys playing in the park found the partially clothed body about 3pm Saturday.

'Wow,' they said in unison, having finished reading the article at the same time.

'I can't believe it,' Morton added, dumbfounded. He couldn't square the old man in his memories, pottering in his allotment in Folkestone, to a Nevada prostitute-slayer. The two men were irreconcilable. 'He would have been sixty-six at that point.'

Juliette shrugged. 'There have been killers a lot older than that, let me tell you.'

'But…but it's my grandad.'

Juliette stood up and placed her hand on his shoulder. 'This is strictly from a non-police perspective now, but do you *need* to do anything more? He is dead, after all, so no conviction can be brought against him.'

'And the police perspective?' he asked.

'You know the police perspective.'

Morton sighed. 'I'll email Aunty Margaret and see if she was aware of her dad ever going to America.'

'Maybe you need to *speak* to her?' Juliette suggested.

'What and ask her opinion on whether her dad might have killed a prostitute in the States in 1980?'

Juliette gave him one of her don't-be-so-stupid looks.

He found himself nodding in agreement but thinking that, actually, there must have been some mistake. A mix-up with results. It was a long time ago, after all. Or, perhaps his grandfather had been a bone-marrow donor and passed the killer some of his DNA. An error made much more sense than his grandfather's having travelled to America and murdered a prostitute. But then he thought of Vanessa Briggs, who had almost certainly been sired by his grandfather, so he clearly hadn't been the man Morton believed him to have been.

He reached for his wine and finished the glass.

His grandfather had murdered someone in cold blood.

Chapter Eleven

4th March 1956, London

Alexander Emmett closed the door to his flat in Lancaster Gate and stepped down onto the lamp-lit pavement. He walked the few paces to his car—a silver Austin Healey—with a confidence bordering on arrogance. He wore a smart pin-stripe suit from Bond Street, complemented by his customary bowler hat. Alexander sought his reflection from the car window and was gratified with the dashing appearance of the man looking back at him; he was exactly the image that Alexander wanted to project. He was as certain as he could be that tonight the invitation, which he had courted for several years, would be forthcoming. He didn't know from where or from whom, but he was sure that it would come. Why else would he have been invited to this party? He splayed his thumb and forefinger over his freshly trimmed moustache, removed his hat and climbed into his car with a smile.

The car was cold and struggled to start. Alexander shivered, switched on the headlights and glanced up at the dense clouds that had hung low over London for the past two days and were now obliterating what little moonlight there might otherwise have been.

The drive to Cambridge Square, along the edge of Hyde Park, took just five minutes. He could have walked quite easily and, in fact, would have enjoyed the stroll, but making an entrance in his new car was part and parcel of the image. He parked the Healey close to the house, reached for his bowler hat and then stepped from the car, guessing and hoping that he was being watched from an upstairs window.

Alexander strode with an air of distinct entitlement, as though this were his neighbourhood, and those people, now entering the house, dressed in their finest attire, were his people.

The truth did not matter.

An erudite young lady, wearing an emerald evening dress with a white fur draped around her shoulders, entered the brightly lit porch of number one Cambridge Square on the arm of a dapper gentleman twice her age: her husband, no doubt, Alexander suspected. He said, 'How do you do?' to the couple, then followed them inside, where a butler, in the traditional black and white livery of his station, checked Alexander's name against the guestlist, took his hat and coat, and ushered him up the stairs into the extravagant apartment of the government minister, Harold Austin.

Alexander's expectation, that he would need to offer an explanatory introduction to the host, was unfounded. He entered a spacious and sumptuous lounge, where more than two dozen guests mingled in lavish apparel, their conversations low and inaudible, falling under the classical tune floating from the grand piano in one corner of the room.

'Alexander Emmett, one assumes?' a softly spoken, short man with a balding crown said to him, extending his right hand.

Alexander smiled, recognising the man as being Harold Austin, the Foreign Secretary, trying not to recoil at his damp, limp handshake. 'An honour to meet you, sir.'

He clearly relished the deference but made a dismissive gesture with his flaccid hand. 'Harold, please.' He studied Alexander for several seconds, saying nothing. 'Your name wafts the murky corridors joining Whitehall and Broadway,' he finally said. Alexander felt that he was trying to achieve a note of enigma.

Alexander's face warmed, not allowing his disquiet over the use of the verb, *waft*, to show in his expression. What was he supposed to say to that? Acknowledge that he knew full well the implications of what had just been said? Whitehall meant government and Broadway meant MI6. Should he feign ignorance? Smile coyly? 'It's a pleasure to be here, sir,' he eventually answered. 'I was rather hoping...' his words trailed off, when he realised that the Foreign Secretary was no longer listening to him. Something behind Alexander was captivating his interest.

Alexander looked over his shoulder to see an exquisite young lady with dazzling green eyes and light blonde hair, wearing a strapless bright red dress which curled up from the backs of her ankles to a height just above her knees. He had to work hard not to show an outward reaction to his surprise at seeing her.

She accepted a flute of champagne from a waiter's elevated tray, smiling thinly as she scanned the room.

Harold, running his tongue over his front teeth like a ravenous dog, flicked the fingers of his right hand towards Alexander in a clear gesture of dismissal. 'Excuse me,' he muttered, striding towards her and cooing, 'Miss Sterling! Enchanted to meet you at last.'

Alexander took several steps back, watching as Harold Austin kissed her on both cheeks. From what he was seeing, the enrapture was mutual.

'Mr Austin—*Harold?*—if I may be so bold?' she asked.

'Oh, my dear, of course,' he answered. *'Flora.'*

As the minister regaled her with some political story which he supposed amusing, she glanced subtly to her left, catching Alexander's eyes. A flicker of recognition to him, then her focus was fully returned to the Foreign Secretary.

The minister's story terminated with his exaggerated guffawing, which Alexander presumed to be for the benefit of showing off to his other guests, who were subtly observing from around the room. Flora laughed politely and placed her white-gloved hand on his.

Alexander had seen enough and beelined purposefully to one of the statuesque waiters, took a flute of champagne from him and then said hello to the closest person to him—a young lady standing alone and absorbed by the energetic pianist's rendition of a notable Beethoven number.

'Oh, hello,' she responded with a warm smile. 'Sorry. I was mesmerised. Wonderful player, isn't he?'

'Yes,' Alexander agreed. 'Are you a friend of the Foreign Secretary?' He nodded across the room in the direction of Harold Austin and Flora Sterling.

The woman grimaced. 'No. It's a kind of a friend-of-a-friend thing,' she explained. 'Except my friend isn't *actually* here. I think I'm a bit out of my depth, to be honest. This isn't my usual *milieu.'*

Alexander smiled and was about to say that it wasn't his usual environment, either, but stopped himself short. 'People here are pretty harmless. Mostly normal.' He laughed, as one gently teasing his own kind laughs, then sipped his champagne. 'Alexander Emmett,' he said.

'Ellen Ingram,' she responded, shaking his hand.

'Nice to meet you, Ellen,' Alexander said.

'She's certainly something, isn't she?' Ellen said, perhaps intuiting his thoughts, or perhaps simply expressing the shared consensus of the room about the woman openly flirting with Harold Austin.

'Our dear Foreign Secretary certainly thinks so, yes,' Alexander replied.

'So, what's your line of business?' Ellen asked him.

'Journalism. Freelance,' he said, turning his back on Harold and Flora, and facing Ellen fully for the first time. Had Flora Sterling not been present in the room, this young lady, with her short brown hair neatly framing an attractive face, might have garnered more attention. 'And yours?'

124

'Boring clerical work,' she said, with a gentle rolling of her eyes. 'Typing, filing, running errands… That kind of thing.'

'I see,' he said, sipping his drink. She did the same and for a moment neither of them spoke.

'Are you from London?' she eventually asked.

'No, born in Port Said, actually,' he answered. 'In Egypt. My father was a Colonial Administrator there but stayed on after independence in some official capacity or other. He died when I was four, so I don't really remember him. I grew up in Port Said as an only child and then came over here in 1946. My mother had died in 1944.'

Ellen laughed. 'Wow, that's quite a specific history, there.'

'Sorry,' he mumbled, flushing with embarrassment at how scripted he must have sounded.

'No, no,' she said, 'it's fine. Just very detailed, was all.'

He laughed but feared how stupid he must be coming across. He told himself to relax. 'Do you think your friend will turn up eventually?' he asked.

Ellen shrugged. 'Are you here alone?'

The answer was much more complex than the simplicity inferred in the question. He'd *arrived* alone, certainly, but the fact that an official invitation, signed by the Foreign Secretary himself, had arrived mysteriously at his house, suggested that he would be meeting someone here tonight. Who that person might be, though, he had no clue. 'I'm by myself,' he replied, checking the room and now questioning whether the invite would happen tonight, after all. He studied the faces of the guests milling around the room, wondering.

'Cheers,' Ellen said, touching her glass to his.

Alexander reciprocated her smile. 'Well, I'm glad that we—'

'Mr Emmett?' someone said, touching his arm.

Alexander looked to his side to see the insipid patronising smile of Harold Austin staring back at him.

'There's someone I'd like you to meet,' Harold said.

'Would you excuse me?' Alexander said to Ellen.

'By all means,' she replied.

Alexander followed the Foreign Secretary across the room towards a tall thin man in a smart suit, who projected prominence in every aspect of his demeanour. Was this the moment?

Ellen turned her back on the room, once again facing the grand piano. Her facial expressions and body language slid into what appeared to be a contented enchantment, lulled by the pianist's dulcet tones. Her eyes, however, were firmly fixed, as they had been before Alexander Emmett had interrupted her, on the large photograph behind the piano. Specifically, on the clear reflection afforded of Miss Flora Sterling.

Ellen's role in A4, the specialist section of MI5, had brought her to the party that evening. Technically, she shouldn't be here, as A4 only operated during the day Monday to Friday. Given that the main part of their role was to follow people suspected of spying and to build a web of contacts for those individuals, Ellen found such restrictions to be unfathomable and often took the initiative, such as she was doing now, of working outside of those outdated, limiting rules. Soviet spies and their contacts did not, as the restrictions placed upon A4 might have suggested, operate only on weekdays during normal business hours.

Flora Sterling had recently come under the suspicions of MI5, after she had been spotted meeting with Nikita Sokolov, ostensibly a second secretary at the Soviet Embassy in Kensington, but who was also known to be a Soviet spy-recruiter and handler. Her superiors were, Ellen knew, on the verge of ending the surveillance into Flora, believing that since no other evidence had come to light, the meeting between her and Nikita had been an innocent one. And yet, Ellen thought to herself, here she was cavorting—no, openly flirting, in fact—with the Foreign Secretary and also with George Kennedy Young, the director of the Secret Intelligence Service operations in the Middle East. A honey-trap of some kind was being set; of that, Ellen was sure. But for whom was Flora Sterling setting it?

In the photograph's reflection, Ellen surveyed the room, unable to locate Flora. She was no longer with Harold Austin; Ellen could see him introducing George Kennedy Young to the journalist with whom she had just been speaking: Alexander Emmett.

She observed Harold walking away from the pair, searching among his guests for Flora, Ellen suspected. Her eyes tracked back to George Kennedy Young, who was now leading Alexander over to the window. She watched as he pointed something out in the street below, then—with the deftness of a professional magician—passed something small to Alexander, before turning on his heel and leaving the room.

Ellen studied Alexander's face in the reflection, as he pocketed whatever he had just been given. Was that a look of satisfaction that he was trying to supress? Over to his left, a group of five socialite women disbanded and, in the void around which they had been gathered, Ellen could see Harold Austin with his hand placed in the small of Flora Sterling's back, as they chatted animatedly.

'They're getting on very well.'

Ellen turned with surprise; Alexander was back and had caught her eyeline trained on the reflection of Harold and Flora. 'An unlikely pairing,' she said, embarrassed to have been caught out, observing them.

'Isn't it just,' he agreed. 'Probably a good thing *Mrs* Austin is out of the country at the moment, or else she might not have agreed.'

'I don't suppose so,' Ellen said, sipping the last of her champagne.

'Would you like another?' he asked. 'Only, I haven't told you about my grandparents and *their* deaths, yet,' he said with a wry smile.

She laughed, relieved to see from his face that he was joking. Maybe he wasn't like these other people, after all. 'No, I need to be getting on my way,' she answered. It was time to leave, lest she should be noticed. She drew in a breath, then said, 'It was nice to meet you, Alexander.' She was pleased to see disappointment on his face.

'Oh, leaving so soon?'

'Early start at the office in the morning.'

'I hope to see you around, some time,' he said, presuming to kiss her on the cheek.

'That would be nice,' she replied. 'Enjoy the rest of the evening.'

'I will. Goodbye.'

'I'm just going to take one final look to see if my friend has turned up,' Ellen lied, providing an excuse for not walking directly to the exit, which would necessitate passing closely to Harold and Flora. She took a convoluted route, pretending to search among the crowds for her imaginary friend.

Ellen reached the exit and left; her work for today was done. She was certain that Flora Sterling was indeed laying some kind of a honey-trap, most likely for the malleable Foreign Secretary. But to what end, exactly?

Alexander appeared at 37-38 St James's Street in Westminster with some degree of trepidation. He paused, looking up at the imposing three-storey building. It was a grand edifice with a Palladian façade and no obvious outward sign as to its name or function. In fact, it was *White's*, the oldest gentleman's club in London. It was a place of some notoriety for its discreetness and exclusivity among the powerful and wealthy. And it was to there that Alexander had been directed by a small card passed to him at the party last night by George Kennedy Young—GK, as he was known.

Alexander was exactly on time. He took in a long breath, checked himself and straightened his tie, then approached the front door.

'Good morning, sir,' an aging doorman in top hat and tails greeted, barring his way. His voice was genial but with an undertone of circumspection.

'Good morning. Alexander Emmett, here to meet with George Kennedy Young.'

Without consulting a list or checking with anyone inside, the doorman nodded and stepped to one side.

Alexander thanked him and entered the entrance hall. Given the size of the edifice, it was small and once again gave no clue as to the building's purpose. It contained just four closed doors, an ornate chandelier and an antique desk, behind which sat another man in a smart black suit. Alexander repeated that which he had just said to the doorman outside.

'Very good. Follow me.' The man—what was he? A maître d'? Footman? Second doorman?—pulled open the door closest to him with his white-gloved hand. 'After you, sir.'

'Wow,' Alexander breathed, as he entered a vast hall-like room with dark-wood panelling and an opulent ceiling. A thin layer of grey smoke was suspended in mid-air, fed by the numerous pipes, cigars and cigarettes protruding from under the moustaches of the hoary white men engaged in discreet conversations at the cloistered booths around the room. Of the back-hand political and business deals now taking place in here, Alexander could hear nothing but a low murmur and the occasional guffaw.

He was led to a two-person booth on the far side of the room, at which was sitting George Kennedy Young.

'Thank you,' he said to the man who had delivered Alexander to him. 'Please, take a seat. I've taken the liberty of ordering you a pink gin.'

Alexander thanked him and sat himself down opposite GK.

'Cheers,' GK said.

Alexander chinked his glass and took a sip of the drink. Should he speak? he wondered, taking a quick glance around him. Whether deliberate or unintentional, nobody else was anywhere near being within earshot.

'I presume, since you're a journalist, that you're keeping abreast of current world affairs?' GK asked.

Alexander wanted to show his sharpness and intelligence, and so, knowing that GK was in charge of the Secret Intelligence Service in the Middle East, took a gamble that his vague enquiry was in fact specifically about developments in that region. 'Yes, I do. I know, for example, about the deal struck last month, where the Soviets agreed to supply two hundred and fifty million dollars' worth of weaponry to Egypt.'

The corners of GK's mouth turned down just a fraction in what Alexander took to be approval. 'And why might this be of concern to me?' he asked.

'Because, Israel, with the unflinching support of Washington, could start a war against Egypt, who clearly have the backing of the Soviets, who in turn want a foothold in the region.'

GK weighed his answer with a tilting of his head from side to side. 'Hmm.'

'And,' Alexander added, 'the Suez Canal is controlled by Britain and, being a crucial part of the shortest shipping route from east to west, is key to our trading and military capabilities in the Middle East.'

GK grinned. 'Yes!'

Alexander sat back and drank more of his pink gin, enjoying the taste.

'In short,' GK said, 'the Middle East is a political volcano; the eruption is not an *if* but a *when.*'

Alexander nodded.

'A journalist's dream come true, some would say,' GK said.

'Yes, it would be.' Alexander met his eyes, waiting.

'You grew up in Port Said, close to the Suez Canal.'

Was that a statement or a question? Alexander nodded.

'So...you know the area well, then?' GK asked.

'Very well,' Alexander lied.

'*And* you're something of an expert in radio communication. *And* you have a pilot's licence. *And* you're considered not to be lacking in intelligence, discretion and common sense.'

Alexander nodded, wondering if he should supplement the list with any of his other attributes and achievements.

'Hmm.' GK turned, raised his right hand and clicked his fingers.

A moment later, a waiter appeared at the table with a deferential, 'Yes, sir?'

'Another pink gin each. Doubles,' he ordered.

'Thank you, sir,' the waiter said, hurrying away.

'Heard of David Astor?' GK asked.

'Yes, he's the editor of the *Observer*.'

'You'll be working for him. Freelance. Three thousand per year. Based in Beirut,' GK said, just like that. No invite. No negotiation. No choice.

'Beirut?' Alexander questioned. 'But I thought Egypt was the epicentre of the troubles?'

'All major political and financial dealings have their origins in Beirut, as you will discover on Monday.'

'Monday? But I haven't even told my current job that—'

'All taken care of,' GK interrupted. 'When you get there, head for St George's Hotel and ask for Alfie Archer. He's a journalist for the *Observer*.'

'Right,' Alexander said, not fully certain if he had just received an invitation to join the Secret Intelligence Service, or not.

'Ah, the drink's here,' GK said.

The waiter placed the glasses down in front of them. GK took his, downed the lot in one go, and said, 'Well, I'd better let you get home and start packing, dear boy. All the best.'

Alexander thanked him, polished off his own drink, shook GK's hand and was escorted from the building by the same man who had conveyed him to the table just minutes before.

Ellen Ingram gripped the steering wheel of her Morris Minor and yawned. She was struggling now. She'd stayed awake all night, staring up at the front door of Harold Austin's flat in Cambridge Square. The party had ended shortly after 3am, although the last guests to leave did not do so for a further two hours. One guest, however, had still yet to leave: Flora Sterling. Ellen looked at her wristwatch. Five past seven. The sun was just beginning to backlight the row of Georgian townhouses.

Ellen was as confident as she could be that the only occupants remaining in the flat were Harold Austin and Flora Sterling. Had the honey-trap been set? Or were there other guests, too, who had also stayed on for legitimate reasons?

She looked up at the flat and noticed that a light had been switched on in the main living room. Ellen slid back into her seat when the shadowed movement of a figure passed by the window. Man or woman, Ellen couldn't tell. She gradually edged forward, looking up, but the person had now moved back away from view.

She sighed. Time was running out. She was due at the A4 office in one hour's time, where she would have to tell her boss, Mr Skardon, about her unofficial trailing of Flora Sterling and file a report into what she had witnessed at the party.

She went through her mental list of the assembled guests—big businessmen, government officials, diplomats, minor royalty and a selection of discreet young women of dubious occupation—only some of whom Ellen would be able to name in her official report.

She remembered Alexander Emmett, a curious chap who didn't quite fit with the other well-to-dos at the party. Ellen couldn't figure him out. He was either nervous around women or he had been lying about his background in Egypt. Inexplicably, she felt that she would leave him out of her report. Then she thought some more. No, she couldn't leave him out: he had been speaking directly to Harold Austin and George Kennedy Young who had clearly passed something to him in secret. Whoever he was, he had to be included in her account of the evening.

Ellen caught sight of movement in her wing mirror. A black Jaguar drove fast along the road behind her, drawing to a sudden stop outside of Harold Austin's flat. The Jaguar passenger door flew open, just as Flora Sterling stepped out of the Foreign Secretary's front door. She was wearing exactly the same outfit as she had worn the night before. Her make-up was now gone and her hair was no longer in the meticulous style that it had been. To Ellen, watching as Flora climbed into the Jaguar, this overnight stay appeared to have been unplanned, or at least made to look that way.

The car pulled away with unnecessary speed, leaving Ellen wondering whether or not to pursue it. She quickly decided against it, believing that the car, on the orders of Harold Austin, would simply be returning Flora to her house, the location of which was already known to MI5.

Ellen had no time to go home and bathe or eat breakfast, despite her being desperate for both. All she could do now was get to work—slightly early—and inform Mr Skardon about her own clandestine surveillance operation.

Half an hour later, Ellen entered Leconfield House, where the A4 Watcher unit operated from a series of nondescript rooms on the third floor. She took the lift and walked the wide corridor, passing various locked doors, behind which she did not know what went on, despite her having worked for MI5 for almost two years. Mr Skardon's office was the only one on the floor to have a window in the door, something that he had apparently insisted on when he had been given an internal office with no external windows.

Ellen tapped on the glass. Mr Skardon was seated behind his desk, smoking a pipe and reading a report of some kind. He looked up and gestured for Ellen to enter.

'Miss Ingram, you're twelve minutes early,' he said, cocking one eyebrow. He was a tall thin man with a thick moustache and the air of a middle-aged gent.

Ellen smiled. 'I need to write a report,' she began.

'Oh?' he replied, knowing full well that her work prior to this moment could not have necessitated her to do this.

'I attended a party at Harold Austin's flat last night,' she revealed.

Mr Skardon sat back in his chair, took a drag on his pipe, then said, 'Go on.'

'Flora Sterling was there...and she stayed the night.'

'Go on,' he repeated. 'But start from the beginning, please.'

So, for the next fifteen minutes, Ellen relayed all that had happened at the party. Mr Skardon listened silently, reserving his opinion on the matter until she had finished.

'You can't write that report,' he said matter-of-factly. 'The surveillance was unsanctioned by either me, or by any other officer in MI5 and, therefore, cannot be designated as official observation.'

Ellen could feel the frustration boiling inside her. She had expected a minor reprimand for acting outside of the section's usual parameters, but not allowing the report to be written at all, given what she had just told him, was lunacy. 'Could it not be sanctioned now, sir, retrospectively?'

Mr Skardon shook his head. 'Sanctioning a Watcher to attend a private party of a top-ranking married government minister? More than my job's worth, dear.'

'But a woman with known...no...proven connections to the Soviets is clearly up to something with the *Foreign Secretary*. Should we not be in the least bit unsettled by this? At a time when tensions are cranking up in the Middle East?'

'*Unofficially*, it's in here'—he tapped his right temple with the mouthpiece of his pipe,— '*officially*, I have no knowledge of the fact that you attended the Foreign Secretary's party, nor of what you learnt by being there. Your shift ended here yesterday at 5pm and you currently have no active casework connected to either Flora Sterling or Harold Austin. Until intelligence arrives, from the powers residing in the floors above us, that, Miss Ingram, is the way things shall stand.'

'Yes, sir,' Ellen mumbled. 'Thank you.' She stood and left the room. She closed his door and walked away from the office, fuming that her intuition and initiative was going to such a waste. More than anything, though, she was frustrated that whatever Flora Sterling was up to, she was free to continue it beyond the reach of the eyes and ears of MI5.

Chapter Twelve

Ellen was sitting cross-legged on the sofa of her two-bedroomed flat in Harrington Square, Camden. It was approaching ten o'clock in the morning and she was still wearing her nightdress. She sipped a mug of tea and hoped to goodness that her mother wouldn't drop by unannounced, as she was prone to doing on a Monday morning, when she knew that Ellen would be off work. Her mother, already deeply suspicious of Ellen's refusal to discuss what her job *actually* entailed, would be horrified to find that she was still in her bed clothes at this time of the day. Ellen was sure that her mother's angst came more from her no longer being able to boast to her church friends about her daughter's occupation, as she had felt able to do when Ellen had worked as a Marks and Spencer store detective. Now her mother dismissed enquiring friends with the nebulous answer, based on that which Ellen herself had given, 'Oh, she does something important in the clerical offices of Special Branch.' As far as her mother and her family and friends were led to believe, she had suffered some kind of humiliating demotion which was generally better left undiscussed; something that, although not true, suited Ellen.

She drank some tea, deciding that even if her mother did call today, she wouldn't answer the door to her. Ellen had work to do: her own investigation work.

Spread out on the coffee table in front of her was all that she had managed to procure—from various sources inside and outside of Leconfield House—on Flora Sterling. Ellen consulted her notes, searching for the date upon which Flora had first come to MI5's attention. According to the reports filed by her A4 colleagues, it had been in December 1955, when a Watcher trailing Nikita Sokolov had followed him to a meeting with the high-ranking Soviet KGB agent and recruiter, Viktor Zima. Flora Sterling had also been present at the meeting, triggering an MI5 dossier to be opened and compiled in her name.

Ellen examined the photostat copy of the file which she had covertly made at work. According to the document, Flora had first been employed at the age of seventeen as a pin-up model, featuring in a selection of insalubrious publications, which had led to a short career as a topless dancer at Murray's Cabaret Club in Soho. The trail of Flora's official employment had ended there in June 1941. What she had done and where she had been in the intervening years to December 1955 was a mystery.

Ellen knew from her time at Special Branch that everything that she had laid out on the coffee table in front of her, coupled with what she had learned from Harold Austin's cocktail party, was at best circumstantial.

The more Ellen studied the paperwork, the more infuriated she became. The answers weren't contained in these documents; they were to be found in constant surveillance into Flora Sterling's every movement, until a web of all of her known contacts and associates had been established, leading to her eventual arrest. The decision by MI5 and A4 not to monitor interactions between Harold Austin and Flora Sterling seemed entirely nonsensical to her. But resources in MI5 were too tight, she had been told, and focus had shifted back to constructing a list of Nikita Sokolov's network of contacts. Nikita was viewed as the lynchpin between the agents operating on the ground in Britain and the higher echelons of the KGB, including his presumed boss, Viktor Zima.

The decision was out of Ellen's hands and there was little point in going over and over the same pieces of paper. She gathered up the documents, placed them back inside the brown envelope and finished her tea. She drew in a long breath of air and then headed to her bedroom to get dressed and ready. Perhaps she would see what her friend Doris was up to later. Maybe they could have lunch together or see what was on at the cinema.

With little care, she pulled her hair back into a loose bun and chose one of her usual outfits: a simple lemon-coloured dress, which she sometimes wore for work, along with an old pair of comfortable shoes. The female Watchers of A4 were sent out to look deliberately ordinary—to blend in—so as not to draw attention to themselves. The men, in some perverse logic that Ellen had never comprehended, were disguised as themselves: all of them donning trilby hats and long raincoats, when conducting surveillance, the idea being that nobody would suspect them of spying because they were dressed as spies.

Ellen left her flat, descended the stairs and opened the front door to be greeted by her mother's scowling face. 'Oh,' Ellen said.

'What do you mean by *that*?' her mother demanded. '*Oh*? That's no way to speak to your mother.'

'Just that I was on my way out, that's all,' Ellen half-apologised with a wooden smile.

'Well, where are you going?'

'To see Doris,' Ellen answered.

'Well, I'll walk with you to the bus stop, then,' her mother said.

Ellen stifled a sigh. 'Lovely,' she said, stepping out onto the pavement.

A blue Ford Anglia, the registration of which Ellen instantly recognised, drew up beside them. It was one of the surveillance cars used by A4. Mr Skardon wound down the driver's window and smiled. 'Morning!'

Ellen flushed with embarrassment, instantly wondering how she was going to dig her way out of this one. Introducing her mother to her boss would inevitably lead to an interrogation of what her job entailed, exactly. 'Morning,' she managed to say cheerfully. 'Just off to see a friend.'

'Ah,' Mr Skardon said. 'I wondered if you fancied accompanying me on a work lunch?'

Work lunch? That was definitely code for something, Ellen thought. Mr Skardon had never called by her home to ask her out for a work lunch in the entire time that she had been with the section. 'Yes, okay.' She turned to her mother, who appeared quite flummoxed by the conversation. 'Sorry, Mother. I'll ring you up later.'

'Oh,' her mother said.

'No, bring her along!' Mr Skardon strangely insisted. 'Jump in the back. More the merrier!'

Ellen looked uncertainly at her mother, whose face lit up. She wasted no time in climbing into the rear of the car. She was delighted, Ellen assumed, to have at last an insight into her daughter's mysterious employment. Ellen got in beside her mother and said, 'Mr Skardon, this is my mother, Mrs Ingram.'

'Sarah,' she said warmly.

'Jim,' he responded.

Ellen rolled her eyes.

'A table has been booked for 1pm at the Dorchester,' Mr Skardon informed them, making careful eye contact with Ellen in the rear-view mirror.

'The *Dorchester*,' her mother gasped. 'Well, how *marvellous*.' She nudged Ellen, beamed and whispered, 'Is this what you *do*?'

Ellen held a fixed smile, whilst trying to determine exactly what was going on. The way that Mr Skardon had said 'A table has been booked...' made her wonder if somebody, whom they were trailing, had booked a table, which required ears and eyes nearby that, for whatever reason, he was unable to achieve himself. She would know for certain, if, upon arrival at the Dorchester, he made his excuses, leaving Ellen and her mother to dine alone. Clearly, if he could have gone into the restaurant himself, then he wouldn't have needed to call for Ellen's services.

'Ellen tells me so little about her work,' her mother complained, as they drove through the busy London streets towards the Dorchester.

Mr Skardon laughed. 'Your daughter is not the ostentatious type, Sarah. She does a sterling job, but it *is* terribly dry.' He went on to communicate to her mother in the dullest of details an account of some fictional role, which he evidently had at the ready for such occasions as this, but Ellen was focussed on his first two sentences. Just a tiny, insignificant change in the timbre of his voice on the words *ostentatious* and *sterling*. Austin and Sterling, she interpreted; it was they who were meeting at the Dorchester at 1pm.

Ellen's mother took a quick sideways glance at her, as if to ask for help in breaking Mr Skardon's deliberately dismal monologue. Ellen simply smiled and allowed him to continue uninterrupted.

'What about you?' Mr Skardon eventually asked. 'What do you do, Sarah?'

'Well, since Ellen's father died, I've been—'

'Oh, look, the Dorchester,' Ellen interrupted, elated to be able to get her mother out of the car. 'We're here.'

They parked up outside the hotel and walked towards the entrance, Mr Skardon taking the lead. Just as Ellen had expected, the doorman stepped into his path and asked, 'Mr Skardon?'

'Why, yes,' he replied, convincingly appearing perplexed at the intervention.

'A message for you: your aunt Lily is terribly ill and you need to return home.'

'Oh, glory,' Mr Skardon said, turning to face the two women. 'I don't know what to do, now.'

'Well, you *must* go,' Ellen's mother insisted. 'No question. And we should come with you to see if we can be of assistance.'

'I don't think that—' Ellen began but was cut off by Mr Skardon.

'*I'll* go,' he said definitively. 'But there's no use us all missing the table'—he lowered his voice considerably—'*as it's all paid for.*'

'Well, if you're sure,' Sarah Ingram said quickly.

'Absolutely. Enjoy,' he said. 'I'll see you back at the office afterwards, Miss Ingram? So sorry.'

Ellen nodded and led her mother inside the hotel. The confusing aroma of cigarette smoke, coffee and cakes drifted from the restaurant when the door was opened to them by an elegantly dressed young lady. 'Do you have a reservation?' she asked.

'Yes, I believe so,' Ellen answered. 'A friend made the reservation but he's unable to make the meal: Skardon?'

The young lady smiled, as she checked some papers on a wooden lectern just inside the door. 'Ah, yes. If you'd care to follow me.'

Ellen glanced surreptitiously at the guests seated around the restaurant, a lavish room with a marble floor and dressed with the rich and beautiful decor of the 1930s, but there were no familiar faces dining here. Had she made a mistake in believing that she had been brought here for surveillance reasons?

The waitress stopped and indicated the two-person table beside her.

No, Ellen had not made a mistake. At the table directly behind the one reserved in Mr Skardon's name, partially concealed behind a tall yucca plant, were seated Flora Sterling and Harold Austin. Ellen tucked her head down and quickly slunk into the chair with its back to their table. Her mother sat opposite her, taking stock of the room.

The waitress handed them two menus and told them that she would return shortly.

'Well,' her mother said. 'This is something, isn't it, Ellen?'

'Yes,' Ellen answered, locating the drinks menu and hastily choosing the first item on it. 'Do you have a compact with you, at all? I've got a lash irritating me.' She tugged down on her left eyelid for good measure.

Her mother nodded, rummaged in her handbag and produced a small gold-coloured disc which she passed over the table.

Ellen opened the mirror and pretended to study her eye, pulling down on her lower lids with a disgruntled sigh. Her focus, however, was entirely on trying to get a glimpse through the yucca branches of the couple behind her. Flora, wearing a stylish low-cut dress, sported a large straw hat which was angled in such a way as to cover most of her face from prying eyes. Harold Austin, with his back to Ellen, had his elbow on the table, his temple resting in the palm of his hand. Plainly, they didn't wish to be seen.

Returning the compact to her mother, Ellen leant back in her chair, feigning to read her menu, whilst she tried to catch the low murmurs of conversation taking place behind her. He was talking. Something about his wife's still being abroad. Someone was unwell. He suggested that Flora stay for a few more days. She laughed and said something that Ellen couldn't discern. She asked if he brought all of his mistresses here. He laughed. No, just her. Something inaudible from him that made her giggle and tell him to stop.

'Well? What are you having?' Ellen's mother asked, with a note of annoyance.

'Iced tea,' Ellen replied quickly.

'Oh, are you? What about to eat? I'm having the Dover sole, since your work is treating us.'

'I'm having the same,' Ellen replied, having given it no thought whatsoever.

The waitress arrived and Ellen, keeping half an ear on the conversation behind her, hurriedly ordered their food and drinks.

Her mother spoke at the same time as Flora asked Harold Austin about his work. Something about what was happening at the moment in the Foreign Office. Ellen strained to hear his reply.

'What's the matter with you?' her mother yapped. 'You're not even listening to me. You're away with the fairies, today. Honestly, I've no idea how Jim gets *anything* out of you. It's really little wonder you're relegated to filing in the basement. Honestly.'

'Sorry. Say it again,' Ellen replied, having just about managed to hear Harold give Flora a dismissive reply, returning their conversation to how splendid she looked in her dress.

'I asked you if you were getting another day off—you know—in lieu of this one,' her mother said, enunciating each word with extra clarity. 'I mean… I realise that it isn't *work*, but still.'

'I expect so, yes,' Ellen replied, just as a light sound of a chair rasping on the marble floor came from behind her. She chanced a subtle glance through the yucca leaves, seeing that Flora and Harold were preparing to leave. Ellen bent down, simulating picking something up from the floor beside her, turning away from their direction. Below the line of the tablecloth, she watched the legs of Harold and Flora passing by her table and disregarded the sound of her mother's demanding to know what on earth she was doing.

'I dropped something,' Ellen explained, as she resurfaced, just in time to see the Foreign Secretary and his mistress leaving the restaurant.

Her mother expelled a breath of disapproving air through her lips.

The waitress arrived with their food and drinks, in which Ellen partook only half-heartedly. Weighing on her mind was the scant detail which she had managed to obtain from their conversation.

'What do you suppose Jim wants to see you back at work for?' her mother asked, slicing a potato in two.

'Something not especially interesting, I shouldn't wonder,' Ellen replied.

'But *what?*' her mother pushed, resting her fork with a piece of potato on it against her plate. 'I just don't understand.'

Ellen rolled her eyes. 'It'll just be some administrative problem that he needs me to sort out.'

'It baffles me, Ellen. It really does. I mean...' She glanced around the restaurant. 'Lunch in the Dorchester...'

'Our department gets given so many free meals per month,' Ellen said, producing the story off the top of her head. 'We get to take it in turns to come here; one of the few perks of the job.'

'Well, you've never said,' her mother replied, finally placing the potato into her mouth.

Ellen laughed. 'It's the first time I've had it. Our department is so big, you see.'

Her mother's face suggested that no, she didn't see.

'What are you going to do for the rest of the day?' Ellen asked, changing the topic and attempting to lighten the mood.

'It's wash day, isn't it?' she answered.

'Right.'

The rest of their meal passed in near-silence and Ellen brought it to a close without ordering desserts. She was keen to get back to the office as quickly as possible. They left the restaurant and Ellen said goodbye to her mother and took a red London bus to Leconfield House, where she found Mr Skardon in a pragmatic mood about how little she had gleaned.

'Well, we just took a chance and that was as close as we could get,' he said, shrugging his shoulders.

'What changed, may I ask?' Ellen enquired. 'To get you to undertake surveillance, I mean.'

'Nothing really. The chaps upstairs were curious to know who the Foreign Secretary's latest courtesan was and, given what you'd told me, I suggested we 'go out for dinner' with him. From what you've said, though, there's nothing to worry about—she's just another in a long line of beautiful young women he likes to parade behind his wife's back.'

'Except, unlike the other women, she's a known associate of Nikita Sokolov and Viktor Zima,' Ellen countered. 'Will she be investigated, now?'

'Not unless something else arises, no,' Mr Skardon answered.

Ellen sighed, realising that she had just handed Mr Skardon the evidence that he needed *not* to continue the surveillance into Flora Sterling and the Foreign Secretary. Was there anything else that she could remember from the cocktail party, or from the Dorchester, which might help? No, nothing that she had not told him already. 'Thank you, sir,' she said flatly, leaving his office.

The taxi—a battered American Buick—drew up outside of the water-front building. Alexander, sweating from the extra ten degrees of heat compared to that of England, was sitting in the back, looking out of his open window.

The driver was a black-bearded Arab, who, either by choice or an inability to speak English, had remained silent for the entire journey so far from the airport. He now turned to Alexander, rubbed his thumb and forefinger together, and said, 'Eight pounds… Lebanese.'

Alexander handed him a Lebanese ten-pound note and said, '*Chokran*,' as he stepped from the Buick, dragging his suitcase across the backseat with him.

He stood on the pavement, as the taxi sped off, then looked up at the building beside him, with *HOTEL SAINT GEORGES* in blue letters on a sign above some entrance steps. Wrapped around each of the five storeys was a white square-grid balcony, which made it stand out from the other more regular-looking oblong buildings in the surrounding area.

Alexander wiped his brow on the back of his hand and entered the hotel. He paused upon entering, responding to a momentary pleasure caused by the ceiling fan directly above him rattling down air as cold as London, but which quickly made him shiver, before he moved further inside. Avoiding the beseeching eyes of the two uniformed ladies behind the reception desk immediately in front of him, Alexander cast his eyes around the place. It looked decent enough. There was an informal seating area to his right with maybe a dozen-or-so vacant chairs, the sole occupant being a young woman nursing a baby in her arms. To his left were two elevators and a staircase. Directly in front of him, the marble-floor stretched out to three open patio doors, which in turn fed onto an enticing terrace.

'Can we help you, sir?' one of the olive-skinned receptionists called over.

Alexander smiled, approached the desk and asked quietly, 'I'm meeting an old friend, Alfie Archer. Is he here, yet?'

'Yes. He's out on the terrace, I believe,' she said, pointing to the open doors behind her.

'Thank you,' Alexander replied, strolling towards the terrace. He stopped just short of actually going outside, set down his suitcase and studied the faces of the twenty-plus people sitting at small tables dotted around the patio. He knew nothing about Alfie Archer beyond his name.

Alexander briefly considered each person in front of him, discounting them if they were female or looked as though they were from the Middle East, which left just one person: a rotund, shirtless man with pasty skin, sitting with his mouth agape, fast asleep. Not at all the type that Alexander had been expecting.

With a deep breath, he picked up his suitcase and started outside, being slapped in the face once again by the hot afternoon sun.

He loomed over the sleeping man, wondering how best to rouse him. Cough loudly? Say his name? He cleared his throat and, at that moment, his name was called from behind him: 'Alexander?'

He turned around and saw a handsome young man with blonde hair and a broad smile on his face, walking towards him.

'Looking for me?' he asked, approaching Alexander with his right hand extended. 'Alfie Archer.'

Alexander shot a look between the two men, as he grinned with relief and shook this man's hand. 'I was told you were outside.'

'I was, but I went in to get you this,' he said, handing Alexander a glass. 'Lebanese wine.'

'Oh, thank you. Are you not having one?'

Alfie shook his head. 'I don't drink... Far too young.'

Alexander laughed. 'Well, yes, you are surprisingly young for a'—he went to say 'spy' but changed his mind at the last moment and finished his sentence with—'journalist.'

Alfie smiled again. 'So I'm told. Shall we sit down? I'll take you to your flat in a while, but you look as though you could do with a drink and a rest first.'

Alexander sipped the wine—enjoying its bitterness to which he was unaccustomed—and followed Alfie to a round two-person table with a parasol, right on the edge of the water. They sat down and Alexander took in the long view over the low stone wall. Nothing but pure azure seas to the horizon.

'Stunning, isn't it?' Alfie said.

'Beautiful,' he agreed. 'Have you been in Beirut long?'

'On and off for two years, now.'

'Right. So, tell me what's what, then,' Alexander said, hoping that, at last, he would learn that there was indeed a dual aspect to his role here as a journalist.

'You've got a day or two to settle in, then you'll begin your first story,' Alfie explained.

'Great,' Alexander said keenly. Lebanon was the only Arab country with good communications and without state censorship. Alexander had a flash-forward to stories interrogating the swelling political discord in the region; to revelations of governmental corruption; of conflict which had rumbled since biblical times between Christians and Muslims; and, of course, the golden article which would encompass almost everything else: the unsettling of the region caused by the rise to power of one Gamal Abdel Nasser, leading Arab nationalist and heir-apparent to the Egyptian presidency. GK was right: this was *the* place to be right now for an up-and-coming journalist.

'And what will my first article be about, exactly?' Alexander asked.

'Cars,' Alfie answered.

'*Cars?*'

'Cars. And how they differ from country to country within the Middle East.'

'Oh,' Alexander said, wondering if he could have come up with any subject less interesting, less appealing to research and write about, than cars in the region. 'They're all either American or French by the looks of the roads from the airport.'

Alfie shrugged.

'Well, that's a fascinating start to my career in the Middle East,' Alexander murmured. 'What about this city? Tell me about Beirut.'

'Well, they don't call it the Paris of the Middle East for nothing. It's hot and exotic. A smorgasbord of cultures, races and religions. The influence of the French can be felt everywhere from the cuisine to the…well…cars.' He grinned.

'It sounds idyllic,' Alexander commented.

'You must know what it's like, though, having been born in Egypt?' Alfie said.

'Yes. Yes, of course,' Alexander replied.

'It has everything you could wish for. Every type of food, bar or restaurant is here. You can ski in the mornings on the *Mzaar Kfardebian* and swim in the sea in the afternoons, here in the Mediterranean, with cocktails in between.'

'Perfect,' Alexander said. 'And what about this place?' He looked up at the back of the hotel. 'Is there a reason you wanted to meet me here?'

'You're sharp,' Alfie commented. '*This* place, my friend…' he turned and pointed to the hotel. '*This* is the city's trading post, where information—*quid pro quo*—flows as fast as the Lebanese wine, between diplomats, ambassadors, journalists and politicians. Where did I first hear that Nasser was planning a confrontation against British influence in Egypt? Here. Where did I first learn of the Soviet arms deal with Egypt? Here. Stories break in Hotel Saint Georges hours or even days before it hits the newspapers and wireless.'

This was the place to be, then, Alexander thought, taking a quick look at the other innocuous-looking people on the terrace, wondering at their occupations.

'Drink up, and I'll give you a quick tour of the city,' Alfie said.

Although Alexander was just beginning to feel relaxed here, he finished his wine, picked up his suitcase and followed Alfie through the hotel lobby and back out of the front entrance, where the taxi had dropped him.

Alfie led with a brisk pace, pointing out places, shops and bars of interest from the white and ochre buildings that they passed. The hot city really was the amalgam of cultures which Alfie had suggested it to have been. On the palm-tree-lined Martyrs Square they passed shops with Arabic signs, French restaurants and even an Odeon Cinema. The busy roads, meanwhile, were crammed with American and French vehicles: Cadillacs, Chevys, Citroëns, Plymouths and Buicks vied for dominance on the city streets.

'An exquisite *bouillabaisse* over there,' Alfie said, pointing at the Hotel Lucullus. 'It's a favourite of the French journalists and diplomats. The Americans and Turks, if you need them, prefer to dine in the Armenian quarter of the city.'

'Right,' Alexander said, making a mental note, but not sure how meeting up with an American diplomat in an Armenian restaurant would help him with an article on cars in the Middle East.

They walked on further still through the broiling city with more cafés and bars being indicated by Alfie as potential locations to meet politicians and government officials. Alexander still could not reconcile a straightforward career in journalism with what he was being told. Not once had Alfie referred to the world of espionage.

'So, this is *Rue Verdun*, on the border between the Christian and Muslim quarters and that, there, is your flat in the *Immeuble Tabet* building,' Alfie said, pointing to a smart-looking, three-storey white apartment block and handing him a door key. 'Number nine. Top floor. Nice view over the city.'

'Perfect,' Alexander said, sensing that Alfie's duty had been fulfilled and that he was now being left to his own devices.

Sure enough, Alfie shook his hand. 'I'll see you around. Good luck with the first article. Mrs Strickland at the *Observer* will give you further instructions. Oh, and your flat is highly likely to have been bugged, or at least will be at some stage in the future, so you'd be wise to keep your mouth shut when you're indoors.'

'Bugged by whom?'

'Oh, flip a coin,' Alfie said with a shrug. 'The Egyptians, the Soviets, the Americans, the Turks, the Israelis, the French, the Syrians or the British. Take your pick. Cheerio.'

Alexander stood on the street corner, sweating, as he watched Alfie Archer strolling away casually with his hands slung in his pockets. Looking at him from behind, he really could have been just a young lad.

Waiting for a break in the stream of traffic, Alexander crossed the road to Immeuble Tabet. He opened the red front door and entered a hot hallway with white walls and colourful Arabian ceramic tiles on the floor. There were three numbered doors to his left and a staircase to his right which he climbed to the next floor that was set out identically to the ground level below. On the top landing, at the far end of the corridor, he found number nine: his new home.

With minor trepidation, Alexander pushed the key into the lock and opened the door, entering a tiny lobby area which led to three closed doors. Shutting the front door behind him, he pushed open the one directly in front of him: a small, windowless bathroom. The door to the right led to a bedroom, containing just a bed, nightstand and a thin, ornately carved wardrobe. He found the final room, a spacious lounge, in semi-darkness, owing to the closed window shutters. From the dimness, he could just make out two chairs, a table and a long dresser. At the far end he spotted a small kitchenette. He put his suitcase down and stepped across the mercifully cool, white marble floor to the windows and threw open the shutters, revealing a fantastic view over the city rooftops to the Mediterranean in the far distance.

Alexander looked around the room and smiled. He would be happy here.

Unlocking the two brass clasps on his suitcase, he pulled it open and took out his Hallicrafter radio set which he had procured from a sale of former RAF stock just before he had left England. He carried the radio over to the dresser, placed it down and then set about rigging up the antenna.

A few minutes later, with his headset over his ears, Alexander was listening in to some inane local chatter. He grinned. With a bit of time and patience, he would be able to communicate over much longer distances outside of the Middle East.

Then he noticed something on the table—a newspaper—that made him realise that, besides the scant pieces of furniture, there was not a single object in the flat. Just a newspaper. Alexander opened it out. It was today's London *Observer*. Was there something to be construed from this being the only item in the place? Was it a not-very-subtle reminder that he had a dreary assignment to write for the paper? Or was a daily delivery of the newspaper, for which he worked, just a routine, regular part of the job?

He remembered what Alfie had just told him about half the world's possibly having bugged the apartment and found himself saying, 'Right, I'll just have a nice sit down,' as he picked up the paper and began to read it cover-to-cover.

Four pages from the end, having otherwise perceived nothing out of the ordinary, an ad in the classifieds jumped out at him:

Wanted: *Lebanese wine for Middle Eastern party. Call Mrs Strickland. Tel. London 35653*

Alexander studied the advert for several seconds, convincing himself one moment that it had nothing to do with him, before settling on the belief that, yes, this advert had been placed there for him: Alfie Archer had told him that Mrs Strickland at the *Observer* would give him further instructions. And here they were. Memorising the phone number, he left his flat in search of the nearest public payphone.

Chapter Thirteen

Morton was in his kitchen, making his third cup of coffee of the day, when the letter box emitted its unhappy moan that a bundle of post was passing through it to the floor. Removing his drink from the coffee machine, Morton entered the hallway and picked up the small stack of letters. He was pleased to see that, among the assortment of post, was a GRO-stamped envelope: Ellen Emmett's death certificate. He headed upstairs to his study on the top floor, sipped his coffee and then opened the envelope.

When and where died: 14*th* December 1957, Harrow Road, Kensal Green
Name and surname: Ellen Emmett
Sex: Female
Age: 30 years
Occupation: Housewife
Cause of death: Blood-loss caused by suicide. Post-mortem, no inquest.
Signature, description and residence of informant: Alexander Emmett, husband, 46a Lancaster Gate, London

Blood-loss caused by suicide, Morton re-read. She'd slit her wrists? He turned to his laptop and ran first a Google search and then an online newspaper search for her suicide but found no reference in either. Evidently, her death had not been newsworthy enough at the time.

Morton stood up, carried the certificate over to his investigation wall and affixed it close to Ellen's name. He added the information to an index card which he placed onto the chronological timeline running at the base of the wall.

Ellen had died, not at her husband's hands, as Morton had entertained, but at her own. His working theory, though, was still that Alexander had fled soon after her death—possibly abroad—and that he had later returned in 1974 under the assumed identity of Maurice Duggan. At that point he had taken a house nearby to his son Christopher's and, once settled back in the area, had organised for a headstone to be placed on his wife's grave space. The motive for changing his name continued to baffle Morton, however. If Alexander had had no part in his wife's death, then why the need to come back under an assumed identity?

Morton returned to his desk and opened the Facebook message which Christopher Emmett had sent at some point in the early hours of the morning.

Yes, I'm connected to the Emmett family you refer to. My father was Alexander Emmett and his father was Geoffrey Emmett. I know next to nothing about either, sorry. Christopher.

Sitting back and enjoying his coffee, Morton contemplated the message and what he might say in response. He was very keen to learn anything at all, no matter how little, from Christopher, but what could he say to justify his further enquiry, without yet giving too much away? He needed to be incredibly circumspect in anything he divulged, since the investigation was still very much ongoing. He placed the coffee down beside his laptop and typed out a message that he hoped might navigate the precarious situation in which he found himself: *Dear Christopher, Many thanks for your reply. I have conducted a little work into your family and could tell you a bit about your father. Perhaps we could exchange information? Kind regards, Morton Farrier.*

He hit the enter key and, almost immediately a tick appeared at the base of the screen, followed by the words *Seen by Christopher.*

Christopher is typing, it read.

Morton drank some coffee and waited. Christopher was either a slow typist or he was writing a very long message.

His focus drifted back to the investigation wall. An active area of research, as denoted by a squiggly pink line around its edge, was the reference to Cabinet Office papers, held at the National Archives, on the funding of British secret intelligence 1957-1958. He had tried to find out more about what might be included in the files but had drawn a blank; the only solution was to request the document at the National Archives. It was a long way to go just to view one file, but one which he keenly felt might justify the effort.

Finally, a ping from Morton's laptop announced that Christopher had sent him a message. He was a slow typist. *Intriguing! Live in the UK? Want to meet for a chat? I work in London (St Pancras), can meet most lunchtimes…Chris*

Morton looked at the time, a plan forming in his mind. *Great! Today any good? I can take the high-speed train up,* Morton replied.

Starbucks in St Pancras station? 1pm? Christopher answered, taking an age.

Perfect—see you there.

149

From St Pancras, Morton could catch the tube out to Kew with just about enough time to access the file on British secret intelligence before the archive closed for the day.

He would need to think carefully about exactly how much he would divulge to Christopher at this point, when so much of what Morton knew was unsubstantiated or still just a working theory.

There was one other job that he needed to do before getting ready to go to London: phone his Aunty Margaret, over which he had thus far procrastinated considerably. He drew in a long breath, picked up his mobile, exhaled and then put it down again. Maybe later. Better that he prepared himself fully for the meeting with Christopher Emmett than get side-tracked with the disturbing addendum to his grandfather's life which had kept his brain active in the early hours of this morning. In the sobering, rational light of day, the conclusions that he had drawn overnight—accepting that his grandfather had probably fathered several children with a variety of prostitutes, whom he had promptly murdered thereafter—had abated somewhat but were still completely conflicted in his mind. He half-wished that he had never uploaded his DNA to the website, but the lid had been firmly blown off that box, never to be resealed. Even if he ignored Maddie's email and never replied, it would take her and her team a matter of minutes to build his family tree and work out the identity of Candee-Lee Gaddy's murderer. In fact, if Maddie thought hard enough, she could probably recall Morton's grandfather's name and even seeing his photograph hanging on the wall of Morton's studio flat back when they had dated. Realistically, all he could do now was to work with Maddie to understand the truth, no matter how uncomfortable or difficult it might be to accept.

The old two-carriage diesel train had heaved its way sluggishly through the Sussex countryside into Kent, arriving in twenty-two minutes at Ashford International where Morton had jumped onto the high-speed train on to London. Thirty-seven minutes later, he alighted at St Pancras International and descended the escalator into the station concourse, in the centre of which, among a run of shops and restaurants, was Starbucks.

Morton immediately recognised Christopher Emmett from his Facebook profile picture. He was wearing a smart dark suit and a red tie, and although he was entirely silver-haired, he didn't look his fifty-nine years. He had a briefcase in one hand and his mobile, at which he

150

was now looking, in the other. In a fleeting double-take, Christopher smiled, pocketed his phone and offered his hand to shake. 'Mortimer Farrier?'

'Morton,' Morton corrected.

'Right,' Christopher said, looking at his watch. 'I've not got terribly long, I'm afraid. Meeting in forty minutes with Green Jumper's people.' He rolled his eyes and led the way inside Starbucks, leaving Morton bewildered as to who Green Jumper's people might be.

'Coffee?' Christopher offered, as they neared the serving counter. 'Or are you one of those decaf herbal types?'

'Coffee's fine, thank you,' Morton said, adding, 'Latte, please,' to the server.

'Just normal coffee for me,' Christopher said.

'What name?' the barista asked.

'Mortimer,' Christopher answered, pulling out his phone and tapping out a message, as he shuffled to the end of the counter, leaving Morton to pay the bill. If two expensive coffees was the cost of procuring any information into Alexander Emmett, then it was well worth it.

'Green Jumper?' Morton asked, joining Christopher, as they waited for their drinks to be made.

'Great band, aren't they?' Christopher said.

They were a band of whom Morton had never heard. He mumbled a noncommittal reply, just as the barista called out, 'Mortimer.'

Morton gave him a wooden smile and took his drink with the name *Mortimer* scribed on the side, following Christopher to a table near to the window.

Christopher looked at his watch again and then, with narrowed searching eyes, said, 'What's your connection to my father, then?'

The question side-swiped Morton's tightly constrained, pre-emptive thoughts on how he was going to broach the subject. 'Er...I don't have a *direct* connection to him. He's on the periphery of some research that I'm doing currently.'

Christopher turned his nose up. Obviously, this wasn't the kind of answer that he'd been hoping to hear. 'Right,' he said, looking at his mobile and sounding to Morton as though the meeting were already about to come to an end. 'So, what *do* you know about him, then'—his eyes flicked to Morton's coffee cup—'Mortimer?'

Morton decided to abandon his gently-gently, skirt-around-the-subject approach. 'I believe that he disappeared soon after your mother's death in 1957, probably leaving the country for somewhere in Northern Europe. I think he returned in 1974 under a false identity, where he took a house on Kilburn High Road, so that he had a direct view of the house in which you were living with your grandmother, Sarah Ingram, in 56 Kingsgate Place.'

Christopher's mouth widened and his face furrowed. He placed his mobile down on the table and stared at Morton. 'Who are you?'

'Morton Farrier,' he said, placing great emphasis on his first name. 'I'm a forensic genealogist.'

Christopher's phone began to ring in an ostentatious racket which drew the attention of most of the shop's customers. 'Danny from Green Jumper,' Christopher informed Morton, looking at the screen. He answered with a gruff, 'Danny, I'll call you back.' He leant across the table. 'My father returned in 1974 and lived nearby, did you say?'

Morton nodded, hoping to goodness that his working theory was indeed correct.

'My God. Why didn't he come and see me, then?' Christopher slouched back, winded by the news which Morton was now regretting having told him in such a blunt and cavalier fashion.

'So, you never saw him?' Morton checked, intrigued by this information.

Christopher shook his head. 'Nope. Never. Are you sure about this?'

'Yes,' Morton replied, although he now feared that the evidence, which he had acquired so far, felt a little thin and he hoped not to be pressed too hard on the matter.

'Wow,' Christopher muttered, staring out of the window, his thoughts evidently mulling the implications of that which he had just been told.

'So, you never had contact with him after your mother died?' Morton probed.

'Nope. My gran always told me that it was his fault that my mother killed herself and his guilt made him run away. She would always end her sentences with 'he's probably dead by now', whenever I asked about him, which was what I too had come to believe. I can't believe he was nearby all along, yet he didn't see me. That's even more tragic, wouldn't you say?'

Morton nodded his agreement. He could certainly see that. From Christopher's perspective, it was all the more heart-breaking that his father had lived across the street yet hadn't made contact. But Morton's gut instinct told him that for him to return and take a house so close must have meant that, for whatever reason, Alexander couldn't let his son know of his existence. Was it fanciful to think that it was because of a connection to the secret services?

'Why didn't he come and see me?' Christopher said pitifully.

'I don't know, but he certainly didn't want to be connected to his former existence for some reason,' Morton replied, withholding the possible connection to the intelligence services. 'I believe he returned in 1974 under the name of Maurice Duggan.'

Christopher twitched. 'There's something familiar about that name. Maurice Duggan?'

'Yes, that's right,' Morton confirmed eagerly. 'Do you know him?'

Christopher shrugged. 'The name rings a bell, is all… But I don't know why.' He repeated the name several times, clearly baffled. 'Nope, I don't know him. Perhaps it's just one of those names which sounds familiar but actually isn't.'

'Perhaps,' Morton said, disappointed that there had been no recollection. The meeting with Christopher had so far generated just one point of interest: that Alexander had not made contact with his son, despite the proximity of their houses. Maybe Christopher had learned something of Alexander's early life from his grandparents? He posed the question.

Christopher sat back and raised his eyebrows, gazing up at the ceiling above him. After a few seconds he said, 'Well, my gran said that he was born in Port Said in Egypt but was a British subject. His father worked in something or other to do with colonies. I think Egypt was a British Protectorate or a colony at the time… Erm, he moved over here after his parents died, which must have been… What? Post-war? Early fifties? Mother was just an office girl and they met at a party; got married in 1957. I came along a little while afterwards. One of those six-month pregnancies that used to be all the rage back then. That's the extent of my knowledge, I'm afraid.'

Morton made a note of what Christopher had said, despite its lacking any firm detail and most of its being already known to him. 'Do you have any photographs of your father at all?' Morton asked.

'My gran always maintained that there were no photographs of him in existence, which, if you think about it, is pretty preposterous. More likely, she destroyed them all once he had walked out. There were plenty of Mother, of course. Here.' He leant to one side and pulled out his wallet, opened it up and slid a small photograph from a sleeve behind an impressive raft of credit cards. 'There she is.' Christopher sighed affectionately for the mother he had never known, as he handed over the picture.

Morton took the photograph, relieved to see that the smiling woman in the photo was doubtless the same person wearing the wedding dress, whom he had identified as Ellen Ingram. 'Do you mind if I take a photograph of it?'

'Go ahead.'

As Morton took a picture on his mobile phone, he realised that, by Christopher confirming his research into Ellen Ingram, he had by definition confirmed his research into Alexander Emmett/Maurice Duggan. It would not be inappropriate, therefore, to show Christopher the photograph of his father, taken from the pilot records.

Scrolling through his camera roll, Morton found the photograph and passed his phone over to Christopher. 'Your father.'

Christopher's facial expression seemed to change two or three times in a matter of seconds: surprise morphed into questioning which transformed into shock. 'But... *That's* Maurice Duggan!' he said, rather loudly.

Now Morton was confused. So, he *had* introduced himself to his son, but under his new identity.

Without once taking his eyes from the photograph, Christopher said, 'He...he used to come into the record shop—Our Price—that I used to work in. Huge fan of George Harrison and the Beatles. We actually had a couple of drinks together in the Black Lion pub on Kilburn High Road to talk about music. *He* was my father?'

'Yes, that's him,' Morton confirmed.

Finally, Christopher looked up and met his eyes. 'But why didn't he say so?'

Morton shrugged. 'At this point, I really don't know.'

'Christ. Will you send that photo to me, please? Wow.'

'Of course,' Morton replied, taking back his mobile and using Messenger to forward the image to him.

Christopher sat back and studied Morton. 'I get the impression you're withholding something.'

'No, I'm not,' Morton lied. 'It's an ongoing investigation, so I genuinely don't know why he didn't reveal who he was to you.'

'But you're trying to find out?'

'Yes.'

'Why? Who are you working for?' he said, a sudden bite to his tone.

There was no way that Morton was going to reveal everything about Clarissa Duggan and how she came to have ninety-thousand pounds of Christopher's father's money, but he knew that there was also no way that Christopher was going to be fobbed off at this point. 'Someone related to the real Maurice Duggan. You see, when your father returned in 1974, he took on the persona of a young man, who had already died some years previous at the age of seventeen. My client wants to know who your father really was.'

'Sounds bloody complicated,' he commented.

'It is,' Morton agreed.

Christopher's ostentatious ringtone suddenly shrieked out from the table. 'Danny, again,' he told Morton, before answering the call. 'Hello? Yes, I'm coming.' The call ended. 'Listen, Mortimer. I've got to go. Will you keep me posted?'

'Yes, I will,' Morton promised.

'Right. Goodbye,' Christopher said, emitting a huge sigh, as he bumbled his way through the crowds and out of the door.

As Morton drained his latte, he realised that he had, in essence, met the requirements set out by Clarissa Duggan: he had found the rightful heir to the money. Yet, the puzzle was far from completed in his mind. Would Clarissa want to continue funding his research, now that he had fulfilled his brief? He would spend a little more time on Alexander's early years in Egypt, see what, if any, connection there was to the secret service files and then make a decision about wrapping up the case. The sooner it was concluded, the sooner he could switch his focus to resolving the situation with Vanessa Briggs and his grandfather.

Placing Mortimer's cup in the bin, Morton headed out of Starbucks and down to the tunnel which connected St Pancras with the underground.

A short while later, he was sitting alone in a tube carriage, heading out to Kew. The journey across the capital would take almost as long as it had taken him to reach London from Rye, so, as soon as the tube was over-ground and allowed him full signal on his mobile phone, he decided to call his Aunty Margaret. He took out his notepad and pen, then pulled her name up on his contacts list. His finger hovered over the *call* button and his decision to speak to her was on a knife-edge, capable of going in either direction. Without thinking any further, he pressed the button and placed the phone to his ear.

She picked up after several rings and wheezed, 'Hello?'

'Hi, it's Morton,' he greeted.

155

'Oh, hello, my love. How are you?'

'Good thank you. You?'

'Much the same… Muddling along. How's my little Grace?'

'A delightful monkey,' Morton answered, wishing that she would use the word 'granddaughter' when asking after Grace.

'Still working on the family tree?' she asked with a chuckle.

'That was why I am calling, actually,' he said, grateful to have a direct in-road. 'Spending a bit of time fleshing out the Farriers.'

'Oh, they were a bunch,' she joked. 'Lots of skeletons in those cupboards.'

Morton laughed. If only she knew. Of course, she would *have* to know, he realised with a horrible sinking feeling. And he would have to be the one to tell her. Was that something that he could do over the phone? He heard himself exhaling noisily and quickly said, 'I don't really remember too much about grandad. Did he travel much outside of Kent for work or holidays?'

Margaret went quiet for a moment, as she thought about his question. 'Yes, I suppose so. Though, I wouldn't say more so than anyone else. He took himself off on cruises around the Med. He went to Italy a few times. Greece. The South of France was a favourite destination. Yeah, and with a few trips around the UK, he didn't do too badly for holidays. Better than me!' She laughed lightly.

'What about further afield?' Morton asked, making careful note of the countries that she had just listed. 'Australia? New Zealand?'

'Oh, no. Never that far. Possibly Canada on one of his visits to America, but that was about as far as he went.'

'Do you recall which parts of America he went to?' Morton probed, a burning nervousness churning his stomach.

'Golly, you're being very specific,' she laughed. 'Erm… San Francisco, one year. What's that place with all the gambling?'

Here it was.

But Morton didn't want to put the words into her mouth. 'Las Vegas?' he suggested.

'No. No. Somewhere in that area, though,' she said.

'Atlantic City?' he offered, emptily suggesting somewhere almost three-thousand miles away on the complete opposite side of the country.

'No…' she said, dragging out the word, as though she had given it considerable thought and was already moving on in her mind.

The line went quiet. Should he say it? he wondered, pen poised above the notepad, ready to write down the word.

But he didn't have to say it.

She did.

'Reno!' she declared with gusto.

Morton wrote the word down, trying to swallow his feelings of nausea. He didn't speak. He couldn't. Any lingering doubts, suspicions that a mistake had occurred, were now obliterated. The mounting evidence was overwhelming.

'I've still got some of the postcards he sent somewhere in the dark vortex that's our loft,' she said.

Morton coughed and tried to clear his throat. Tears were welling in his eyes and he was choked. Without saying another word, he ended the call.

Chapter Fourteen

It took Morton several minutes to control his unexpected rush of emotion. During that time, his Aunty Margaret had tried calling him back four times. There was no way that he could speak to her again for the time being. So, he sent her a text message which he hoped was suitably jovial and explanatory: *Sorry, bad signal on the tube! Nice to speak to you. Would you mind hunting down those postcards from your dad? Interested in any / all he sent. Love, Morton xx.*

She replied several minutes later with the semi-cryptic *Into the abyss we go! x,* which pretty well summed up how Morton felt about what was looming on the horizon.

The rest of the tube journey to Kew passed in spiralling imaginings of his grandfather's exploits on his travels. In Morton's warped narrative, Alfred Farrier had travelled America and the Mediterranean, leaving a slew of dead women in his wake.

The wind was whipping the fallen leaves from the gutter, as he strode the ten-minute walk from the station to the National Archives. And as he strode, he chastised himself for allowing his thoughts to run amok; his grandfather had been implicated in a single murder, he told himself. He was hardly a modern-day Jack the Ripper. But then Morton remembered the brutality of the report—*...Ms. Gaddy had died from multiple stab wounds...*—and the sick feeling promptly returned.

He entered the archives and stood impatiently waiting whilst an overweight security guard just inside the main entrance rummaged in his bag. Having passed the check, Morton walked apace towards the cloakrooms. He stowed his jacket and bag in a locker and carried his laptop, notepad and pencil upstairs to another security check, whilst he swiped his reader's ticket to enter the lobby area of the Document Reading Room. He headed over to the translucent orange lockers and opened the door to the one that corresponded to the seat which he had pre-selected on his train journey to London. Inside was the single file that he had ordered. He carefully removed the manila folder, which was about a quarter of an inch thick, placed it on his laptop and carried the two items into the Document Reading Room, a vast open space filled with octagonal desks, at which several dozen researchers pored over a range of historical records.

Morton sat at his usual seat—10B—and set the file down on the desk in front of him, deeply curious to know how Alexander Emmett might figure in the papers contained within it.

The file was fastened together by a treasury tag in the top-left corner and the document reference, *CAB 301/118* was handwritten in black letters across the middle. At the top, written in pencil, were the words *Secret Service Reserves 1957-58*.

Morton carefully opened it to the first page, where he found a short, typed letter, headed *TOP SECRET*:

London, S.W.1
1ˢᵗ October 1958

Dear Compton,
We have now heard from the Bank of England that the gold has been sold. The proceeds, amounting to £55,859.5.2 have been transferred to Glyn, Mills & Co., Whitehall, and credited to the "C" Deposit Account. They will be shewn in the statement at the end of the month.
Yours sincerely

The name of the sender had been redacted by a white sticker. At the bottom, in large typed red letters was stamped: *THIS IS A COPY. THE ORIGINAL IS RETAINED UNDER SECTION 3 (4) OF THE PUBLIC RECORDS ACT.* Had that not been the case, Morton might have been tempted to peel back the sticker to reveal the author's identity. He photographed the letter, not having the foggiest what it pertained to, then turned the page. Another letter, also marked *TOP SECRET*, dated 23ʳᵈ September 1958.

Dear Compton
1. *I am writing to confirm, for the record, the points discussed at our meeting on September 17ᵗʰ.*
2. *It was agreed that the proceeds of our accumulated Deutschmark holding should be added to the "C" account.*
3. *It was also agreed that the proceeds of certain S.I.S. holdings of foreign currency, going back to the war and immediate post-war period, should be regarded as "unofficial reserves" and added to the "C" Deposit Account.*
4. *It was confirmed that the Bank of England holding of gold on behalf of this service was to be regarded as "unofficial reserves" and sold for sterling and the proceeds added to the "C" Deposit Account.*

159

5. *The decisions have all been ratified by "C".*
6. *Arising out of these decisions, the following action has been taken. Glyn, Mills & Coy. have been instructed to transfer to the "C" Deposit Account the sum of £320,284.17.11d.*

Yours sincerely

Again, the signatory's name had been redacted. The whole file, which so far made little sense to Morton, was seemingly arranged in reverse chronology.

He photographed the page, still none the wiser. One thing was clear, though: an awful lot of unofficial money was going into the bank account of someone called C. Wasn't C the chief of MI6? Or was that just in the James Bond movies, Morton wondered, opening up a search page on his mobile. Yes, the internet was in consensus that C did indeed stand for Chief of MI6 in both the James Bond movies and in real life.

Interesting as it might be to wonder at what the unofficial funds might have been used for, it so far revealed no connection whatsoever to Alexander Emmett or the Duggan Case in general.

Morton turned to the next page. More discussion about the sale of the gold and the unofficial reserves. The following page was a letter, signed by C himself, written on the 15th August 1958 advising that Coutts bank was transferring £118,363 to his account.

More letters followed and Morton photographed them all, even though they seemed irrelevant at this moment in time.

On the subsequent page, a copy of the contents of C's deposit account in June 1958 took Morton slightly aback. The balance of this so-called *unofficial reserve* stood at £1,039,655. He couldn't help but Google what the equivalent funds in 2019 might be: £24,088,678, apparently. Was it normal for the head of MI6 to have this astronomical figure in his deposit account which was classified as *unofficial?* What did that even mean? He hoped the documents that followed might enlighten him.

Further through the file, another letter offered some explanation as to the definition of *unofficial reserves*; though this raised more questions in Morton's mind as to the funds' origins.

The present distinction between official and unofficial reserves stems from the sources from which the funds came. The official reserves consist of money voted by

Parliament. The unofficial reserves are not derived from money voted by Parliament but were "subscribed by well-wishers of the service". In addition to the regular budgets of the Secret agencies, provision must be made, all from the Reserves, to finance Special Political Activity (S.P.A.) projects. Our present estimate of the cost of S.P.A. in 1958/59 is £455,000. To some extent this includes proposals which have not yet passed political or financial scrutiny…Only the smallest number of people know of these reserves. They were reported to the Chancellor (Mr Butler) in 1953 and to Mr Macmillan in 1956. So far as we know, their existence is not known to any other Minister.

In other words, Morton pondered, it was a truckload of money, donated by goodness only knows whom, to fund *Special Political Activity* projects abroad, beyond Parliament's remit. But what were those projects? he wondered. They certainly sounded suspicious. A hint towards an answer to that question came a few pages later, in the form of yet another letter.

TOP SECRET AND PERSONAL
FOREIGN OFFICE, S.W.1.
October 25, 1957

Dear Sir Edmund,
Would you please refer to Hoyer Millar's letter of July 18 and mine of August 1, both about current projects involving the secret reserves.
I have now been asked to let you know that Hoyer Millar has approved a further £75,000 for SAWDUST, and a further £50,000 for SCANT.
The exact financial position of the two operations is at present as follows:

(a)   SAWDUST
   1.   £375,000 authorised
   2.   £275,000 spent
   3.   Leaving £100,000 in hand for current operations

(b)   SCANT
   1.   £200,000 authorised
   2.   £150,000 spent
   3.   £50,000 in hand for current operations

Yours sincerely,
R.L. Wade-Gery
(Private Secretary to the Permanent Under-Secretary)

Morton studied the piece of thin paper for a few moments, once he had photographed it. Two secret operations, taking place somewhere overseas, which commenced in September and October 1956, were the main points that Morton took from the letter.

He moved through a further series of exchanges until he came to one that included the name for which he had been searching.

TOP SECRET
FOREIGN OFFICE, S.W.1.
November 10th 1956

Dear Sir Edmund
I write following our meeting this afternoon regarding Operation "SAWDUST". As suggested, I have contacted Alexander Emmett, who attested that the current strategic approach has failed. He therefore will not be drawing on the fund at the present time.
Yours sincerely
R.L. Wade-Gery

Could it be him? Morton wondered. *His* Alexander Emmett? Involved in Special Political Activity abroad, namely Operation Sawdust? He thought for a moment. How could he be certain that he had found the correct person? The answer was the only way he knew how: to turn over every single stone until he found proof either way, hopefully. Perhaps, he thought, the three or four pages left in the file might contain details of what exactly Operation Sawdust had been and what role Alexander Emmett had played in it.

What he found, however, when he turned the page, were more letters concerning the financing of the reserves, from which Operation Sawdust drew, but nothing that revealed the nature of the operation itself. Nor did he find any further mention of Alexander Emmett.

Morton closed the file, pushed it to the back of the desk and opened up his laptop. In Google he typed *Operation Sawdust* and hit enter.

About 5,070 results.

The top results presented by Google were three Woody Woodpecker films. Below them was a Wikipedia entry about Operation Sawdust, which, it stated, was the 47th animated cartoon in the Woody Woodpecker series, released in 1953. Brilliant.

162

Morton sniggered and continued scrolling down the list of results. Nothing in the first ten pages except references to the famous American cartoon. As he abandoned this fruitless search, he wondered if that operation name had been chosen as a further, deliberate obfuscation of its true nature.

There was notoriously little in the National Archives' records about MI5 or MI6, for obvious security reasons, but surely there was some further mention of what Operation Sawdust actually had been and who the Alexander Emmett had been, involved in it. He opened up the search page on their website and typed in 'Operation Sawdust.'

One record. Just one.

Morton clicked to view it and spotted its irrelevance instantly. It referred to a document from 1871, which contained the phrase, *120 bags of sawdust.*

He returned to the main page. A search for MI6 brought up 4,710 results, the majority of which had that number and combination of letters within its document reference but actually nothing whatsoever to do with that particular branch of British Military Intelligence. Part of the problem, too, was that most documents held by the National Archives, and which *were* publicly available, had yet to be indexed. Therefore, Alexander Emmett and Operation Sawdust could actually be contained in a whole raft of open but unindexed files. It was worse than a needle-in-a-haystack situation: he was wasting time searching a giant haystack for a needle which may have zero relevance to the Duggan-Case focus.

Clearing the search box, Morton re-entered CAB 301/118 and then navigated up one level in the reference hierarchy. He was now presented with all documents within the subseries of CAB 301 – ORGANISATION AND FUNDING OF BRITISH INTELLIGENCE: GENERAL. He read down the list of records with interest: reports into the Burgess and Maclean affair; the enquiry into the disappearance of Commander Crabb, Royal Navy frogman; intelligence activities in Commonwealth countries; and funding from the Secret Vote 1940-1948.

There were a few documents listed that he would order. One in particular struck him as possibly containing information on Operation Sawdust: *Miscellaneous correspondence on secret funding 1955-1962.* He clicked through to order it.

Document ordering has closed for the day.

'Damn it,' Morton muttered, slumping back in his chair.

He opened his pad and read through various notes that he had made during the Duggan Case. Other than to establish what exactly Operation Sawdust had been and to determine if the Alexander Emmett involved in it had been the same person, whom he was researching, there was little left to do on the case other than to find out whatever he could about Alexander's early years in Egypt.

Morton located the notes which he had made from Alexander's aviator's certificate. According to the record, Alexander had been born 7th December 1927 in Port Said, Egypt. Crucially, however, he was stated to have been a British subject, which should imply that, despite his birth's occurring in Egypt, it would have been registered in Britain.

Morton picked up the CAB-file from his desk and carried it back out through the glass double-doors to the returns desk, where a member of staff happened to be loading up a trolley with returned boxes, books and folders.

'Excuse me,' Morton said. 'Do you know anything about records for births overseas?'

The young man grinned. 'Nothing whatsoever.'

'Oh, right.'

The man looked at the open space which ran behind the desk and the lockers, then called out, 'Paula! Could you pop over here a second, please?'

Paula, a sprightly lady with Harry-Potter-style glasses, a nose-piercing and short bleached hair, arrived with a spring in her step and a smile on her face. 'Yes!'

'This gentleman wanted...,' he turned to Morton. 'What was it, again?'

'Overseas births,' Morton said. 'Specifically, the birth of a British subject in Egypt in 1927.'

Paula smiled. 'The *easiest* way to locate foreign births is on any of the computers in the building, using Findmypast to access the overseas births collection. That'll give a reference code that you can use to order with the GRO; like you would any other British birth certificate.'

'Oh, okay,' Morton said. 'Thank you.' That was easy. He returned to his desk, opting to use his own subscription to Findmypast, and pulled up *British Armed Forces and Overseas Births and Baptisms*. He typed Alexander's name, year and country of birth and was more than half-surprised, given all of the deception that had occurred in the man's life, to find that a record of his birth actually existed.

Name: Emmett, Alexander
Station: Port Said
Vol: 20
Page: 318
Year: 1927

Morton scribbled down the reference, then opened a web-browser tab, logged onto the General Register Office website and, just as simply as Paula had attested, ordered Alexander's birth certificate.

With the inability to order further documents at the National Archives, and rush-hour fast approaching, it was time for Morton to pack up and leave. He shut his laptop lid, gathered up his things and left the Document Reading Room. He passed through the exit security check and made his way back downstairs to the cloakroom. Although he hadn't found out as much as he would have liked to have done, the day's research had certainly moved the Duggan Case forward.

Morton left the archives and headed home.

'Shhh!' Juliette hissed the moment Morton stepped through the front door. He took the pre-emptive rebuke as a warning that Grace was asleep. He was disappointed to have missed her, but the commute across London to St Pancras had been a veritable nightmare, taking much longer than he had anticipated.

'Is she asleep?' Morton whispered, carefully shutting the door behind him.

'Yes,' Juliette replied in a hushed voice.

'Daddy!?' came a yell from upstairs.

'*Was*,' Juliette corrected. 'Over to you.'

Morton removed his shoes and headed up to Grace's bedroom. 'You're supposed to be asleep, young lady,' he said quietly, approaching her cot-bed.

Grace was standing up, her hands on the rail with a wide grin on her face. 'Daddy!' she repeated, holding out her arms.

Morton picked her out and squeezed her to him. 'What a lovely cuddle. Have you been a good girl for Mummy, today?'

'Yes,' she replied. 'Daddy tree work.'

He wasn't exactly sure what that meant. 'Yes, Daddy's been doing family tree work.'

'Oh,' Grace said. 'Painting?'

'No, not painting this time,' he answered with a smile.

'Oh.'

'Right, Grace needs to go to sleep now. Give Daddy a kiss.'

Grace obliged, then allowed him to lower her back into her cot-bed.

'Goodnight, Grace.'

'Night, Daddy.'

Morton pulled her door shut, then headed downstairs to the kitchen. 'Hello,' he said, kissing Juliette.

'Good day?' she asked.

'Tiring,' he replied, before bringing her up to speed with his work on the Duggan Case.

'Spies,' Juliette commented. 'How exciting.'

'Maybe. Maybe not. It's a shame I ran out of time at the National Archives, though. It means another trip up there to try to find out more about Operation Sawdust and what Alexander Emmett had to do with it; if anything.' In his pocket, his mobile phone vibrated. He ignored it, but then it vibrated again and again. He took his phone out and looked at the screen: WhatsApp messages from Aunty Margaret with photo attachments.

Juliette was talking, but he didn't hear what she was saying, as he unlocked his phone to view the images.

The fronts and backs of six postcards, some slightly out-of-focus but clear enough to discern: Florence, Italy; Santorini, Greece; Cannes, France; Cornwall, England.

Then the final images: Reno, America.

Morton clicked to view the reverse of the postcard, splaying his fingers to see the date.

He passed the phone to Juliette and interrupted her. 'Look. A postcard my grandad sent from Reno.'

'Twenty-first of December 1980,' she read, turning to face Morton. 'And when was Candee-Lee murdered?'

'The day before,' Morton replied, feeling suddenly very sick.

Chapter Fifteen

18th June 1956, Port Said, Egypt

The tide is turning quickly...

No, that made it sound too regular and too routine, Alexander thought, striking a line through the sentence. What was happening here was much more significant than that opening line to his article would imply.

~~*The tide is turning quickly*~~. *The political volcano is about to erupt.*

He wrote this on his notepad and considered it a moment longer. Metaphors involving volcanos and politics were old and hackneyed. Dull. Dull. Dull. It bore no resemblance to what he was seeing right here, right now in Port Said.

~~*The tide is turning quickly*~~. ~~*The political volcano is about to erupt.*~~

He needed to keep thinking.

It was hot and Alexander, wearing a short-sleeved shirt and light pair of trousers, was leaning on the balcony of a tiny room which he had been renting for the past few days in Hotel Dakhla. In the street below him, thousands of people—no, thousands of *men*, he realised ominously—were gathering, pouring in from every side-street. The high-spirited shouts and calls, rising around Alexander, held the buzz of excitement and promise, as more and more buildings spilled their occupants out onto the roads.

The room was dingy, without any kind of cooling system, and stood in the shadow of a giant oil refinery. But what this ring-side view could do for his journalism career was unparalleled. Change was happening in Egypt right now.

Alexander studied the crowd and jotted down some notes on his pad. The men were predominantly young—below forty years of age—and were either wearing shirts and trousers or the traditional *galabeya*, full-length robes.

There was a momentary audible ripple from the crowd, akin to a shared intake of breath, and then cheering. The loudest cheering,

Alexander believed, that he had ever heard. He craned his head over the balcony and could see, heading in his direction about a hundred yards along the street, an open-topped car led by a motorcycle through the crowds.

Car—Buick? he scribbled quickly. *Thousands of <u>men.</u> Young. Buzzing atmosphere. All cheering. No booing. Implications?*

The crowds, who had gathered directly below his balcony, were now being divided by the approaching motorcycle, like some biblical parting of the waves.

Alexander could now clearly see the identity of the man standing in the back of the car, waving at the fervent masses: *Colonel Gamal Abdel Nasser.*

The cheering achieved a deafening crescendo, as Nasser's car passed by the hotel. Nasser himself glanced up at the balcony and, for the briefest of seconds, caught Alexander's inquisitive stare, perhaps wondering why he was not joining in with the frantic waving and cheering all around.

As the car progressed further down the street towards the canal zone, the parted crowds folded back together, running behind the Buick.

Grabbing his notepad and pencil, Alexander dashed through his hotel room, down the stairs and onto the street, joining the rear of the animated horde. As they continued onwards, Alexander correctly guessed at Nasser's destination: Navy House, overlooking the harbour. The Union flag, until last Tuesday designating the grand waterfront building as the British headquarters in the city, was now gone.

The procession slowed and Nasser's car once again performed its parting-of-the-seas miracle, this time being granted admittance through a thick line of white-uniformed Egyptian soldiers.

Alexander began to feel the crushing weight of the dozens of men, who had joined the crowd behind him, as he struggled to stretch up on tiptoe to see what was happening in front of Navy House. Nasser had climbed down from the Buick and was moving in the direction of the barren flagpole.

Although he could not see what was going on, Alexander knew that *something* was afoot from the way in which the crowds' cheering had dramatically escalated. Then he saw it: a flag was being hoisted up the pole.

The roar of commendation and approval reached a fever pitch when the flag attained the top, unfurling to reveal the red, white and black horizontal stripes of the 1952 Egyptian revolutionary flag.

A metallic crackle drew Alexander's gaze to a loudspeaker affixed to Navy House. Then came Nasser's voice and the crowd settled to a near silence.

'This is an immemorial moment of a lifetime,' he announced, to more cheers. 'We have dreamed of this moment which had been denied to our fathers, grandfathers and our brothers, who have fought for years to achieve this moment and to see the Egyptian flag flying over our land. We pray to God that no foreign flag ever flies in our skies again. May God guide you.'

The men went wild and, for the first time, Alexander heard shouts of dissent. Not dissent towards Nasser, though, but towards the British and French. To his right came a yell about evicting British imperialists from Egypt.

Alexander suddenly felt a shudder of vulnerability. Were the sneering men pressed close to him noticing him for the first time? Or was he just being paranoid? He lowered his head, just as a crack of gunfire rang out. He flinched, as another, then another shot was fired into the air. A gun salute, he realised, as his heart raced.

It was time to leave. He turned to try to push his way through the crowds, the end of which he could now not see, then paused a moment. He thought that he had heard his name being called. He scanned around him, trying to tune out the gunfire and the city's clamorous approving cheers. He couldn't hear his name being called again, but that which he could hear—and now see—were several aircraft, flying in at a low altitude across the sea towards them.

'Alexander!'

There it was afresh. Somebody *was* indeed calling his name. It sounded as though it had emanated from the direction of the line of soldiers.

He turned, carefully eyeing the crowd for as far as he could see. Then, through the heaving heads and shoulders in front of him, he spotted a tuft of blonde hair belonging to someone who appeared to be in difficulty with a growing number of men surrounding him. He was fairly certain that it was Alfie Archer, who was struggling to get his attention.

Using his right shoulder as a barge, Alexander shoved himself forwards, navigating a route towards Alfie, just as nine aircraft flew

169

seemingly inches above the canal-side buildings, receiving a rapturous applause from the gathered men.

Alexander felt as though he were wading through treacle in trying to reach his colleague. As he drew closer, he could see that Alfie had been encircled by a group of men, taunting and shouting in Arabic. One of them jabbed him in the chest, sending him backwards onto another man, who then shoved him forwards.

Alexander pushed closer. Although he couldn't understand the words that the men were using, he understood the tone well enough.

'British scum,' one of them spat, squaring up to Alfie. Well, the intention and meaning encapsulated in that was perfectly clear.

'He's not British,' Alexander said, taking on some obscure, vaguely American accent. 'He's American.'

The Americans had so far kept a low profile in the escalating tensions in the Middle East and this information seemed sufficient to cause the men to pause and stare at each other, as if they were no longer sure how to proceed. Americans, generally, were well-regarded here.

Under the roar of another flypast overhead, Alexander reached in and grabbed Alfie by the arm, dragging him through the crowds. He turned to see that the men, who had been taunting Alfie, having abandoned their confrontation, were now pushing instead to get a closer view of Nasser.

'Thanks,' Alfie said breathlessly, as they made it to a quiet side-street. They stood under the cool shelter of a first-floor balcony. Alfie whispered, 'I don't like this anti-British feeling in the air with Nasser's visit. Can we lie low at one of your family members' houses…or maybe a friend's place? You must have plenty of contacts here.'

'I do,' Alexander answered in a similar hushed tone, 'but I don't think the situation's going to improve when Nasser buggers off back to Cairo. If anything, it's going to get worse. I think we need to return to Beirut as soon as possible. Besides, it's not safe to write from here about what we've seen today.'

'True enough,' Alfie agreed. 'I mean, did you…' he stopped himself short when two Egyptian men walked past them, then continued. 'Did you see the planes they used in the flyover?'

Alexander nodded.

'Russian MiGs, for God's sake,' Alfie seethed. 'You need to get us out of this place. I'll be outside your hotel entrance in an hour. Be ready.' He walked quickly, keeping his head down, back to the main street.

Alexander stood, watching him leave and wondering how Alfie knew at which hotel he was staying. Despite having undertaken work for British intelligence for the last three months, they still hadn't fully accepted him into their ranks. The pattern had been identical each time: the *Observer* would send him out around the Middle East, ostensibly undertaking research in order to write some innocuous article for the newspaper, but soon after each story had been commissioned, an advert would appear in the paper's classifieds—where Mrs Strickland would be buying or selling something or seeking a new lodger—and he would telephone the number and receive instructions about what additional task he should undertake.

In Iraq, he had been required to fraternise with a female cipher clerk from the American Embassy, to try to establish the US position in the event of the UK-managed company, Iraq Petroleum's being nationalised. In Syria, Alexander's task had been to identify pro-Western members of the government, who could be used as scapegoats and blamed if a clandestine plan for Iraq to annex Syria were to fail. In Yemen, having identified a tractable administrator in their security services, he had bribed him for blueprints of the second residence of the country's leader, Imam Ahmad, which Alexander had assumed was with a view to regime change. What was interesting to him now, though, was that, despite having been tasked with writing a story about the people's view of the upcoming presidential referendum, he had yet to be called upon by Mrs Strickland for any supplementary services.

Alexander walked back to his hotel purposefully, all the while thinking about how odd the past two months in the Middle East had been. Was this how it was, working for MI6? Did spies not refer to themselves or each other in that explicit way?

In his hot hotel room, Alexander packed quickly and then sat on the bed, making notes about what had happened today. At 1.58pm, he looked over the balcony at the hotel entrance: Alfie wasn't there, yet. He looked up and down the street, but there was no sign of him. So, he went back inside, stowed his notepad in the side pocket of his suitcase, and then returned to the balcony, thinking that he would wait there until Alfie arrived. He glanced down to the entrance to find that he was already there, looking up at him with a smile. Not only did he know in which hotel Alexander was staying but he also knew in which room, apparently.

171

Alexander waved, picked up his suitcase and headed out through the hotel.

'Over to you,' Alfie said, when Alexander had reached him. 'Get us out of this hell-hole.'

'Right,' Alexander said, looking up and down the street. 'I rather thought we'd head straight for the centre and get a bus to the border.'

'Too risky,' Alfie retorted. 'On the way here, I was asked if I was English by this pair of thugs. Said I was Australian, of all things, which seemed to satisfy them. Take us the back ways—you know, the rat-runs and back alleys that nobody uses—and we'll pay some local man with a decent Mustang to get us over to Israel.'

'Okay, let's go,' Alexander said, leading the way determinedly down the thin passageway which ran beside the hotel.

'There you go,' Alfie said with an Australian accent, slapping Alexander between the shoulder blades. 'That's what I like to hear.'

The passage wound its way around the back of the hotel, to what appeared to be a courtyard servicing the rear entrances to several large buildings, including those of the oil refinery. Thankfully, the street was deserted.

'This is more like it,' Alfie commented, keeping up the accent, as he followed behind Alexander to where the road terminated at a narrow perpendicular path.

Alexander paused at the junction, looking in both directions.

'Lost?' Alfie asked.

'No,' Alexander answered. 'Just deciding which way's best.' After deliberating a moment more, he chose to go right and they continued in that direction for some time, passing behind a long ochre apartment block and a rundown car garage.

'How did you know where to find me?' Alexander asked pointedly, in the hope that Alfie might finally open up about his involvement in British intelligence.

Alfie smiled. 'Well, as Rudyard Kipling once said, "If you truly wish to find someone you have known and who travels, there are two points on the globe but to sit and wait and sooner or later your man will come there: the docks of London and Port Said."'

Another cryptic answer which failed to answer the question. Alexander repaid Alfie's smile with a look which he hoped expressed the uncertainty that he felt in his role out here.

They took another turning which ran behind some squat white houses, and then they reached a main road, busy with men buoyed from the recent display down at the canal zone.

Alfie reached out and grabbed Alexander's arm. 'But…we're back where we started,' he said, pointing down the street. 'That's the oil refinery beside the Hotel Dakhla.'

'Oh, damn. We should have turned left back at that junction,' Alexander admitted. 'Bugger. Sorry.'

'Look,' he said, pointing to the canal zone at the end of the road, where Nasser had raised the Egyptian flag. 'The party's over and people are starting back in our direction. We need to get out of here, pronto. Let's just put on our best Australian accents and get a bus out of the city as quickly as we can.' Marching in a near-run, Alfie headed a few paces ahead of Alexander along the main road towards the bus station.

Alexander hoped that his carelessness wouldn't be relayed to whomever Alfie Archer reported. He was being entrusted with crucial British intelligence, which he detected was about to intensify. With the unsettled times ahead, that intelligence would be gold-dust.

Five days later, Alexander headed down to St George's Hotel, where he took a seat on the terrace, watching the red sun arcing down towards the horizon, and sipped his fourth pink gin, the taste for which he had first acquired at the meeting with GK at White's Gentlemen's Club. He had just finished reading the *Observer* from cover to cover, scanning for any references to Mrs Strickland, or any other names which might jump out at him, but there was nothing.

To his side a figure was approaching, and Alexander turned to see that it was a thin-faced man with a scraggy moustache and unkempt thinning hair. Their eyes met, but neither of them spoke, until the man had slid into the chair opposite him. 'I have read your stories in the *Observer*, Mr Emmett. Very interesting,' he murmured in a heavy Baltic accent.

'That's very kind of you to say so,' Alexander replied.

'I think you have good insight into the region's troubles.'

Alexander eyed him, waiting for the words that he knew were coming.

'Perhaps we could meet sometime to discuss your feelings on a common market of the Arab countries?'

'Yes,' Alexander replied.

'Thank you for your time,' the man said, rising from the table. He shook Alexander's hand. 'Goodbye.'

Alexander nodded, watching as the man turned to leave. He opened his hand and looked at the fragment of paper, upon which was written *SU2FG*.

'Oh, by the way,' the man said with a sniff, 'the referendum result will be announced shortly: Nasser is the new president of Egypt.'

Alexander sat back and sank the last of his pink gin, just as the muezzin's call to prayer wafted out over the city from the mosque's loudspeakers. He emitted a long sigh, which expressed a mere fraction of the complexities of his upcoming role in Middle Eastern politics. He looked again at the snippet of paper to confirm that he had memorized it correctly, then rolled it into a tiny ball and jettisoned it over the wall into the sea.

With a simple but subtle hand gesture, Ellen's Watcher colleague, Paul Reynolds, handed the surveillance of Nikita Sokolov over to her. Paul would now head back to Leconfield House and log a report on the progress of his observations this morning. The trailing of Sokolov and piecing together of his associates was now A4's main priority. Something, which was as yet unknown to MI5, had given rise to increased activity in Sokolov's movements in the past two months, coinciding with a quantity of high-grade secret intelligence being leaked to the Soviets. Whatever was going on today, Sokolov was going to great lengths to evade surveillance by dry-cleaning himself of pursuers or *proverka*, as it was termed in his own KGB jargon.

But today, A4 had managed to maintain a constant watch from his flat in Bayswater, right across to the east of London, to where he was now, striding through St James's Park.

Through a gap in the cluster of people, which Ellen tried to maintain between them, she caught a glimpse of Sokolov's long black overcoat. Fifty feet or so behind Ellen, was another female Watcher, ready to take over when Ellen felt that she had been pursuing him for too long, or, in the worst-case scenario, if Sokolov actually clocked her presence.

MI5 had no idea of Sokolov's plans, but something was imminently afoot, of that Ellen was certain. You didn't spend your entire morning zigzagging across London for an innocuous lunch with a friend, returning a library book, or to pay your electricity bill. Could he be leading them, at last, to the person responsible for getting whatever intelligence, which he had somehow obtained, out to the Soviets? MI5 were very much under the impression that Sokolov knew that he had been under twenty-four-hour surveillance and was now only acting as an intermediary.

Sokolov suddenly looked over both shoulders, forcing Ellen to side-step to the left so that the two women in matching brown suits, walking a few feet in front of her, obstructed his view; although it may have been too late. When she shifted her weight over to one side, so that she could see past one of the women, she noticed that he had stepped off the main path and was walking diagonally across the grass. He stopped and placed one hand on his hip. The other hand, acting as a sunshield, he held just above his eyes, as he started to shuffle a full circle.

He was about to get a full view of everyone who had previously been walking behind him.

Ellen increased her pace, quickly drawing alongside the two women. She beamed widely and turned to them. 'What a miserable old day,' she laughed.

The one farthest away simply looked at her, bewildered, whilst the closest to her smiled politely, and replied, 'Isn't it.'

'Typical British summer,' Ellen laughed, continuing to walk with the two women, as she entered into Sokolov's line of vision.

'I just wish it would make up its mind, one way or the other,' the woman next to Ellen said.

'Off anywhere nice?' Ellen asked, hoping to keep her place beside them until she would have passed completely out of Sokolov's sight.

'Back to work,' the other woman answered with a frown. 'Why do you ask?'

Ellen laughed. 'Oh, just being friendly.'

'Well, if you don't mind, we were right in the middle of a private conversation,' the woman said.

'Terribly sorry,' Ellen replied, making no effort to change her speed or direction of travel. Just a few more yards and she would be behind a cluster of cherry laurels.

'Look,' the less friendly of the women snapped. 'Push off, now, will you?'

'Cheerio,' Ellen said cheerfully, as she hastily cut behind them and cowered in the shadows of the shrubbery. She took a breath, then began to insert herself into the bushes, gradually and slowly parting the branches until a small window had formed overlooking the open

175

stretch of grass on the other side. It took a moment for her to locate Sokolov. He was sitting on a bench, with his legs crossed at the ankles, whilst he spoke to the person sitting beside him: Flora Sterling.

Ellen was delighted to have proof that something serious was going on with Flora Sterling and Nikita Sokolov and simultaneously frustrated that the pair of them were sitting on a bench with nobody and nothing around them but a wide expanse of grass and Buckingham Palace framed in the background at a distance.

She felt completely helpless and had a cold flash-forward to the debrief with Mr Skardon, where she would be unable to tell him anything other than that the pair of them had met on a bench in St James's Park. She could hear him now, 'That's proof of nothing, Miss Ingram. Any names revealed as to how state secrets are being obtained and passed to the Soviets? No? Any agents identified? No?'

Ellen removed herself from the bushes and looked around her. She spotted a young boy of perhaps eight or nine years of age, kicking a balled newspaper along the path.

'Hey, you,' she called to him. 'Want to earn some money?'

He nodded.

'I'll give you one pound if you kick that ball of yours over to the bench on the other side of this bush, where a man in a black coat is sitting with a pretty young woman. I need you to very carefully listen to what they're saying whilst you kick the ball in front of them, then put it in the bin beside them, then come back to me. Don't rush, but don't hang around, either. Make it look like you're just dilly-dallying and not really listening to them at all.'

The boy stared at her, saying nothing and looking puzzled.

'You mustn't tell them anything. In fact, don't even speak to them.' She repeated the instructions and asked if he understood.

He nodded and proceeded to kick the ball of newspaper around the bushes.

Ellen trod back inside the greenery and parted the branches for a view of the boy doing exactly as she had asked. In the performance, which she couldn't have scripted any better, the boy lingered a few feet in front of the bench, kicking his ball and paying no heed to Nikita Sokolov and Flora Sterling. In that moment Ellen wondered if perhaps he really was paying no attention to them and that she had expected far too much of a child.

She continued to watch the spectacle through her small viewing gallery. The boy kicked the ball one last time, then scooped it up and, taking his time, placed it in the bin beside the bench, just as Sokolov stood up and began to stride away from the meeting.

Ellen faced a dilemma. The Watcher, who had been following Ellen, would have, upon seeing her seemingly abandoning her surveillance, consequently ended her own, leaving nobody to continue trailing Sokolov. This meeting with Flora Sterling might have been the entire reason for his spending the morning dry-cleaning himself, but it was also possible that he was going on to an even more significant meeting. But if she left in pursuit of Sokolov, then she would never know what the boy might have heard.

He arrived back, panting slightly. 'Done it. They just talked about cars. That's it. Can I have my money, now?'

Ellen's heart sank, as she realised that she had made the wrong call. Sokolov was now out of sight and the boy had nothing to say. She crouched down in front of him. 'Okay. Think *really* carefully about what you heard. Try and tell me *exactly* what the man and the woman said to each other, even if it doesn't make any sense to you. Okay? So, who did you hear speaking *first*?'

The boy thought for a moment. 'The woman. She said something about a car.' He shrugged.

'Pretend you're her,' Ellen directed. 'Say what she said exactly.'

The boy, rendering his best theatrical impersonation of a posh lady, said, 'I haven't been able to get much out of the old Austin. He's very'—the boy dropped his impression—'she used some word what I ain't heard before'—then returning to her voice—'he's very something or other.'

'Austin: is that the car you referred to?'

The boy nodded.

'I see. And what did the man say back to her?' Ellen pushed.

'He was quite miserable and had a funny-sounding voice, like he's foreign or something.'

'Pretend you're him. What did he say?'

The boy's chin sank into his chest and he scowled, as he pushed his voice as low as he could manage, 'We must pass this at once to'—he looked up in thought, then continued—'Jericho.'

'Jericho?' Ellen said, wanting him to confirm this significant piece of information.

The boy nodded.

'Right, then what was said?' she pressed.

177

The boy thought more and replied in his own voice, 'One of them said something about sawdust.'

'Sawdust?' Ellen queried.

'I think so. Then the man said, goodbye.'

'Is there anything else you can remember?' Ellen asked.

The boy shook his head and held out his hand. Ellen placed the promised one-pound note in his outstretched palm and thanked him. Her parting words to him were meant sincerely: 'You should be on the stage.'

As she hurried to the closest tube station, she thought over that which she had learned. Flora Sterling was gleaning secrets from her affair with Harold Austin and then passing them to someone by the name of Jericho. Mr Skardon finally had the proof that he needed. But what did 'sawdust' mean? Had the boy heard correctly?

Chapter Sixteen

24th July 1956, London

Flora Sterling was lying on her back, wearing her crimson nightie. Her head was hanging over the end of the bed, as she puffed small halos of smoke into the air above her.

Harold Austin entered her vision upside down in his white vest and pants. His unattractively squat figure and overhanging belly was even more frightful from this unflattering angle. He bent down and kissed her on the lips.

'I've a meeting with the PM this afternoon, then another one after that with my department, which is likely to go into the small hours,' he said.

Flora feigned disappointment. 'The Middle East Crisis, *again*?' she cried. 'When's it going to be over?'

'Hmm,' Harold replied. 'There's an interesting question. Let's just say things are afoot and leave it there.'

Flora had learned quickly not to ask too many political questions. In fact, the more she had feigned ignorance on a subject, the more detailed the information had been that she had been able to procure from him in his condescending explanations. Little snippets of information about the British government's intentions in the Middle East had been inadvertently exposed one evening over expensive cocktails, when she had professed great surprise in learning that Egypt was a real country and not a lost, ancient civilization like the Aztecs. Harold had then spent much of the evening drawing maps on napkins and using the old days of the Empire as justification for the continued British presence in the region.

But those titbits of information had not been sufficient for her handlers; they wanted firm, concrete plans for the area, which could be passed on to their agents in the Middle East. And that's exactly what she was getting, slowly but surely.

Harold removed the cigarette from Flora's lips with an admonishing glare. 'Filthy habit, you bad girl,' he said, then promptly took his own long drag, before placing it back between her lips. 'I'm going to bathe, if you'd care to join me?'

'In a while,' Flora replied with a smile.

Harold grinned and strolled from his bedroom down the corridor to the bathroom.

Flora closed her eyes, continuing to smoke, as she listened carefully for the sounds emanating from the bathroom. Harold was humming, as he filled the bath with water. She pictured him, standing in front of the cabinet and admiring his own reflection, and wondered how *he*, an insipid little man with no personality, had come to have one of the most important jobs in the country at one of the most important times in history. He, romping around with a beautiful young woman half his age and who accepted his depravities in the boudoir.

Hearing the minor groan of pleasure, which Harold usually gave, as he sank down into the bathtub, Flora stood up, stubbed out her cigarette and padded towards the door. She listened carefully and, sure enough, heard that he was bathing.

Hurrying over to her vanity case, she tipped her makeup onto the bedspread, then ran the nail of her forefinger down the side of the base until she found the leather flap, which she lifted, revealing the small cavity below, housing a silver Minox sub-miniature camera. She prized the camera free from the hollow, then returned to the door with it in her hand, where she paused to listen again. Harold could just be heard, singing flatly in the bathroom. She stole from the bedroom and into the lounge, where his locked briefcase was perched on the edge of the coffee table. Placing the camera down, she rushed over to his suit jacket and fumbled for his wallet in the inside pocket. She pulled it out and opened it wide. Tucked at the back of the wallet, behind a secure flap, Flora removed a cardboard-framed photograph of Harold's wife. Tipping the picture over to the side with the slit in it, she banged it onto her hand until a small brass key plopped out into her palm.

She quickly placed the key into the twin locks, then popped open the briefcase. Before she did anything else, she replaced the key in the photograph frame and returned the wallet to Harold's suit pocket. In the open case was a file, containing several documents marked with *SUEZ* on the front.

Next, she removed the stack of documents from the case and quickly thumbed through them. There were far too many to photograph and, besides which, the camera film could only take fifty frames. She needed to prioritise.

'Flora, darling!' Harold called from the bathroom. 'Harold needs a back rub.'

'Oh, shut up, for God's sake,' Flora said to herself, as she took the papers out one at a time, making sure that they remained in the correct original order, until she reached the first one marked TOP SECRET. She ran her eyes down the sheet. It concerned two secret operations: Operation Scant, a black propaganda radio station based in Cyprus; and Operation Sawdust, an examination of the possibilities of regime change in Egypt. This was exactly what Sokolov had requested of her.

She took a photograph, wound on the film, then repeated with the document below it.

'Oh, Flora, darling. Where *are* you?' Harold sang. 'Don't make me come and find you!'

Flora snapped another two documents.

'You're hiding, aren't you?' Harold declared, evidently settling on the idea that she was indeed enticing him into some seedy game of naked, wet hide and seek.

She took one more picture, then shouted, 'Just coming, darling!'

'Oh, okay...' he responded, sounding dejected that his idea of what might be happening actually wasn't.

'Come on,' Flora told herself, hurrying to take more photographs.

'Flora Sterling!' Harold yelled impatiently.

She knew that, if she took any more time, he would come looking for her. Taking one last photograph, she returned the paperwork precisely as it had been, closed the briefcase and ran across the flat to the bedroom, where she secreted the camera back in the base of the vanity case and haphazardly threw the make-up in above it.

She placed the vanity case back on the bed and turned to see Harold standing in the doorway, naked and dripping bathwater. His face revealed nothing. How long had he been there? Had he seen her concealing the camera? She quickly applied some lipstick, as if for him, and made her best attempt at a coy, seductive smile. 'You found me.'

He grinned. 'I did indeed. It's bath time.'

She did her best impersonation of a woman, delighted to find herself confronted with a nude, squat, overweight, paunchy man, with beads of water running from the thick hair of his front and back. For the next hour or so, she would endure this revolting creature. Then, when he went off for his important meeting with the prime minister, she would take the film cartridge to the dead drop.

Mrs Strickland had still not requested his services, a fact that was making Alexander increasingly anxious. The more he thought about it,

181

the more he blamed the lack of contact on his dismal performance in getting Alfie Archer and him out of Port Said.

It was dusk and he was enjoying his fifth pink gin of the evening, sitting on the terrace at the rear of St George's Hotel, not taking his eyes from a slender young woman with long black hair and wearing a turquoise dress. He was watching and waiting, using his own initiative to sniff out a story for the *Observer* on the sudden collapse this morning of British and American funding for the construction of the Aswan Dam on the River Nile in Egypt. All day long it had been the currency of conversation on the journalism circuits. Every bar, hotel and meeting point was reverberating with the news. Seventy million US dollars of funding withdrawn overnight with little explanation. The general consensus, among those with whom Alexander had spoken, was that the money had been removed owing to President Nasser's growing alliance with the Soviets. But what Alexander had yet to find out from his investigations was what the Egyptian government intended to do about it.

Nadia Ibrahim—the woman in the turquoise dress—was standing with two acquaintances beside the stone palisade wall, laughing at something that one of the two had said. She glanced over, connected with his eyes, and did a double take. Was that recognition? he wondered, maintaining eye contact with her. He smiled, but she looked away and turned her back on him. Evidently, the suggestion by an American journalist that she might be a compliant informer had been incorrect and his hopes of procuring information from her were not looking likely. She was the eldest daughter of one of Nasser's closest advisors, a man who was rumoured to be dissatisfied with the country's rapid shift towards hard nationalism.

He watched her closely, finding her very attractive.

Her two friends left her side and entered the hotel. Nadia turned her head in his direction and stared at him impassively. Then, she marched towards him, the collection of silver bangles on her left arm jangling, as she walked.

'Can I help you?' she asked.

Alexander was slightly taken aback at the directness of her question and her apparent frostiness. 'Can I get you a drink?' he asked.

She smiled, but there was something disingenuous about it. 'I say yes, and then you schmooze me, flatter me, and you try subtly to steer the conversation towards politics and what happened today with the Aswan Dam. And then you feign great surprise when I tell you that my father is in Nasser's government, and you buy me more drinks and flatter me more still, until you eventually ask me what it is exactly that the Egyptian government plans to do in response to this news. Then a story will be published in the *Observer* from *our man on the ground, Alexander Emmett*. Is that about right?'

Alexander nodded.

'Then, let's skip to the end. I'll tell you what I know, which is this: Nasser is planning something big, but what it is, I don't know. My father doesn't even know what it is.'

'Would you tell me, if you did know?' Alexander asked.

Nadia shrugged. 'Goodbye, *man on the ground*.' She turned and walked back gracefully to her friends, who had returned from inside the hotel.

'The flattery would have been quite genuine, by the way,' he called after her.

She made no response and continued away.

Alexander finished his gin and stared out to sea, wondering what big thing it could be that President Nasser might be planning.

Three days later, an advert appeared in the *Observer*. Mrs Strickland was requesting holiday lodgings in Beirut. Alexander phoned the number and was told, in the briefest of terms, to be at Chez Temporel—one of Beirut's most fashionable and expensive restaurants—at seven o'clock this evening.

He looked at his watch, as he took two steps up into the white, water-front restaurant: two minutes to seven. He had no idea what he was doing here, nor whom he was meeting; so, it was with a somewhat blank expression that he approached the podium of the smiling maître d', a middle-aged Arabian man with a thick black beard.

'Hello. Welcome,' he greeted. 'Do you have a reservation, sir?'

'Yes,' Alexander answered. 'The only bother is that a friend of mine had someone at their work book the table... So, I'm not quite sure under which name you'll find me.' He laughed, edged around to the podium, and said, 'May I?' He looked down at the reservation sheet, expecting to see the name of Strickland. 'That's the one,' Alexander said, pointing to the surprising name of GK Young.

'Ah,' the maître d' said, seemingly also surprised. 'Come with me.'

The restaurant, Alexander noted, as he was being led through the sea of tables, was occupied by formally dressed men and women, and

183

he was glad to be wearing his best shirt, a plain red tie and a pair of navy trousers.

GK, wearing a smart black suit, was sitting alone at a table for two beside one of the large, arched windows which offered an enchanting view across the azure waters of the Mediterranean. Once again, whether by accident or by design, the table was well out of the earshot of the nearest diners.

GK stood up when he spotted Alexander heading to his table. 'Good to see you, old chap,' he greeted, giving Alexander's hand a rigorous shake. 'Take a seat.'

'Good to see you, too,' Alexander responded.

'Well, how's it been?' GK asked, as they sat down.

'Interesting,' Alexander answered.

'*Interesting?*' GK parroted, drumming the fingers of his left hand on the table. 'I've had *interesting* stays in Bognor Regis, not in the Middle East. You're living in the cross-fertilization point of East and West, a crossroads of cultures, the epicentre of Middle Eastern politics, and all at a pivotal moment in history and your choice of adjective to describe it is *interesting.*'

Alexander offered an austere smile, deciding to confront the situation head-on. 'And yet, GK, here I am currently writing an article on Lebanese cuisine...'

'Well,' GK interjected, 'You won't find much better food than in here. Steak au poivre vert and Syrian truffle salad. Nothing better. You must somehow get *that* into your article.'

'Hmm,' Alexander said, elbows on the table and fingers interlaced, staring at GK. 'Well, that's all well and good on a surface level, isn't it? A mediocre newspaper journalist producing run-of-the-mill drivel on trite subjects with a vaguely Middle Eastern theme for a British readership.'

GK shrugged, feigning ignorance of a greater implication.

'What exactly, though, is below the surface? What am I? Mrs Strickland's errand boy?'

GK emitted a squashed laugh. 'What is it that you think you're doing?'

Alexander took a quick look around the restaurant, then lowered his voice: 'Below the surface of producing run-of-the-mill drivel for the *Observer*, I've been tasked with gathering low-grade intelligence from around the Middle East, which would ostensibly appear to be passed to the Secret Intelligence Services.'

'Ostensibly appear...?' GK questioned.

'Yes. I'm fairly certain that the past three months have been an extended probation period...a test of sorts.'

A knowing grin from GK. 'Well, you're almost there. The intelligence you gathered—not necessarily always low-grade, I hasten to add—*did* wind up in the gloomy offices on Broadway. But you're quite right in that your performance in the Middle East has been being closely monitored.'

That was the first acknowledgement that the information, which Alexander had obtained, had indeed ended up at the MI6 offices in London. 'And did I pass?'

Another chuckle from GK. 'We don't quite operate like that, old chap.'

'Then how *do* you operate?' Alexander asked.

Before GK could answer, a waiter appeared, ready to take their order.

'Two double pink gins,' Alexander ordered. 'And we'll both take the steak au poivre vert and Syrian truffle salad, please.'

GK laughed heartily. 'Good man. Good man.'

With the waiter gone, GK sank back in his chair. 'Do you think you and I would be sitting here if you hadn't *passed?*' he asked, emphasising the final word of the sentence.

Alexander thought for a moment. 'No, I suppose not. And your being here now is somehow connected to yesterday's news, I presume?'

GK sat up, suddenly serious. 'Listen, we would like to formally invite you into the fold.' He reached into his jacket pocket and tossed a piece of paper and pen down on the table in front of Alexander. 'Your signature, if you will.'

The paper was a long, typed document headed with the words OFFICIAL SECRETS ACT. Without reading anything further, Alexander scribbled his name at the bottom of the page and slid it back over to GK.

'Marvellous. Erm, yes... I am here on business concerned with yesterday's news.'

Yesterday, in a two-and-a-half-hour-long speech, President Nasser had announced the immediate renationalisation of the British- and French-controlled Suez Canal, sending shockwaves through the British government. The move, Nasser had declared, was in order to fund the construction of the Aswan Dam after the British and Americans had pulled out, despite the Soviets' having stepped in with an unconditional loan to cover the project. The big news, at which Nadia Ibrahim had hinted, could only have been surpassed by an outright declaration of war. Indeed, to some in the diplomatic circles in which Alexander mingled, renationalising the Suez Canal *was* akin to a veiled declaration of war. The ball was back in Britain's court.

'Now that you're one of us, I'm not going to beat around the bush,' GK began. 'Behind the scenes in Whitehall, every diplomatic, political and military option is currently—and with much fervour—being explored. Our dear PM is *very* keen to stem this septic anti-British tide, emanating from Cairo, by all possible means. The most obvious, but perhaps most problematic way of so doing, would of course be to excise the tumour at its root.'

'Nasser?' Alexander clarified.

'Nasser. But, as I say, all options are being considered. And, as part of the Special Political Activity under my authority—as director of the Secret Intelligence Service in the Middle East—several new operations in the area have been instigated...' GK paused as the waiter returned, placing two glasses of pink gin on the table, then resumed. 'And... in one of these new operations, I would like *your* active participation.'

Alexander nodded. 'Yes, of course.'

GK smiled, picked up his glass, and said, 'To Operation Sawdust.'

'Operation Sawdust,' Alexander echoed, glancing his glass with GK's, and feigning an ignorance of Operation Sawdust which was actually far from the truth of the matter.

Following the meal with GK, Alexander returned to his flat, switched on his Hallicrafter radio set and listened out for SU2FG on the airwaves.

Chapter Seventeen

Morton parked his Mini beside the triangular green at the centre of the Kentish town of Westerham.

Pulling his bag from the passenger seat beside him, he stepped out from his car into a cold, misty drizzle and took a moment to look around himself. Surrounding the green were an assortment of old properties and quintessentially quaint shops and boutiques. A charming place on a sunny day, he thought, shivering.

With a quick step, he hurried along the pavement in search of Vanessa Briggs's home. He soon found the ground-floor flat in what appeared to have once been a shop of some kind, judging by the elaborately large front windows. He knocked on the black door and waited.

A few moments later, a slim woman with long brown hair, wearing a blue and orange patterned dress, answered the door.

'Hi,' Morton began. 'I'm looking for Vanessa Briggs.'

'That's me!' she replied excitedly. 'Are you Morton?'

'Yes, nice to meet you,' he said, extending his hand.

She ignored his offer of a handshake and threw her arms around him.

Morton smiled at her greeting.

'Come in, come in!' she said, encouraging him into a small lounge. 'Tea? Coffee?'

'Coffee would be lovely,' Morton answered. 'Thank you.'

'Take a seat and I'll be right there; then we can get started,' Vanessa enthused, disappearing through a door on the other side of the room. 'Milk or sugar?' she called out.

'Just milk, thank you,' Morton answered, taking out his notepad and pen. He settled back in the chair and looked around the room, whilst he waited for Vanessa to return. On the bright yellow walls were hung several attractive ink and pen sketches of countryside vistas. There were two small sofas, which were covered in floral throws, facing a small television and on one wall was a tall bookcase, rammed with books on art, animals and nature. This was an optimistic, positive person's house, Morton reasoned, liking the initial impressions of his new half-aunt. He noticed that there were two large floral suitcases next to the front door.

Vanessa returned and handed him his coffee. 'Choccy bic?'

'No. I'm fine, thank you.'

'No. Me neither. I'm trying—and failing, mostly—to be healthy.' She sat down on the other sofa and smiled. 'Where do we begin? You're the expert. Sorry. Don't mean to sound like a stalker, but I Googled you and found your name attached to some pretty hairy stories over the years.'

'Yes,' he acknowledged. 'I do seem to have had a habit of running into trouble.'

'Well, hopefully our family connection will be less problematic,' she joked, tucking her hair behind her ears.

'Hmm,' he said.

'You wouldn't believe the journey that I've been on in the past twelve months,' she began.

'Tell me.'

'Right…' she said, drawing in a dramatically long breath. 'I was found in a shoebox outside Woolworths in Sevenoaks a few hours after I was born.'

'Good opening line,' Morton said, detecting her own black humour about what was undoubtedly an awful situation.

'That's going to be the start of my autobiography,' Vanessa said with a laugh. 'I was very lucky, though, compared to the other…' she cut herself short. 'I'll come to that. I was left in the shop doorway, just before it opened, fortunately. So, it wasn't long before the assistant manager found me, phoned for an ambulance and I was whisked off to hospital, where I stayed for a few days whilst something more permanent was found for me. Luckily for me, I was placed almost immediately with a lovely child-less couple, who couldn't have been better parents.'

'That's good,' Morton said, detecting that a 'but' was on its way. He had a raft of questions but he held back from asking them, sensing that Vanessa had more to say.

'Yeah… I really can't fault their parenting, except in one way: they kept the truth about my birth hidden from me and I didn't know anything at all until my dad passed away last year, having survived my mum… Oh, that didn't sound right! You get what I mean, though. And, whilst clearing out his flat, I found a newspaper cutting about a baby found in a Clark's shoebox outside Woolworths the week I was born. It didn't take a genius to work out that that little abandoned girl was me. Since then I've been trying to get my head around the facts of the matter and trying to find out who my biological parents really were.'

Morton actually found himself gulping with guilt by proxy.

'And I'm hoping you can tell me more about my father,' she continued with a smile. 'You said it was on your paternal Farrier side?'

'Yes,' Morton replied, unsure of where to draw the line in his knowledge. He had debated telling her about the murder in Reno for the entirety of the drive over to Westerham but could not reach a firm conclusion on the matter. Was it her right to know? Was it his place to tell her? Should he wait until more facts had been established? He didn't know. 'So... Your biological father was my grandfather, Alfred Farrier.'

'Oh, right,' Vanessa said, clearly taken aback. 'When were you born, then?'

'Nineteen seventy-four,' he answered.

'I was born a year later,' she said with a perplexed frown. 'So, that makes me your half-aunt?'

Morton nodded.

'Okay,' she said, still frowning.

'My grandmother—Alfred's wife—had died in childbirth, you see,' he explained, knowing that it actually didn't explain anything.

'But how old would he have been when I was conceived, then?' she queried.

'Sixty.'

'*Sixty*?' she repeated. 'Wow. That's quite old to be fathering a child... And what can you tell me about him?'

'How about I start with these?' Morton said, taking three photographs of Alfred Farrier from his notepad and passing them over to her.

Vanessa gasped as tears instantly welled in her eyes. She bit her lower lip, rotating through the three images. 'Wow. My father...' A few moments passed, then she looked up at Morton and asked, 'What was he like...as a person?'

God. Now what? 'Well, I understand from my Aunty Margaret that, as a father, he could be a little on the tyrannical side when she was growing up—'

'But not towards *your* father?' she interrupted.

Oh, yes, another can of genealogical worms: his biological mother, having been aged sixteen when she had fallen pregnant, had given Morton to her brother and his wife to raise; a fact which Morton himself had only discovered at the age of fifteen. 'I'll come to that another time.'

'Oh, right. Sounds interesting. Do you not remember him, then?'

'Yes, I do,' Morton confirmed.

'What was he like towards you?' she asked.

'He was just a normal grandfather, as far I was concerned. Took me out on occasion. We watched cowboy films together. He taught me how to play chess. I helped him out down his allotment.' Morton shrugged, unable to remove the stain of the murder from his memories.

Vanessa smiled, which unnerved him somewhat. 'That's nice to hear.'

'Well...' Morton said, teetering on the edge of blurting it out. 'He was a very complicated man... There's something, which has come to light in recent days, that suggests that he might not have quite been the man that I knew.'

'Oh? Sounds intriguing. Go on!' she encouraged with a smile.

'I will,' Morton said. 'But, do you mind first telling me what you've found out about your maternal side? You mentioned in a message that you had higher DNA connections on GEDmatch, is that right?'

Vanessa nodded and sipped her drink. 'Yeah, basically I've found two new half-sisters. We all share the same mother.'

'Wow,' Morton uttered. 'And have you found out who she was?'

'No idea whatsoever. The other two were found in very similar situations: dumped and unwanted. The differences with them, though, were that they went through a series of horrible children's homes and foster homes, and not having the stable base which I was lucky enough to have had.'

'Is there anything else you know about her?' Morton pushed.

'Literally nothing. Because of the circumstances of our births, none of us has an adoption file or anything official that might have named her. It's weird, all three of us were clearly not wanted in the slightest, to the point that we could very well have died as a result of our mother's actions, and yet each of us are desperate to find out who she was and what made her abandon us.'

'Why do you think she did that?' Morton asked, really not enjoying his position as possessing potentially greater knowledge.

Vanessa sighed and looked at the window. 'So... I was found in Sevenoaks. Liza was found in Croydon and Billie was found in Manchester. She was a woman who moved around a lot, with the ability to give birth at least three times unnoticed by officials... I'm afraid, given that your grandfather is implicated in all this, that we all think she was very likely to have been...a prostitute.'

'I thought the same thing,' Morton agreed.

'Oh, right. What led you to that conclusion, then?' Vanessa asked, clearly puzzled.

He realised at that moment that he had just inadvertently revealed something more than that which he had thus far been prepared to disclose.

'Morton? What are you not telling me?'

God. How was he supposed to say it? It was his turn to sigh. 'After you messaged me to say that you had close relatives on GEDmatch, I logged my own kit back in to allow law enforcement usage and I suddenly had a DNA match stronger than my match with you. I emailed the person and got a response to say that the kit, to which I matched, had been uploaded as part of a cold-case investigation into the death of a prostitute in 1980.'

'My mother?' Vanessa stammered, jumping to the wrong conclusion.

'No, no,' Morton responded. 'This was a woman in Reno, Nevada.'

'Sorry, I'm lost. Who did *your* DNA match with, then?'

'My grandfather.'

Vanessa threw her hand to her mouth. '*He* killed the prostitute?'

Morton nodded.

'Oh, my God! A *complicated* man, you said... Wow...'

In the lengthening silence that followed, Morton drank his now lukewarm coffee. Vanessa sat in silence, cuddling her knees and quietly sobbing. He wondered if he should go over and comfort her. She was his half-aunt, after all and he had just relayed some pretty unpalatable news.

'Do you think he killed my mother, too?' she asked.

He desperately wanted to be able categorically to say no, to exonerate his grandfather of further wrongdoing, but, how could he? He had stabbed a prostitute to death. Why couldn't he have done exactly the same to others? 'I really don't know,' was the best answer that he could give.

'Well, that's the second line of my autobiography sorted, then,' she said with a short laugh. After a pause, she asked, 'Where do we go from here?'

191

'I need to pluck up the courage to email the cold-case team in America and hand over Alfred's name as the suspect, if they haven't worked it out already…which I imagine they probably have.'

'Will you help me, Morton, to find out what happened to my mother? For good or for bad?'

'Yes,' he heard himself saying. 'I'm in the middle of a case at the moment, but as soon as that's done, I'll try and help you to find out what happened to her.'

'Thank you,' she said, sobbing once again. 'I'm going away for six weeks, travelling around Australia and New Zealand, anyway. So, you've got some time before I start pestering you for answers.'

Morton was back at home, feeling emotionally drained. The same feeling of nausea came over him in waves when his thoughts returned—regularly and often of their own volition—to his *grandfather's situation*, as he was euphemistically dubbing it.

He couldn't delay it any longer: he needed to email Maddie and offload some of the burden onto her. Part of his reluctance stemmed from the unknown implications, which would follow his naming his grandfather, but he realised that they would not be his load to bear.

Sitting at his study desk, he opened up his laptop and scrolled down his emails until he reached the one from Maddie. He clicked reply and then stared at the screen for a few seconds. Then, he headed down to the kitchen and poured himself a large glass of red wine. Then, he went to the toilet. Just as he was going back upstairs, his mobile phone began to ring in his pocket. An unfamiliar landline with the dialling code of *01342*.

'Hello?' he answered, continuing up to his study.

'Is that Morton? It's Winnie, here.'

It took him a moment to register that he was speaking with the woman who lived in Priory Flats in Ardingly. 'Oh, yes… Hello. How are you?' he asked.

'Not bad, thank you. Mustn't grumble,' Winnie replied. 'I'm calling about that photo you sent. Yes, it's definitely Maurice, the poor old sod.'

'You're completely sure, are you?' Morton pressed, sitting at his desk and sipping his wine.

'One hundred percent; it's him.'

Well, it might have been the man whom you *believe* to be Maurice Duggan, Morton thought, but actually his name was Alexander

Emmett... But he wasn't about to start down that convoluted explanation.

'May I keep the photo?' Winnie asked. 'Only, it's a little bit clearer than mine, see.'

'Of course. Thank you for letting me know,' Morton said, about to end the call and begin writing the dreaded email to Maddie.

'I've kept looking at it because it reminds me of someone,' Winnie continued. 'Maybe someone famous? Like a film star of the day?'

Morton brought the image of Maurice on the pilot's licence to mind but couldn't agree that he looked like any film star of whom he could think. He picked up the pair of glasses that had belonged to Alexander during his time posing as Maurice Duggan and put them on.

'When was it taken?' Winnie asked.

'I don't know exactly, but it was used on his pilot's licence in 1948. So, some time before that.'

'Clark Gable?' Winnie suggested to herself. 'James Stewart? What was that chap in that Hitchcock film?'

Morton stifled an impatient sigh, not wanting to listen to a list of film stars from the 1940s.

'Cary Grant? No... That's not him.'

'Right, I'd better get on,' Morton cut in. 'Thanks for letting me know about the photo.'

'You're very welcome. I'll keep thinking about that—'

'Thank you,' Morton said. 'Bye.'

He just caught the words, 'David Niven,' as he ended the call.

The email in reply to Maddie was still onscreen, the cursor flashing, impatiently waiting for him to type something.

Dear Maddie,

Then he stopped, drank some of his wine thoughtfully and stared at the laptop.

It was the first time that he had written her name in a *very* long while.

He sat back in his chair, looking at the word *Maddie*, recollecting when he had first met her. It had been in his final year at University College London and she had been on some kind of an exchange programme from the US, appearing out of the blue one day in a Photo Forensics lecture, held by his favourite teacher, Dr Baumgartner. He had been instantly struck by her. Yes, she had been attractive, but there had been something much more than that, which had drawn him to her. She had a self-assured attitude but without any accompanying arrogance, a trait which was manifest in her conduct, confidence and in her dress sense. Morton could still remember exactly what she had been wearing on the day when they had met: a straw trilby hat, stone-washed jeans covered with lacerations and a baggy white shirt. The look was accessorised by a small silver nose-stud and knee-high leather boots. He snorted at the mental image, thinking how totally opposite she had been to Juliette, which might go some way to explaining why he and Maddie had failed where he and Juliette were succeeding.

Having admired her from afar for the entire term, Dr Baumgartner had paired them together on the final project, where they had to identify the precise date and location of an aerial photograph, giving them no additional information than that which could be gleaned from the picture itself. Morton smiled, still able to bring to mind the very photograph. It was centred on a detached bungalow, with an average-sized garden, sandwiched between two similar bungalows, both built in a similar style. Morton and Maddie had worked hard on identifying the date, using all the techniques that they had learned from Dr Baumgartner. The types of trees—deciduous or evergreen—had informed them of the season. The length of the shadows had told them the time of the day. The make and registration of a car on the driveway suggested a year following which it had to have been taken, therefore. When they had zoomed in on a white van parked outside the neighbouring property, they had just about managed to glean that it was a local dog-walking company, providing them with the approximate geographical area. An analysis of the collection times of the wheelie-bin, perched on the pavement edge, pointed to a particular day of the week. A combination of all of those results had led them to just one day and one location when the photograph could have been taken. They had fulfilled the task with ease.

But that hadn't been enough for Maddie. It had also been her idea to try to establish who had lived at the property, which had seemed to Morton like an unnecessary extra task, but one with which he had willingly gone along, delighted to be spending even more time in her company. Using electoral registers for the area, they had discovered that the bungalow in question had, in fact, belonged to Dr Baumgartner's sister. They completed their report with an addendum that a small flat-roofed extension to the rear of the property would have required planning permission, where none had been granted. The project had received full marks and a commendation from Dr Baumgartner. He had also told them, with a wry grin, that he would inform his sister that she needed to obtain retrospective planning permission for her new bathroom.

Then, they had started dating. Not long after that, they had moved in together and everything had been perfect. Or, so it had seemed to Morton. But one day, as miraculously as she had appeared in his life, so had she disappeared. Just a short note had been left, with no real explanation, saying that she would be returning to America.

He hadn't heard from her ever since.

He wasn't at all surprised to read in her email that she had established her own cold-case investigation company. With that dogged determination of hers, coupled with her unquestionable research skills, she would be unstoppable.

Dear Maddie,

Was it inappropriate now to ask why she had left him? Would Juliette accept that he was asking purely to know *why* and that he had no ulterior motive? After all these years, did it even matter why? What good could come of asking or knowing? For some reason, which he couldn't quite articulate, he decided that, yes, it did still matter.

He sighed, then sipped and set down his wine.

Just keep it professional, he told himself, positioning his hands above the keyboard.

Dear Maddie,
Thanks for getting back to me — wow, small world!
I'm sure by now you have worked out the identity of LZ025. In case not, he was my grandfather, Alfred Farrier. I have been working on trying to establish more facts and have had it confirmed that he was in Reno at the time of Candee-Lee Gaddy's murder. What happens next?

He ended the email *Best wishes*, then promptly deleted it. Best wishes? He was writing to confirm that his grandfather had been a murderer.

Kind regards,
Morton

He read the email back, finding it strikingly odd how formal it sounded, given their past relationship. He began to dissect his choice of words and the possible ways in which the email could be read, then quickly hit *send*, and it was gone.

Morton exhaled at length and finished his wine.

From downstairs, he heard the front door open and Grace immediately calling out his name. He grinned. Whatever the reason was that Maddie had left him, he might never know. What he did know, however, was that he wouldn't change a single thing about his life right now and, one way or another, it had all led him here.

Chapter Eighteen

Morton was sweeping a pile of broken plates and bowls into a dustpan. The kitchen floor resembled some Greek taverna after a particularly pleasing post-dinner plate-smashing party. In what must have been record-breaking speed, with Morton and Juliette both out of the room for less than a minute, Grace had managed to destroy the entire contents of the crockery cupboard. Just one pathetic bowl and two small plates had survived the massacre.

'She's asleep,' Juliette whispered, entering the kitchen.

'She needs it after that rampage,' Morton replied. 'Or she needs exorcising.'

'Morton, you really need to fix those cupboard doors. It's so dangerous.'

'I will, I will.'

'Today?' she asked.

'Well, probably not *today*. I'm off to TNA.'

Juliette rolled her eyes. 'Is this for the spy man or your killer grandad?'

'Spy man,' he answered, not sure if he liked Juliette's monikers for the two cases currently dominating his thoughts.

'Anything back from Maddie, yet?' Juliette probed, as she filled the kettle with water.

'No, which is worrying.'

'But there's nothing they can do now: he's dead. What's to worry about?'

Morton shrugged. He didn't know much about the US legal system to know whether his grandfather would be posthumously found guilty of the murder, given the overwhelming evidence, or whether the case would simply be dropped.

'Do you want a drink?' she asked.

'No, thanks. I'd better get ready and head to Kew,' he replied, leaving the kitchen. Sitting on the doormat in the hallway was a single item of post, stamped with the long-familiar GRO logo. Morton tore open the envelope, intrigued. It was the first British birth certificate registered in Egypt that he had ever ordered. Its content was overwhelmingly disappointing, being almost identical to the standard British birth certificates.

When and where born: 7th December 1927 at Port Said
Name: Alexander Emmett
Sex: Male
Name and surname of father: Geoffrey Owen Emmett
Name and maiden surname of mother: Alexandria Emmett, formerly Hassan
Rank, profession or occupation of father and claim to citizenship of the United Kingdom and Colonies or British Nationality: Colonial Administrator. British subject by birth, born Kings Lynn, Norfolk
Signature, description and residence of informant: G.O. Emmett, father of the child. Port Said.
When registered: 22nd December 1927
Signature of consular officer: L.H. Hurst, H.M. Consul

The certificate was interesting, to a point, but added little to his overall investigation into Alexander Emmett's life and the reasons why he had taken on Maurice Duggan's identity. Morton hoped that, following another trip to the National Archives today, he would have an answer. Although the Duggan Case had been fascinating thus far, he had—with the discovery of Christopher Emmett—effectively fulfilled the brief set out by Clarissa Duggan, who simply wanted to know the rightful inheritor of the £89,692,92. Morton doubted very much that Clarissa would be interested in whatever involvement it was that Alexander had had in Operation Sawdust. He decided to see how the research today would go and then would consider drawing the case to a close.

Morton folded the certificate into his bag, put on his coat and shoes, then returned to the kitchen to say goodbye to Juliette. 'See you later,' he said, kissing her on the lips.

'Have a good day,' she said. 'Don't get into any trouble.'

'As if…' Morton responded, picking up his bag and heading out of the front door. He hurried down the steps to the street and jumped with fright when someone touched him on the shoulder. 'My…God!' he shrieked.

'Morning! Any updates for me?' It was Clarissa Duggan, standing there and wearing an unnecessary transparent rainhat and matching mackintosh, as if she had been conjured by his thoughts just a moment before. Had this woman not heard of telephones? Had she really come all this way from Horsham on spec, just for an update?

'Erm…well, I'm still working on the case,' he explained. 'In fact, I'm off to the National Archives right now.'

Clarissa's eyes bulged. 'Oo! How exciting. You've still not found out who he was, then?'

Technically, yes, but was he really about to stand on his doorstep and try to explain all that he had discovered so far? No. He made a point of not divulging his discoveries mid-way through a case, if at all possible. 'It's very complicated, and I hope it won't be too much longer until I can give you a full report with all that you require.'

'An heir!' she cried.

Morton nodded evasively.

'And a reason?' she enquired.

'Not yet,' he said, trying to show through his body-language that he was wanting to move off.

'Funny, isn't it?' she mused.

'Well, it's certainly an odd one,' Morton agreed. 'I'd better get on, if there wasn't anything else…'

'Oh, yes, of course. Off you go!' Clarissa said.

He said goodbye and climbed into his Mini, which was parked beside the house, removed his coat, started the engine and then slowly pulled away over the cobbles of Mermaid Street.

In his rear-view mirror, Clarissa Duggan was still standing in the middle of the road, looking rather lost and ghost-like. He was still unsure if she had come all the way from Horsham just for that short exchange. With all of its peripheral characters, the Duggan Case was one of the strangest genealogical investigations on which he had ever worked, he thought with a wry smile, as he drove to the archives.

Morton pulled up at the new car park barriers at the National Archives, waiting whilst the automatic number plate recognition cameras scanned the front of his Mini. The barrier lifted and Morton entered and found a space. He gathered up his belongings and marched into the building, passing through the security check, through the foyer and into the locker room.

Having stowed his coat and bag, he headed directly to the first floor, where he removed the two pre-ordered documents from locker 10B and walked through to the adjacent Document Reading Room.

There was an air of quiet busyness to the place, with the usual increase in researchers, owing to its being a Saturday. Three other people were sharing a slice of 'his' octagonal desk, one of whom, having noticed his arrival, he acknowledged with a smile, as he set his things down in his designated section in front of him.

The brown file, similar in appearance to that for which he had searched the last time he had been here, bore the casual black pencil scrawl: *CAB 301/278*. Above it was written *MISCELLANEOUS CORRESPONDENCE ON SECRET FUNDING 1955-1962*.

The file, comprising multiple pieces of paper varying in size and colour, was held together by a treasury tag in the top left corner. Morton opened it to the first page. It was a small blue letter, headed *TOP SECRET*.

Box No. 500
Parliament Street B.O.,
London. S.W.1.

26th October 1957

Dear Norman
In connection with the examination of my estimates I have written a letter giving some account of Security Service activities during the last year. I think you might be interested to see this, and I am therefore sending a copy to you and should be grateful if you would return the copy to me afterwards.
Yours ever,
Harold Austin

The Right Hon. Sir Norman Brook,
Cabinet Office
Great George Street, S.W.1.

Before turning the page, Morton quickly ran a Google search for the two men named in the letter. Harold Austin had been the Foreign Secretary under Anthony Eden's premiership and Sir Norman Brook had been head of the Home Service.

Morton photographed the letter, then eagerly turned the page to see what kinds of overseas security operations had been conducted, especially looking out for any mention of Operation Sawdust.

Instead, what he saw was a white form, headed with the National Archives name and logo, giving the document reference at the top. Below it was a series of boxes, each containing a reason why the expected file was absent. *Closed under FOI exemption. Temporarily retained.*

Missing at transfer. Number not used. A scribbled signature and the date *14/2/17* had been written beside the box marked *Retained under section 3(4) of the Public Records Act 1958.*

Redacted. Brilliant.

He turned the page to see another letter, promising enclosures regarding foreign operations in 1956, but that too was followed by a complete redaction.

With increasing frustration, Morton worked through the file. Where documents had not been entirely removed under the Public Records Act, most had undergone some kind of censorship, with sensitive names generally being whited out.

Despite the lack of progress, Morton waded his way through the remainder of the file, diligently photographing each page, just in case it might later prove to be of interest.

He reached the end and sighed with annoyance.

He had ordered two other files from the CAB series, each purporting to be connected to the Foreign Office during the 1950s, but his hopes of discovering what Operation Sawdust actually had been were now dwindling. Other potentially interesting documents, which were listed in the online catalogue, could not be ordered at all. His delight upon seeing *CAB 301/409 – Authorisation of intelligence operations* quickly sank when he read that it was closed to public inspection.

It took over an hour for Morton to plod through the two files. By the end, he had learned nothing more about the nature of Operation Sawdust and there had been no further reference to Alexander Emmett.

He sat back in his chair, with the files closed on the desk in front of him.

He yawned, which was never a good sign. Time for coffee.

He placed the three files onto his laptop and carried them out into the foyer, then set them down on the Returns Desk, passed through the security check and down the staircase to the ground floor.

With another yawn, he joined a small queue at the café. His tired eyes, drifting aimlessly over the open-fronted bookshop opposite the café, settled upon a placard advertising the National Archives' current season on the Cold War. From his place in the queue, Morton couldn't make out any of the titles on the promotional stand and decided to head over to take a closer look.

The bookshop was advertising a whole range of offerings connected with the Cold War. Surely, he thought, one of them had to

201

mention operations in Egypt. He picked up the top-most title on the stand and checked the index for either Alexander Emmett's name or Operation Sawdust. Neither was listed. He repeated the task with the next book, and then the next. The fourth book, which he checked, was entitled *Disrupt and Deny. Spies, Special Forces, and the Secret Pursuit of British Foreign Policy* by Rory Cormac. In the index was a reference to Operation Sawdust.

Morton smiled, paid for the book and carried it back over to the café queue, which had now all but dispersed. He ordered a large latte and carried it over to one of the few free tables in front of the café. Thumbing his way to the index, he found that there were in fact three references to Operation Sawdust and three to Operation Scant; both being listed on the same pages across two chapters: *Covert action before Suez* and *Covert action after Suez*.

Morton read the chapters intently, making notes as he went. Scant was clearly defined. It was a black radio station based in Cyprus, broadcasting propaganda against the president of Egypt, Gamal Abdel Nasser for six hours a day. Operation Sawdust, on the other hand, was much more nebulous, being an over-arching broad plan to undermine Nasser. The task, so the book explained, had been handed to the man in charge of SIS in the Middle East, George Kennedy Young.

'Wow,' Morton muttered to himself. He didn't know too much about the Suez Crisis, but whatever President Nasser had done, he had certainly irked the British government.

'Thanks, Rory,' he said, closing the informative book.

Was it so outlandish, Morton wondered, to believe that the Alexander Emmett, noted as having somehow been involved in Operation Sawdust, was the same man who had later assumed the identity of Maurice Duggan? He had been born and raised in Egypt, after all. Outlandish, no, but he had zero evidence to corroborate it, never mind anything resembling the Genealogical Proof Standard.

The book and the lack of available records on Operation Sawdust had presented Morton with more questions than they had answered.

What could he do now? he questioned, given that so little clearly existed on the specifics of the operation. After some deliberation, he concluded that there was little point in expending further energy in exploring the possibilities of this avenue right now, given that it had nothing to do with what Clarissa had requested of him.

Instead, he decided to make best use of his time at the archives and try to find anything more about Alexander's early life. When had he left

Egypt? He drank his latte, as he went back over his notes on the case. According to Alexander's aviator's certificate, he was living in London by August 1948.

Turning to the *UK, Incoming Passenger Lists, 1878-1960* record set on Ancestry, Morton typed in Alexander's name, with an embarkation point of Egypt. At the top of the results list was the one which he had hoped to see. He clicked to view the original image, a colour scan of a double-page excerpt, giving a typed list of passengers travelling on the Pacific Steam Navigation Company ship, *Orbita*. Morton ran his finger down the alphabetised list and found him:

Port of Embarkation: Port Said
Port at which Passengers have been landed: Liverpool
Arrival date: 20th May 1946
Names of Passenger: EMMETT, Alexander
Age of Passenger: 18
Proposed Address in the United Kingdom: 46a Lancaster Gate, London
Profession, Occupation or calling of Passenger: Journalist
Country of last permanent residence: Egypt

It was undoubtedly the correct person. Everything tallied together. Morton downloaded the page, made a brief note of it on his pad, and then reminded himself about what he knew of Alexander's life prior to this point. On his marriage certificate, he had stated that his father had been Geoffrey Owen Emmett (deceased), a Colonial Administrator.

Returning to the indexes for deaths overseas, Morton typed in Geoffrey's name, finding that he had died in 1931. Next, he searched for his mother, Alexandria, and found her death in Port Said in 1944. He queued the two documents to print out when he returned home, wondering if it had been his parents' deaths, which had prompted Alexander to move to the UK.

Chapter Nineteen

5th November 1956, Port Said, Egypt

A distant noise pulled Alexander from a deep sleep. He rolled over, pushed the thin white sheet from his clammy body and curled up into a foetal position. Closing his eyes again, he quickly began to drift back off.

He was staying in the same room of the Hotel Dakhla in Port Said in which he had been staying when Nasser had boldly raised the Egyptian flag outside of Navy House almost five months earlier. At this moment in time, Alexander was here in his capacity as a journalist, not as a spy. He had been sent here from Beirut six days ago, when Israel had launched a surprise attack on the Egyptian Sinai region, receiving a twelve-hour joint ultimatum of a cease-fire from Britain and France, which had gone unheeded. Alexander had been present on the Port Said bank of the Suez Canal when President Nasser had ordered the scuttling of all forty ships which had been passing through it at the time, rendering it entirely unusable.

Alexander's subsequent report into the escalating crisis had made the front pages of the *Observer*. Four days ago, in response to this audacious move, the RAF and the Royal Navy's Fleet Air Arm had begun to bomb targets across Egypt. Alexander had witnessed Valiants and Canberras flying low over the city on sorties, destroying Egyptian military targets, airfields and oil fields. The attacks were ostensibly in reaction to Nasser's ignoring of the cease-fire demand but, in Alexander's opinion, they were the prelude to much larger attacks to oust the president and change the regime for one more favourable to Britain's interests.

The same sound, which had roused him moments ago, occurred again somewhere in the distance. This time, Alexander sat up and listened.

It sounded like gunfire.

He swung his legs from the bed and hurried over to the internal shutters, which he hastily tugged open. He shielded his eyes for a moment, as he opened the door to his balcony and the light of early dawn pierced into his room.

Through squinted eyes, Alexander looked up and down the empty street. More noise drew his attention and then he saw the skies, maybe a mile or two away, filled with small black objects falling to the ground. Those objects, he realised, when his vision had fully adjusted to the light, were soldiers being parachuted to the ground.

Alexander returned to his room, pulled on a pair of trousers and a white cotton shirt, then dashed from the hotel in the direction of the invasion, sweeping his hand through his blonde hair in lieu of any time to style it.

'Damn,' he cursed himself. He'd forgotten his notepad. He paused to consider going back but decided against it. He made a mental note that the attack had begun at around 5.15am, with hundreds of paratroopers being dropped in to the El Gamil airfield.

The streets were largely deserted and those people, whom Alexander did encounter, were focussed on fleeing in the opposite direction. The closer he drew to the airfield, the more he could see that the objects tumbling from the sky were a mixture of hundreds of paratroopers and large containers, filled, presumably, with ammunition and supplies. Alexander was not witnessing a warning shot to President Nasser; he was seeing here the start of a whole-scale military invasion.

As he continued down the main street towards the airfield, he felt his dichotomic allegiances pulling inside of him, as tangibly as though they were a physical part of his biological structure. Where was this invasion going to lead? The outward actions of the British, French, Egyptians and Israelis would go some way in determining the course of this conflict, but, behind the scenes, the positions taken by the Soviets and the Americans would be pivotal to the eventual outcome.

Any intelligence that he could obtain on the ground could be crucial.

He hurried along the Saad Zaghloul, which bordered the very edge of the Mediterranean Sea, the airfield just visible in the distance. He pushed on, breaking into a run until he reached the tall wire boundary fence which encircled El Gamil airfield, arriving at the far end of the single tarmac runway. He laced his fingers through the wire and stared up at the tiny black dots, slowly metamorphosing either into armed paratroopers or elongated barrel-shaped containers. The soldiers, who had landed, were advancing in a line of machine-gun fire towards the main airfield building, receiving an ever-dwindling amount of return fire from the Egyptians. The control tower was ablaze, black smoke billowing from the windows overlooking the airfield.

Pressing his face to the mesh, Alexander strained his sight to attempt to identify the nationalities of the dead bodies that were littered across the airfield. He couldn't be completely certain, but it seemed as though both sides had suffered casualties.

From his peripheral vision, Alexander spotted movement. He turned to see a soldier running in his direction, jerking a machine gun at him and shouting something.

Alexander stood still, waiting as the soldier drew nearer.

'Get back! Get back!' the paratrooper yelled angrily. Then, when he was closer, added, 'What do you think this is, an outdoor theatre show?'

Alexander held up his hands. 'I'm a journalist with the *Observer*,' he said. 'British.'

'I don't care who you are, pal,' the soldier retorted, now within two metres of Alexander. 'You need to get the hell out of here. Can't you see what's going on?'

'The opening shots of World War Three?' Alexander suggested.

The soldier glared at him.

'You're from the 3rd Battalion Parachute Regiment, yes?' Alexander asked, noting his uniform.

The man's face tightened, and he slowly shifted his gun to face Alexander. 'Move...on.' His words came out, slow and deliberate, rather like the final warning issued by a livid headmaster, right before exploding with anger.

Alexander held up his hands in a conciliatory way and backed away from the fence.

When he was a safe distance from the airfield perimeter, he spun around. The soldier was running back towards the action, which was now constricting in a tighter circle around the main building with diminishing resistance.

The early morning skies above the airfield were painted in a single shade of pale blue and were now no longer peppered with the tumbling black speckles which portended a looming war.

When Alexander reached the main thoroughfare into the city, the previously quiet streets had become hives of chaotic activity. People were hurrying around, conversing with strangers in a fast, high-energy babble, with constant repeated looks and gestures towards the canal and airfield beyond. Word was spreading and, although Alexander could not understand what was being said, the implication was obvious: nobody knew what to do next. Hands were thrown up in the air. A woman began to cry. An elderly man, stooped over a stick, shouted something angry and defiant to anyone willing to listen. More and more people joined the throng, as they learned from neighbours, friends and strangers what was happening at the airfield.

A low thrum, growing increasingly loud, rose from the north of the city, drawing the attention of some of the crowd. Then, there was a booming explosion, which thundered through Alexander's core, shaking the ground beneath his feet and giving rise to a united shriek of fear from the gathered crowds.

The scenes of chaos were now channelled into a common focus on escape. To where, though, Alexander had no idea.

Another scream rang out as a large aircraft approached from the east. The people around him began to yell and run haphazardly in all directions.

Alexander recoiled, searching around him for a place of relative safety. He was surrounded by buildings, each as unsafe as the next.

He looked up at the plane, swooping low overhead. He blew out a tight breath, which he had unconsciously been holding, when he saw that the aircraft was a Vickers Valetta, primarily used for troop transportation, not bombing.

Alexander hurried back to his hotel, replaying in his mind what he had just witnessed from the various perspectives which his position here demanded of him. One thing was certain: the level of military organisation, which he had seen, showed a high degree of pre-planning; not some knee-jerk reaction to a disregarded ultimatum issued just six days before.

Until his services as a spy were called upon—and he was certain that they would be at any moment, given what was occurring here—he was going to spend the day working on a story for the *Observer*. First, he needed his notepad and pen.

He approached the hotel, reminding himself of the facts, as he strode. Over five hundred soldiers from the 3rd Battalion Parachute Regiment had parachuted into El Gamil airfield at dawn this morning, receiving low-level resistance from the Egyptian army. Bombing raids were taking place in Port Said. Troops were being moved around the country.

Just as he stepped inside the hotel lobby, another bomb was detonated somewhere in the city, shaking the entire building.

'Mr Emmett!' someone called to him.

Alexander looked over to the origin of the voice. It was the hotel concierge.

'Mr Emmett, you must take shelter in the basement. We have special concrete shelter ready-built for Israeli attack. Come, come!'

Alexander waved him off dismissively. Now was not the time to be taking shelter; now was the time to be on the ground, observing the beginnings of the war first-hand. He continued up to his room, opening his door to see GK sitting on his bed, looking affectedly down at his fingernails.

'GK,' Alexander said, trying not to sound startled. 'Nice surprise.'

GK took a moment, then looked up and met his gaze. He was dressed in his usual ostentatious dark suit and Homburg hat. He smiled. 'It's started,' he uttered, as if Alexander were somehow unaware of what was taking place outside.

'I realise,' Alexander said, just as another bomb exploded nearby.

GK looked towards the window. 'Oh, not *that*. That's nothing to do with me. That's the military flexing their muscles to the world, as they're wont to do every twenty years or so. Every generation needs to see what the great Empire is capable of.' He smiled again. 'No, I was referring to Operation Sawdust. Much more discreet and subtle but with the potential to be much more powerful.'

'Getting rid of Nasser?' Alexander asked.

'Well—not to put too fine a point on it—yes, exactly. Which is where you come in.'

Alexander remained outwardly unmoved. 'Right,' he replied flatly.

'Several methods have been contemplated: pumping nerve gas into the ventilation system of his headquarters; using a poison dart; sabotaging his electric razor so that it explodes; and poisoning his food. But we'd like something more *natural-looking*...to outsiders, at least.'

Alexander was thinking hard, as a raft of questions and conundrums raced through his mind. He was also trying to get one step ahead of GK and predict where this conversation might be leading. But he had no idea.

'Something...say...like his aircraft crashing mid-flight...would be one possible scenario,' GK mused, as though the idea had only just occurred to him.

Alexander's involvement in Operation Sawdust suddenly crystallised. He was being asked for ideas of how to sabotage President Nasser's plane. 'Excise the tumour at its root', as GK had put it at their last meeting.

'What did you have in mind, exactly?' Alexander asked.

'Given your experience, I was rather hoping that *you* might be able to answer that question.'

'You want his plane brought down but with little or no evidence, which something like a bomb might create, that could be traced back to the British government?' Alexander clarified.

'Exactly!' GK confirmed.

Alexander raised his eyebrows, thinking hard about a myriad of implications, which this latest development engendered. But now wasn't the time. GK was staring at him, seemingly wanting him to be able to hatch an assassination plan, involving an aircraft, off the top of his head.

'Well,' he began, 'You could put a small nick in a propeller, which would eventually lead to a stress fracture, which in turn would bring the plane down; but the problem there is the uncertainty of when exactly that would occur. Plus, there's a real possibility of it being discovered in the pre-flight checks.'

GK screwed up his face. 'Listen, you have a little think and get back to me. Just don't take too long over it. His plane is a Soviet—*obviously*—Ilyushin IL-14 twin-engine and its flight plans are in the hands of one of his top advisors, Karim Ibrahim.' GK clasped his hands together. 'I'm sure if you get yourself over to Cairo, you can figure out a way to procure them.'

Alexander nodded. GK was referring to Karim Ibrahim's daughter, Nadia, upon whom his last attempt at allurement had failed so deplorably.

GK blew out a long breath and stood from the bed. 'You've got'— he glanced down at his wristwatch—'about thirty minutes to get out of here. Just enough time to pack your bag. Oh, and brush your hair: it looks ridiculous.'

'I don't understand.'

'Airfields, military installations and oil refineries are being targeted today and tomorrow,' GK half-explained, as he stepped towards the door.

It took Alexander a moment to realise that he was referencing the refinery next to the hotel, which, by all accounts, was about to go up in smoke.

'Good day,' GK said, leaving the room.

About thirty minutes to pack up and leave. He wasn't going to take any chances, given the lack of defined margins in that statement, and rushed around the room throwing his few belongings into his canvas bag.

Fifteen minutes later, with his bag slung over his shoulder, Alexander left the hotel. He stood motionless outside, listening. Intermittent gunfire persisted from the canal zone, but now lacking in its previous intensity. The road was bustling with an odd mixture of those people calmly going about their normal lives and seemingly oblivious to the embryonic war unfurling around them, and those fiercely intent on fleeing the city as quickly as possible, dragging cases and even items of furniture with them.

Alexander walked up the street, intending to catch a train to Cairo in order to track down Nadia Ibrahim, then to begin figuring out how he was going to answer GK's request.

As he walked, he brought the image of an Ilyushin IL-14 twin-engine to mind. He knew its specifications, although he had not flown one before. He began to think of its mechanics, just as two Vickers Valiants flew low overhead.

Alexander flung himself to the ground, pulling his canvas bag over the top of his head, knowing what was coming next.

The explosion, which detonated a moment later, was massive, rippling the ground beneath him for several seconds. A series of smaller explosions echoed from the refinery and then came the stretching groan of buildings collapsing around him.

Alexander held his breath, as a choking cloud of dust and debris swept over him. Pushing his chin as far down into his chest as he could manage, he took a short gritty breath which made him cough and wheeze.

A brief, eerie silence was broken by the sound of an alarm ringing from somewhere nearby and a male voice shouting something and calling somebody's name.

He pulled himself up onto all fours, sending the bag to the ground, and coughed loudly, thumping his chest with a balled fist, as he did so. He turned around to see, through the veil of thick dust, that the Hotel Dakhla was no longer standing where it had been just minutes before.

Flora was walking through St James's Park with the gait of a fashion model for whom time was an alien concept. She was dressed in a navy-coloured dress with matching high-heeled shoes. Her lips were plump and painted bright red, and her light blonde hair was styled immaculately under a hat set on a fashionable tilt. Over her shoulder was a lavish handbag which she had purchased for good money from a boutique on Bond Street. She feigned ignorance of the appreciative glances from some of the men, whom she passed, maintaining a general air of aloofness. All of this was despite the discomfort emanating from her brassiere, which contained another film cartridge from her Minox sub-miniature camera.

Last evening, having plied Harold with a steady quantity of red wine, mixed with large doses of benzodiazepine, she had waited for the tell-tale grunting of his discordant snore, then silently risen from the bed. From the amount that he had consumed, Flora had known that Harold would be in a very deep sleep for a good many hours. To be sure, though, she had jabbed a finger into his fleshy belly several times, but he hadn't stirred in the slightest. Flora smiled faintly at the recollection. She hadn't rushed the next part and had taken her time in opening his briefcase in the kitchen. Once she had opened it, she had read through each document slowly and carefully. Her instructions from Nikita Sokolov had been to obtain as much information as she could about the plans for Operation Sawdust, which was precisely what she had done. She had taken her time choosing and photographing with great care. The fifty frames of copied images on the film cartridge were now securely held inside her undergarments, causing her an aggravation which she could not mollify without attracting unwanted attention.

She watched a policeman passing her, his eyes roving her body, as he walked. If only he knew what was hidden under her dress, she thought with a wry smile.

Using a street-craft technique taught to her by Nikita, she removed her compact from her handbag and, moving her head slowly from side to side, feigned an inspection of her lipstick, eye shadow and rouge, all the while identifying the people walking immediately behind her. She was clear. A different set of people from a few minutes ago when she had used a café window for the same purpose.

She lowered her mirror and, as she did so, caught a fleeting glance of someone—a woman whom she had definitely seen before. Not today, but a few days ago. Damn. It could be a coincidence, but, in a city of eight million people, what were the chances that this same woman was walking fifty paces behind her twice in the same week, when the routes Flora chose were always deliberately arbitrary?

Flora continued along Birdcage Walk until she reached Whitehall. The road was unusually busy, and then she saw why: just ahead of her was the tail-end of a protest march, which spanned the entire width of the road, moving slowly towards Trafalgar Square. Great. Now the buses, tubes and pavements would be even busier than usual, meaning that it would take her much longer to reach the dead drop.

As she looked at the heaving mass of people, she had the idea that, actually, she could use the protests to shake off the tail.

Increasing her pace, it took Flora just a moment to join the back of the march. As she edged her way through the masses, she looked up at the banners waving above her: *LAW NOT WAR. STOP THE AGGRESSION. EDEN MUST GO!*

Oh, the irony. She was marching with the anti-war protesters! Nikita would find this most amusing when she told him at their next rendezvous.

She sidled her way between the hordes of people, impressed by the great number who had gathered to protest. The pace of the march had slowed almost to a standstill and she could see ahead of her that the crowds were spilling into Trafalgar Square, centring their demonstration at the base of Nelson's Column. Disparate shouting and mantras began magically to unify in to a single, definite chant: 'Eden must go! Eden must go! Eden must go!'

Flora jostled through the stagnant masses, half-grinning again about the potentially explosive material concealed in her bra. The ammunition that it would give these people! It would certainly be enough to stop the war and end Eden's premiership, and enough to bring down the British government.

'Eden must go!' she joined in with pleasure. She continued to chant, as she edged her way across the road to the Strand, where yet more people with placards and banners were thrusting towards her. 'Eden must go!' she yelled, a biting ferocity underlining her words. 'Eden must go!'

At last, the crowds were thinning, and Flora chanced a casual look behind her. There she was, that wretched woman. She was good, Flora had to admit, to maintain her surveillance through so many people. Now what? She could carry on trying to shake her off, but pretty soon she would be replaced by another unknown Watcher. With such high-grade material on her person, it was far too risky to continue. She had to abort. Charing Cross Station was just across the road. It was time to lose the tail properly in the simplest and most illogical of ways: to catch any train out of London. It was a known fact that the MI5 Watchers only operated within the boundaries of London and no covert operation undertaken by this unit had ever broken this incredibly ill-conceived rule.

Flora crossed the road and entered the station, seeing the female Watcher in the reflection of a shop window. Inside on the concourse, she took a moment to look at the information boards. A train would be leaving for Dartford in five minutes. Close by to Dartford was a safehouse of which she could make use overnight. She hurried over to the ticket booth, purchased a ticket and passed through the invisible frontier of the MI5 Watcher section.

With a subtle raising of one eyebrow, Flora glanced at the woman standing on the other side of the barrier and actually felt a little pity for her, as she boarded the train.

She would try again tomorrow.

But so might she.

Ellen emitted an audible sigh. 'Absolutely ludicrous!' she complained to herself, as she watched the train shambling out of Charing Cross Station towards Dartford. That the Watchers were unable to pursue suspects outside of London was another of A4's rules that had always irked Ellen, but today it was plain anger and frustration that she felt.

She stood in front of the barrier, watching the train until it was completely out of sight. Flora had clearly worked out that she had been followed and knew precisely what to do about it. Now there was no telling when she might return to London. Flora knew that the A4 unit did not have the resources to maintain a constant vigil at Charing Cross, waiting for her return; she could very easily jump off the train at the next station and then take the next one back and A4 would be none the wiser.

Ellen walked through the busy station and back out onto the Strand, wondering how Mr Skardon was going to take the news that Flora Sterling was fully aware that she had been under surveillance. Would he maintain it in order to keep up the pressure? Or would he terminate it, finding it a waste of meagre resources? She would find out when she returned to Leconfield House.

The protest was now in full, noisy swing. Only on this very spot on VE Day had Ellen ever seen as many people as were gathered here together, protesting against Eden's war. The parallels, of course, didn't end there. Directly owing to the Suez Crisis, petrol-rationing was due to commence once again the following month, with an allocation of fifty miles per week per car.

As she edged into the thronging mass of people, she took her time to look around. She was surrounded by men and women of all ages and social classes, and who all desired the same outcome: to stop the war in Egypt and to oust Eden as prime minster. It was a sentiment that Ellen shared with them. 'Get Eden out,' she whispered to herself. As much as she would have liked to have joined in fully with the demonstration, first and foremost she was on duty for MI5, where one's personal politics had to be disregarded.

She pushed through the crowds out of the top corner of Trafalgar Square and onto Pall Mall. As she walked, she was deep in thought about where Flora Sterling might have been headed. They had followed her from Harold Austin's flat on an obviously random route around London. But where would she have gone, had she not realised that she was being followed? Ellen needed to look at a map.

Twenty minutes later, Ellen entered Leconfield House on Curzon Street and took the stairs to the third floor. For the moment, she wanted to avoid having to tell Mr Skardon that the surveillance operation had been unequivocally compromised during her watch, and so she headed into the general office of the A4 section. On guard at the entrance to the room, maintaining sentry over the four telephones on her desk, was the bullish secretary, Miss Brogren. As always, she was wearing a smart white blouse and navy skirt, and her spectacles, with glass as thick as a submarine porthole, were perched on the bridge of her nose.

'Good morning,' Ellen greeted.

Miss Brogren offered an icy smile. 'Morning,' she replied, tonguing a boiled sweet from one side of her mouth to the other.

The office was spacious with large windows which, had they not been so terribly filthy, would have given a view over the Georgian houses opposite. In her two years of working here, the glass had never once been cleaned, making Ellen wonder if perhaps it were another way of helping to safeguard the secrets within. More likely, though, it was due to budget constraints. Whatever the reason, the end result was that the overhead strip lighting was nearly always switched on, giving the room an artificial, slightly oppressive atmosphere. Again, perhaps it was a deliberate choice. There were twelve desks in the centre of the room, each having two seats, thus giving a workstation for all twenty-four members of the A4 Watcher section, were they ever to be present in the room at the same time. Around half of the seats were currently occupied. The walls of the room were lined with several bookcases and locked filing cabinets.

Instead of going to her desk, Ellen headed to the rear of the room, where there were three large blackboards, procured from a recently closed local junior school. Affixed to the centre blackboard were photographs, covertly taken by the section, of Flora Sterling, Harold Austin, Nikita Sokolov and various other associates and known connections. The right-hand blackboard contained numerous notes, pieces of intelligence and scribblings in coloured chalk. Above it all, in white letters, were the words THE STERLING RING.

Ellen's eyes were drawn to a single word, handwritten in red letters further down the board: *Jericho??* The recent addition of two question marks by an unknown hand underlined the uncertainty of the intelligence which she had obtained from the boy in St James's Park, where Nikita Sokolov had, according to the child, said that he would have to pass information to a person of that name. However, a search of the registry indexes matched nothing at all to that designation, and doubt among the men of A4 that the intelligence was reliable was becoming more vocal. Uncertainty had crept into her own thinking and she had to reassure herself on several occasions that she *had* heard the boy correctly. In fact, she had repeated the name Jericho back to him to ensure that she had understood properly. Of course, *he* could have been mistaken, or completely fabricating what he had heard; but the boy had correctly identified Harold Austin, and Mr Skardon had confirmed that an undercover operation *did* exist by the name of Sawdust. So, why should Jericho not be real, too?

Ellen glanced at the men around the room. Most were at their desks, smoking and typing up their surveillance logs. For the majority of them, Jericho was not an active line of enquiry.

'You bored, Miss Ingram?' one of them—John Potter—called over to her with a smirk. 'I could do with a coffee, if you don't mind.'

Ellen smiled. 'The refreshments room is just along the corridor, third door on the right. You'll find everything you need there.'

He snarled, rolled his eyes and moodily returned to stabbing his forefinger at the typewriter keys, whilst drawing on the pipe dangling from beneath his greying moustache.

She slowly cast her eyes across the photographs of the main players in this unfolding drama: Harold Austin; Flora Sterling; Nikita Sokolov. But, she reasoned, it couldn't be a case of intelligence passing—wittingly or otherwise—along a simple three-person chain, and then

215

out to Moscow. Nikita had known for a very long time that he was under MI5 surveillance; there was no way he would be the person responsible for getting the intelligence out of the country. Was it really so outlandish to think that the reason for Flora Sterling's taking regular convoluted routes around London was to dead-drop the intelligence to a person, codenamed Jericho? But then how did Jericho get it out of the country?

'Miss Brogren?' Ellen called, receiving a scornful over-the-shoulder glare. 'Might I have the keys to cabinet 42, please?'

Miss Brogren dutifully unlocked a drawer of her desk, removed a set of keys and strolled over to the run of filing cabinets under the windows.

Ellen matched her pace and they arrived at cabinet 42 at the same moment. Miss Brogren unlocked it, took a step back and watched, as Ellen pulled open the top drawer.

Trying to ignore the heavy scrutiny of the secretary, Ellen ran through the file dividers until she came to one marked *SURVEILLANCE LOGS*. She thumbed through the sub-dividers until she reached *FLORA STERLING*. Pulling out the file, she offered a wooden smile to Miss Brogren and headed to the open bookshelves at the side of the room, whence she removed a London Street Atlas. Behind her, she could hear the cabinet being hastily relocked.

Back at her desk, Ellen opened the file of surveillance logs, containing pages and pages of forms, labelled *B.2.A.*, which were typed descriptions of the reconnaissance conducted by the A4 section. The first was written by her colleague, George Caldwell, and was dated 7th March 1956.

Flora STERLING
Observation was taken up at Number 1 Cambridge Square at 5 p.m. and half an hour later STERLING came out and walked home.
Twice during the evening, the police were called by local residents to our men.
Observation withdrawn at 11 p.m.
G. Caldwell

Number one Cambridge Square was Harold Austin's residence. Flora had left his flat and gone home. Nothing more, apparently. Ellen turned to the next log. This one was longer, starting at Cambridge Square and tracing her back and forth across London in an obvious attempt to shake off any potential Watchers. On this occasion, she had succeeded, giving the Watcher, Geoffrey Partridge, the slip at Layton Place in Kew.

Ellen located Layton Place in the Street Atlas, noting that it was very close to Kew Gardens railway station, a likely escape route.

Taking a pencil from a handle-less mug which now served as her stationery receptacle, Ellen drew a wonky circle around Layton Place, then returned to the surveillance logs. The next three showed Flora going to the cinema alone, going shopping and meeting an unidentified female for lunch. The fifth log commenced at Cambridge Square and, once again, involved a complex route, which Ellen followed on the atlas. It screamed out to her as an obvious attempt not to be followed, whereas, in the previous three logs, Flora had taken a direct route to the cinema, shopping arcade and restaurant and then had gone straight home.

Ellen sat up with deepening interest. This log was in two parts. In the first part, the Watcher, Angela Jones had lost sight of Flora on Mortlake Road and consequently withdrawn her observation at 3.33pm. By chance, Flora had then been spotted at Kew Gardens railway station, where the Watcher had followed her all the way home. The Watcher's signature was scrawled at the bottom of the log: *John Potter*.

'Mr Potter,' Ellen called over. 'Still want that coffee?'

John Potter pulled the pipe from his mouth. 'Spitting feathers, here, love.'

Ellen smiled and carried the surveillance log over to his desk, placing it so as to bar the keys of his typewriter.

John Potter looked up uncertainly at her.

'I'll make you a coffee while you remember everything you can about when you first caught sight of Flora Sterling in this report.' She gave another exaggerated smile and headed to the refreshments room to make him a coffee. It seemed a fair exchange and would be the last waitress service that she would be providing him for a time to come. She made him his coffee perfunctorily, her mind occupied by that which she believed she was finding revealed by the surveillance logs.

Ellen returned to the general office and passed John the cup of coffee.

He held the log in the air and asked, 'Why the interest?'

'Just working on a possible line of enquiry,' Ellen replied.

'Not Jericho?' he sneered.

Ignoring the comment, Ellen said, 'So, what do you remember?'

217

'Well, it's all here, isn't it,' he said, handing her back the log. 'That's rather the point of them, Miss Ingram.' He took a sip of coffee, winced at the temperature and then returned to squinting at the piece of paper curled inside his typewriter.

'You said in your report that you spotted Flora Sterling approaching Kew Gardens railway station,' Ellen said, disregarding his attempt to dismiss her.

John Potter huffed and shot her a look of annoyance.

'From which direction was she walking? Only, you never stipulated that in the log.'

He remained silent and Ellen couldn't tell what he was thinking. Finally, he exhaled a long breath and then said, 'North Road.'

'Sure?'

'Very—she was coming up the steps to cross the bridge into the station.'

'Are you absolutely certain of the time you first saw her: 3.55 in the afternoon?'

'Yes,' he answered exasperatedly. 'Listen, love. I've been doing this job a *very* long time. Much longer than you, in fact. I know that I need to log times accurately and that's just what I did.'

'Do you think she saw you, or knew that she was being followed?'

'In my assessment, no,' John said.

'And she went directly home: no stopping at a shop or meeting a friend?' Ellen asked.

'Does it say so in there?' he said, nodding to the document in Ellen's hand.

She shook her head. 'Nothing else you can recall that didn't end up in your log?'

'No.'

'Thank you,' she replied, heading back to her desk. She located Mortlake Road on the atlas with ease, just a few streets from North Road, where John Potter had picked her up.

Studying the map carefully, Ellen couldn't fathom why the journey from Mortlake Road to North Road had taken twenty-two minutes; it appeared that it should take no more than five to ten minutes, depending on where it was on Mortlake Road that Angela Jones had lost sight of Flora. Unfortunately, Angela was off sick with a slipped disc in her back, so Ellen was unable to ask her.

She continued looking through the surveillance logs, finding a further three in the vicinity of Kew Gardens railway station. She

218

became increasingly convinced that the dead drop was somewhere in that geographical area. She stood up, about to run her theory past another of her colleagues, when Mr Skardon entered the office.

'Could I have everyone's attention, please,' he called across the office. Mr Skardon fiddled with one end of his moustache, as he waited for the cacophony of typing, chatting and paper-shuffling to diminish to near-silence.

'With the unfolding developments in the Middle East, pressure is being placed rather heavily upon this office to get results fast.' He sighed and glanced down at the ground. 'It seems that our delightful Miss Sterling has rumbled that she's being followed. As a consequence, anyone, who has conducted observations into Miss Sterling in the past month, is herewith prohibited from so doing until further notice and will be assigned to other priorities. I realise that this will place rather a stretch on the rest of the team, but we have little choice. Thank you.'

Ellen looked up to see a smug grin on John Potter's face. 'Jerich-oh! Cheerio.'

Chapter Twenty

6th November 1956, London

It was Ellen's day off from work. She needed to go shopping, she needed to get a haircut and she needed to catch up with the friends, whom she had been neglecting because of her work. Instead of doing any of those things, however, she was now walking amongst a glut of commuters, descending the stairs into North Road, Kew. She hadn't bothered making much effort with her appearance this morning; she had cursorily run a brush through her hair and pulled on the first dress that she came across in her wardrobe, which she wore under her teal-green, knee-length jacket.

She reached the bottom of the steps and allowed the crowd of people to disperse around her. From her raffia bag, she took out photostats of the surveillance reports into Flora Sterling, which she had covertly made at work, and a London Street Atlas. She had annotated the map with various locations extracted from the logs. Once Mr Skardon had issued the directive that everybody, who had monitored Flora Sterling in the past month, was barred from continuing in that capacity, Ellen had mooted her theory to one of her A4 colleagues, Paul Reynolds. He had taken one look at the atlas and dismissed her out of hand. 'Mortlake Road runs for nearly a mile!' he had derided. 'Of course, it could take twenty-two minutes! Christ, my missus would take double that with her gammy legs.'

Even though Flora Sterling did not have 'gammy legs', he still had a point, Ellen had been forced to concede. Mortlake Road *was* a very long one. So, last night on her way home from work, Ellen had called in to Angela Jones's house, thrusting the map under her nose on the doorstep and asking approximately where she had lost sight of Flora Sterling on that road during her surveillance. 'Somewhere on the approach to West Park Road,' Angela had remembered, pointing at a street that spurred off of Mortlake Road. 'In fact, I wondered if she'd gone to the train station, so I walked in that direction, but there was no sign of her. So, I withdrew observation and took the train back to Leconfield House. Luckily Mr Potter picked her up by chance.'

'Yes,' Ellen had agreed. 'But that was twenty-two minutes later. Are you sure about the time you lost her?'

Angela had nodded vehemently. 'Absolutely.'

The steps down from the bridge behind her led precisely to the elbow-joint where North Road met West Park Road. At the far end of West Park Road—directly in front of her—Ellen could see Mortlake Road. She looked at her wristwatch, scribbling down the exact current time on the bottom of one of the log photostats, then began to walk down the road. She closed her eyes briefly to try to recall Flora Sterling's gait and pace, matching it with her own. Not too slow and not too fast.

It took three minutes and twenty seconds to reach Mortlake Road, where Angela Jones had lost sight of her. What had Flora been doing, which could have taken the remaining nineteen minutes?

Ellen looked around her. The area was residential, comprised largely of smart semi-detached 1930s housing. Could one of these houses be the dead drop…where Jericho, responsible for getting the information out of the country, lived? How did he do that?

Spinning around, Ellen walked back on herself. This time, she walked slowly, taking in every house that she passed. They all looked so ordinary, the type of house owned by a respectable middle-class family who kept their windows washed and their front gardens tidy. Not one house was out of keeping; but then it wouldn't be, would it? she reasoned. If her suspicions were correct, then the owner and the house would need to blend in seamlessly. There was a good chance, therefore, that Jericho *was* middle-class, British and ordinary.

She passed a derelict site, where a pair of conjoined houses had once stood. Bombed during the war, she guessed. Now all that remained were two hillocks of shattered brick, glass and wood. A good potential site for a dead drop, she thought, craning her neck over the remains of the low front wall.

Ellen continued walking, making a mental note of anywhere that might be used for a dead drop: a plane tree with a small cavity, just at arm's length; a run of four garages, one open and filled with rubbish; another uncleared bomb site; several empty houses; a wheel-less caravan. Any of them would have been perfect.

She turned up the first of two roads which linked between West Park Road and Mortlake Road, studying the properties, as she walked. Then, she turned left onto Mortlake Road and back down Burlington Avenue towards West Park Road.

Half-way down the street, Ellen stopped in her tracks. Could this be it? she wondered, as her heart rate began to increase markedly.

Number thirteen Burlington Avenue had an aerial mast protruding from the chimney stack. Was this how Jericho got the information out of the country? Directly opposite was a derelict house, with a low brick wall and a hand-written wooden sign with *DANGER! DO NOT ENTER!* in red painted letters. The perfect place for a dead drop.

She didn't know what to do but knew that she couldn't just stand here, staring at the house and drawing attention to herself. She made some lame attempt at a mime of scanning across the run of houses, feigning enlightenment upon discovering the one for which she might apparently have been searching. Continuing with her performance, just in case she was being watched from inside number thirteen, Ellen walked up to the front door of number seventeen and pretended to press the doorbell. When nobody answered, she walked with a disappointed face back in the direction of West Park Road.

Once safely out of sight, she exhaled a long puff of air. She was certain that this could be the dead-drop location, opposite Jericho's house, but she wanted to check one last thing.

Walking quickly, Ellen returned to the junction of West Park Road and Mortlake Road, where Flora Sterling had given Angela Jones the slip. She wrote the precise time down on the copy of the map and began to walk at an average pace back towards Burlington Avenue. She stopped slightly short and out of sight of number thirteen, where she paused for a moment, before turning back on herself to head towards the railway station.

Ellen looked at her wristwatch when she reached the location where John Potter had picked up Flora's trail again: exactly twenty-two minutes.

The thin white stripes on the opposite wall, announcing the arrival of daylight through the slatted blinds, made Alexander think of a prison cell. If this was what prison was like, he thought, then it would be okay if ever his crimes were to catch up with him. He was in bed in a luxury Cairo hotel, with Nadia Ibrahim lying beside him. She was sleeping on her side with her back to him, her long black hair splayed out on the pillow.

He shifted and reached out to touch her. She stirred, rolled onto her back and opened her eyes.

'Good morning,' Alexander said.

She smiled, which he found a relief, given how much they had had to drink in the hotel bar the previous night. He had feared that she might wake up with a regretful groan. 'Morning. What time is it?'

He had no idea. He leant down to his pile of clothes beside the bed and picked up his wristwatch. 'Nine thirty-seven.'

Nadia gasped and sat bolt upright. 'I've…got to go,' she said, jumping out of bed and prancing about, picking up her clothes, which were scattered between the door and the bed.

'Come on, stay for a quick breakfast with me,' Alexander said, not quite ready for her to leave him. He had genuinely enjoyed her company but he had yet to even begin working on his primary objective: attempting to acquire the upcoming flight schedules for President Nasser's private plane. Nadia had been very adroit at keeping their alcohol-fuelled conversations away from the current political turmoil. Given that her country was currently under siege from France and Britain, it was almost certainly deliberate. He would have to do that which he had been unwilling to do last night: ask her directly.

Nadia sighed, pulling her hair so that it hung over her left shoulder, standing in her underwear and deliberating his question. 'Half an hour,' she said, pulling on her dress. 'Maybe in that time you might manage to tell me what exactly it is you want from me.'

Alexander swung his legs from the bed. To deny an ulterior motive would be to thwart his task, disrespect her and undermine her intelligence. 'Yes,' he conceded. 'I shall do that. Then, perhaps once this is all over, we could have dinner together.'

'Perhaps,' she answered expressionlessly.

Five minutes later, they were seated in the plush marble-floored restaurant at a table, chosen by Alexander for its isolation from the other dozen-or-so diners.

A waiter arrived and said something in Egyptian Arabic.

'What would you like?' Nadia translated.

'Coffee, please,' Alexander answered.

'And to eat..?' she said. 'I'm having *ful medammes*.'

'What's that, exactly?' Alexander questioned.

Nadia frowned. 'You grew up in Port Said and you don't know what ful medammes is?' She laughed, said something in Arabic that satisfied the waiter, and he left.

Alexander grinned and tapped his belly. 'Egyptian by birth, British by palette, I'm ashamed to admit.'

Nadia raised her eyebrows.

Alexander, wishing to change the subject, placed his hands on the table and laced his fingers together, pushing himself closer to her. In a quiet voice, he said, 'I really enjoyed last night with you and I'd like to see you again—'

'But,' Nadia interrupted.

'Not a *but*, more an *and*,' he corrected. '*And*, I wonder if you are able to assist me.'

Nadia gazed at him, saying nothing.

'It would be of great assistance if you were able to get access to the upcoming flight schedules...for Nasser's private plane.'

Nadia laughed and began to tap various parts of her body, as though she had lost her purse. 'Now, where *did* I put those... I'm sure I have them here somewhere...'

Alexander smiled. 'Your father is privy to the flight plans,' he clarified.

'You are right,' Nadia whispered. 'But you are forgetting several important things: one, the schedules change often and sometimes with little notice; two, this country is currently at war and Nasser is hardly likely to be taking pleasure flights; three, my father would not risk sharing them with anyone, least of all his daughter; and four, you assume that I would be willing to pass them to a British journalist without any idea of what he intended to do with them.'

'One is not a major problem, as far as I can see. Two, Nasser will be needing to fly more than ever during such a crucial time; morale boosting and such like. Three, I'm very sure you have ways of getting what you need from your father. Four, the schedules would be used to help achieve the outcome desired by you, your father and millions of others: a change in regime.'

Before she could reply, the waiter returned, carrying two plates, which he set down in front of them. He said something in Arabic, to which Nadia responded with a smile and the familiar words for 'thank you.'

The dish contained steaming beans in a reddish-brown liquid with a boiled egg split open in the centre, a chunk of bread and half a lemon set to the side of the plate.

'I hope your British palette enjoys it,' Nadia said, picking up her knife and fork.

'What is it, exactly?' he asked, taking his first mouthful.

'Fava beans, slow-cooked in an *idra* with oil and salt. It's a very popular dish in Egypt. I can't believe you have never tried it.'

'Tasty,' he acknowledged, dipping the bread in the oil, which had begun separating from the rest of the liquid.

Nadia said something, but Alexander didn't hear. He was staring at his plate, as an idea began to crystallise in his mind. 'Sorry,' he said, when he realised that he hadn't heard what she had said. 'Say that again.'

'I said that it will be almost impossible to get the flight schedules. You need to think of another way, I'm sorry.'

'What about his pilot?' Alexander mused, thinking about the vast sums of black money reserved for Operation Sawdust. 'Is he bribable?'

'If the money is right, you will find most people attached to the government here are bribable.'

Alexander smirked. 'Do you know his name?'

'He has several pilots on his staff, but Ahmed Mahmoud is probably your best bet. He is a weak-minded man who has a large family to support and a wife with a terminal illness.'

Ahmed Mahmoud sounded very much as though he would take a bribe in exchange for a couple of pieces of paper. Alexander now needed to get back to Beirut and inform GK that he had found both a potential avenue from which to obtain his flight schedules and, something that had just occurred to him whilst Nadia had been speaking, a method of sabotaging Nasser's plane. His goal had been achieved. He reached across the table and took Nadia's hand. 'Thank you.'

'Will I see you again?' she asked. '*Really*?'

'I very much hope so.'

Nadia ate more of her breakfast, then asked, 'Are you going to tell me who you really are, *Alexander Emmett*?'

Alexander sipped his coffee and stared at her, unsure of the direction of her question. He contemplated his answer but didn't need to give it, as the waiter returned with a serious look on his face. He spoke directly to Nadia in Arabic and, although Alexander could not understand a single word, he could tell from the tone that he wasn't politely asking if their ful medammes were to their liking.

Nadia dabbed her mouth with her napkin, thanked the waiter and stood from the table. 'There is an urgent message waiting for me,' she said.

Alexander followed her out of the restaurant and into reception, where they found a middle-aged man in a smart cream suit, nervously fiddling with his black beard.

'Mohamed… What is it?' Nadia demanded.

Mohamed leant over and whispered something in Nadia's ear. She gasped, raised her hands to her mouth and began to sob.

Alexander was suddenly unsure of his place and so withheld comforting her, despite his desire to put an arm around her shoulder. Mohamed and the waiter looked on with equal uncertainty.

Finally, Nadia turned to Alexander and, in a broken sobbing voice, managed to say, 'My brother was killed this morning in Port Said… Killed by his own people…'

'I'm so sorry,' he offered quietly.

Nadia drew in a quick breath and wiped her eyes. 'I must go.' She moved towards the hotel entrance.

'What about your things?' Alexander called after her.

She paused, turned and said, 'Give them to me when we meet next time.'

Alexander said goodbye, as he watched her disappear through the revolving doors.

It was time for him to pack up and get back to Beirut.

'Miss Ingram?' Mr Skardon said with surprise, looking up from his typewriter at the knock on his open door.

'Mr Skardon,' Ellen greeted, fearing how her own private investigations would be received.

'Forgotten that it's your day-off, today?'

'No, sir,' she said with a smile. 'May I sit down, please?'

'By all means,' Mr Skardon said. 'Push the door shut. It rather sounds as though a confession, resignation or grievance is forthcoming.'

Ellen closed the door and sat opposite him.

'Not John Potter again, is it? Getting all handsy, was he?' Mr Skardon enquired.

'No,' Ellen replied. 'I think the whack I gave him last time probably did the trick once and for all.'

'Ah, good show.' Mr Skardon slouched back in his chair and placed his hands in his lap. 'So, what is it I can help you with, then?'

On the tube ride out of Kew Gardens into Central London, she had rehearsed what she was going to say over and over again, but, now that she was sitting in front of him, her prepared speech evaded her. 'I think I know where Jericho lives,' she said, breaking the one rule that she had set herself; that of not mentioning the word Jericho.

'Ah,' Mr Skardon said. 'And where might that be?'

Ellen pulled the photostats of the London Street Atlas from her raffia bag, along with her written notes from the surveillance logs, and set about explaining to him her theory and its provenance.

To his credit, Mr Skardon listened intently, without interruption and deferring judgement but rather making his own notes, as she relayed every detail of her jaunt this morning and her suspicions about number thirteen Burlington Avenue.

Ending her explanation, she sat up straight, braced for his reaction.

Mr Skardon nodded. 'A perfectly reasonable theory, Miss Ingram.'

'But…?' Ellen said.

'No buts, Miss Ingram. In fact, I've not been long out of a meeting which proves Jericho's existence.'

'Really?' Ellen said.

Mr Skardon nodded and fiddled with the tip of his moustache. 'Some pretty high-grade intelligence has been intercepted from someone operating under the cryptonym Jericho. Obviously, I'm not at liberty to divulge the content but, suffice it to say, it pertains to the situation in the Middle East, which would fit perfectly with Jericho's being the terminus of the Sterling Ring.'

'Now what?' Ellen asked.

'I shall immediately apply for a telephone check, a Home Office Warrant on post going to the address, and, as soon as I get the occupiers' names from a check of the current voters' lists, observations on the property will begin. Brilliant work, Miss Ingram. Sterling, in fact, so to speak. Well done.'

Ellen could feel the warm rise of blood in her flushed cheeks: Mr Skardon had seldom been so effusive.

He picked up his telephone, pressed a button, then said, 'Miss Brogren, I'd like a check in the voters' lists…immediately, please. Yes. Number thirteen Burlington Avenue, Kew. Yes. Thank you.' He placed the receiver down and smiled. 'As soon as that's back, I'll apply for an H.O.W. and we'll get cracking on this Jericho fellow.'

Flora Sterling allowed the train carriage to empty entirely before she even bothered to stand up. It terminated here, at Charing Cross, and there were more than twenty minutes before it headed back out into Kent, where she had spent the night in the safehouse in Dartford. She had deliberately seated herself in the last seat of the last carriage, to prevent any Watchers from waiting behind her.

227

She sighed, then cautiously made her way over to the door and peered out at the empty platform. She climbed down from the carriage, as certain as she could be that she was the last to disembark the train. She walked steadily beside the line of carriages, scrutinising each, as she passed. It was unlikely that anyone had waited in the station overnight for her to return, and highly unlikely that anyone had followed her out of Kent and into London this morning, but, given that the film cartridge was once again tucked inside her bra, she would need to take a longwinded route to the dead drop, just to be sure.

Flora exited the railway station and hailed a taxi.

'Where to, love?' the driver asked, directing his question to the rear-view mirror.

Flora sighed. 'Oh, er… Maybe Bond Street?'

'Well, maybe or definitely?' he retorted. 'I ain't getting all the way over to Bond Street for you to turn around and change your mind.'

'Definitely Bond Street,' she replied curtly. 'I need a new hat.'

'Don't we all, love. Don't we all.'

Ellen couldn't concentrate. She was sitting at her desk in the general office on the third floor of Leconfield House, attempting to type up a report. She had been so sure of her theory, but, now that most of the department were deployed in uncovering Jericho's identity, doubt began to skulk into her mind. What if she were wrong? Right now, a whole group was assembling, readying to begin surveillance on thirteen Burlington Avenue: a van with shaded windows and a photography team were already on their way to the address; the radio inside the house was being monitored; and negotiations were occurring with a letting agent to take over number nineteen.

'Damn,' Ellen cursed, making her third mistake in the first sentence of her report. She wound the paper through the typewriter, crushed it into a ball and threw it into the bin below her desk.

The office door swung open and Ellen shot a look across. John Potter entered with a knowing grin on his face. He pulled his pipe from his mouth and said, 'You look worried, Miss Ingram. Almost like you might've set half of MI5 running around on this wild goose chase of yours.'

She went to defend herself, to repeat the evidence that Mr Skardon had made her announce to the whole office, when he had stated that the direction of the investigation would be shifting to a new focus on Jericho and number thirteen Burlington Avenue, but what was the point? Time alone would tell if she were right and nothing that she could say at this precise moment would convince John Potter and others like him that there might just be something to her theory.

The door opened again and Mr Skardon entered the room, holding aloft a piece of paper. He cleared his throat, about to ask for quiet, but the fifteen members of staff present had already fallen silent upon seeing his entrance.

'*William Gilmour* is the registered occupier of thirteen Burlington Avenue,' he relayed. 'Does that name mean anything to anyone here?'

His question was met with a stony silence.

'He's got no criminal record, but I've put in a Registry Action Slip to see what we can find on him,' Mr Skardon said, glancing in Ellen's direction expressionlessly.

Ellen squirmed inside. Having no criminal record was not conclusive, but when her theory was judged to be so flimsy in the first place, it served only to intensify the doubt now weighing heavily on the room.

'I've put in for a Home Office Warrant on his post and a telephone check is going through at this very moment,' Mr Skardon continued. 'If Miss Ingram *is* correct, then we could very soon be netting ourselves the missing link in the Sterling Ring of treachery, stretching from the heart of our government out to the USSR. It *will* be broken.'

'Isn't it time Harold Austin is told who his fancy-piece really is and what she's been up to? Stop these state secrets getting anywhere near Burlington Avenue in the first place?' Frank Tilsbury asked.

Mr Skardon scowled. 'Definitely not, no. We need Miss Sterling to keep doing what she's doing so we can pull the whole ruddy network down in one go… Sweep the country clean.'

'High hopes, Mr Skardon,' John Potter called, eyeing Ellen as he spoke. 'Very high hopes.'

'Yes,' he agreed, turning and leaving the office.

Ellen drew in a long breath, inserted a fresh piece of paper into her typewriter and tried again with her report.

Flora's calf muscles were biting. She had spent more than two hours criss-crossing London in taxis, buses, tubes and an exceptional amount on foot. She had just stepped off the tube at Kew Gardens and was making her way across the bridge and down the steps into North Road. A dozen-or-so people alighted from the tube at the same time as she had, but by the time she had reached the bottom of the steps, over half

229

of them had dispersed. She did something next that she knew was generally unadvisable: she looked over her shoulder, taking stock of the five people walking behind her. She didn't recognise any of them and none of them paid her any attention, but that meant nothing; that was exactly what the Watchers were trained to do.

Flora spotted a black Austin FX3 taxi, sitting idle beside the road. She approached it and tapped on the passenger window. The driver looked up from his newspaper, leant across and wound down the window.

'Hello,' Flora greeted pleasantly. 'Could you tell me where Broomfield Road is, please?'

'Yeah,' the driver said. 'You've gone and come out of the wrong exit from the station. It's basically over on the other side. If you go back through the station, then turn up Royal Parade, it's diagonally opposite.'

'Oh, right. Thank you very much,' Flora said, stepping back from the car to affect searching for something in her handbag. With a subtle glance around her, she could see that the five train passengers, who had alighted behind her, had all now departed. In fact, there was nobody but she and the taxi driver anywhere in the immediate vicinity. Her delaying tactic had worked.

As she walked away from the station, she concluded firmly that there was no way that she had been followed here.

The stillness in the air was broken when the taxi driver yelled across the street, 'You're going the wrong way, Miss!'

Flora turned and waved dismissively, continuing along West Park Road to the junction of Burlington Avenue. She walked briskly at first, opening her jacket as she went. Once she had turned into Burlington Avenue, her pace slowed. Moments later, with a deft movement of her right hand, she quickly pulled the film cartridge from her brassiere and released it at the dead drop without a moment's pause or faltering. To any casual observer, the action was so swiftly executed that it would have gone completely unnoticed.

Her heart was rising in her chest and her breathing was short, as she continued walking down Burlington Avenue, picking up her stride along the way.

To get herself away from the dead drop as quickly as possible, Flora walked a loop back to Kew Gardens station, where she took the first tube train back into Central London.

Forty-five minutes later, she pressed the entry buzzer to Harold Austin's Cambridge Square flat.

'What?' he barked.

'It's me,' she purred.

There was a pause. Something was wrong. He always admitted her. And straight away. Often the sounding of the entry buzzer would be accompanied with some sleazy greeting or other. 'Harold, darling, are you there?' Had his wife returned home? Did he suspect her? She could hear his breathing. Yet, he wasn't responding. 'Darling…?'

The door lock released with a loud buzz, and Flora stepped inside the entrance hall, perplexed by his lack of greeting her arrival. The front door clunked shut behind her and Flora stood still, wondering if she might be about to walk into a trap. Craning her neck, she gazed up the stairs but could see and hear nothing at all. She turned back towards the front door and placed her hand on the latch, about to flee. Then she assessed the situation and told herself that she was being stupid. If she were walking into a trap, then Harold would have been behaving normally to coax her in. Something was wrong, but she was prepared to take a risk and assume that she had not been unmasked.

Climbing the stairs with a false confidence, she found Harold waiting at the flat door, his shirt and tie dishevelled and a heavy frown on his face.

'Took your time getting up here,' he grunted.

She pouted, pumped her chest forwards and placed a lingering but delicate kiss on his repulsive lips. As she did so, she gazed over his shoulder into the flat. Nothing looked amiss or out of the ordinary.

'What's the matter, darling?' she asked quietly.

Harold puffed out an exasperated breath. 'I'll tell you inside,' he mumbled, standing to one side to allow her in.

Whatever was wrong had nothing to do with her, Flora realised, as Harold closed the front door. She followed him into his lounge, where a raft of paperwork was scattered on the coffee table alongside a glass of whiskey. The problem was work.

Harold slumped into his chair with another sigh and took a large gulp of drink.

Flora flung her coat onto a chair and stood behind Harold, gently massaging his shoulders. 'What is it?' she asked, feeling the tenseness retreating under the pressure of her thumbs.

'It's the PM,' he said in a thin voice which Flora could barely hear.

'What about him? He's alright, isn't he?' Flora said with syrupy concern.

'I'm sure some would attest to the contrary; but, yes, he's alright.'

'Then, what is it?' Flora asked, engaging her child-like, imbecilic tone of voice, which often prompted Harold to over-divulge inadvertently.

Another sigh, mixed with a groan of pleasure, then his head sank forward and he muttered something unintelligible.

'Pardon, darling?'

'He's about to call a cease-fire in the Suez,' he repeated.

'A cease-fire?' Flora parroted. 'Really?'

'Yes.'

'But why?' Flora said, consciously keeping her voice neutral, since Harold had not yet disclosed his own opinion on this surprising new development.

'The Americans,' he answered flatly.

'What about the Americans?' she asked.

'They've threatened Eden with devaluing the pound, if he doesn't pull out of Egypt and leave Nasser to his own malevolent devices.'

'How can they do that?' she asked, sounding naïvely innocent, bordering on stupid.

Harold sighed, taking his time to answer. 'By selling their sterling bond holdings. And, given that we're at crisis point with our oil reserves, we need a loan from the International Monetary Fund, which the Americans have refused to grant without a cease-fire. They've also gone scurrying off to the United Nations, requesting their intervention.'

'Oh,' Flora replied, her thoughts running with the implications of this news. Should she try to get a message to Nikita, ahead of any official announcement, or let him find out when the rest of the world would be told?

Alexander entered Immeuble Tabet and wearily climbed the stairs to his apartment, eager to get home, following two days of heavy travel from Cairo back to Beirut via Port Said. He wanted to pour himself a pink gin and relax for what was left of the evening but, really, he would have to make a start on his report into that which he had witnessed this morning at the Suez Canal. The British and French had been relentless in their naval bombardment of the area, which had been followed immediately by the Royal Marines' landing in amphibious vehicles at

Port Said. Centurion tanks from the Royal Tank Regiment had landed, assisted by men from 45 Commandoes, who had been helicoptered in from *HMS Ocean* and *HMS Theseus*. In a surprise twist, and despite unquestionably winning the battle, the British prime minister had ordered a complete cease-fire. Port Said, when Alexander had arrived there this morning, was ominously devoid of gunfire, yet puzzled British and French troops continued to patrol the smouldering city, in seeming bewilderment at London's directive. They had been just days, possibly even hours away from regaining complete control of the Suez Canal.

With a satisfied exhalation, Alexander entered his apartment and closed the door. He set his small suitcase down and entered the sitting room. Opening the shutters and windows, the stifled air became instantly substituted for the noise of the humming city.

It felt good to be back, he thought, moving to the kitchen and pouring himself a large pink gin. Once he had immediately refilled the glass, he returned to the sitting room and sat down at his Imperial Model T typewriter. As he did so, he noticed a brown envelope tucked underneath the typewriter, which had not been there when he had left for Cairo. He carefully removed it. It was thin and lightweight, and on the front was written *Almost impossible*.

Alexander tore the end of the envelope and withdrew three stapled sheets of paper which he identified immediately as being President Nasser's schedule for the coming ten days. Nadia Ibrahim had, for whatever reason, changed her mind. Perhaps he had beguiled her with his charms, or perhaps it had been precipitated by her brother's sudden death.

With a self-satisfied smile, he read through the listed activities for each day, which stated the president's entourage and mode of transport.

Alexander scrutinised the itinerary. In two days' time, President Nasser was due to fly in his Ilyushin Il-14, piloted by Ahmed Mahmoud, from Cairo to Port Said in order to *assess damage and tour local hospitals*. It would be the perfect opportunity. He needed to pass this information and his idea about how to sabotage the aircraft to GK without delay.

Sinking the pink gin in one, Alexander found a new surge of energy. Placing the itinerary back into the envelope, he hurried from his apartment to the one place where GK was most likely to be: St George's Hotel.

233

There was a subtle change to the atmosphere, which Alexander immediately noticed, as he strolled out onto the terrace of St George's Hotel with another pink gin. It was a difference that only someone who had been coming here regularly would have picked up on. It was somewhat busier than usual, but today, the suited diplomats were engaged in muted high-energy conversations. Crucially, these discussions were taking place across the usual political and geographical divides. A top-level Yemeni diplomat was conversing with his US counterpart. A bizarre conversation between French, Israeli, Syrian and Egyptian diplomats, taking place at the far side of the terrace most intrigued Alexander. What characterised each of the men was a look of general bafflement.

'This is disgusting,' a familiar voice said behind him. Alexander turned to see Alfie Archer, in a cream shirt and white trousers, holding up a glass of wine and sneering. 'Egyptian Bordeaux,' he said. 'One to be avoided.'

'Good to see you, old chap,' Alexander said, shaking his hand. 'Keeping well?'

'Trying to,' Alfie replied.

'Look at that,' Alexander said, nodding his head towards the diplomats across the other side of the terrace.

'Strange times, indeed,' Alfie observed. 'I rather think Eden's announcement has caught everyone off guard. Apparently, even the cabinet had no idea that he was going to issue a cease-fire. Now everyone's wondering what the hell is going to happen next.'

Alexander lowered his voice. 'What *is* happening? With Sawdust, I mean.'

'Oh, Sawdust is still very much happening in the background. More so, in fact, now that the heavy-handed military endeavours might have failed.'

'I need to see GK,' Alexander said. 'Urgently.'

'You don't need to go too far; he's in the bar, chatting up some leggy Cypriot,' Alfie revealed.

'Thanks,' Alexander responded, making his way inside the hotel. He spotted GK, resting his hands on the bar, as he watched a tall thin brunette sashay away from him.

'GK,' Alexander said.

Without turning to see who was behind him, GK continued to stare at the departing woman, wistfully saying, '*Married* or some such excuse.'

With unnecessary drama, Alexander placed the brown envelope down on the bar in front of GK.

'And this is?' he enquired, finally turning to face Alexander.

'Nasser's flight schedules for the next ten days,' he disclosed.

GK nodded but said nothing.

'*And*...I've got a method for you,' he began, thinking back to his breakfast of ful medammes. 'It's simple, really: pour water into the two oil tanks prior to take off. At some point during the flight the water will reach boiling point and turn to steam, expanding and building so much pressure it will blow the caps off the oil tanks. With the caps gone the slipstream will suck the oil out of the tanks, aided by the steam furiously pushing up from below. Soon after, the engine will seize up solid. The sudden stoppage will tear it apart, causing major damage to the airplane, or even a fire. One such calamity the crew might handle, but two? Even if by chance what's left of the plane is spotted in the open desert, there'll be no survivors.'

GK grinned. 'Perfect. Absolutely perfect. Good work.'

Alexander smiled in return. 'Thank you.'

GK slid the envelope across the mahogany bar back to Alexander. 'Let me know what you need in terms of manpower and resources, although it sounds as though all you require is a cup and good old-fashioned water.' He laughed. 'Let me get you a drink.'

'What do you mean manpower and resources...?' Alexander questioned. 'You want *me* to sabotage the plane?'

GK looked stupefied. 'Of course. Who did you think was going to do it?'

Alexander shrugged.

'Not going to be a problem, is it?'

'No... No, not at all,' Alexander answered with a smile which he hoped belied the severe inner conflict dominating and ravaging his thoughts. He needed to get back to his flat and get a message out to SU2FG.

Chapter Twenty-One

Cheddar and peanut butter; that was the flavour of scone which Morton was currently trying to figure out whether he liked or not. He was sitting in his usual spot in Granny's Scones with his brother-in-law, Guy Disney, eyeing him like a hawk from the front counter. Morton gave him the thumbs-up, still not sure whether it was a hideous flavour or strangely pleasant. Weird: that was his general assessment, as it had been with most of the concoctions dreamed up by Guy and Jeremy. Guy grinned and reciprocated with a double thumbs-up.

Morton's laptop was open and he was mid-way through writing up the Duggan Case, which, he had decided yesterday, could now be concluded. He had fulfilled Clarissa Duggan's brief and presumably, once she had read his report, she would be passing a cheque for £89,692.92 to Christopher Emmett. Quite how she was going to explain herself and how she had fraudulently obtained his father's money, Morton was entirely at a loss; but that wasn't his problem to worry about.

He sipped his latte and thought excitedly about getting this report into the post later today and then being able to move on to finding out more about his grandfather's situation, which both horrified and thrilled him in equal measure.

He took another bite of the scone with a slight grimace, then continued to type the report. There were still gaps in the puzzle, which he didn't like, but they were only gaps that existed for him because he knew the context of the wider picture. Operation Sawdust and Alexander's possible involvement in it was irrelevant to the job which he had been tasked to do by Clarissa.

He typed in a summary of Alexander Emmett's marriage to Ellen Ingram, then inserted a copy of the original certificate as an appendix at the back of the report. As he did so, he noticed something. Ellen's occupation had been listed as a *Civil Servant, Leconfield House*. At the time of discovery that place had meant nothing to him, but now it rang a bell. He was sure that he had come across it in his research over the past few days. But where? He could not recall.

Opening up a web browser, he ran a Google search for Leconfield House. According to Wikipedia, it was a building in Mayfair, London, used as the headquarters of MI5 from 1945 to 1976.

Morton mentally kicked himself for such an obvious and revealing oversight.

He looked at the marriage certificate again, impressed. Ellen clearly wouldn't have been able to state her actual involvement with MI5 but, by saying that she was a civil servant working at Leconfield House, she had given a subtle though clear hint to future historians that her occupation had been significant. Even her son, Christopher, believed that his mother had been 'just an office girl'. But what did she do at Leconfield House? Did her job have something to do with her death?

Morton's inquisitiveness got the better of him and, with slight reluctance, he clicked the small red cross at the top of his concluding report for Clarissa Duggan and closed the document. Even though Ellen's employment was irrelevant to the Duggan Case, he simply couldn't help himself; he needed to investigate further.

He switched his focus to running a series of internet searches for Ellen Ingram with connections to MI5 or Leconfield House in the 1950s.

After a good while of searching, he had found nothing relevant, which wasn't overly surprising. Ellen's role in the secret services appeared to have been as veiled and mysterious as that of her husband.

Morton finished his latte and took the final bite of the odd-tasting scone, then pulled up the website for the National Archives. Clicking *search our records*, he entered Ellen Ingram's name.

Fifty results.

Morton scrolled down the first suggestions.

Order of removal of Ellen Ingram. Easter 1779. Lancashire County Quarter Sessions. Nope.

Probate of will (dated 22 Mar 1867) of Elizabeth Frederica Crofts. Nope.

Ingram v Brauche. Court of Chancery 1386-1558. Nope.

Ashton in Makerfield. Order of filiation and maintenance of Ellen, bastard child of James Prescott. 1781. Nope.

The Security Service: Personnel Files (PF Series). Communists and suspected Communists, including Russian and Communist Sympathisers. November 1956. Yes! Morton thought.

He clicked the hyperlink and felt pleased beyond measure that the record was available to download for the sum of £3.50 and did not necessitate another visit to the National Archives. Bargain.

'See… I flamin' knew you'd enjoy it!' Guy called over in his heavy Australian accent.

'Pardon?' Morton questioned.

'Your face: look at it! *That* is what this shop is all about,' Guy said smugly. 'Pure, unadulterated culinary joy.'

Morton grinned, unable to break the news to his brother-in-law that actually the joy on his face was caused by the PDF file currently downloading onto his laptop and not by the peanut butter and cheddar scone.

'Do you want another?' Guy asked. 'I've got plenty.'

'As lovely as it was… I'm stuffed,' Morton answered, patting his growing belly as proof. 'I've just about got time for another latte, though. Thanks.'

'Coming right up,' Guy said, scurrying over to the elaborate coffee machine behind the counter.

Morton watched absent-mindedly, as Guy attacked the coffee machine like a professional barista, pressing buttons, wiping protruding pipes, banging grout-containers and attempting to create some kind of frothed-milk work of art on the top of his drink. When Morton's attention snapped back to his laptop, he saw that the file had finished downloading. He smiled, as he scrolled to the first page. It was a short, typed, un-headed letter.

B.5.

With reference to my telephone conversation this morning, I should be grateful if you could let me have the Voters' list for 13 Burlington Avenue, Kew, Richmond.

J. Skardon
A4
6.11.56

As far as Morton could tell, the letter was inconsequential to his interests. He moved down to the second page, just as Guy arrived carrying his latte.

'Ta-da!' he said enthusiastically.

'An onion?' Morton queried, angling his face, as he stared at the milky design on top of the coffee.

'No, it's not a bloody onion,' Guy countered. 'Look, it's a *heart*.'

'Oh, I see,' Morton said, not really seeing. It looked like an onion. 'Thank you very much.'

Guy smiled weakly and drifted back to the counter.

Morton dipped his finger in the froth of his drink, cutting a small indentation in the top of the onion. 'There, *now* it's a heart.' He turned his attention back to the PDF, eager to see how Ellen Ingram might appear in it. The second page was another typed document.

13 Burlington Avenue, Kew, Richmond

According to the current voters' list the following person is residing at the above address:-
William GILMOUR
The following particulars respecting William GILMOUR *were obtained from the Richmond Food Office:-*
William GILMOUR
Born 18.7.1928
Moved to his present address on 19.4.1952

Morton looked at the name William Gilmour. It was familiar, but he couldn't place how or why. Had he been one of the witnesses to Alexander and Ellen's marriage, perhaps? Or someone named in Rory Cormac's book? Or someone who had cropped up in his research at the National Archives?

He scrolled to the third page.

TOP SECRET

6th November 1956

Dear Colonel Allan,
I am now applying for an emanating H.O.W. on William GILMOUR *or Any Name of 13 Burlington Avenue, Kew, Richmond. Individuals at this address are strongly suspected of espionage and we should like to have copies of all correspondence going there.*
Yours sincerely
W. J. Skardon
A4

Colonel M.P. Allan, M.B.E.
G.P.O

The letter contained so many acronyms and cryptic descriptions that Morton failed to make much sense of the page. He turned to Google for help and found that H.O.W. stood for Home Office Warrant and that G.P.O. meant General Post Office. Morton's deciphering of the document was that J. Skardon—from an obscure section in MI5, called A4—had applied for William Gilmour's post to be intercepted because of possible espionage. Still no relevance at all to the Duggan Case and still no sign of Ellen Ingram. Morton pushed on to the next page.

I attach herewith for signature, if approved, an application for a telephone check on Richmond 4758 which is installed at 13 Burlington Avenue, Kew, Richmond. The subscriber to this number is William GILMOUR.
We do not know whether there are any other residents at this address apart from the person named above, but it is hoped that a telephone check will give us information regarding the present activities and contacts of the occupants.
W. J. Skardon
A4

Poor William Gilmour, Morton thought. His post was being intercepted, his phone was being tapped and, as he saw when he moved on to the next page in the document, he was also under twenty-four-hour surveillance.

A4. Joseph Tandy
William GILMOUR
6.11.56

Flora STERLING observed depositing an object in the front garden of the empty property directly opposite 13 Burlington Avenue at 5.40 p.m.
GILMOUR left his house at 5.48 p.m. and was seen sitting on the wall of the property opposite his house. Observed retrieving an object from behind the garden wall. 5.51 p.m. he returned to his house.
Nothing further was seen of him during the evening or overnight.

Morton picked up his latte and sipped away the bottom of the onion-heart. The next two pages in the document had, frustratingly, been entirely redacted and replaced with the now-familiar National Archives insert THE ORIGINAL DOCUMENT RETAINED UNDER SECTION 3(4) OF THE PUBLIC RECORDS ACT 1958. What it could contain, which might

240

still have held currency in 2019, baffled Morton, as he moved to the next page. At last, he saw Ellen Ingram's name.

A4. Ellen Ingram
William GILMOUR
7.11.56

Observation was taken up at 13 Burlington Avenue at 6.30 a.m. GILMOUR left at 12.25 p.m. and went shopping in Richmond and was home by 12.50 p.m. Nothing further was seen of him up to 11 p.m. when observation was withdrawn.

Morton paused his reading of the file and returned to the internet, running a search for *MI5 A4* to try to understand the precise nature of Ellen's work there. The first few results on Google agreed that the A4 section of MI5 was physical surveillance teams, or Watchers, as they had been known. Between 1953 and 1961, the section had been headed up by William James Skardon.

Morton gaped at the screen, deep in thought. Prior to their marriage, Ellen had worked for MI5 and Alexander had worked for MI6. Ellen had committed suicide in 1957 and Alexander had fled the country. Sixteen years later, Alexander had returned to London under an assumed identity and then also committed suicide in April of this year. *Dubious* was a grossly understated description, Morton thought, not at all convinced by the official verdicts into the couple's deaths. Despite his misgivings, there was nothing whatsoever to link Ellen's role in A4 to anything that Alexander had got up to as part of Operation Sawdust. She was simply undertaking surveillance into this guy, William Gilmour, whose name continued to bug Morton.

The next pages in the file contained further observation logs.

A4. Ellen Ingram
William GILMOUR
8.11.56

Observation was taken up at 13 Burlington Avenue at 4.45pm. GILMOUR observed leaving house and walking thirty-five minutes to the Ritz Cinema on Sheen Road, Richmond. He went in at 5.20 p.m. and was out again at 8.40 p.m. He was alone and so far as could be seen, made no contacts. He came out and walked to Richmond, where he was observed purchasing a copy of the Daily Worker. He walked home and reached 13 Burlington Avenue by 9.15 p.m. No further sightings until 11 p.m. when observation was withdrawn.

Morton ran a search to confirm his belief that the *Daily Worker* was a British Communist Party publication and found that indeed it was. Given the quantity of manpower and resources thrown into surveillance, Gilmour was obviously suspected of a much deeper involvement than a casual interest in communism.

Finishing his drink, Morton looked at the time: he only had another few minutes left before he would need to head back home. Juliette would be collecting Grace from nursery right about now, he thought. Despite not seeming to be relevant, the file continued to intrigue him, and he made a mental note to send it on to Christopher, once the dust had settled on the case. It would certainly bring him a fresh perspective on his mother.

Morton scrolled to the next page in the file, which was a log of intercepted post for 13 Burlington Avenue.

CONFIDENTIAL

The undermentioned packets have been intercepted to-day. It was not considered necessary to photograph them.

Name and address: *William Gilmour*
Origin: *S.W.1*
Date: *7th November '56.*
Short summary of contents: *Brochure from Royal Institute of International Affairs*

Name and address: *William Gilmour*
Origin: *Liverpool*
Date: *8th November '56.*
Short summary of contents: *Littlewoods Pool Coupon*

A page, entitled REGISTRY ACTION SLIP, came next, which Morton read with interest.

REGISTRY. *Please look-up the name(s) marked below and return with further information.*

An innocuous enough employment history, when viewed in isolation, Morton thought, but taking into account all the documents which had preceded it, offered a rather more ominous interpretation.

From the table, his mobile phone pinged with the arrival of a text message. It was from Juliette: *Home xx.* He took that single innocent-sounding word and decoded it as *You need to get home now. It's your turn to make the dinner and put Grace to bed. I'm pregnant and tired. xx.*

Morton closed his laptop and placed it with all the loose paperwork into his bag.

'Thanks, Guy,' he said, on his way out.

'See ya,' he replied. 'We won't be seeing you tomorrow, will we? Good luck!'

Morton gazed at him blankly.

'The scan!' Guy reminded him.

'Oh, yes,' Morton said, having clean forgotten about it, once again. 'We'll let you know.'

He stepped from the shop, surprised to discover that darkness had almost fallen. A cold greyness was draped over the town and a fine drizzle was blowing down the High Street, obliging Morton to zip up his jacket and to hurry home as quickly as possible.

Ten minutes later, he arrived at his house, gratefully closing the front door behind him. He entered the kitchen, finding Juliette picking labels from some new crockery and loading them into the dishwasher, whilst Grace was sitting in the middle of the floor, naked on her potty and holding a ukulele.

'Hi,' he greeted, kissing them both.

'Daddy,' Grace said. 'I sing.'

'You're going to sing? Go on, then,' he encouraged.

Grace smiled and began to strum the strings and sing something bearing a possible, passing resemblance to *Twinkle Twinkle Little Star*.

Morton clapped enthusiastically. 'Take a bow.'

Grace bent forwards over the ukulele, and giggled.

'Naked ukulele playing?' Morton said to Juliette. 'She must get that from you.'

Juliette smirked. 'Good day? Nice scones?'

'Peanut butter and cheddar,' he answered.

Juliette turned up her nose. 'Case closed?'

Morton took a breath and she rolled her eyes. 'Sort of. Almost.' Over the din of Grace's next song, he explained his recent discovery about Ellen's working for MI5.

'But if it's nothing to do with what you were asked to do, then why are you carrying on with it?' Juliette asked, closing the dishwasher with a long exhalation.

Morton shrugged.

'Because you're nosy; that's why,' Juliette said, answering her own question.

He nodded with agreement. 'But, as someone not generally interested in history and genealogy, doesn't it intrigue *you*?'

'Yeah,' she conceded. 'But you're essentially working on your own interest...for free.'

'To be honest, once I've finished reading through this document, I'm done. I'll get the report finished and move on to my grandad's situation. Right, go and sit down and I'll get the dinner on,' Morton suggested. 'What do you want to eat, Grace?'

'Carrots,' she replied, then started singing a song with the word *carrots* repeated on an endless loop.

Juliette laughed and took herself off to the lounge.

'First things first: wine.' He joined in with Grace's carrot song to mask the sound of his uncorking a bottle of red. 'Carrots, carrots, carrots,' he chanted as the liquid passed from bottle to glass.

'Wine!' Grace shouted, when she saw what was in his hand.

'Morton!' Juliette chided from the lounge.

'What?'

'You know what,' she replied.

'Wine!' Grace repeated.

Morton quickly managed to sneak a little, out of view, before secreting it behind a packet of cereal. 'Blackcurrant,' he said to Grace.

'No. Wine,' she corrected, embarking on a new song involving that single accusatory word.

Morton rolled his eyes and tried to open the fridge, but it was yanked back closed by a newly installed child-lock, which took him a good few seconds to figure out how to open. 'Who put the child-locks on the cupboards?' he called, moving his way around the kitchen, tugging on each cupboard door.

'Me,' Juliette answered. 'Who do you think?'

'Thanks,' he muttered. 'I'm already looking forward to the day we can take them off.'

Juliette laughed. 'Well, with Baby Farrier not even arriving until February, that will be a long while off, yet.'

Morton groaned. 'Can't believe we'll find out what it is, tomorrow,' he said, hoping for some recognition or praise for having remembered the date.

'Did you just get a calendar alert on your mobile, or something?'

'Ha…ha.'

Grace stood up from the potty and then tipped the contents onto the floor. 'Finished,' she declared.

Morton sighed and drank some wine, unhidden this time. It was going to be a very long evening.

The household was asleep. Morton was sitting in his study on the top floor of the house, listening to the creaks and moans that the old house articulated from time to time. Directly under his desk lamp was a glass of red wine, his fourth of the evening. He savoured the notes of grape and oak, as he clicked to read the email from Lazarus, which he had discovered a few moments ago when he had first sat down to finish reading the Security Personnel files downloaded from the National Archives website.

Dear Morton

Thanks for your email.

Yes, my team had worked out the identity of LZ205, but thank you for confirming. I realise this can't have been easy for you.

245

Regarding what happens next, I have passed our report to the Reno police who will inform the family about the progress of the case. Often what happens is that the police will release a statement to say that the identity of the perpetrator is now known and, because he is deceased, the case is now closed. But that's really a police matter and out of my jurisdiction.

Best,

Maddie

Morton hoped desperately that the Reno police wouldn't release a public statement, which would forever be out there on the internet, for anyone who ever searched for it: Alfred Farrier, the cold-blooded murderer of Candee-Lee Gaddy. He considered contacting the police and requesting of them not to do it for the sake of his family. What was he going to say to Grace or Baby Farrier when they asked him about his grandparents? Spin them the lie which he had believed his whole life? Or tell them that someone sharing their genetic coding had barbarically stabbed a prostitute to death? Or simply never speak about him, which somehow felt much worse than the previous two ideas.

Morton pulled up the Security Personnel file and instantly yawned. It was late, and tomorrow they had to be at the hospital at 9am. He picked up his empty glass, closed his laptop and switched off the lamp. It was time for bed.

Chapter Twenty-Two

Juliette was lying on the hospital bed with her head propped up on two pillows, her t-shirt rolled up and tucked into her bra, exposing her swollen belly. Morton was standing beside her, holding her hand and, without realising it, also holding his breath. They were in a small room in the maternity unit of the William Harvey Hospital and a petite Asian sonographer was pushing a joystick-like device into the jelly smeared on Juliette's stomach, whilst looking up at the ultrasound screen just above the side of the bed.

A sort of baby-like object appeared on the grainy screen, and the nurse smiled. 'There!' she said, grinding the scanner into Juliette, as though she were crushing herbs with a mortar and pestle. Another smile from the nurse. 'A strong heartbeat. It's good.' She looked from Juliette to Morton and asked, 'Do you want to know the baby's sex?'

Morton nodded and replied enthusiastically, 'Yes.'

'No,' Juliette said.

'What? I thought we'd agreed,' Morton asked, slightly taken aback.

'We did,' she said with a grimace. 'I've changed my mind. Is that okay? I just think it'll be a nice surprise to wait.'

'Er...yeah...okay,' Morton stuttered, trying to work out if he really cared to know the baby's gender today, to be able to decorate the bedroom and shop for appropriate clothing, or minded waiting four more months and rushing around in a mad panic. He raised the point to Juliette, as the sonographer gave an impatient smile.

'What, pink for a girl and blue for a boy?' Juliette said. 'Really?'

He shrugged and clapped his hands together, quickly coming to a realisation. 'The baby's healthy. You're healthy,' he said. 'Let's go home.'

'Hang on one moment and I'll print you some scan pictures.'

'Perfect,' Morton said.

Juliette took his hand and kissed it. 'Thanks.'

'Are you sure you're okay with it?' Juliette asked, as she opened the front door to their house. 'Not knowing, I mean.'

'It took me by surprise but, yeah, it's fine,' Morton replied.

'It took *me* by surprise, too,' she confessed. 'Right up until I saw the baby on the screen, I thought I wanted to know.'

'You know who *will* mind,' Morton said.

Juliette winced. 'Guy and Jeremy.'

Morton nodded. 'They still think we're going to have a grand gender-reveal party at Granny's Scones.'

Juliette patted his arm, and said, 'I'll let you break the news to them.'

'Thanks,' he mumbled. 'Maybe not today; I can't face it. Plus, I want to finish reading that document and then get the concluding report written for the Duggan Case.'

'Good, I was hoping you were going to do some work. It means I can put my feet up and catch up with Netflix,' she said with a grin.

'You do that,' he replied kissing her on the lips. 'I won't be too long.'

Juliette shuffled into the lounge, and muttered, 'He said…disappearing into a genealogical vortex, never to be seen again…'

'Ha, ha,' he replied, heading up the stairs.

In his study, he sat down at his desk and, as he waited for his laptop to wake up, looked at the four framed photographs on his desk: one was of Grace in his arms, moments after being born; the second was a photo of his and Juliette's wedding day, three years earlier; the third was of his brother, Jeremy, and their parents, his adoptive family; and the final image, taken in January 1974, was of his biological parents together. From his back pocket, Morton removed the scan photograph of Baby Farrier and leant it up against the picture of Grace. His new son or daughter, he thought with a warm smile, as he gazed at the sepia, alien-like creature, currently residing inside Juliette.

His laptop was now alive and, on the screen in front of him, there was the document pertaining to the surveillance of William Gilmour, open exactly where he had left it last night. The page was headed NOTE FOR FILE, written by the head of the A4 section, William Skardon.

I interviewed William GILMOUR *at Richmond Police Station at 3 p.m. on 9ᵗʰ November 1956. I introduced myself as an officer of the Security Service and stated that I wished to ask him a number of questions. He was subdued and morose throughout the interview.*

I began by asking him why copies of the Daily Worker and literature from the British-Soviet Friendship Society had been discovered during a search of his house. He said that he had an interest in international politics and differing ideologies. I asked whether he subscribed to the ideologies of communism and he said that he did but protested that this was not a crime nor a reason to be arrested.

I asked if his interest in communism had arisen from his time working in Moscow. He said that it had not; it had started when he was around the age of 16. I asked what had caused this to happen at such a young age, but he refused to answer the question. I asked whether he had undertaken political activities during his youth, and he again refused to answer. From this point in the interview, GILMOUR became increasingly withdrawn, declining to co-operate or to give any answer at all to my questions.

I asked why he had left the DWS in 1952 and from what source did he now derive his income. He refused to answer.

I questioned him as to his current political activities; he refused to answer.

I asked what he had collected from the garden opposite his house on the 6th of November; he refused to answer.

I asked what he knew of Flora STERLING; he refused to answer.

I asked what he knew of Nikita SOKOLOV; he refused to answer.

I asked if he went by the cryptonym JERICHO; he refused to answer.

I asked if he was responsible for transmitting communications of intelligence to a foreign Power; he refused to answer.

I posed other benign questions about his family, upbringing and current hobbies, all of which he refused to answer.

At the end of the interview, GILMOUR made little acknowledgement when told that he would be indicted with five charges under the Official Secrets Act and that he was facing a lengthy prison sentence.

The file then came to a surprisingly sudden end. The remaining four pages in the document had all been redacted and replaced with that maddening placeholder: THE ORIGINAL DOCUMENT RETAINED UNDER SECTION 3(4) OF THE PUBLIC RECORDS ACT 1958.

Morton sighed.

He sat back in his chair, gazing up at his investigation wall and back to his laptop. The date of Ellen Ingram's involvement with this William Gilmour troubled him. It was so very close to the dates of Alexander's possible involvement in Operation Sawdust. Or was Morton trying too hard to connect two unrelated things? Maybe Juliette had been right: he was just inherently nosey and was actually now wasting time pursuing something of no relevance to that which Clarissa Duggan had requested of him. *Inherently nosey*; he preferred the term *professionally curious.*

He drummed his fingers on the desk, weighing the decision.

His professional curiosity won the day and Morton convinced himself that he would just spend the rest of the afternoon investigating and, if that came to nothing, then he would draw a line under the case and move on. Simple.

Taking three pieces of plain paper from the printer beside him, Morton wrote WILLIAM GILMOUR in the centre of one sheet, FLORA STERLING in the centre of another and NIKITA SOKOLOV in the middle of the third.

He started by searching for William Gilmour in the National Archives database, thinking that such a man, accused of such serious crimes, would have other files against his name. When Morton filtered the search down to include only results from the 1950s onwards, the three hundred and seventy-two hits reduced to just fifteen. The results were dominated by Medal Listings for a variety of different men with the name William Gilmour, who had been awarded decorations in the Second World War. The remainder of the results pertained to documents where the words *William* and *Gilmour* had occurred in the same file, but which were not actually adjacent to one another.

Odd, Morton thought. Perhaps Gilmour had been released without charge.

Next, Morton ran a search for his name in the British Newspaper Archive. Scrolling down the list of results, one leapt out at him with the headline of *SPY SUICIDE*. He opened the article, dated 14th November 1956. Above the short story was a headshot of a man who appeared to be in his early-to-mid-twenties. He was youthful and handsome but had what Morton interpreted as a mournful look in his eyes, as though he had known little happiness in his life. He lowered his gaze from the image to the text.

SPY SUICIDE
DOWNFALL OF AN EX-CIVIL SERVANT
The downfall of an ex-civil servant was described at a Richmond (London) inquest to-day on William Gilmour (29), who was found hanging in his prison cell in Richmond Police Station three days ago.
Mr Gilmour, latterly of 13 Burlington Avenue, Kew, was being held in police custody following serious charges of communicating information of value to a foreign power.
The police-sergeant who found Mr Gilmour's body said that the deceased had fashioned a rope from his socks and had suspended himself from the window bars. He estimated the prisoner to have been dead for a matter of minutes.
The coroner was told that the prisoner had barely spoken since the charges were brought against him. He recorded a verdict of 'Suicide while of unsound mind.'

Whatever secrets William Gilmour had been communicating to a foreign power had died with him, prior to his court case; any further connection to Ellen Ingram or possible link to Alexander Emmett was unlikely to be unearthed, Morton reasoned, as he returned to the results list. He took his time idly reading through other newspaper articles, which had also covered the suicide story, making relevant notes on the sheet of paper with William's name in the centre.

As Morton scribbled down the information, he couldn't help but feel that there was something amiss. Something he wasn't quite getting. He studied the notes that he had just made, then looked searchingly up to the investigation wall in front of him. Was there any other connection between Gilmour and Ellen Ingram, or was it simply that she had played a small part in the surveillance operation into his activities?

Morton set the piece of paper to one side and selected the one with Flora Sterling's name in the centre. As the British Newspaper Archive was open on screen, Morton started by searching for her there.

Your search returned 51 articles.

He could see from the first results that they were irrelevant and way out of being the correct time period. He filtered the results to 1950-1959, which narrowed the list to just five articles. The first article contained two contiguous adverts within the *Evesham Standard & West Midland Observer*, one advertising a *Flora "Viceroy" odourless paraffin heater*, the other advertising *Sterling Chicks: Britain's Best Birds*. Nothing to do with a person, named Flora Sterling, then.

The other references, Morton found, were identical. Whoever she was, Flora Sterling had not done anything newsworthy in the 1950s. Just to be certain, he expanded his search to the 1940s and 1960s but found nothing that was obviously attributable to this woman.

Google returned a similar verdict on her.

The National Archives website offered one promising result. It was a file within the KV 6 series, forming part of the Security List, which related to investigations carried out on individuals between 1929 and 1972. The file was a free download.

Seconds later, the PDF document was open in front of him. The coloured scan commenced with the file reference of *KV 6/147*, and below that was typed, *FLORA STERLING*.

Morton scrolled down to see a full-page, black and white photograph of a strikingly beautiful woman. A handwritten label appended to the image declared the woman to be Flora Sterling. She was truly captivating, staring out at the camera with beguiling eyes, as though she were a Hollywood movie star. She appeared to Morton to have been around the age of twenty-five when the photograph had been taken, which in his initial supposition he placed in the late forties or early fifties. She had light-coloured hair, fashioned in a forties-style waved pompadour, and, despite the monochrome image, it was obvious that she was wearing heavy make-up.

Wow. William Gilmour had refused to answer the question of whether or not he knew of this woman, but Morton doubted very much that she was someone whom you could easily forget.

The next page in the file was something all too familiar to Morton: redacted. Except this white page did not say that it had been retained under the Public Records Act, as had the others which he had viewed. This was designated as *Missing at transfer*.

The following two pages were also classed as missing.

Morton raised an eyebrow, as he scrolled on to the next document, headed IMMIGRATION BRANCH, HOME OFFICE and dated 9th November 1956. He read the typed letter carefully.

To the Immigration Officer

Flora STERLING

The above-named person should not be permitted to leave the country. You are advised to contact Scotland Yard immediately if this person should attempt to depart from the United Kingdom. This instruction will hold good until further notice and the following entry should be made in the Suspect Index:-

STERLING, Flora. Female. Born 1921. Photographer's model. Passport number: 15559

F. J. Ralfe
H.M. Chief Inspector,
Immigration Branch.

All ports.
Scotland Yard.
M.I.5.

Two days before William Gilmour had committed suicide, an all-ports alert had been issued, preventing Flora Sterling from leaving the country. What intrigued Morton most about this page in the file was that the word CANCELLED was stencil-stamped in large red letters diagonally across the letter.

The subsequent page confirmed the termination in a short-typed communication, again from the Immigration Branch of the Home Office to *all-ports*.

12ᵗʰ November 1956.

The following name is no longer required to be included in the Home Office Suspect Index:-

STERLING, *Flora. Passport number: 15559*

Please remove with immediate effect

F. J. Ralfe
H.M. Chief Inspector,
Immigration Branch.

What had changed in such a short time? Morton wondered. Whatever the reason had been, the following pages gave no indication. Seven pages, containing those ominous words, *Missing at transfer*, took the document to its end.

Morton sat back, dissatisfied.

The piece of paper in front of him contained almost zero useful information about Flora Sterling. He wrote, REDACTED. REDACTED. REDACTED. in a circle around her name, then slid the paper to the bottom of the pile.

He had one last person to investigate: Nikita Sokolov.

The National Archives website declared that it had *0 Records* corresponding to this search.

The British Newspaper Archive told Morton that his search *returned 0 articles*.

Google, however, found 667,000 matches for the name.

Morton worked his way through the first few pages of results which broadly related to a Russian football player, born in 1995. He amended his search to exclude the word *football*, bringing the total results down a few thousand. Now the list was populated with references to a Russian hockey player, so Morton subtracted out the word *hockey*. He was now down to 538,000 hits. Racing and athletics were another popular link with the name Nikita Sokolov, so Morton excluded those from his search, too. But still the results were too numerous and unwieldy. When he added the word *spy*, the number of matches dropped dramatically and the top result was one which Morton clicked with interest. It was a Wikipedia article relating to something called the Mitrokhin Archive, which sparked a distant memory.

Morton leant closer to the screen, as he read that the archive was a collection of 33 boxes of handwritten notes made secretly by a KGB archivist, named Vasili Mitrokhin. The documents, numbering 25,000 pages, detailed secret operations from the 1930s to the 1970s, naming several notable KGB spies, global undercover operations and assassination attempts. Morton vaguely recalled that the archive had made headline news twenty or so years ago, when it had been first publicly revealed.

He found Nikita's name under the section *Prominent KGB spies named in the files*.

Nikita Sokolov (16th December 1912 - 23rd March 1974) a Second Secretary at the Soviet Embassy in Kensington, London. KGB recruiter and handler.

Morton wrote the information on the piece of paper with Nikita's name in the centre. Then, he spent some time conducting further research, now that he had some biographical material to go on. He trawled various websites, following many links, which ultimately drew him to the same assertion: that the specific details of Nikita's life as a KGB spy were contained in the Mitrokhin Papers. Papers which were held at the Churchill Archives Centre in Cambridge and, Morton read with frustration, were written entirely in Russian. Morton's knowledge of the Russian language began and ended with the word *vodka*. Great.

He sat back, spread the three sheets of paper out in front of him, and wondered. He contemplated how they all might relate to one another. The most logical answer was that Nikita Sokolov had recruited William Gilmour and Flora Sterling who between them were gathering state secrets and transmitting them to the Soviets. Morton also wondered if there was a point in continuing to pursue this line of enquiry, when the next step would undoubtedly be to cart himself off to Cambridge, which in turn necessitated finding a translator. It was more time and more money. And for what, exactly? Yes, it was compelling, but this was also pure indulgence.

He felt foggy-headed and stood up to stretch. With a giant yawn, he looked at the timeline on his investigation wall, then exhaled: he needed fresh eyes.

Morton ambled downstairs to the lounge, where he found Netflix in full swing, broadcasting an episode of *The Crown* to Juliette who was lying on the sofa with her head back, mouth open and eyes closed. He grinned and pressed the pause button on the remote control.

Juliette woke with the gasp of someone who had been underwater for as long as their breath could possibly take it. She wiped a line of dribble from the side of her lips, and snapped, 'Hey, I was watching that.'

'Yeah,' Morton replied. 'It really looked like it.'

'Finished?' she asked, her question morphing into a yawn.

'Well… I was hoping to ask your opinion on it, actually,' Morton began. 'But I think probably we both need to get some sleep.'

Juliette stood up, widened her eyes and blew out some air. 'Nope, it's fine. Tell me what the problem is.'

Morton led the way up to his study and then explained his latest discoveries, punctuated throughout by both of them yawning.

'Right…' Juliette muttered, turning to face the chaos of his investigation wall.

Morton remained silent, leaning on his desk and watching her, as she bent down, scrutinising each piece of evidence in turn.

She unstuck something from the wall and turned to face him with a frown of confusion. 'So, you said that Alexander probably left the country at some point after his wife, Ellen's death, then returned to the UK in 1974 under an assumed identity…and then died this year.'

'Correct,' Morton said with a chuckle. 'Confusing, isn't it?'

'Yes,' she agreed, glancing down at whatever she had removed from the wall. 'But you've stuck this up, which says that Alexander died between 1941 and 1945.'

'What?' Morton replied, reaching out for whatever was in her hand. She passed it over. It was the indexes for deaths overseas. Morton laughed. 'No, this Alexand*ria*,' he explained. 'She was his mother—' he stopped talking when he saw what she had seen.

GRO Consular Death indices (1849 – 1965)

First names: Alexander
Sex: Male
Last Name: Emmett
Death year: 1941-45
Birth year: 1927
Type: Consular / Overseas
Country: Egypt
Place: Port Said
Page: 121
Age: 16

How had he missed *that*? He had missed it because he had been searching for Alexandria's death and, once found, he had printed the reference page from the indexes but not actually looked closely at it. It could, of course, pertain to somebody else, but what really were the chances?

If, as he strongly suspected, Alexander Emmett had died in 1944, then who on earth was the real identity of the man he had been researching?

'Is that not him, then?' Juliette questioned.

Morton nodded slowly. 'I need to order the certificate to be sure, but…yes, I think it is.'

'So,' Juliette began, gazing to the ceiling to clarify her thoughts, 'the guy pretending to be Maurice Duggan was actually also pretending to be Alexander Emmett. That right?'

'It looks that way.'

'So, who was he, really, then?' she asked.

Morton shrugged. He had no words.

Chapter Twenty-Three

9th November 1956, Port Said, Egypt

A city in limbo, Alexander wrote on his notepad. *45,000 British and 34,000 French troops armed and impotently marching the streets. Muzzled tanks cruising the bombed roads. Restlessness and defiance among the goading local population – hungry, looting shops.*

Alexander had positioned himself in a corner of the bar, close to the door of the backstreet hotel in which he was staying, in case he should need to make a quick exit. It was possibly the worst time in history to be British in Egypt and he had been forced to use the side streets to get around, keeping his head down and using his dubious American accent, if required to speak.

He swigged from his third double gin, as he looked around the bar. The room was small, with just half-a-dozen tables, and poorly illuminated by two stumpy church candles perched on the bar top. 'No electricity,' the barman had complained to Alexander, when he had ordered his first drink. 'Five days. No electricity.'

Just one local man, slurring infrequently to himself in Arabic, shared the room with Alexander and the barman whose face was now hidden behind a broadsheet Egyptian newspaper. Alexander couldn't understand the headline, but the image of Nasser waving valiantly to crowds of several hundred Egyptians revealed the gist of the story.

Nasser victorious, Alexander wrote. *United Nations Emergency Force being requested to fill the void. What next?*

He knew what next. He would wait there in that gloomy bar until sundown and then he would make his way to the El Gamil airfield, where, once inside, he would find President Nasser's Soviet Ilyushin Il-14 waiting on the tarmac, following his whistle-stop tour of his beleaguered country. Tomorrow morning at first light, the plane would depart for Cairo but would never land.

On the floor beside Alexander was his canvas bag containing everything that he would need to sabotage Nasser's plane. He still couldn't quite believe that those were his orders as part of a variety of tactics aimed at regime change under the umbrella of Operation Sawdust.

It seemed incongruous that here he was on the verge of an assassination attempt at the same time as the military attacks had mysteriously screeched to a grinding halt despite a unilateral consensus that the British and French would have been victorious. Ironically, Eden's cease-fire appeared to have spurred on the rise of nationalism sweeping Egypt: Nasser was more popular than ever.

Alexander finished his drink and approached the bar. He ordered another.

'Where you from?' the barman asked, unable to hide a curious glower. 'Your accent is strange.'

Alexander smiled, realising that he had ordered the gin without disguising his voice this time. He swallowed hard and then spoke with a softer, diluted version of his attempt at sounding American. 'Yes,' he said through a laugh. 'My father is Australian; my mother is from California; but I grew up in Texas.'

The barman nodded but continued to frown. 'Be careful, my friend,' he warned. 'To sound British is not good here now.'

'British?' The semi-conscious man, slumped at the bar, awoke and looked between Alexander and the barman. 'Who's British?'

'Nobody,' the barman said. 'This man is American.' He stared at Alexander with cold, unblinking eyes, then said something in Arabic to the other man.

The man snorted and dropped his head into the crook of his elbow, resting on the bar top.

'Be careful,' the barman reiterated, sliding the glass of gin across to Alexander.

'Thanks,' Alexander replied, taking the drink back to his table. As he walked back, he peered outside. Darkness had almost fallen.

He sat down and sipped his drink, noticing the light tremor in his hands. He drank more.

At that moment the door opened and a group of six young lads, wearing galabeya and babbling animatedly in Arabic, entered the room.

Alexander watched, as they splayed out across the front of the bar. He interpreted, from their body language alone, that the man in the centre, who looked as though he might be their leader, was seeking drink choices from his friends. He spoke to the barman and then Alexander caught a subtle nod in his direction. The Egyptian in the centre turned and stared at him.

It was time to leave. He downed his drink, picked up his bag and hurried from the hotel.

Outside, the lack of lighting cloaked the streets in total blackness. He walked as quickly as he could in the vague direction of the airfield, relying more on the memory of his previous visit than from that which he could actually discern. Tepid water, pumping unrelentingly into the streets from shattered pipes, lapped over the edges of his shoes.

His blood ran cold as a firm hand landed on his left shoulder. 'Hey, American.'

Alexander stopped, preparing to swing his canvas bag at the man, who, he was certain, had just followed him out of the bar.

'Where do you rush to, American?' the faceless voice demanded, the hold on his shoulder remaining.

'Away from here,' Alexander replied sternly.

'I want to get you a drink,' he said.

'Why would you want to do that?' Alexander asked.

'You're on our side,' the voice answered.

Alexander emitted a short, gruff laugh. 'Goodbye.'

The weight on his shoulder fell away and Alexander pushed off into the darkness, his heart pounding. He exhaled sharply and pointlessly squinted ahead of him, trying to distinguish where the road split. Fortunately, at that moment, a car swung around the corner, its headlights momentarily raising concealed people, buildings, palm trees and tanks from obscurity and then returning them to their previous eerie darkness. He was left alone, pressing on towards the airfield, with his bag slung over his shoulder.

His pace was painfully slow, having to rely on passing motor traffic to keep check on his progress. But the absolute drape of night had played into his hands: his ethnicity went unchallenged and, more significantly, not a single person could attest to having witnessed his journey to the airfield.

As he left the confines of the invisible city along the Saad Zaghloul, the atmosphere began to change imperceptibly around him. He shuddered, wondering what was so different now. He sensed that he was no longer surrounded by buildings and tried to picture his location, as it had been when he had walked here that morning when the paratroopers had landed.

It was the Mediterranean, he realised, just a few feet away to his right. El Gamil, therefore, could not be far away. In the far distance he could see the faintest of lights which, he guessed, were probably Cyprus.

He paused, dropped his bag to the floor and rummaged blindly inside until his hand touched the cold metal cylinder. For the first time, Alexander chanced switching on the torch, but he did so steadily, shielding the majority of the light with his left hand. It was enough to see that the tall wire fence, which formed the perimeter of the airfield, was just up ahead of him.

He switched off the torch but kept it in his hand and, with renewed confidence, he strode to the airfield boundary. Then, keeping his right hand on the wire, walked away from the roadside, so that he would be well out of sight before he attempted to gain access.

This interregnum period, with the country awaiting the arrival of the United Nations Emergency Force, had assisted him greatly. The British, no longer on a war-footing, were maintaining a notional skeleton presence at the airfield. Alexander was convinced that, even if he were to be caught by a British soldier, a simple phone call to Security Intelligence Middle East would likely see him instantly released, whilst a blind eye were turned to his activities.

Alexander stood still and listened carefully for a few seconds. In so far as he could tell, he was very much alone. He risked switching on his torch, once again muting the light with his left hand. He was at the far end of the runway. He extinguished the light, placed the torch down beside him, then felt inside the canvas bag for the wire-cutters.

It was too risky to keep the torch illuminated whilst he cut through the fence, he thought. So, he began a repeating pattern of cutting a section of wire, then shining the light fleetingly onto his work, before cutting on blindly once again.

Alexander stopped suddenly. From the far side of the airfield, he spotted a pair of white lights. Moving. Moving towards him. He froze. The lights were moving quickly, and the accompanying drone of an engine confirmed to him that they belonged to some kind of patrol vehicle. Maybe the airfield wasn't as abandoned as he had allowed himself to believe.

The vehicle continued in its trajectory towards him.

Alexander threw the wire-cutters and torch back into the bag and then ran with it as fast as he could away from the fence. His chest was achingly tight, as he ran, causing the tools inside the bag to rattle and jostle against one another.

Glancing over his shoulder, he saw that the vehicle was just twenty feet from the hole that he had begun to cut.

Alexander dived down into the sand, tucking himself into the foetal position with his back to the fence, in the hope that if he were spotted, he might just be mistaken for one of the rocks and boulders bestrewn around the area.

He held his breath and tensed every muscle, as the patrol vehicle passed.

He listened for the tell-tale sound of deacceleration; but none came. The vehicle continued to circuit the perimeter.

He exhaled, stood up, picked up his bag and rushed back to the fence, wondering how long it would take the patrol to return. However long it took for them to get back, Alexander needed to work fast.

Pulling out the wire-cutters once more, he hacked quickly at the fence.

In just a few short minutes he had cut two parallel lines two feet apart. The incisions would hopefully appear indistinguishable under a casual glance from the passing security personnel, but the hole that he had created was sufficient for him to pass through into the airfield.

Alexander pressed his face to the fence, searching the gloom for the vehicle, but it was not to be seen. Yet.

He decided to go for it and stowed the wire-cutters in his bag, lifted the fold of wire and passed it through to the other side. Then, with the wire flap leaning against his head, he pushed himself into the airfield.

He was in. He stood up and took in a long breath, almost—and quite ridiculously—expecting that the air might feel different on the inside of the airfield.

Picking up his bag from the grass, he began to jog in the general direction of the main airfield buildings, where he had previously seen the light aircraft stowed, on standby.

As he ran, Alexander turned to look behind him. The fence was lost to black murkiness and he felt a sudden stab of a fear of his not being able to find the hole again in order to get away. He could, he reasoned, just cut a fresh hole, but if he needed an immediate escape, in the event that he had in any way been detected, then that would be an impossibility.

Fifty yards up ahead of him, Alexander could see intermittent lights flickering in the control tower and he could hear the low thrum of a generator working nearby. He saw flashes of outlines of men inside the tower. Armed by all accounts, judging by the appearance of their silhouettes.

The quivering light was just adequate to determine that Alexander was standing on the tarmac apron used for parked aircraft. But there was a problem: there was not a single aeroplane here.

The lights in the control tower went out and Alexander felt a tightening in his chest. He *had* to find Nasser's plane and go through with his task. But where was it? Maybe Nasser's itinerary had changed and he had left already.

The lights flashed on, much brighter than they had been before, and the generator kicked into a new rhythm, like a car changing down a gear too soon.

Alexander whipped around, taking advantage of the extra brightness, to confirm that there were definitely no aircraft on the airfield. As he turned back towards the control tower, he spotted the large hangar on the other side of the buildings. If Nasser's plane was here at all, then it had to be in there. Getting to it, however, meant passing directly in front of the tower, which contained, by his estimation, at least half-a-dozen armed men. What those ominous silhouettes had yet to reveal to him was the nationality of the men projecting them.

The lights were becoming a problem for Alexander, their intensity surging and falling with increasing irregularity. If he passed in front of the control tower at the wrong moment, he could suddenly find himself, like an actor in a stage spotlight, illuminated for all to see. Conversely, if he took the long way around to avoid the lights, he would be adding unnecessary time and could risk his being spotted by the patrol vehicle.

He settled on an idea and hurried towards the hum of the generator, situated directly beside the tower. Ducking down behind it, he peered inside the building, scarred and burned from the invasion: he spied seven idle-looking soldiers with guns on their shoulders.

Egyptian soldiers.

Alexander pulled out the torch and ran the beam over the generator. It was about the size of a domestic refrigeration unit on two wheels, with a thick cable projecting from the rear. He moved along the side of the machine in an awkward crouching shuffle until he reached the back. There, his torch beam illuminated a control panel with several switches, the exact function of which was explained in Arabic. Just as he placed his hand on the largest of the buttons, the side door to the control tower burst open, spilling out light and an energetic conversation between two men.

Alexander dropped to the floor and wriggled back around to the other side of the generator, praying that he wouldn't be spotted. Barely allowing himself to breathe, he heard the striking of a match. Moments later he smelt the repugnant odour of Egyptian cigarettes wafting over him.

One of the men said something that made the other laugh.

From his uncomfortable position on the floor, Alexander attempted to discern something of the men's conversation, but he couldn't understand a word. They were just two guards on their break. If they stayed put, then he should be okay.

Time dawdled with painful sluggishness, as the two soldiers smoked and chatted.

A niggling cramp in Alexander's left calf muscle began to bite harder. He gritted his teeth against the pain. There was no way that he could stretch his leg as his muscles were demanding. The burning increased and Alexander grimaced from the pain. He opened his eyes to see a cigarette butt plop down onto the tarmac, right beside his face. Another he heard land somewhere near the back of his head.

More conversation between the two men was followed by Alexander's being plunged back into darkness, as they closed the control tower door behind them.

'Ah!' Alexander groaned, stretching out the cramp from his leg. 'Jesus.'

He exhaled noisily and took a moment to catch his breath.

But he didn't have a moment; the patrol vehicle was making its way towards him.

If he didn't move quickly, he would be sandwiched between the patrol vehicle and the illuminated control tower. He needed to act but, with the vehicle not far away, he couldn't risk using his torch again.

Fumbling breathlessly and without vision, Alexander ran his hands over the generator's control panel. His fingers gripped around the largest switch, which he turned clockwise, plummeting the control tower into instant darkness. From the soldiers inside, he heard a collective groan.

Alexander grabbed his bag and ran as fast as he could, directly under the control tower window, hoping that, thanks to his diversion, he wouldn't be seen or heard.

He could tell from the looming shape just in front of him that he had almost reached the hangar.

Chancing a look behind him, he saw that the patrol vehicle was just thirty feet away and about to turn in his direction.

With the last of his energy, Alexander pushed himself into a flat-out sprint, reaching the hangar just in time. He pressed himself into a recess in its outer wall, watching as the patrol vehicle—a military-style jeep—sped past.

He had a good few minutes until it would return, so allowed himself a few seconds to recover. He bent over, resting his hands on his knees, as beads of sweat erupted on his forehead and ran over his temples and down his cheeks.

Once he had recuperated sufficiently, Alexander stepped out of the recess, into which he had been tucked, and found that he had been standing close to a side door to the hangar. Pressing his ear to the door, he stood quietly, trying to shut out the sound of his own whirring blood. He couldn't hear anything from inside, but that didn't mean much in an aircraft hangar of that size. He knelt down and ran his fingers along the base of the door. There was a good half-inch gap between it and the concrete hangar floor. No light appeared in the space in between.

Alexander stood up and gently pushed down on the door handle. Unlocked. As slowly as he could manage, he edged the door ajar, then paused. No sounds. No movement. No lights. He was as confident as he could be that the hangar was unguarded.

He pulled the door open wide, stepped inside and closed it gently behind him. Despite the quietness with which he had shut the door, the sound still echoed terribly around the hangar.

Again, he waited. Seconds ticked by. Then, he took out his torch and shone it into the palm of his hand. The illumination was negligible but it sufficed to show that there were three sleeping aircraft in here.

He moved the torch light steadily but swiftly around the hangar. The huge main doors at the front were closed. There were no windows and no adjacent rooms which might have contained airfield personnel. Alexander concentrated the beam on to each of the aircraft in turn. Nasser's plane, the gleaming silver Soviet Ilyushin Il-14, was the closest to him.

What Alexander had forgotten about this particular type of aircraft was that it had tricycle gear and having its shape and a nosewheel meant that the aircraft sat entirely raised and parallel with the ground: there was no way that he could clamber up onto the wings without some kind of assistance.

He threw the torch beam around the hangar. There had to be a ladder here somewhere. Then he spotted one, mounted to the wall on the other side. Setting down his bag beside the plane, he loped over, removed it from its hooks and carried it to the aircraft. He propped the ladder into position behind the left wing, picked up his bag and ascended. At the top, he side-stepped onto the back of the wing, placed the torch in his mouth and then proceeded carefully forwards towards the left engine. Putting his bag down noiselessly, he knelt at the oil door. It was eight inches in diameter and held shut by three quarter-turn screws. Turning each of them ninety degrees, he was able to open the round flap. With the torch in his left hand, Alexander worked his fingers into the oil door, finding another screw cap, which he turned and removed, placing it down beside him.

He took a breath, removed the jerry-can from his canvas bag and unscrewed the lid. Slowly and cautiously, he began to pour the contents into the oil reserve. He continued pouring until he heard the rising notes, announcing the liquid's nearing the top of the tank. Then, he screwed the cap back on to the jerry-can, fixed the first oil cap in place and turned the three locking screws on the outer case.

If he had walked away at that point, then there would have been a very good chance that this engine would suffer catastrophic damage in flight; enough damage to bring down the plane. But a very good chance wasn't quite good enough, Alexander knew, stuffing the torch back into his mouth and stepping onto the ladder. He scaled down quickly, dropped his bag just below the right wing, then slid the ladder under the fuselage of the Ilyushin Il-14, before bracing it against the edge of the right wing to repeat the manoeuvre. He climbed quickly and more adroitly, perhaps because of a growing confidence or perhaps through fear of taking too long.

Kneeling at the second oil door, Alexander quickly rotated the three quarter-turn screws, opened the flap beneath and then proceeded to pour a second jerry-can of water into the oil tank until the coalesced liquid bubbled at the surface. It took just a moment to reseal both caps and descend from the aircraft. Not wasting a second, Alexander lowered the ladder and repositioned it on the wall, ensuring that it was hanging on exactly the same rungs as those which had held it when he had found it. He picked up his bag and then swept the torch over the aircraft and all around the floor, ensuring that there was no trace of his having been there.

The circle of white light lingered on the Ilyushin Il-14. Tomorrow, that aircraft would take off from this airfield and never land. He had done his duty.

Switching off the light, Alexander allowed his eyes a few seconds to adjust to the darkness, before gingerly opening the door a few inches.

Outside was silent.

He decided that, given the level of security at the airfield, he would wait there until the patrol jeep had passed, before making a wide arc around the front of the control tower and heading back to the hole in the perimeter fence.

'Come on,' he muttered, staring into the night, willing the pair of lights to make an appearance around the corner.

It felt to him as though several long minutes had passed before the patrol jeep finally emerged on the horizon.

Alexander inched the door closed, leaving just a narrow gap from which to observe the approaching vehicle. As it drew closer, he pulled the door completely shut, then waited a few seconds before reopening it. The jeep had gone, continuing its circuit around the airfield.

He opened the door wide and stepped outside. Hearing nothing out of the ordinary, he closed the door behind him and walked in a straight line away from the hangar. Reaching the tarmac runway, he turned left and began to run directly for the fence. The control tower, with its flickering lights, passed by to one side.

Alexander's body was soaked with sweat and he was wheezing for breath by the time he reached the fence. He pulled out his torch and began quickly to sweep the beam across the bottom of the wire, searching for the hole.

'Where is it?' he stammered, starting to wonder if he should just start to cut a fresh one. He took a glance behind him and gasped when he spotted the patrol jeep in the distance, heading towards him. There was no way that he could cut a new hole through which to escape.

A nervous panic rose in his chest, stifling his breathing. 'Come on. Come on,' he said, running along the fence line, as the beam of light bounced and leapt across the wire. The hole had to be here somewhere. He slowed his pace, fearing that he might overshoot it in his haste.

The jeep had reached the corner of the airfield and was about to turn to move in his direction.

He considered flattening himself to the ground, or pulling himself into a vague rock shape, as he had done earlier, but knew that this time his position would fall directly into the illuminated curve of the jeep's headlights.

Then, he saw the hole. He was right beside it. Hurriedly, he lifted the wire flap, threw his bag out to the other side, then scurried through himself. He grabbed the bag and ran as fast as he could. At the last moment, he dived to the ground, knocking the remaining breath from his lungs.

The patrol jeep passed by without pausing.

Alexander stood up, panting for breath. He'd done it. Now it was time to get back to his hotel and prepare to leave first thing tomorrow.

Every time the door opened there was an instantaneous transformation in the office atmosphere: discussions paused; typing stopped; phone conversations were halted; and all eyes of the dozen members of staff turned to verify who had entered the room.

'It's only me,' Paul Reynolds remarked, strolling into the office with his hands in the air, as though he had been arrested.

Ellen sighed, her gaze switching from Paul Reynolds back to her typewriter. This was a team effort but she, more so than anyone else in the room, was feeling the pressure of the surveillance operation into William Gilmour and Flora Sterling.

She stared at the sheet of foolscap, wound through her typewriter. Blank. She could think of nothing else but that which was currently underway in Richmond Police Station, where Mr Skardon was in the process of interviewing William Gilmour. The surveillance at Gilmour's home had been planned to last much longer, in order to try to round up as many individuals connected with him as possible, but the decision to raid the house yesterday and arrest him had been taken after suspect messages had been monitored being transmitted from the radio inside thirteen Burlington Avenue. Gilmour had been heard speaking to a man with a Soviet call-sign. Their conversation, recorded onto acetate gramophone records, was ostensibly banal. However, among the facileness were obviously coded phrases, such as 'The birds are singing tonight,' 'The full moon falls on the even numbers' and 'The lighthouse is waiting to flash again.'

The subsequent raid on the house had led to Gilmour's arrest and a vanload of evidence being removed. The greatest priority from the hoard had been the film cartridge, believed to have been deposited yesterday by Flora Sterling. It had been found concealed under Gilmour's bedroom floorboards and taken off to the MI5 labs to be developed.

Ellen shot a look across to the office door, as it opened again. Angela Jones entered, carrying two mugs. 'Just me,' she clearly felt compelled to say, when the entire room once again held its collective breath and stared in her direction. She perched herself on the edge of

Ellen's desk and offered her one of the mugs. 'Thought you could use a nice cup of tea.'

'Thanks. I could use something stronger, actually,' Ellen replied.

Angela smiled sympathetically. She was of a similar age and outlook to Ellen, and the two of them got along well together. Their natural rapport with one another often saw them undertaking surveillance work together, the theory being that they appeared like two normal friends, not Watchers from MI5. 'He'll be back soon enough.'

'How long does it take to interview one man, for goodness' sake?' Ellen asked, sipping the drink.

'Depends how much he has to say, I suppose,' Angela answered. 'Did you hear that there were more leaks about the Middle East three days ago, presumed to have come from Jericho?'

'So I heard,' Ellen said.

'What are you working on at the moment?' Angela asked, looking at the blank sheet of paper in Ellen's typewriter, and then adding, 'sorry, what *should* you be working on at the moment?'

'Logging yesterday's surveillance,' Ellen answered. 'Tracking Flora to the Foreign Secretary's flat. I mean, how stupidly naïve can that man be? Does he really think that someone like *her* would be interested in *him*?'

Angela laughed. 'I'd love to be a fly on the wall when MI5 eventually goes in and tells him that his bit on the side has been squirreling away his state secrets and passing them through Jericho to the Soviets. Think he might need to step down *on health grounds* afterwards.'

'Yeah, I think so, too. I don't imagine that his wife will be—' Ellen stopped herself short, as the door opened once again. It was Mr Skardon, face solemn, as though he were carrying a heavy burden. In his right hand he held a manila file. He didn't need to call the office to silence today.

'I've just come back from interviewing Gilmour,' Mr Skardon began. 'Unfortunately he was less than cooperative. He refused to answer questions regarding his connections to Flora Sterling, Nikita Sokolov, or whether or not he operated under the codename Jericho to pass state secrets to a foreign power.' He held up the file. 'A transcript of the interview is in here, should anyone wish to read it.' He drew in a long breath before continuing. 'The film cartridge left at the dead drop by Flora Sterling and collected by William Gilmour has been developed'—he glanced at Ellen and briefly smiled—'and, as suspected by Miss Ingram, contains top-secret information unequivocally obtained from the Foreign Secretary. Among the documents copied by Miss Sterling, which we must presume Gilmour communicated to the Soviets, were details of a highly important undercover operation currently underway in Egypt.' Mr Skardon drew in his lower lip, implying that he had finished speaking.

'So, what's the plan now, then, sir?' Joseph Tandy called across the room.

Mr Skardon raised his eyebrows. 'To have another go at getting something from Gilmour, to get the operations concerned in the Middle East shut down and to get any endangered agents repatriated.'

'What about Flora Sterling?' John Potter asked.

'Ah, yes. The police are on their way to arrest her right now.'

'So, our job on this case is done?' Angela asked. 'Jericho's captured; Flora is about to be arrested; presumably the Foreign Secretary will be getting a wrap on the knuckles.'

Mr Skardon agreed with a gentle nod of his head.

'What about Nikita Sokolov, though?' Joseph Tandy enquired. 'Surely he'll just recruit others to replace Gilmour and Sterling?'

Mr Skardon grinned. 'We're keeping him under close watch for the time being, but I *believe* that once we've got enough on him, he's going to receive a visit where he'll be presented with two options: leave the country…or change his paymaster.'

'Defect?'

'We shall see,' Mr Skardon replied. 'One thing is for certain, though. We wouldn't be where we are, with Jericho facing a lengthy prison sentence, were it not for Miss Ingram.' He turned in her direction, smiled and nodded his head. 'Well done.'

There were murmurs of agreement from around the office, then Mr Skardon placed the file on Miss Brogren's desk and left the room. A raft of animated babble erupted around the office.

'Good job, Miss Ingram,' John Potter called over to her, struggling to articulate his words around the pipe protruding from the side of his mouth.

'Thank you,' she replied.

'Yes, good work, Miss Ingram,' Angela agreed with a grin.

'I'm just relieved that my hunch proved to be correct,' she said, standing up. 'I want to read that transcript, even if nobody else does.' She walked over to Miss Brogren's desk, picked up the file and began to read it, as she returned to her own desk. 'There's not much to it.'

'It doesn't sound like Gilmour's going to be very cooperative,' Angela said, craning her neck to read the typed text.

'Maybe Flora Sterling will be,' Ellen replied.

'We'll find out when the police bring her in,' Angela said, moving off the desk. 'Right... Back to it, Miss Ingram.'

Ellen smiled. 'Thanks for the tea.' She set her fingers on the typewriter and began to type up her surveillance log.

Flora was in her nightie, lying on the sofa in Harold Austin's apartment, with her legs crossed at the ankles. In one hand she held a tumbler of whiskey and in the other the last smokable remnants of a Gold Flake cigarette. She smudged the butt into the glass ashtray balanced on her stomach, then reached over to the coffee table beside her for the cigarette packet.

'God,' she muttered, scrunching the empty pack in one hand and tossing it to the floor.

Harold's eyes danced from *The Times*, which he had been reading, to Flora, to the discarded cigarette packet, then back to Flora.

'Are you going to be working *all* evening?' Flora asked, draining the last drips of the whiskey. 'I rather thought we might go out somewhere for a nice dinner.'

Harold tweaked his glasses. He was sitting opposite her, still wearing his suit, shirt and black tie from his day in parliament. He sniffed. 'We need to be more discreet, Flora, dear.'

Flora frowned. 'Why? Are you embarrassed of me?'

'Why? Because I have a wife. And, with all that's going on in the Middle East right now, I've got half of Fleet Street following my every move. So, I just need to be judicious with my *social* engagements.'

'Judicious with your social engagements,' Flora parroted. 'Wow.' She stood up in annoyance and walked over to the window. She parted the curtains and gazed out. 'When is *Mrs* Austin due to return, anyway?'

'Next Sunday, I believe,' he answered without looking up.

'Then what?'

'Then what *what*?' he asked.

'What about us?' Flora demanded.

Harold shrugged. 'Well, obviously you can't carry on here, as you have been. I'll find us a nice little place somewhere. Look, could you come away from the window, please, darling.'

Flora rolled her eyes and went to obey. As she did so, she caught sight of something below. It was a turquoise Hillman Minx, parked directly below the flat. From the light of the nearby streetlamp, she could just make out a copy of *Men Only* magazine on the dashboard.

Flora stifled a gasp. The magazine was a signal to her, an unequivocal instruction to get out…right away.

Recoiling from the window, Flora dashed through the lounge to the front door, where she threw her coat over the top of her nightie and slipped her feet into her shoes which weren't the most practical for a hasty retreat.

'Where are you going?' Harold called.

'To get cigarettes,' she snapped, slamming the front door and running down the stairs as briskly as her heels would permit.

Flora opened the front door to the building and could hear the sound of sirens very close by. 'Damn it,' she said, throwing her shoes into the gutter and breaking into a run. She just reached the corner of Cambridge Square, as two police cars entered at the opposite end. She hurried up the steps to the nearest house, tucking herself under the portico entrance and peering around a pillar at the two police cars braking dramatically outside of Harold's building.

She watched as six police officers jumped out and ran to the house.

Taking a deep breath in, Flora stepped down onto the pavement as calmly as she could manage. She thrust her hands into her coat pockets and strolled in bare feet out of Cambridge Square, leaving the blue lights flashing dramatically behind her.

Alexander entered the hotel lobby. Five thick candles threw ugly shadows across the ceiling, which was scarred with fracture lines from the recent bombing raids. The concierge on duty behind the desk raised his hand towards Alexander. 'Mr Emmett: a message for you.'

Alexander approached the desk and took a folded piece of paper from his outstretched hand.

In the bar
AA

Alexander thanked the concierge and walked the short corridor which ran out of the lobby and entered the bar. The six lads from earlier had gone, but the drunk slumped at the counter remained. Alfie Archer was sitting in the same strategic spot in which Alexander had been seated earlier in the evening.

'Alfie,' Alexander said, taking the seat beside him.

'You need to leave,' Alfie whispered.

'I am,' Alexander said. 'In the morning. I've got a—'

'No. Now,' Alfie interrupted. 'There's a car waiting out the back.'

Alexander nodded. 'I'll go and get my things.'

'They're in the car,' Alfie said, rising from his chair. 'Let's go.'

'Can I ask what the urgency is?' he said quietly.

'Sawdust has been compromised,' he answered, as he ushered Alexander out of the bar. 'We're not safe here.'

'Will heading back to Beirut tonight, as opposed to tomorrow morning, really make a difference?'

They were outside the hotel already. Alfie pointed at an old Cadillac, its engine running. 'We're not going back to Beirut; we're returning to London.'

Alfie climbed into the front of the car and Alexander in the back.

As the car sped away from the hotel, Alexander stared out of the window, wondering if he was being sent back to London because they had discovered his secret.

Chapter Twenty-Four

Ellen was in the refreshments room on the third floor of Leconfield House, pouring tea from a pot; tea which, judging by its stew-like colour, had been made a good while ago. On a worktop behind her, the wireless was broadcasting the Home Service from the BBC. She dipped her finger into her cup. Tepid. It would have to do, since she didn't have the time to make another pot from scratch. She cocked her head towards the wireless, thinking that she had heard the news reporter talking about the awful plane crash in Egypt of the preceding day. She turned up the volume dial and listened.

Someone entered the room. It was her colleague, Jill Bradley. 'Morning!' she greeted cheerfully, placing the kettle on the gas-ring.

'Shh!' Ellen replied, placing her ear closer to the wireless speaker.

'Charming,' Jill muttered.

'...confirmed that the plane, scheduled for transporting President Nasser, had been in fact transporting a group of nurses to hospital facilities in Cairo. The plane came down a few miles out of Port Said and no survivors have been found. The cause of the accident is currently unknown...' the news reporter went on.

Ellen turned down the volume dial. 'Sorry,' she said to Jill. 'I just wanted to hear that story.'

'Terrible, isn't it,' Jill said. 'Sixteen young nurses.' She lowered her voice and leant in closer to Ellen. 'Shame it wasn't Nasser himself, to be honest.'

'Hmm,' Ellen said, her thoughts running off into the wilds of her mind. Leaving her mug of tea behind, Ellen hurried along the corridor and knocked on Mr Skardon's office door.

'Come in,' he called.

Ellen entered the office. 'Sorry to disturb you, Mr Skardon. Do you have a minute?'

Mr Skardon issued a short laugh. 'Of course, Miss Ingram. You're top of the class at the moment. More theories?'

'Well... Yes, actually,' she said. 'Nasser's plane that came down yesterday... Was it full of nurses, instead of Nasser himself, because of a tip-off?'

273

Mr Skardon shifted in his seat, looking rather irresolute about what he might say next. 'That's certainly very likely, yes.'

'Would it be wide of the mark to suggest that the tip-off came from Jericho?' Ellen asked, knowing that she was requesting more information than that usually permitted her in her role.

Mr Skardon said nothing but nodded.

'And were details of Nasser's flight mentioned in the intelligence found on the film cartridge Flora Sterling had passed to Gilmour, sir?'

Mr Skardon gritted his teeth and leant forwards onto his elbows, evidently feeling that he should not divulge anything further. 'Miss Ingram, this is in no way a reflection on you or your conduct, but I really am not in a position to share with *anyone* in this section the nature of what was contained in those photographs. As you will appreciate, they were highly classified, top-secret files pertaining to current, live political activity overseas.'

Ellen nodded. 'I understand, sir.'

'What's bothering you, exactly?'

'President Nasser received a tip-off from Jericho that his plane had been sabotaged, right?'

Mr Skardon opened his hands and shrugged.

'But *Gilmour* couldn't have done that. *He* never got to develop the prints. We did.'

'What are you trying to say?'

'Maybe Gilmour *isn't* Jericho,' Ellen ventured quietly.

Mr Skardon laughed. 'Believe me, Miss Ingram. If you'd seen the kind of evidence we've removed from his house, you would *not* be saying that. We've got enough to put Gilmour away for the rest of his life. He's been passing a lot of state secrets to the Soviets for a good number of years. And thanks largely to you, he's now behind bars. I think you're reading too much into all this. Men like him would have several sources of information, Flora Sterling being just one of them. And as much as I'd like to sweep every last mole, double-agent and spy from the country, it simply isn't going to happen overnight.'

Ellen nodded. He was probably right, and she was trying to make connections where none existed.

There was a sudden knock at the door with sufficient ferocity to startle Ellen.

'Come,' Mr Skardon barked.

Miss Brogren opened the door, appearing quite flustered. 'Urgent telephone call, Mr Skardon,' she said, a boiled sweet rattling fiercely against her teeth, as she spoke.

'Put it through,' he said, his hand hovering over the receiver.

The telephone rang once before he picked up. 'Skardon here... What? When? Well why the dickens wasn't he supervised? For God's sake, man!' He slammed down the receiver and glowered at Ellen. 'I'll be two minutes,' he said, hurrying from the office.

Ellen couldn't recall Mr Skardon ever looking so flustered as he had just then. She sat forwards in her chair and noticed something. On Mr Skardon's desk was a brown envelope with William Gilmour's name on it. She turned to the open door behind her, wondering. Did that file contain the photographs taken by Flora Sterling? And if so, was she brave or reckless enough to take a look? She glanced at the door again and then, without further deliberation, leant across the desk and opened the file. It was mainly comprised of loose sheets of foolscap paper, but at the back she saw photographic prints. Craning her neck around, she saw that the first image was of a letter, headed *TOP SECRET*.

Casting her eyes quickly down the document, she could see that it was a memo from the prime minister, Anthony Eden to Harold Austin. The subject, in bold underlined letters was *OPERATION SAWDUST*.

From the corridor outside came muted conversation.

Ellen quickly closed the file and sat back in the visitor's chair, studying her fingernails, just as Mr Skardon re-entered the office. Ellen feigned surprise at his arrival and asked, 'Everything alright, sir?'

'Gilmour's dead.'

'What? What happened?' Ellen asked.

'Hanged himself in his cell,' Mr Skardon replied. He huffed, raised his eyebrows and said, 'Well, now we'll never bloody know, if he was Jericho, or not.'

'Unless the police find Flora Sterling,' Ellen countered.

Mr Skardon huffed again, as though he thought that an unlikely scenario.

Ellen sensed that it was time to leave. 'Thank you, sir,' she muttered, making her way out of the office and closing the door behind her.

Back at her desk, Ellen was unable to shake the question mark which she had placed over Gilmour's head. A few days before, she had been the only person in this office to believe Jericho to have been a codename used by William Gilmour. Now, she was the only person in this office who doubted that fact.

She walked to the back of the room and stood in front of the three large blackboards. The board in the centre, containing photographs of Flora Sterling, Harold Austin, Nikita Sokolov and William Gilmour, had been updated with recent developments. At any moment, Mr Skardon would come in and announce to the office that Gilmour was dead and somebody would add an annotation to the board to reflect this fact.

Above Flora Sterling's photograph was written in red chalk letters, URGENTLY SOUGHT.

Ellen stared, unblinking, at Flora's picture.

Flora was bored. She was more bored than at any time she could recall in her life prior to this dull exiled existence. She was staying in the Dartford safe house, a dreary, post-war, prefab bungalow, which, although only twenty miles outside of Central London, might as well have been a thousand miles from any form of civilisation. It was set in its own run-down grounds, accessed via a much-neglected country lane.

She was standing at the open kitchen door, shivering at the chill November winds whipping up from the nearby River Thames, not half-a-mile away. Given that Nikita had said that there was an all-ports alert out for her, it was crazy to think that, following a short walk from here, she could just hop onto a boat and be out in the English Channel in a matter of minutes, with MI5's being none the wiser. She grinned at the idea that her name and photograph was pinned up at every port and airport in the country. How far she'd come. From her days as a mannequin model and topless dancer at Murray's Cabaret Club to being in possession of sufficiently damaging intelligence, capable of bringing down the British government. And that was her trump card which would see her getting out of here within a day or two: one telephone call, which she would make later today to dear Harold about all that she knew, and the nationwide hunt for her would be instantly over.

She stared into the grey abyss over the Thames, reflecting on how Nikita Sokolov had first recruited her in 1940 at the age of nineteen to act as a 'swallow'. At first, her personal charms and beauty had been used to recruit intelligent but pliable young men to the cause of communism, who could be guided through careers in the British Secret

276

Intelligence Services, where they would have routine and regular access to unparalleled material, secrets and espionage networks around the globe.

Her position had progressed quickly from manipulating susceptible young men to working on British diplomatic officials who, having fallen for her charms, could be blackmailed into rendering further service. Nikita had seen further potential in her and, from there, Flora had begun to gather her own intelligence. And here she was, the mistress of the Foreign Secretary at a time of great national crisis, procuring high-grade intelligence.

One telephone call to the hacks on Fleet Street, and she would be set financially for the rest of her life: her story, with the accompanying proof which she had carefully hidden, would be worth a small fortune. There would never have been a scandal like it, she thought with a wry smile. The public exposure would instantly bring an end to her espionage career, but perhaps it was coming to an end anyway, she thought; she could hardly show her face at gatherings of high society and cocktail parties, given what the establishment would come to know about her in due course.

Whatever the future held, for the moment Nikita had told her to lie low until the situation had settled. So, she was imprisoned in this dull hellhole of a place, which didn't even have electricity. If Harold could see her living here! Poor, sordid, little man: she actually felt sorry him. She could see him now, sheepishly taking in the news from the police and MI5, wondering how he could have been so stupid and reckless; wondering how much of his private life would end up as front-page news; wondering how to save his precious job in government and what on earth he would tell his wife.

Flora laughed feverishly, as she stepped inside and closed the door to the cold November day.

Alexander's eyes rolled and his eyelids danced up and down, before finally surrendering and closing completely. His muscles relaxed and the empty tumbler in his right hand dropped to the floor. The thud, as it struck the carpet and smashed, jolted his eyes back open. In those few fleeting seconds his memory reset and he felt anew the deep horror of when he had learned of the plane crash. His mind had cruelly—or perhaps justifiably and deservedly—created a perfect, mind's-eye image of the last moments of those nurses' lives. Since, he had spent every moment re-hearing the details of the 'accident'—for that was how it was currently being described—numbed by anguish and alcohol. But still, through this haze of intoxication, his brain had delighted in replaying over and over again its fantasy version of the plane's demise. The real details, he had tried to avoid. Names, ages and back stories of the nurses involved had begun to filter into the Egyptian news.

How could they have done that? To him and to those women? *How?* That had not been what was supposed to have happened.

Alexander's head tipped to one side, as drunken sleep dragged him in.

Instantly, he was ravaged by the horrendous, filmic detail of his nightmares. Real snippets—his pouring water into the oil tanks—were seamlessly spliced with fictitious imaginings: each of the propellers failing in turn; fire billowing from the engines; the Ilyushin Il-14 plummeting to the ground and the sheer terror on the women's faces.

Sleep was no good. Alexander reached to the bottle of pink gin on the chair beside him. Empty. He stood up and walked into the kitchen of his flat in Lancaster Gate. He hadn't been back in London very long and, after all that had happened whilst he had been away, it felt slightly other-worldly to be there. Perhaps the physical distance was a good thing.

As he searched in his cupboards for more alcohol, he heard a strange buzzing sound. He paused and listened. It was a familiar noise, yet he could not place it. It buzzed again and he realised that it was his door entry system.

In the hallway, Alexander pressed the button to speak, his mental and physical worlds spinning. 'Hello?'

'Alexander? Mrs Strickland here,' came a strong female voice.

He laughed. 'Mrs Strickland! How are your holiday lodgings in Beirut?' he called through the intercom. 'And the Lebanese wine?'

'Might I come in, please?' she asked, although there was little question in her tone.

Alexander laughed and stubbed his finger in and around the button which permitted entry.

He opened the door to his flat, intrigued.

The woman, who appeared, was not how his imagination had designed her. She was in her early sixties with tightly curled white hair, a pair of round dark-rimmed glasses and a stern judge-like demeanour. She wore a long blue raincoat and held a tartan handbag clamped to her side. She extended her right gloved hand towards him. 'Mrs Strickland.'

'Alexander,' he said, mesmerised and slightly baffled. 'Come in.'

She entered his flat and he closed the door. As he directed her into the lounge, he said, 'I didn't think Mrs Strickland was real. I thought it was just a codename.'

Mrs Strickland made a moue, as she prepared to sit down, noticing at the last moment the empty bottle of pink gin and the smashed glass on the floor. Plucking the bottle neck between forefinger and thumb, as though it were a dead mouse, she placed it down beside her.

'Mr Emmett,' she began. 'I should like—'

'How did it happen?' he interrupted.

'Pardon?'

'How did it happen that President Nasser was replaced at the last minute by sixteen nurses?' he asked, concentrating hard in order to produce a near-coherent sentence.

Mrs Strickland slowly inhaled. 'It's not yet known. Certainly, he received a tip-off, but from where and whom is currently under investigation. I'm afraid, like all civilian casualties in war, it is a regrettable par for the course, as it were.'

'I don't imagine their families seeing it like that,' he retorted, slowly climbing towards sobriety.

'No, but neither would President Nasser's family, nor the poor pilot's.'

'What do you want, exactly?' Alexander asked.

'A further application of your expertise and knowledge of Egypt,' she revealed.

'Huh?' he replied. 'Another assassination attempt?'

'Not at this time, no. This is more intelligence-related.'

'I don't feel very intelligent,' he found himself mumbling.

'Operation Sawdust has, in light of recent events and the changeable situation in Egypt, had to change direction somewhat.'

'Sawdust is still running?' Alexander asked.

'Very much so, yes.'

'Wow, this government must *really* hate Nasser and his regime,' he muttered. 'So, what is it you want from me? I thought my presence in Egypt was too dangerous.'

'It is,' she confirmed. 'We want you to work from here for the time being.'

'Doing what, exactly?'

'Attend the Czechoslovakian Ambassador's Ball tonight.'

Alexander shrugged. 'That doesn't sound too difficult.'

Mrs Strickland gave him a brief, false smile. 'Yesterday, the United Nations General Assembly passed Resolution 1003—'

'To send out the first-ever international peacekeeping force,' Alexander interjected.

'Precisely that,' Mrs Strickland confirmed. 'The first troops will be sent out in three days' time.'

'And what's that got to do with me?' he asked, the lifting fog in his head seemingly preventing clarity of thought.

'Yugoslavia is sending an entire reconnaissance battalion to the area, headed up by Colonel Zoran Pavlovic.'

'And...?'

'Colonel Zoran Pavlovic will be attending the Czechoslovakian Ambassador's Ball tonight.'

'And you want what from me?' Alexander asked, still none the wiser.

'To use your charm, wit and knowledge of the area to procure from the good Colonel anything and everything about the organisation of his battalion, to whom the reconnaissance will be sent and in what format, and the locations of their bases.'

'Right.'

Mrs Strickland pressed the clasp of her handbag and removed a black and white headshot of a man in his early fifties, wearing unfamiliar military regalia. He had fierce, vicious eyes and the appearance of a soldier capable of anything. 'This is he.'

'Pleasant-looking chap, isn't he?'

Mrs Strickland held the photograph in front of him, as though he should be engraining the man's face onto his memory, then returned it to her bag.

'Anything else?' Alexander asked.

'Enduring trust and friendship.'

'In one evening,' Alexander remarked.

'Yes,' Mrs Strickland said. She stood to leave. 'Good luck.'

Alexander followed her to his front door. She opened it and, on the landing outside of his flat, bent down to pick up a suit bag. 'You'll be needing this,' she said, handing it over to him. 'And for God's sake have a shave, take a bath and sober up.' She turned and descended the stairs without a word or a glance back.

'Bye,' he muttered, staring at the tuxedo which had been miraculously delivered to his door. On top of the black bag was a gold-rimmed invitation to the ball with his name written in the centre.

Was he really up to this? The plane crash had been the first blood spilled, which had been directly attributable to him. Sixteen civilians were dead because of what he had done. Did he need to harden himself, as Mrs Strickland had said, to see the bigger picture?

He had no choice.

Alexander walked towards the magnificent white building of the Czechoslovakian Embassy. It was located at the far end of Hyde Park at the exclusive address of 6-7 Kensington Palace Gardens. The buildings around him were exquisite, situated around the palace itself, the birthplace and childhood home of Queen Victoria and now the official residence of the Duchess of Kent.

He strolled with an affected gait, assuming the role and comportment that his bowler hat, tuxedo and polished shoes demanded of him. He had obeyed all of Mrs Strickland's instructions: he had bathed, shaven and not touched a drop of alcohol all day, despite his dark thoughts pressing him to do so.

Two men, wearing bright-red livery with white ribbing, offered a pleasant but guarded welcome when he reached the door. It was clear from their demeanour that if his name appeared on the list, then he would be very welcome to enter the ball, but if it were not, then they would cheerfully and forcefully remove him from the premises; possibly even from the vicinity.

'Alexander Emmett,' he said.

The man on the right checked his name from a list on a wooden podium beside him. 'Welcome, Mr Emmett,' he greeted, gesturing inside the entrance.

Alexander went to move but stopped and asked, 'Has my friend arrived yet, Zoran Pavlovic?'

Whilst the doorman examined the guest list, Alexander needlessly added, 'He's a colonel in the Yugoslavian army.'

The doorman shook his head. 'He has not arrived, yet, sir.'

Alexander thanked him and entered the opulent lobby, where the passionate notes from an unseen orchestra's concluding crescendo drifted in.

A young man in livery stepped forward and took Alexander's hat and coat, directing him to the attractive young woman at the far end of the lobby, who stood with a fixed smile and a silver platter of flutes raised precariously but deftly on her fingertips.

'Welcome,' she said, with a slight deferential curtsey. 'Champagne for you, sir?'

Alexander thanked her, took a glass and proceeded through the open doors into a vast hall. On the left, lit by magnificent crystal chandeliers, were between twenty and thirty round tables, each set for eight people. On the right of the room, presently adorned with a twelve-piece, all-female orchestra, was an open space which, perhaps later, would act as a dancefloor but which, for the time being, was occupied by at least eighty men and women wearing their finest tuxedoes and ballgowns, mingling with polite diplomacy.

He passed slowly through the crowds, casually scrutinising the guests as he went, wondering if everyone here was a marionette with a hidden agenda, subtly probing below the surface of refined conversation to elicit information for a higher power. From the appearance of the diplomats, ambassadors, ministers and government officials, whom he was passing, the answer was no; convivial smiles and prosaic conversations were all that he could discern. Perhaps he was being too cynical and the banal conversations around him were actually sincere, whilst laying the foundations for potential future ambush or collusion.

His thoughts were interrupted when someone tapped his arm and said, 'Hello, stranger.'

Alexander stopped abruptly, almost spilling his champagne. 'Oh, hello,' he replied. 'This is a nice surprise.'

The woman smiled and kissed him on the cheek.

'Ellen Ingram,' he said, pleased to have remembered her name.

'Alexander Emmett,' she said, touching her glass to his. 'What brings you here, then? Are you a friend of the Czechoslovakian ambassador?'

Alexander laughed and considered what he should tell her. There was little sense in lying, he thought. 'I need to meet with a Yugoslavian colonel who's going to be here tonight.'

'Oh, right. Sounds terribly exciting.'

He grinned, unsure whether she was being sarcastic or genuinely thought that meeting Zoran Pavlovic was an interesting prospect. 'What about you? I didn't think this was your *usual environment*,' he said, recalling what she had told him at their last meeting eight months previous at Harold Austin's cocktail party.

She rolled her head, contemplating his question. Then, she sipped her champagne. Eventually, she answered. 'People-watching.'

'Cryptic…' he replied.

'Look at them,' she said, scything her flute in the air at the guests around her. 'All of them speaking through fixed smiles, talking about nothing at all of significance, yet determined to hear something of terribly grave importance.'

'That was the conclusion I just came to,' Alexander agreed.

He studied her face, thinking her more beautiful than the last time that he had seen her. She too had a hidden agenda; a woman with a simple clerical job and a blatant disdain for such occasions would not find herself accidentally at the Foreign Secretary's cocktail party nor the Czechoslovakian Ambassador's Ball.

'I rather hoped we might have bumped into each other after meeting in March,' she said, coyly.

'Me too,' he agreed. 'I've been out of the country, though, as a correspondent.'

'Oh, where have you been?' she asked.

He noticed that, as she spoke, she was surreptitiously glancing over his shoulder at something or someone behind him. He was minded to turn and look but didn't want to betray that he had perceived it. 'I've been based in Beirut,' he replied.

Ellen raised her eyebrows, impressed. 'The epicentre of all the crises,' she commented.

'Yes, very much so,' he said. 'Journalistically speaking, it's been fantastic.'

'I'm sure,' she said, snatching subtle glimpses behind him. 'Did you report on Suez at all?'

Alexander nodded. 'Yes. Terrible situation out there.'

Ellen finished her drink. 'And all those poor nurses killed on that plane yesterday.'

'Hmm,' he mumbled, draining the last of his champagne and feeling the nausea reawaken inside him. 'Do you want another drink?'

'Yes, please,' Ellen replied.

He turned hastily, throwing his eyeline in the direction to where Ellen's attention had been drawn. Two older ladies, chatting and laughing together, were directly in the line of sight. Was it they, by whom Ellen was captivated? As Alexander walked in their direction, one of them stepped backwards, offering a snapshot of a man hunched awkwardly at the bar. Could it have been him?

Alexander stood next to the man, acting obliviously and ordered two further glasses of champagne. In his peripheral vision, he could see the man's head swaying, as he knocked his drink back in one. 'Another,' he demanded of the barman.

Alexander turned, as if now suddenly aware of him. The man was suitably attired, but still somehow his unkempt balding hair and grey unshaven stubble gave him a dishevelled appearance. 'Evening,' Alexander said, with a light nodding of his head.

'Good evening,' the man replied with a slurred Baltic accent. When he spoke, he revealed a prominent dead tooth in the front of his mouth, conferring on Alexander the certain knowledge of the identity of this man, whom he had never met. Was Ellen here because of him? Intriguing.

'Which country are you representing tonight?' Alexander asked with a warm smile.

'I am second secretary at the Soviet Embassy here in London,' he wheezed. There was a hardness to his voice, but also a suggestion of arrogance.

'Alexander Emmett,' he introduced, offering his hand. 'Journalist for the *Observer*.'

The man shook his hand impassively, as the barman slid another glass of drink in front of him. 'Nikita Sokolov.'

'Nostrovia,' Alexander said, raising his glass and wondering if Ellen were trailing this man for whomever her employer was.

'Na Zdorovie,' Nikita replied, meeting Alexander's glass with his.

'Have a good evening,' Alexander said to him, standing up with the two drinks of champagne.

He retraced his steps back to where Ellen had been, but she was gone. Feeling unexpectedly forlorn, Alexander scanned the crowds in search of her, but she was nowhere to be seen. He wondered if his speaking with the drunk Soviet secretary had necessitated, for whatever reason, that she abscond.

Alexander took a long drink and cast his gaze slowly around the room in search of either Colonel Zoran Pavlovic or the mysterious Ellen Ingram. He could see neither and drank more, mercifully beginning to lose himself to the effects of the alcohol; effects which were becoming ever harder to attain.

Ellen had watched the interaction between Alexander and Nikita, fascinated. What on earth could they have been saying to one another? She saw Alexander return to where he had left her. She saw the crestfallen look of disappointment on his face and she smiled. This was followed by his searching the crowds for her.

He turned towards the orchestra and she walked up behind him, placing her hand on his elbow. 'Looking for me?'

He twirled around and grinned. 'Thought you'd abandoned me,' he said, handing her a flute.

'I was just making some subtle changes to the dining arrangements,' she revealed.

'Oh?'

'A little presumptuous, I know,' she went on, 'but you've now got *me* sitting beside you instead of some dreary German diplomat. Don't worry, your colonel is still sitting on your other side.'

Alexander raised his glass conspiratorially. 'Cheers to that. Good work!'

'He's not here, yet, by the way,' she added.

'Who's not?'

'Your colonel friend,' Ellen answered. 'I asked at the door for you.'

She was thrilled by his reaction when he shrugged and said, 'It just means I get more time to talk to you.'

From her position in front of Alexander, Ellen could still just make out Nikita Sokolov sitting propped up at the bar. He was drinking a lot but only talking to the barman. He was making no obvious attempts to contact or link up with anyone else, least of all Flora Sterling, as had been the hope at Leconfield House after she had vanished two days earlier.

A tip-off had come from inside the Soviet Embassy that morning that Nikita would be attending the Czechoslovakian Ambassador's Ball and two tickets had been urgently procured. Also in the room, operating independently, was her A4 colleague, Paul Reynolds. Twice already they had passed each other, acting as apathetic strangers.

'Is the colonel a friend of yours?' Ellen asked, keen to understand Alexander's reasons for attending.

'No,' he answered. 'It's really rather boring. I need to speak to him for a piece I'm writing on the United Nations Emergency Force.'

'Ah,' Ellen said, 'Resolution 1003.'

Alexander grimaced. 'How do you know about that?'

'It's all over the news,' she replied.

'Yes, but—'

'But…because I'm a woman, I shouldn't take an interest? Or I shouldn't understand the situation in the Middle East?' she said, giving him a gentle smile.

He declined to reply but instead said, 'What are you *really* doing here, Ellen?' he probed.

Rather inexplicably, Ellen was almost wanting to tell him. Almost. 'I told you, boring clerical work.'

'It seems we're both here for very boring reasons,' he observed with a wry smile, nudging obliquely at the truth.

Was he guessing as to the nature of her employment, as she was guessing his? There was one thing of which she was sure: he wasn't just a journalist with the *Observer*. Like many people in this room, his purported job was merely a façade. 'Let's leave it there, then,' she suggested, chinking her glass against his again.

Over his shoulder, Ellen watched, as Nikita slipped off the bar stool and fell onto the floor. Her reaction evidently had shown on her face, for Alexander turned.

'Oh, God,' he said. 'Do you think I should go and help him?'

'No,' Ellen said, decisively grabbing his wrist. 'He'll be okay. He's just drunk, is all.'

With a coincidentally rousing number from the orchestra as an accompaniment, they watched Nikita trying to stand up. The music serendipitously managed to render the scenario farcical and completely out of place. The barman was talking to him, calling over a waiter who slung Nikita's right arm over his shoulder and began to walk him towards the door.

Damn it, Ellen thought. She should pursue him, but how could she without its being entirely obvious to Alexander? She didn't know what to do, watching as Nikita and the waiter disappeared from view.

Alexander glanced at her, perhaps also wondering what she was going to say or do next.

Thankfully, in that moment, the decision was taken away from her, as she spotted Paul Reynolds heading out of the door behind them.

'Well…' she said, turning on her heels and facing Alexander. He seemed to be about to speak, but at that moment the orchestra brought the symphony to an end and the Master of Ceremonies—a short rotund man with a white beard—breathed heavily into a hand-held microphone, then bade everyone welcome to the ball. He announced that the first course would be served in ten minutes' time, making a quip about the ladies just having time to powder their noses before taking their seats.

'Well, I don't need to powder my nose,' Ellen whispered to Alexander. 'You?'

He shook his head. 'Shall we go and sit down?'

A violinist began to play a piece of emotive music, as the guests began gravitating towards their tables.

Ellen led Alexander to their place-settings and they sat down.

'Still no sign of him, then,' she said, pointing to the vacant spot beside Alexander.

'Maybe he had a better offer,' he replied.

Ellen picked up the menu from the centre of the table. 'What could be better than'—she held the menu closer to her face—'char siu duck with cucumber and spring onion salsa? Or galantine of corn-fed chicken with beetroot, girolles and golden raisin purée?'

He laughed and whispered, 'What the hell's galantine and girolles?'

She giggled. 'No idea. Or char siu duck.'

A refined-looking lady—in a purple ballgown and a glittering tiara—sat down beside Ellen with a scowl, evidently disapproving of the conversation that she had inadvertently entered. Her husband—a dashing gentleman with a thin black moustache and swept-back hair—tucked in her chair, then she leant towards Ellen and articulated quietly, 'Char siu is a *marinade*, don't you know.'

'No, I didn't,' Ellen replied, not sure how to take the woman's condescending tone. She turned to Alexander and quietly said, 'There's an amazing fish and chip shop near to my flat in Camden.'

He laughed and whispered, 'At least we'd be able to understand the menu.'

Her eyes lit up and she inclined towards him. 'Shall we?'

'Are you serious?' he said, taking a quick glance to the empty chair beside him.

She nodded. 'Come on.' Synchronised, they stood up and finished their champagne, before excusing themselves and heading to the cloakroom.

'Oh, I do hope that nothing is the matter,' the attendant said, handing back their coats.

'I'm afraid my husband is feeling rather unwell,' Ellen teased, placing a concerned hand on Alexander's arm.

Alexander played along, nodding and stroking his stomach.

'Oh, dear. Well I do hope the situation improves. Such a pity,' the attendant said.

'Isn't it just,' Ellen concurred, threading her arm through Alexander's and heading out into the cold November night.

'Thanks, Wife,' Alexander laughed the moment they were away from the embassy.

'You'll thank me later when you're tucking into the best rock and chips in London.'

'Even better than char siu duck?' he joked.

'*It's a marinade, don't you know,*' she replied, pushing her face close to his.

He leant in and kissed her gently on the lips.

Ellen pulled him closer, feeling his breath on her lips, then opened her mouth and kissed him with a passion that startled her as much as it did him.

It took a few seconds for Alexander's thoughts to catch up for him to place his surroundings into a context which he understood. His head was aching, but he managed to sit himself up and look around. The sight of Ellen Ingram asleep beside him brought the memories of last night cascading back. They had taken a taxi to Camden, bought fish and chips and eaten them here in her flat. She had opened a bottle of cheap white wine, at which point his recollection of the rest of the night grew somewhat foggy.

He climbed out of the bed naked, in desperate need of a glass of water. Ambling over to the bedroom door, he quietly pulled it open. In front of him was a small hallway with three closed doors. His memory of last night provided him with no clarity as to which would be the kitchen.

The first door, which he opened, led to a tiny bathroom. He urinated, scowled at the horrendous person scowling back at him in the mirror and then backtracked into the hallway. Pushing open the second door, he could see that it was a box room containing a single bed, stack of boxes and a chest of drawers. He was about to close the door when he noticed the wall. What on earth was *that*?

He moved inside the room, his tired eyes darting over the photographs, typed reports and handwritten notes, which were sellotaped to the wall. What was all this?

One black and white photograph, clearly taken without the person's knowledge, confirmed whom Ellen had been following the night before: Nikita Sokolov. Another undercover photograph was of the Foreign Secretary, Harold Austin, and sandwiched between the two men was an image of Flora Sterling. A single line of red wool, fixed to her image, draped across to Harold Austin's photograph, then continued on to Flora Sterling before firing off diagonally to a small photograph that made him gasp: William Gilmour. Below the image of Gilmour was written a word which sent a chill to Alexander's core: ~~JERICHO~~.

The word was repeated on its own separate sheet of paper, followed by an ominously large question mark. Below it were newspaper cuttings pertaining to Nasser's crashed aeroplane and the words *Operation Sawdust.*

Alexander reached for the chest of drawers, feeling suddenly nauseous.

This woman, to whom he was genuinely attracted, was clearly not employed in clerical work. What was she? A private detective? MI5?

Chapter Twenty-Five

'Wow,' Morton said to himself. Although it wasn't a major surprise, holding Alexander Emmett's death certificate for 1944 still took him aback. He was standing in his kitchen, dumbfounded.

'What is it?' Juliette asked, looking up from reading her book.

'Alexander Emmett's death certificate,' he answered. 'You were right, he *did* die in 1944.'

Juliette pulled a smug face. 'You're welcome.'

The certificate left no room for doubt that the Alexander Emmett, whose birth certificate Morton had fixed to his investigation wall, had died eighteen months before apparently being resurrected and sailing on the Pacific Steam Navigation Company ship, *Orbita*, arriving in the UK on the 20th May 1946.

Morton was, to all intents and purposes, back at square one. The man, who had masqueraded as Maurice Duggan, had also masqueraded as Alexander Emmett.

But who was he?

Morton exhaled, wondering if he had ever encountered a case more complex than this one. If he had, then he certainly couldn't bring it to mind.

This man, whoever he had been, had gone to great lengths to cover his tracks and Morton was running out of avenues to pursue in order to identify his real self. One area, where this interloper could not hide his identity, was through his DNA which he had passed on to his son, Christopher. An Ancestry DNA kit, which Morton had sent by expedited delivery, should be with Christopher at any moment.

He looked down at the death certificate again, as if he might somehow glean new information which might contradict his firm assessment that Alexander had died in 1944.

When and where died: 14th November 1944, Port Said, Egypt
Name and surname: Alexander Emmett
Sex: Male
Age: 16
Occupation: Student. Legitimate issue of Geoffrey Owen Emmett (deceased), a British Subject by birth
Cause of death: Trauma following car accident

Signature, description and residence of informant: L. H. Hurst, H.M. Consul

Now what? he wondered, carrying the certificate up to his study. He had spent the great majority of yesterday trying to find anything on Alexander Emmett's early life in Egypt but could find barely anything. All that he had discovered was that Alexander's father, Geoffrey had arrived in Egypt from London in 1922 and had married Alexandria Hassan in 1925.

Morton stood in front of the timeline fixed to his investigation wall. There was no space left to add a summary of the information on the certificate, which was now rather crucial evidence. He knelt on the floor and began unpicking the earliest documents from the wall, intent on rearranging the timeline.

From downstairs came the sound of the doorbell. Morton paused for a moment and craned his neck towards the door. Juliette was talking to the person; a woman, it sounded like.

He resumed his removal of the documents, reminding himself of the content, as he did so. Maurice Duggan's baptism entry in Ardingly in 1927. His burial in 1944. The newspaper report into his drowning.

Morton became distracted: someone was heading up the stairs. With the newspaper report in his hand, he stood up, expecting to see Juliette. He quickly realised from the effortful breathless shuffling, however, that it was not her. Even in her current state of tired pregnancy, she wouldn't be making the racket currently emanating from the person climbing the stairs. Brilliant.

Clarissa Duggan entered his study and stared wide-eyed at his investigation wall. 'Oh, my word!' she screeched. 'It's like I've stepped into some television police drama and you're the mad stalker-serial-killer.' Her astonished eyes roamed the wall and then looked suspiciously at Morton.

'Right,' he said, not sure how to respond to her comment.

From the floor below, he heard Juliette giggling and couldn't manage to stifle his own small grin. He would be sure to thank her, later.

'I was going to ask how you were getting on,' Clarissa said, still trying to make sense of what she was seeing. 'But... I mean...' She made a noise of incredulity, as she blew out her puffed cheeks. 'Well.'

Morton looked at his watch and then at the newspaper report in his hand. Two words suddenly leapt off the page at him: a name. He did a quick double-take to confirm that which he had just read.

Clarissa was talking, but Morton ignored her and re-read the whole article.

DUGGAN BOY DROWNED WHEN ICE GAVE WAY

Maurice Duggan, the son of renowned local businessman, Gerald Duggan of Knowles, Ardingly was drowned on Saturday afternoon when the ice on which he was playing at Westwood Lake gave way. This tragedy was attended by a deed of great pluck and heroism by a 17-year-old boy, named Hubert John Spencer from 2 Street Lane, Ardingly. He was nearby and plunged into the icy water to Maurice's rescue. He succeeded in getting Maurice onto his back and, holding him with one hand, swam to the edge of the lake. Hubert continued his heroic endeavours to get Maurice out of the water but he suddenly slipped out of his grasp and disappeared under the ice. Hubert, himself well-nigh exhausted by the cold and his strenuous efforts, managed to scramble out. Another of the boys' friends, William Gilmour sent for P.C. Foster, and after attempting to reach the hole in the ice, ran half a mile to fetch a ladder. Sub-Divisional Inspector Martin and other officers made efforts to get to the boy. They procured a boat which they launched, quickly finding Maurice Duggan's body. Attempts to revive him were made whilst still in the boat and continued when he was on the bank. A resuscitator was also used until the arrival of Dr Rooney, who pronounced life extinct. At the inquest of Wednesday, Mr J. Baily-Gibson, Deputy Coroner recorded a verdict of "Death by misadventure."

William Gilmour.

Morton didn't understand. Working under the presumption that Gilmour's name appearing in the report was not simply a coincidence, then this document provided a link between him and Maurice Duggan. But still it made no sense.

'You're not even listening to me, are you?' Clarissa accused.

'Sorry,' Morton said, returning. 'Could you say it again, please? I just got a bit distracted.'

'Is all this'—she gestured to the investigation wall—'*really* necessary? It's never this complicated on *Who Do you Think You Are?*'

'No,' he agreed, it wasn't. How could he explain the case to her, when he didn't understand it for himself? He rubbed his eyes and said, 'Look, the man posing as your brother was a very complex person. I'm in the process of trying to pull all of this together, but it is still ongoing. I'm going to need a little more time before I can get the report to you.'

Clarissa frowned and whispered, 'I just can't sleep with that cheque hanging over me. It's *a lot* of money.'

Now that he was fully focussing on her, Morton could see that her face was more drawn and lined than the last time that he had seen her. Hypothetically, he *could* tell her what she wanted to hear: that the man, who had pretended to be her dead brother, had a son, Christopher, to whom she could hand the cheque for eighty-nine thousand pounds, which she had fraudulently obtained. But what if there were more children out there? He posed a question to her, which had been troubling him somewhat: 'Can I just ask you something?' he began. When she nodded, he continued, 'What will you do when you hand the money to the rightful heirs of this man, if they then decide to tell the police?'

'Take it on the chin, I suppose,' she said. 'What else *can* I do?'

'Look, I don't mean to alarm you, but they might feel that's their only option. If they don't report it and then take the money, essentially they're aiding and abetting the crime.'

'Hmm,' she said. 'What if I were to cash the cheque and then give them the money anonymously somehow?'

'I don't know,' Morton replied honestly. It was an ethical minefield. He had visions of Clarissa feeding bundles of fifty-pound notes through Christopher's letterbox in the middle of the night.

'How much longer?' she asked.

An Ancestry DNA test could easily take up to six weeks. Sometimes more, sometimes less. 'A month?' he ventured optimistically.

She groaned and steadied herself on the door. 'Good gracious. I'm not sure my poor nerves could stand it.'

'I just can't conclude the case,' he repeated. 'Not yet.'

Another heavy sigh from Clarissa. 'I suppose I'd better go. I've got the removals men coming tomorrow—thank goodness—to get rid of all that junk from my house,' she said, moving off but then pausing to study the investigation wall once more. She looked Morton in the eyes. 'You really are a strange fellow and I'm not sure what the police would say about all *this*,' she said, jabbing an accusatory finger at the wall.

Morton smiled, probably appearing all the stranger. 'Thanks for popping in.'

Clarissa continued to mumble, as she made her way down the stairs.

For the third time, he read the newspaper report into Maurice Duggan's drowning, certain that he must be missing something crucial. He couldn't make his brain join the dots together. Ellen Ingram had worked for MI5. She had followed Flora Sterling, a suspected spy to the house of William Gilmour. Gilmour had been arrested and then had committed suicide. Around the same time, the reincarnated Alexander Emmett had something to do with the secret MI6 mission, Operation Sawdust. Ellen had then married Alexander. Ellen had committed suicide and Alexander had fled. Alexander had returned under the dead double-identity of Maurice Duggan, who had drowned in 1944 despite the best efforts of William Gilmour and Hubert Spencer to save him.

It wasn't so much a jigsaw puzzle as three or four jigsaw puzzles of similar design, with different pieces missing, all jumbled up in the same box.

'Why can't I break this?' he said to the wall. But the wall didn't answer, it just showed him a whole raft of documents, which he had accumulated in the course of his research, making his head spin.

The next step, he thought, would be to find the evidence that the two William Gilmours were one and the same person.

Leaving his timeline in pieces on the floor, Morton sat at his desk and started up his laptop. He remembered that there had been several newspaper reports mentioning William Gilmour's death, but at the time Morton had had little to link him to the Duggan Case and so had not searched too deeply beyond the first results.

Opening up the British Newspaper Archive online, he entered Gilmour's name and the keyword *spy* into the search engine.

From just outside his door came a cackling, "Oh, it's like I've stepped into a police drama and you're the mad serial-killer!"

Morton laughed and Juliette stuck her head around the door, clutching the bottom of her distended belly. 'Oh...that did make me laugh, Morton,' she said, giggling again. "I don't know what the police would make of all this!"

Morton shook his head. 'She's got the audacity to say that *I'm* strange. Honestly.'

'Although it is lovely to come up here and mock you, I actually came up to ask if you're around tomorrow to pick Grace up from nursery?'

Morton grimaced. 'I'm booked at the Churchill Archives in Cambridge and I've got a translator reserved, as well. Sorry. Why's that?'

Juliette gave a dismissive wave. 'Doesn't matter. Lucy wanted to do something, but we can arrange a different time. Why do you need a translator?'

'A crucial file I need access to is written completely in Russian. Have you heard of it: The Mitrokhin Archive? It exposed loads of Soviet spies from the Cold War when it was released in 1999.'

Juliette thought for a moment and then shook her head. 'Don't think so.'

'Yes, you have. There was that old lady, Melita Norwood, who'd been spilling secrets to the Russians about her work at some research lab.'

'Oh, yes...' Juliette recalled. 'I do. There was a newspaper headline I remember: *The Spy who came in from the Co-op.*'

'Yeah, that's the one,' Morton confirmed. 'And there was a Scotland Yard detective, a journalist and an MP, who were all revealed to have been spies. Nikita Sokolov is mentioned in that file somewhere.'

'Exciting,' she said.

'It could be,' he replied, not sure whether she was being sarcastic or not. 'I'll be down shortly.'

'Heard that before,' she retorted, heading downstairs.

Turning back to his laptop, Morton clicked on the first newspaper report into William Gilmour's suicide. It gave nothing about his background but did state that he had been aged twenty-nine, which tallied with the date of birth that he had discovered in the National Archive file on Gilmour.

As Morton worked through the list of results, he noticed that many of the newspapers had run almost identical stories, particularly the provincial titles. A thought came to him. He returned to the search menu and filtered the results, first by county, then by newspaper. He selected the *West Sussex Gazette* and the *West Sussex County Times.* If any newspaper had written more about Gilmour's background, then it would have been a local one.

Two results.

The first was an article in the *West Sussex Gazette* about Gilmour's suicide. He scanned down the text and found something: ...*Yesterday, the young misfit who hailed from 2 Street Lane, Ardingly, West Sussex, who used to sing so sweetly as an innocent, surpliced choir-boy, was found dead in his cell…*

There it was: Ardingly.

Then another thought struck him and he opened the photo app on his mobile phone, scrolling back until he found the pictures which he had taken at Ardingly church. He found the image of Maurice Duggan's baptism and moved up the page, scrutinising the other entries, which had occurred in that small parish at that time. Sure enough, at the bottom, he found William Gilmour's baptism.

Both Maurice Duggan and William Gilmour had been born in the village and would likely have gone to school together and been friends.

Still unable to figure it out, Morton continued reading the newspaper report, copying into his notes another intriguing paragraph:

…In 1945 Gilmour joined the Royal Corps of Signals, completing initial training in the Middle East, where he wrote to a friend in London: 'I have a little library of my own, including 'The Soviet Caucasus' and 'Land of the Soviets.' But how I long for a film magazine or 'Daily Worker!'…

Morton pored over the text, wishing that it made more sense. Gilmour had spent time in the Middle East: could that be what connected him to the real Alexander Emmett and the fake Alexander Emmett?

'What am I not seeing?' he said to himself.

His mobile phone pinged with the receipt of a Facebook message. Morton looked at the screen. Christopher. He opened the message. *Mortimer, spat & sent. Christopher.*

Spat & sent. Nice. An abridged version, Morton assumed, of his having taken the Ancestry DNA test and posted it off.

Great! Thanks, Morton, he replied, wishing that there was the ability to underline his name within the app.

Christopher is typing…

Green Jumper YouTube classic up!

Morton responded to the nonsensical message with a thumbs-up emoji, hoping that that constituted a satisfactory response.

He was tired and was also tired of going around in circles. He simply didn't have enough information at his disposal to figure out the connections between these people. He hoped that the Mitrokhin Archive might shed some further light on matters the next day.

He was about to shut his laptop lid when an email from Lazarus came in. It was short and concise.

296

Morton,
The Reno police have released their statement.
Maddie

Below her name was a hyperlink to the Reno Police Department.

Chapter Twenty-Six

Morton had travelled to Cambridge and was sitting on a low concrete wall, gazing into a rectangular pond which ran underneath a paved walkway leading to Churchill College. The building to his left was an unimaginative two-storey brick affair with a pyramid of yellow steps rising to the entrance.

He looked at his watch: he was five minutes early for his arranged meeting with Tiana Dudnik, a Russian translator, whom he had hired to assist him with the Mitrokhin Archive.

His eyes tracked the listless movements of a large goldfish, until it disappeared beneath a cluster of lily pads, and his brain made the leap to his grandfather's fishpond, dredging up a memory of helping him to smash a hole in a thick crust of ice, which had formed following a freezing winter's night. He must have been—what?—eight years old at the time. Right around the time when Alfred Farrier was frequenting prostitutes and two years after he had murdered Candee-Lee Gaddy. The memory was fuzzy but it was real. And now it was irrevocably tarnished.

He opened the email from Maddie on his mobile phone and once again clicked the hyperlink, which she had sent.

The Reno Police Department
Your Police, Our Community

Media Update
City of Reno
Reno Police Department

<u>*For Immediate Release*</u>

The cold-case murder investigation of Miss Candee-Lee Caddy, who was murdered December 20, 1980 has been closed by RPD after DNA evidence successfully identified the perpetrator. He is named as Alfred Farrier, a British national who was aged 66 at the time of the murder but who has since deceased. No further action.

The report was thankfully brief in its description of both Morton's grandfather and the horrific nature of the crime. But still, it was out

298

there on the internet for all the world to see forever. His prostitute-murdering grandfather.

Once he had digested the news and had shown it to Juliette, Morton had forwarded it on to Vanessa Briggs.

'Morton Farrier?' a female asked, her shadow looming over him.

He turned and smiled. 'Yes. Tiana Dudnik?'

'That's me,' she replied in a surprisingly posh English accent. He had expected broken English in a Baltic pronunciation. She was in her early twenties with her long dark hair pulled up into a ponytail.

'You sound very…'

'English?' she answered.

'Well, yes,' he said, standing and offering her his hand.

'My dad was Russian and my mum was English, so I had both languages from birth, and then I studied Russian at university.'

'Oh, right.'

'But, I ken britend if you vant,' she said in an exaggerated accent, revealing a silver-stud tongue-piercing. 'Ve are looking at spy file, yes?'

Morton nodded. 'Your normal voice will do, though,' he said with a laugh.

She tilted her head to one side and clapped her hands together. 'As you like.'

'Shall we?' Morton said, gesturing towards the ugly building.

They walked side-by-side up the yellow steps and into the entrance. To the left was a porter's lodge, where three men, wearing black trousers and white shirts, were sorting four giant stacks of post.

'Can I help you?' one of them asked.

'We've got an appointment at the Archive Centre,' Morton said.

The man walked over to the window and pointed outside. 'You see that covered walkway? Go along there, then turn right and you'll see a building covered in concrete strips—looks a bit like a prison—it's in there.'

'Right,' Morton answered. 'Thank you.'

'So, what is it that you're hoping to find, exactly?' Tiana asked, as they followed the directions towards the Archive Centre.

As briefly and concisely as he could manage, Morton relayed to her what he hoped to find in the documents. He had written on his notepad, in clear capital letters, the names of all the key players involved in this case, which he would place on the desk as a constant reminder for Tiana.

A prison-like building shrouded in thin concrete pillars came into view. Morton opened the door and they took the staircase up to the first floor, where they were confronted by a glass door on which was etched *CHURCHILL ARCHIVES CENTRE.*

'I'll just put my stuff into a locker,' he said, taking out his laptop, notepad and a pencil, and then locking up his bag and coat.

Morton led the way down a short corridor which terminated at another glass door. He pulled on the handle expecting it to open, but it didn't budge. He tried to push it, but nothing happened.

Tiana looked through the door into the archive and waved at a lady sitting behind a desk. The lady smiled and pressed a button which released the door, and Morton was able to pull it open.

'Thanks,' he said, entering the archive. It was a small room with six wooden desks pushed together in the centre, surrounded by bookshelves dominated by volumes written by or about Winston Churchill.

'You've booked to see the Mitrokhin Archive?' the lady behind the desk asked pleasantly.

'Yes, that's right. And this,' Morton replied, 'is the Russian translator.'

'Okay. If I can just get you both to read through the rules of the archive,' she said, sliding a green sheet of paper in front of them.

Morton pretended to read it but guessed the rules would be the same as most other places.

'Okay,' Tiana said.

'Yep,' Morton agreed.

'And if you can complete one of these each, please,' she said, handing over two white forms and two pencils. 'This will be your reader's ticket, which is valid for three years.' She reached down below the desk and produced two pieces of pink paper. 'And these are extra rules pertaining to the Mitrokhin Archive. If you could read these and then sign the bottom.'

The opening paragraph made Morton hopeful. *I acknowledge that the Mitrokhin collection includes sensitive personal information about individuals...*

He finished not reading the extra rules and signed at the same time as Tiana. Now, they were ready to get cracking.

But the archivist lady had other ideas. 'And if you could both just sit down at that computer in the corner and watch a short document-handling video.'

'Okay,' Morton said, swallowing down his eagerness.

'Oh, and you can't use that notepad,' the archivist said. 'Sorry. We have yellow legal pads for two pounds, if you'd like one of those?'

Morton nodded. 'Yes, please.'

'And it's one pound for a photo licence, if you were intending to take pictures?'

Morton placed three pounds down on the desk. 'I'll just go and put this in my locker,' he said.

Having stowed his notepad away, Morton returned to the archive room, where Tiana and the archivist were waiting for him at the computer terminal.

'Ready?' the archivist asked, with much more gravitas than Morton felt was necessary, given the content. When he and Tiana had nodded their agreement, she leant over and started the video. She stood behind them whilst the film played, hands placed on her hips, as though she were ready to tell them off, if they stopped paying close attention. When it had finished, she clicked an icon to return them to the home screen. 'So, to order up from the Mitrokhin Archive, you need to click through the Janus search portal...' Her voice trailed off and Morton realised that she was issuing instructions that he was expected to be following.

Morton obeyed.

'Then click *Advanced Search*...then type in *Mitrokhin*.'

A long list of matching files were presented on screen.

'Write down the full document reference on one of the request slips that are situated on each desk, and then hand them to me and I'll get the files to you.'

'Is there much of a wait?' Morton asked, becoming increasingly aware that he was paying Tiana by the hour and, so far, she had done absolutely nothing to earn her money.

The archivist glanced at the empty tables. 'No.'

'Thank you,' Morton said, hoping that she might now leave them alone. But she didn't. She stood behind them, observing as he began to inspect the details for each document within the Mitrokhin Archive. Without the pressure of time and the language barrier, Morton would have been intrigued to read any number of the files in the categories presented before him. *Afghanistan. Iran. Pakistan / Bangladesh. United States of America. Canada. France.* The topics within in each sub-category were equally as intriguing: *The Church*; *Communists*; *Dissidents*; *Agents*; *Active measures*; *Illegals*; *Directorate K.*

301

One file, *MITN 1/7* stood out. It pertained to Britain, Ireland, Australia and New Zealand. He clicked to view the headings of the document and smiled.

Britain: 1 –118
Appendix 1: KGB agents, contacts and cultivators 119-130
Appendix 2: KGB officers and co-optees 131-138
Appendix 3: Footnotes 139-161

Details about Nikita Sokolov had to be contained within those pages. Morton stood up, grabbed a handful of white document request slips, then proceeded to complete one for this file.

'Shall I take that and go and find it for you?' the archivist asked.

'Great, thanks,' Morton said, handing her the piece of paper.

'I thought she was never going to go,' Tiana whispered, once the archivist had disappeared into a room behind the help desk.

'Me neither,' Morton agreed. 'I think it's the sensitive nature of the archive that's making her a little wary of us.' He stood up. 'Any preference as to where we work?' he asked.

'Here?' she suggested, taking a seat at the closest table.

Morton sat beside her and, since he had been unable to use his own notepad, rewrote the names of everyone involved in the Duggan Case, including codenames and known pseudonyms.

'Are you expecting to find *all* of those names?' she asked.

'No,' he clarified. 'But keep your eyes peeled. Nikita Sokolov is definitely mentioned in there but the rest… I don't know.'

'Dis is vedy interesting,' Tiana replied.

'Fingers crossed,' Morton said, hoping that that, which they would discover in the files, would warrant his trip to Cambridge and his paying a hefty hourly rate for a translator.

The archivist returned with a smile on her face and carrying a blue folder neatly wrapped in a white ribbon. She placed it down between Morton and Tiana, then took great care to untie the bow and lift open the wallet. 'There we go,' she said, stepping back, as though she had just revealed an original copy of the Magna Carta.

Morton thanked her, took a fleeting glance at Tiana, and then turned the first page of the ring-bound volume. The page was typed in Cyrillic. 'Hmm,' Morton said, 'that's that, then,' as he slid it across the table so that it was directly in front of Tiana.

She leant closer to the text and began to read.

Morton waited impatiently for any kind of reaction or response. He hated the dislocation, which he felt profoundly, caused by his inability to read the document. Tiana might well be an excellent speaker and translator of Russian but she wasn't a genealogist and might miss any number of partially hidden clues or inferences which the file might provide.

He clasped his hands together to stop himself from drumming his fingers on the desk, as he stared at a life-sized bronze bust of Winston Churchill looking moodily into the distance.

She turned the page and continued reading.

Morton surreptitiously looked at his watch. Assuming that Tiana's work had started the moment that they had met outside the college, he already owed her almost one hour's pay.

'I'm reading as quickly as I can,' she said, without taking her eyes from the text, having evidently caught his not-so-surreptitious glance.

'No, it's fine,' he lied. 'I was just seeing what the time was.'

Tiana looked at him. 'So, this is basically talking about the history of Soviet espionage in Great Britain and, so far, about the organisation and structure from just before the Second World War.' She looked doubtfully at Morton. 'Do you want me to keep reading every word of these hundred and eighteen pages, or skim-read, or do you want me to skip to the appendices, where you will most likely find Nikita?'

This was the problem. If he instructed Tiana to skim-read or skip whole passages, who knew what he would be missing? But she was quite right in saying that Nikita would most likely be found among the final pages. 'I think skim-read through to the appendices, but please keep an eye out for any of those names,' he said, drawing a pencil circle around the list at the top of the yellow notepad.

Tiana nodded her agreement and returned to reading.

Morton watched, as she ran her index finger carefully down the page, then on to the next. He could only hope that he was doing the right thing.

As she scanned the text, she muttered highlights of what she was reading: 'Buildings used... Methods of recruitment post-Second World War... Priorities shifting to the United States... nuclear, scientific and technological main concerns during the Cold War...'

Interesting but very nebulous, Morton thought, as he digested her bullet-point summaries.

Tiana worked through the file until she reached the first appendix on page 119. She sat back and looked at Morton. 'So, now it's on to the agents, contacts and cultivators.'

'Okay,' Morton said, nodding his encouragement and feeling bizarrely nervous.

Tiana read for a moment, then said, 'This page is for an agent called Eduard Ivanovich Koslov, codenamed Yevdokimov. Do you want me to translate the details? It seems to give a short biography of his life.'

Morton shook his head. 'Just double-check that the biography doesn't include any of those names,' he said, reiterating the list of players in the Duggan Case.

Tiana nodded, checked the biography, then said, 'No.' She read the opening sentences of the next page, 'Aleksei Nikolayevich Savin, codename Ruslan?'

Morton shook his head and, once she had scanned the information relating to him, turned to the next page.

'Melita Norwood, codename Hola?'

'The Spy who came in from the Co-op,' Morton commented.

'Pardon?'

'Nothing. No, not her.'

Tiana nodded, skim-read her two-page biography and then moved on to the next agent: 'Arne Herløv Petersen, codename Kharlev?'

Morton shook his head.

'Detective Sergeant John Symonds, codename Scott?'

Morton shook his head.

'Arkadi Vasilyevich Guk, codename Yermakov?'

Morton shook his head.

'Nikita Sokolov, codename Stefan?' she asked with a wry smile.

Morton nodded his head and grinned. 'Do you mind if I record your translation?' he asked and, when she had consented, switched on the voice-recording app on his mobile phone which he placed on the table close to her. He sat with his pencil poised over the yellow pad. 'Okay.'

Tiana re-read his name and codename, then began to read the single biographical paragraph recorded on this Russian agent: '*Born in Czechoslovakia in 1912. Arrived in Britain 4th April 1936 as an agent for the OGPU. Lived at Redcourt Hotel, Bedford Place, W.C.1. Worked initially as an assistant to an illegal agent and intelligence officer in the KGB, Viktor Zima. After WW2 Sokolov employed as Second Secretary at the Soviet Embassy in*

Kensington, London. Recruited several notable agents, including James Hart (HECTOR), a clerk in the Underwater Weapons Establishment at Portland, and Flora Sterling (MEDUSA), mistress to Harold Austin. Handled several agents, including MERCURY, *a chemist recruited in 1954;* YUNG, *an aeronautical engineer recruited in 1952;* AKHURYAN, *a nuclear physicist recruited in 1949; and* LONG, *an operator in the Diplomatic Wireless Service, recruited 1944. Defected to the UK December 1957. Given new identity. Further details unknown.*' She stopped reading and looked at him.

Morton was running over the significance of what he had just heard. 'Defected December 1957,' he repeated. '*And* Flora Sterling's handler…'

'Was that what you were hoping to hear?' she asked.

'Er…' he muttered, thinking. 'Harold Austin, you said?'

Tiana looked back at the text. 'Flora Sterling was *mistress to Harold Austin.* Is he someone I should know?'

Morton shrugged. 'Depends on how interested you are in the Conservative government of the 1950s.'

She screwed up her face. 'Not so much.'

'He was the Foreign Secretary,' Morton clarified, recalling one of the heavily redacted documents which he had recently examined at the National Archives.

'Do you want me to read on?' Tiana asked.

'One second,' Morton answered, pausing his audio-recording and opening up a Google search for Harold Austin. 'Foreign Secretary from 1955 to 1956.' Morton frowned. 'But to *when* in 1956?' The agreed date shared by the internet of Harold Austin's last day in government was the 12th November 1956, when he had stepped down on health grounds.

That date rang a bell. 'Hang on, I just need to check something,' Morton said, rising from the desk and heading over to the door. He nodded to the archivist and she buzzed it open for him. At his locker, he pulled out his pad and flipped back to look at the notes that he had made on the KV 6 file on Flora Sterling, which he had downloaded from the National Archives website.

A wonderful coincidence! Harold Austin had resigned the very same day that the all-ports alert which had been in force for his mistress—Flora Sterling, a known Soviet spy—had been lifted.

He re-entered the archive room and sat down beside Tiana.

'Okay?' she asked.

'Yeah,' he replied. 'I think so.' He was thinking hard. 'Could you re-read the paragraph on Nikita Sokolov, please?'

'Sure.' And she did.

Morton clicked his fingers. 'An agent in the Diplomatic Wireless Service, recruited 1944. William Gilmour?'

'Pardon?' Tiana said.

He began to scribble his thoughts down on the yellow pad.

Flora Sterling - known Soviet spy, mistress to Harold Austin
Harold Austin - Foreign Sec, in charge of operations overseas, inc. Middle East.
Suez Crisis November 1956. Resigned 12 Nov '56
Alexander Emmett – Operation Sawdust – undermine Pres. Nasser
William Gilmour - Diplomatic Wireless Service. Communist. Worked Middle East 1945. Handled by Nikita Sokolov. Charged with communicating secrets to the enemy
Nikita Sokolov – recruited Flora Sterling. Handled William Gilmour? Defected Dec '57

Morton exhaled. It might not quite cross the threshold for Genealogical Proof Standard, but he felt that the evidence before him was sufficient to confidently argue that Flora Sterling had obtained state secrets about the Middle East, specifically the Suez Crisis, which she had left, in whatever format, in the garden opposite William Gilmour's house on the 6th November 1956. Gilmour, with his training in the Diplomatic Wireless Service and obvious communist beliefs, had transmitted these secrets to Moscow. Harold Austin had resigned but, Morton assumed, had first granted immunity to his mistress, Flora Sterling.

The narrative was becoming more robust, yet Alexander Emmett's role was still defying clarity. His original identity still remained unknown, but he had taken on the dead double of Maurice Duggan, who had grown up in Ardingly with William Gilmour. Alexander had grown up in Port Said, the epicentre of the Suez Crisis. And, finally, Alexander had ended up marrying a member of MI5—responsible for the surveillance of Flora Sterling—who happened to kill herself in the same month as Nikita Sokolov had defected to the UK.

Morton saw the overlap between all of this disparate information as a series of Venn diagrams, but where the central portion, which unified them all, was empty. But he was getting closer, of that he was certain.

The archivist, he noticed, was staring at Tiana because she was staring at him and the hurried squiggles that he had been making on his yellow legal pad. Morton smiled to them both in turn and then said, 'Carry on.'

Tiana tucked a piece of errant hair behind her ear, then turned the page and began to read. 'Sirioj Husein Abdoolcader, a clerk in the Greater London Council motor licensing department?'

'Nope,' Morton answered.

'Terrence McMillan, Labour MP?'

Morton shook his head.

She flicked the next page, read a few lines and then turned to him with a wide smile. 'Alexander Emmett.'

Morton rolled his chair closer to her and peered over the text, none of it legible to him. 'What does it say? What does it say?'

Tiana frowned. 'It's terribly hard to read. I don't think I can make this one out.'

'What?' he asked incredulously, before noticing her mock-grimace. 'Very funny.'

Tiana laughed. 'So, it says this—'

'Hang on,' he interrupted, restarting the voice-recording app.

'*Born in 1927. Recruited in 1944. Returned to UK 20th May 1946, working as a journalist. Lived at 46a Lancaster Gate. Sent to Middle East to cover Suez Crisis. Active lead on Operation Sawdust to undermine government.*'

'"Active lead'… Did it not give his codename, at all?' Morton asked.

Tiana checked the file again. 'Oh, yes. Erm…' She glanced at him with an ominous look on her face.

Morton asked, 'What is it?'

'It's Jericho.'

Chapter Twenty-Seven

Ellen was at her desk on the third floor of Leconfield House, discreetly drying her eyes with a handkerchief scrunched in her left hand. Her desk was all but empty. All that remained now was the pathetic handle-less mug which had dutifully served as a receptacle for her stationery since her first day here. The keys of her faithful typewriter were currently being pounded across the room by her younger, more glamorous replacement, Gladys Perrier.

'Gonna miss us, ay?' John Potter called over to her, his pipe bouncing in the corner of his mouth, as he spoke.

'Some of you, yes,' she answered, sniffing back another surge of emotion.

'Tough act for her to follow,' he replied, nodding to Gladys, then licking his lips. 'Reckon she'll fit in nicely, though.'

Ellen took a long breath in. Her work in the A4 section of MI5 was over. On Saturday she would be marrying Alexander Emmett and, adhering to another of the nonsense rules which governed operations here and elsewhere, she was unable to continue working as a married woman. Quite why, nobody had been able to tell her. Her mother, when Ellen had raised the question with her on her last day off, was mortified that she would even contemplate the idea of carrying on with her work after marriage. 'Why on earth would you want to do *that*?' she had asked. 'Your role as a housewife is a much more important duty than…than whatever it is you do at the moment. Goodness me, what a suggestion.'

But Ellen's enquiries and mild incredulity were actually hypothetical: she could no longer work in her condition, as she was now beginning to show. Yesterday, Angela Jones had made not-particularly-subtle enquiries as to why her blouses were no longer loose-fitting around the midriff, as they had always been. Ellen had managed to brush aside the comments, she hoped, by mumbling something about eating a lot more since having met Alexander.

Despite her sadness at the prospect of leaving the section, she was very much looking forward to getting married. The last three months with Alexander had been a whirlwind of dinners, romantic walks and out-of-the-way weekends in country hotels. 'But it's ever so quick,' her mother had said pointedly. 'Do you know enough about him? I've not even met him, yet, for heaven's sake.'

'Yes, Mother. I do,' she had responded, not quite truthfully. When she and Alexander spoke, it was always about the present moment or their future plans together, never about either of their pasts. She had guessed a long time previous that, in common with her, he was unable to discuss certain aspects of his job. She strongly suspected that he was working for MI6.

'Do you love him?' her mother had pressed.

'Yes,' Ellen had answered, this time honestly. He was somewhat of an enigma, but, so far as her limited experience had shown, so were all men.

She looked around the office at the men at work today; all of them were enigmas in their own way. Perhaps only Mr Skardon was the straight-forward man that he presented himself to be.

Ellen stood up and wandered aimlessly over to the blackboards at the back of the office. A whole new espionage network was now under investigation. Two black and white photographs, labelled *Harry Houghton* and *Ethel Gee*, were at the centre of the boards and thus at the centre of the new enquiry.

Following William Gilmour's suicide and Harold Austin's resignation, the investigation into the Sterling Ring had been formally closed. Even the prime minister, Anthony Eden, had resigned on health grounds. But still two things bothered Ellen: one was why, on the 12th November, Flora Sterling had turned herself in to MI5, being released just hours later with no charges having been brought against her and no further investigation into her associates; two, the definite identity of Jericho had still remained unsolved. It was an anomaly which had been strangely disregarded in the office since the collapse of the investigation. Some still believed that Gilmour was Jericho, some didn't care, some presumed him deceased and some, under hushed whispers, proposed that Jericho's identity was being protected by higher powers. Ellen had her own theory: that Jericho was an agent in the field, loosely connected to the so-called Sterling Ring, and only being contacted when intelligence gathered from other sources had a bearing or impact upon Jericho's own operations.

Maybe it no longer mattered, since all intelligence regarding Jericho had fallen silent.

Ellen turned around, about to head back to her desk, when she noticed that everyone in the office had gathered together and were staring at her with inane grins on their faces. 'What's going on?'

Mr Skardon stepped forward, carrying a large cardboard box, which he set down in front of him. 'Miss Ingram,' he said. 'I would just like to say, on behalf of everyone in the section, how much we have valued working with you. You have been an outstanding agent for A4, bringing great intuitiveness, discretion and aptitude to the role. Your keenness—and sometimes forthrightness—has been a great asset to the security services. Your dogged determination late last year brought about a swift and fantastic conclusion to the Sterling Ring, making this country a much safer place. And so, on behalf of all your colleagues in the section, I would like to wish you all the luck in the world for your forthcoming marriage—'

'You'll need it!' John Potter chipped in.

'And,' Mr Skardon continued, ignoring the comment, 'we would like to present you with these gifts by way of our appreciation for all your efforts. Thank you, Miss Ingram.'

The office burst into applause, as Ellen, with her cheeks flushed, stepped forward to the box. 'Thank you very much,' she muttered. 'Shall I open it now, or after the wedding?'

'Oh, as you like,' Mr Skardon replied, over general murmurs that she should open the gift now.

Ellen lifted the lid of the box. Inside were two items: an Electrolux Vacuum Cleaner and a carriage clock. 'Wow, thank you very much,' Ellen said, trying to muster some enthusiasm.

'Don't want you to not have *time* to clean up after your husband,' Paul Reynolds said, with a titter.

'Lovely,' Ellen said, feigning great admiration for the contraption.

'We felt practical presents would be the order of the day,' Mr Skardon enthused.

'Yes, thank you very much,' Ellen repeated, as tears of mourning for her career welled in her eyes.

'Right, back to work, everyone,' Mr Skardon said. 'We've got spies to catch.'

The gathering around Ellen dissipated and she dragged the cardboard box over to her desk. She sat down glumly and gazed at the grimy windows, wondering how on earth she was going to cope with the void left by work, as she became a wife and mother.

Back at her flat, Ellen entered the spare room. One wall was still obscured by the large quantity of intelligence relating to the Sterling Ring and her attempt to identify Jericho. When the investigation had ceased at work, Ellen had covertly made photostats of the entire file and added it to the collection on her spare room wall.

Alexander had been nagging her for some time now to take it down and get ready to move into his flat on their wedding day. Up until now, she had resisted, hoping that some new intelligence might come to light, but the time had come for its removal.

She stared at it as a whole picture, then looked again at each piece of evidence, as she began to unstick it from the wall, hoping that she might see something that she had previously missed. How many times had she stood here like this, though? Dozens and dozens of times, for hours on end. Some of the intelligence she could even recite verbatim; there was nothing here that she hadn't already analysed a hundred times over.

Maybe she should just accept the narrative which was generally shared and agreed within the corridors of MI5 and MI6 regarding the Sterling Ring: that top-secret documents pertaining to operations in the Middle East had been stolen from the Foreign Secretary by Flora Sterling and passed to William Gilmour, who had transmitted them to the USSR. Not a ring at all, in fact, but a very simple linear chain, which had been completely dismantled.

Where nobody could assuage her doubt, however, was regarding the film cartridge which Flora Sterling had deposited at the dead drop in Burlington Avenue. It had contained top-secret intelligence relating to Operation Sawdust, destined to be transmitted by William Gilmour to the Soviets, but, crucially, that transmission had never actually occurred. Mr Skardon had all but confirmed that Jericho was indeed responsible for tipping off President Nasser that his plane had been sabotaged. Perhaps, as Mr Skardon believed, Gilmour was indeed Jericho and had at his disposal several sources of information, Flora Sterling being just one of them. Perhaps.

With reluctance, Ellen continued to clear all of the intelligence from the wall, placing it carefully into a cardboard box. After a few minutes, the wall was cleared, and only rashes of brown Sellotape residue gave any indication that the investigation had ever existed.

Ellen sealed the box and placed it on to a growing stack of her belongings, all of which would be transported to Alexander's flat in the next day or two.

311

She touched her swollen belly and smiled. It was time for the next phase in her life.

Great torrents of freezing rain lashed down on Tudor Street, changing direction at the whim of the gales currently thrashing London. Alexander, wearing a bowler hat and a long black coat, left the *Observer* office, driving his umbrella into the air above him.

He had just completed his final story before the wedding: a piece about the effects of the recent fuel rationing and the hope that the Suez Canal might be reopening next month.

No more work for three weeks, until he and Ellen had returned from honeymoon in the South of France. He smiled to himself, nervously excited about the coming days. Last November, when they had first got together, his immediate concern had been how he would prevent Ellen from discovering his double-identity, which she had seemed on the verge of doing. In the end, she herself had solved the problem by announcing that she was pregnant. He had proposed, there and then, knowing full well that marriage and a child would bring an end to her career at MI5 and, thus, put an end to this bizarre obsession in which she had to try to unmask Jericho. But now, he couldn't wait to marry her; true love having arrived almost immediately following the night of the Czechoslovakian Ambassador's Ball.

'Mr Emmett,' a voice, which he recognised, called from behind him.

Alexander stopped, his face stern, as rain dripped from the front of his Homburg, and turned around to face GK.

'I hear congratulations are in order,' GK said, without so much as a hint of sincerity, an echo of their last meeting, which had not been a pleasant one.

'Thank you.'

GK shot a look around, waited for an old man to shuffle out of earshot and then said, 'We've got a new job for you. One which, given all this'—he glanced upwards at the inclement weather—'will, I'm sure, be met with approval from your new wife.'

'I'm listening.'

'Second Secretary at the British Embassy in Istanbul: it's the new Beirut, the new centre of Middle Eastern politics.'

Alexander frowned. 'But my identity was leaked.'

'We'll create a new one for you,' GK answered, as though it were as simple as that.

Six months ago, he would have jumped at the opportunity. In fact, it was precisely the kind of role which would give him unparalleled access to a wealth of intelligence relating to the Middle East. Every covert operation, every plan and every clandestine conversation would be at his disposal. But such a role would come with definite and explicit expectations about the sharing of information by the Soviets. He was done with spying.

'Not going cold on us, are you?' GK asked. 'Don't let the fiasco of the Ambassador's Ball trip you up.'

'It wasn't a fiasco,' Alexander countered. 'I left feeling unwell.'

GK rolled his head. 'Not *quite* what happened, now, is it? I heard from a reliable source that you left with a tart from MI5 and our single opportunity with Colonel Zoran Pavlovic was lost.'

'Well, your source was unreliable,' Alexander countered. 'I've got to go.' He set off, but GK locked a grip on his forearm.

'Look, do you want this job, or not?'

Alexander tugged his arm free. 'Not.' He walked away, listening for and anticipating the sound of pursuit, but it never came. He strode away with all the confidence in the world, all the while trying to prevent his hands from shaking.

A smile crept over his face in a surge of emotional freedom. Sixteen years of firmly held convictions swept to the side because of one woman! The beliefs were still there, in all actuality, but the deeds, which they had prompted, had ended.

From a wind-battered market stall on the corner of Fleet Street, Alexander selected a bunch of red roses from a tin bucket of miserable-looking flowers.

His past and his future—so utterly opposed to one another— tangled his thoughts all the way to Harrington Square: the two, he concluded, as he pressed the doorbell to Ellen's flat, were unreservedly irreconcilable. The past was destined to be buried for the foreseeable future.

'Hello?' Ellen said over the intercom.

'It's your terribly attentive and terribly wet fiancé,' he said.

'What's your name, please?' Ellen asked. 'I *do* have a fiancé, but he's not terribly attentive.'

'Well, he's sufficiently attentive to have brought you flowers,' he replied with a smile.

'Oh, alright, then.' The door buzzed open and Alexander collapsed his umbrella. He emitted a long sigh, as the dry warmth wrapped around him. He bounded up the stairs two at a time and found her leaning on the doorframe to the entrance of her flat. She was dressed in what she termed 'her shabby work clothes', without make-up and without pretence, precisely how he found her at her most attractive. Of course, she looked stunning when she was dressed up, but the naturalness on display right now in front of him was honest and real.

'For you, madam,' he said, offering Ellen the roses. 'Sorry, they're a little wind-swept.'

'Beautiful,' she said, taking the flowers and standing to one side. 'Come in, do.'

Alexander hung his coat and bowler on the hat-stand and then leant in to kiss her. Her warm lips drew him in. 'It's really good to be here.'

'You might not say that when you see how little's left in the place,' she commented.

'There's only one thing here I need,' he said, kissing her again.

'Corny,' she responded. 'But probably true.'

'Are you almost done clearing the flat?' he asked.

'Nearly there. That stack there'—she pointed to four cardboard boxes and three black bags—'is all rubbish, which I was wondering—since you're already soaked—if you could take down to the bins for me?' She grinned hopefully.

'Sure.'

He followed her towards the sitting room and, as he did so, he spotted that the spare room had been packed up and the wall stripped of her Jericho investigation. Thank God. 'You've binned all that stuff off the wall, I see,' he said.

'Well, not binned,' she answered. 'Boxed up in the spare room, just in case.'

'Just in case of what?' he enquired.

Ellen shrugged. 'You never know. And *this* box,' she said, pointing, 'contains my leaving gifts from work.'

Alexander peered inside the box, laughed, then covered his mouth. 'Sorry, didn't mean to mock.'

Ellen giggled. 'No, but that's the right reaction. A vacuum cleaner and a carriage clock! Nobody in the whole office thought they were weird things to be buying me as a joint leaving-wedding gift.'

'Well, we don't want you wasting time or neglecting your duties as a housewife, now, do we..?' he joked.

'I'm not going to be one of *those* wives, by the way,' she retorted.

'Good,' he said, kissing her again. 'Now, how much longer is my blessed dinner going to take?'

She smirked. 'Just long enough for *you* to take out the rubbish, darling.'

He watched, as she disappeared into her small kitchen, then he hurried into the spare room. His fear that he might not be able to locate the box quickly enough was dispelled when he saw, at the top of a small stack of boxes, one labelled *JERICHO*.

He picked up the box, carried it into the hallway and, scooping up the items destined for the rubbish bin, headed out of the flat, down the stairs and out into the rain.

Beside the building were several large black bins. Alexander lifted the lid of the closest one and threw in the bags, followed by the boxes, leaving just the one labelled *JERICHO* in his hands.

With the rain tipping down around him, he pulled open the box and removed the top item: a newspaper report into William Gilmour's suicide. He started to read the article but, as the tears in his eyes melded with the falling rain, the words became indistinct. He read the word *Ardingly* just as the wind tore the sodden paper in two.

Ardingly. The village where he had been born and where he had grown up. The place where he and his two best friends had first discovered communism. He, William Gilmour and Maurice Duggan.

A lifetime ago.

Chapter Twenty-Eight

'Oh, that's just marvellous,' Morton said to his laptop. 'Just the news that I wanted to have to break.'

He was alone in his study, cuddling a large cup of coffee, gazing at the screen absent-mindedly. Four weeks after having taken the DNA test, Christopher Duggan's results had just been posted on the Ancestry website. Morton had still yet to analyse them to try to determine exactly who Christopher's father had really been, but one thing was immediately obvious: Christopher had a sixty-three-year-old half-brother, named Fayez Alexander Ibrahim. His middle name hinted rather heavily that the relationship connection was on Christopher's paternal side.

Morton continued the one-sided conversation with his laptop: 'Hello, Christopher. Mortimer, here. A mad old lady owes you the best part of ninety thousand pounds because your father, whilst working as a spy for MI6 but also in the employ of the KGB, was pretending to be a man who was pretending to be her brother who had died in 1944. Oh, and by the way, you have a half-brother, who has already sent me three messages, desperate for further details. Cheerio.'

Maybe he needed to work on his delivery a little.

Setting down the coffee, Morton began the process of trying to work out the birth name of the man who had been posing as Alexander Emmett and Maurice Duggan.

Before delving into the unknown, he needed to eliminate the known by removing as many of Christopher's maternal matches as he possibly could. Once they were taken out of the equation, only those matching on his paternal side would be left, making the hunt that much easier.

Morton searched his notebook and located the information which he had previously found on Ellen Ingram's family. Her parents were named as Charles Ingram and Sarah Atcherley. Using a variety of online genealogical sources, Morton spent time creating a pedigree chart for Ellen Ingram, taking each of her maternal lines back three generations. He then spent some time creating a skeleton tree for each name.

Once completed, he clicked the search button on Ancestry DNA and typed *Atcherley*, the first of Ellen's eight great-grandparents, into the *Surname in matches' trees* box. A list of ten people appeared where the name had occurred within their online family tree. For each match, Morton clicked *Shared Matches*, producing a triangulated list of other people who shared DNA with Christopher via the Atcherley surname. To each of these shared matches, Morton assigned a joint colour group, so that they could be eliminated from the main results list.

It was a long and arduous process, but after several hours, when Morton returned to the master list of all of Christopher's DNA matches, around half of them he had managed to link to Ellen Ingram's family. Rather unsurprisingly, Fayez Alexander Ibrahim had not matched with a single person on Christopher's maternal side.

Morton clicked on the shared matches between Christopher and Fayez: all of them had to be on their shared paternal line. He scanned down the list of names to see if any stood out as being either familiar or dominant: *Carter; Wright; Spencer; Turner; Wood; Gregson; Monks; Horsfall; Cato…*

Nothing familiar and nothing dominant. He was going to have his work cut out but he had done this type of methodical work before, many times. His task would be to work through the long list of shared matches, building up several skeleton trees as he went, slowly finding the connections between them all: hours and hours of further research.

Just as he was contemplating taking a massive short-cut by asking Fayez Alexander Ibrahim who his father was, another message from him arrived in his inbox: *Christopher, I see that you have logged in today! Please respond! I am your half-brother and I hope that you might help me to find out who my father is. I was born in Egypt 7th August 1957. My mother was Nadia Ibrahim. I live in Cairo. Please reply. Affectionately, Fayez.*

Morton looked at the screen. He had turned into one of *those* people who never replied to messages. Could he answer him, though, before telling Christopher? Was that ethically sound? He didn't feel as though it were something that he could or should do.

Two things the message confirmed: one, Fayez also did not know the identity of his father; two, it provided further evidence that the man posing as Alexander Emmett was indeed in Egypt in 1956. Morton worked back nine months from Fayez's birthdate in August 1957.

November 1956, the crucial month which linked so many of the important people in the Duggan Case.

Morton stretched and yawned. He had just a couple of hours left until Juliette and Grace arrived home. It was an impossible task to be achieved in that amount of time, but he at least needed to make a start.

The highest paternal match shared between Christopher and Fayez was a second cousin, Karen Gaulden, who had a strong 236 centiMorgans of shared DNA. The family tree, which Karen had uploaded, included all eight of her great grandparents: *Benson; Parker; Spencer; Stamp; Wood; Smith; Nickalls; Gaulden.*

One of those names *could* be the surname of Christopher and Fayez's father.

Two hours later, surrounded by a raft of paperwork, each containing a huge family tree, Morton heard the front door slam shut.

'Daddy!' Grace yelled at the top of her voice. 'I home!'

Morton smiled, rubbed his eyes, stood up and yawned. Although he had all of these elaborate family trees in front of him and had established a good number of connections between the people who shared DNA with both Christopher and Fayez, he had yet to determine a single family name for their father.

He looked down at the mess of papers and wondered if, even once he could finally attach a name to Christopher's father, he would ever really know *why* this man had felt the need to take on the dead double of two people and live his life vicariously through them.

'Daddy! Daddy! Daddy!' Grace shouted. 'I *home!*'

'I coming,' he replied, making his way down the stairs.

She was waiting behind the baby-gate with a big grin on her face. 'Daddy!'

Morton picked her up and held her close to him. 'Have you had a lovely day, Grace?'

'Yes,' she answered. 'Play with me.'

'Okay. What do you want to play?'

'Peppa Pig.'

'Oh, my favourite,' he said, carrying her into the kitchen, where Juliette was jabbing a knife with alarming ferocity into the film lid of a ready meal. Morton mimicked the *Psycho* music, receiving a glare from his wife.

'Microwave dinner for us, tonight,' she announced.

'Bad day at work?' he ventured, fearing that the knife blade might actually go all the way through the tray.

She glowered at him. 'I don't want to talk about it.'

'Non-alcoholic wine?' he asked.

She turned with a deep frown, still brandishing the knife. '*Not* helping.'

He sat down on the floor, waiting, as Grace turfed a selection of her plastic Peppa Pig characters out of her toy box. Then, she pulled out their house, car and a boat and began to assemble them in some kind of illogical way which presumably made sense to her.

'Do you really want the boat in the bedroom?' Morton asked her.

'Yes,' Grace answered, adding the figures to the boat.

'How's the case going?' Juliette asked, throwing the dinner in the microwave, whilst Grace began rooting around in her toybox again.

Morton sighed. 'Dragging, to be honest. I still can't identify—' He stopped short, noticing that Grace was pushing one of the figures around a mini ice-rink. 'Ice-skating.'

'Grandpa Pig ice-skating,' Grace confirmed.

'Hello? Anyone there?' Juliette said, waving her hand in front of his eyes.

'Give me two minutes,' Morton said, leaping up.

'That's about all you have got until dinner's ready.'

'Daddy?'

Taking the stairs two at a time, Morton darted up to his study, where he crouched down at the timeline fixed to his investigation wall. He pulled off the newspaper report into Maurice Duggan's drowning in 1944 and re-read it for the umpteenth time: '…*This tragedy was attended by a deed of great pluck and heroism by a 17-year-old boy, named Hubert John Spencer from 2 Street Lane, Ardingly… Hubert continued his heroic endeavours to get Maurice out of the water but suddenly slipped out of his grasp and disappeared under the ice…*'

Hurrying around to his desk, Morton rifled through the pile of loose paperwork until he came to one of the family trees which he had compiled this afternoon: that of the Spencer family.

Morton ran his eyes all over the tree and then saw the name: *Hubert John Spencer.*

'Dinner!' came Juliette's shout from downstairs.

'Daddy!' Grace echoed.

'Damn,' Morton muttered. Given Juliette's current mood, this would not be a good meal to skip in favour of work. 'Coming,' he returned with great reluctance. He padded back down the stairs and entered the kitchen. 'I think I've just found him.'

'Daddy, play,' Grace said, thrusting George Pig at him.

'Who?' Juliette asked, slopping something that looked vaguely like a lasagne onto two plates.

319

'The man… The man who pretended to be Alexander Emmett and Maurice Duggan,' he said, squatting down and placing George Pig into the driving seat of the car, which Grace had positioned on top of the boat in the bedroom.

'And?' Juliette said.

'No!' Grace scolded, removing George Pig from the car. 'Not drive, Daddy.'

'Sorry,' he answered Grace, before turning back to Juliette. 'I think it could be Hubert John Spencer, but I need to use *What are the Odds?* to check that the numbers work out.'

'I know that name, don't I?' Juliette asked.

'George in *toilet*,' Grace insisted.

Morton obeyed and placed George Pig inside the bathroom. 'Yeah, he was the boy who tried to save Maurice Duggan from drowning.'

Juliette gazed at the ceiling, clearly trying to make sense of it all. 'So… William Gilmour, Hubert Spencer and Maurice Duggan were all friends from Ardingly, right?'

'Right,' Morton confirmed.

'And Maurice drowns in 1944, despite his two friends' best efforts to save him. Then, Hubert decides later in life to turn into his friend but in the meantime pretends to be Alexander Emmett. How does *he* fit into the group? He was from Egypt, not Ardingly.'

'No idea.'

'And this guy worked for the KGB *and* MI6.'

'Yep.'

'Right, my brain's frazzled,' Juliette said. 'Let's eat.'

The house was silent. Grace and Juliette were sound asleep and Morton was sitting in his study, working under the yellow lamplight at his desk.

The numbers did add up. Hubert John Spencer could very well be the father of Christopher Duggan and Fayez Alexander Ibrahim. But so could several other men across the family trees which Morton had found or created. Morton was convinced that he had found him, though. The chances of his name's appearing in the tree of someone matching both Christopher and Fayez were just too great to be coincidence.

The coincidence was even greater still, given that which he had just discovered: that the Hubert John Spencer in the brothers' DNA-linked second cousin's family tree had been born in 1927 in Ardingly. In such a small village, there was no doubt that this man had been the friend

320

who had tried to save Maurice Duggan from drowning. Perhaps it was a display of remarkable profoundness, Morton thought, that Hubert had resurrected his childhood friend for the latter years of his life.

He looked at his investigation wall. With the addition of the facts from the Mitrokhin Archive, there was no longer a single inch of space left on the wall. Never before had Morton encountered a genealogical investigation quite as complex as this. Just when he thought that he was starting to understand the picture, a new document or search result came along and completely skewed his perspective. The man was, if nothing else, a fascinating enigma and, even though Christopher wasn't the client, Morton felt that he owed him his own report.

He wanted to beef up his knowledge of Hubert's early years. Perhaps something in the records might shed light on the extraordinary path his life took out of Ardingly.

As Morton began to search all the major online genealogical websites, an email from Vanessa Briggs pinged into his inbox. He clicked to read it: *Hi Morton. I'm back from my travels! I've contacted my two half-sisters and they'll be adding you as a collaborator on their DNA results soon. Hopefully that will enable you to find our elusive mother... Hoping you're well. Love, Half-Aunty Vanessa xx.*

Although he was eager to get cracking with finding their mother, a nervousness was growing inside him that it would be opening up a whole new Pandora's Box. What if he were to discover that his grandfather had murdered her, too?

It was irrelevant for the moment, anyway; he still had work to do in order to close the Duggan Case.

He returned to his previous searches. According to the birth indexes, Hubert had had no other siblings. Switching to the death indexes, Morton ran a search for Hubert's parents. He quickly found that his father had died in the September quarter of 1944. On the same page of the same quarter of the same year, Morton also found Hubert's mother's death.

Curious, Morton thought, wondering if maybe their deaths had been war-related.

He ran a Google search of their names, along with *1944* and *Ardingly*.

The top result was a local history website which detailed all the bombing raids that had occurred in the area during the Second World War. The page upon which Morton had landed showed a grainy black and white photograph of several mounds of bricks and rubble, the caption reading, *Numbers 5 and 6 Street Lane*. Morton read the short description below the photo:

On the 6th August 1944 a V1 rocket (doodlebug) fell on Ardingly. The rocket had been destined to wreak havoc on London but was intercepted by a quick-thinking American P-51 Mustang pilot. The pilot, believing that he was bringing the doodlebug down in open countryside and thus doing no harm, actually sent it crash-landing on Street Lane, killing Mr and Mrs Ronald Spencer in their home at number 6. Their only son, Hubert narrowly avoiding death at his friend's house at number 2 Street Lane.

Poor guy, Morton mused. Was the horrific death of his parents enough to turn Hubert into a spy for the Russians? It didn't strike Morton as a natural step to take, somehow.

Something else struck him from the website story. Being by now *very* familiar with the newspaper report into Maurice Duggan's drowning, Morton was certain that it had said that Hubert Spencer had been living at 2 Street Lane in 1944, which, according to this website, was actually his friend's house. Could that friend have been William Gilmour?

Morton got out of his seat with a light groan. His limbs were aching and it was way past his time for bed. He ambled over to the investigation wall and located the newspaper report on William Gilmour's death from the *West Sussex Gazette*. Yes, he had lived at 2 Street Lane in Ardingly.

He sighed and looked at the wall as a whole. He grinned when he recalled Clarissa Duggan's reaction upon seeing it: it was a *little* peculiar, he had to admit.

His focus settled on the doleful image of William Gilmour. The Security Service personnel file on him, held by the National Archives, said that he had been recruited by the Soviets at the age of seventeen, which would have been in 1944. The file in the Mitrokhin Archive on the man posing as Alexander Emmett had attested that he, too, had been recruited in 1944.

But this was all nothing more than supposition and conjecture. It was hardly something that he could write in his report without concrete evidence. What he really needed was to speak to someone who knew the three boys at that time.

Morton looked at his watch: 1.24am. Far too late—or early, depending on how you looked at it—to make phone calls, but in the morning he planned to call both Clarissa Duggan and Winnie Alderman from Priory Flats. Hopefully they would know something of the three boys' interest in communism. When he thought of Winnie and replayed their last conversation in his mind, another thought struck him. But it really would have to wait until tomorrow.

Morton parked his Mini at the rear of Priory Flats and walked around to the front door. He pressed the button for number fifteen and waited.

'Hello!' Winnie's voice crackled through the intercom, in a familiar way which suggested she was not exactly inundated with visitors. He had telephoned her this morning and asked if he could swing by and see her.

'Hello, it's Morton Farrier,' he said.

'Come in. The lift's broken, though,' she called, as the door buzzed open.

Morton entered the building and climbed the stairs to the top floor. He strode along the corridor to number fifteen and could hear chains rattling on the other side of the door.

'Oh, goodness,' Winnie said, shocked to see him at the door already. 'I'm not used to people getting up those stairs so fast. Come in.'

'Sorry,' Morton said, entering the warm flat. 'I won't keep you a moment. I just had a couple of questions for you.'

'Right you are,' she said. 'Would you like a cup of coffee?'

'I'd love one,' he began, 'but I need to get on to Horsham. So, not this time, thank you.'

'Well, take a seat, at least, won't you?' Winnie said, pointing to one of the two armchairs in the small lounge.

'Thank you,' he said, sitting. 'So, do you know much about the friendship between William Gilmour, Maurice Duggan and Hubert Spencer?'

Winnie smiled. 'Oh, they were as thick as thieves, them! Honestly, they did everything together. Not surprising, really, in a little village like ours. They were all of a similar age, I suppose. Went to the village school together...' She paused. 'I think William and Hue went to the secondary school nearby, but Maurice's family were quite well-off, so he went off to a private school, if I remember rightly. Don't quote me on that, though,' she said, eyeing Morton, as he made notes on what she was saying. She laughed. 'It was *rather* a long time ago.'

323

'Thank you,' Morton said. 'And, do you know their political persuasions, at all?'

Winnie pulled a face. 'Like the rest of us, I suppose: all against Hitler and what-have-you…'

'What about prior to the war?'

Winnie shrugged. 'I couldn't tell you. Sorry.'

'That's okay,' Morton replied, rummaging in his bag and withdrawing the photograph which he had previously shown to her of Alexander Emmett on his pilot's application form in 1948. 'This picture—'

'Dear Maurice,' she said with a warm smile.

'You said that he reminded you of a film star.'

'Yes. And do you know… I racked my brains for days afterwards. I even started watching a load of old, black and white films to try and jog my poor memory, but nothing did the trick. I thought it might have been Robert Wagner for a spell, but no, not him.'

'Could he have reminded you of Hubert Spencer?' Morton asked, not liking that he was putting ideas directly into her head but feeling that he had no choice.

Winnie studied the photograph for some time, then looked up at him. 'Do you know… Yes, it could well be him that he reminds me of. But how could that be? I'm quite confused.'

Morton exhaled. 'Tell you what, I will have that cup of coffee and I'll try and explain.'

Winnie stood, clearly delighted. 'Lovely! *And*… I've got some fruit cake which I made yesterday, special.'

Morton watched her leave the room and breathed out. He looked at the photograph. Winnie's response had hardly been convincing; just yet another 'maybe'.

After a few moments—not long enough to have made a drink—Winnie reappeared, beaming, carrying what looked to Morton like a rectangular piece of cardboard. She silently passed it to him.

It was a sepia photograph of twenty or so children, sitting solemnly outside a brick building. White lettering at the bottom of the image said, *ARDINGLY SCHOOL 1937.* Morton could immediately identify Maurice Duggan from the picture leant to him by Clarissa. He was standing at the back, one of the eldest in the shot, flanked by two other boys. He was fairly certain that William Gilmour was standing to Maurice's left.

'Whole-school photo. That's me in the bottom row and that's them…in the older class,' Winnie said, pointing at the picture and naming each boy in turn. 'Hubert Spencer, William Gilmour and Maurice Duggan.'

Morton held the photograph closer, studying Hubert Spencer's face, then he held up the picture which the man posing as Alexander Emmett had used on his aviator's licence. With the two images side-by-side, there was no doubt whatsoever that they were one and the same person.

'So…' Winnie began, looking at the two pictures and trying to understand, 'Hubert Spencer pretended to be my friend, Maurice?'

Morton nodded.

'Well, I feel like such an old fool. I didn't know Hue all that well but, my goodness, you'd think I would have recognised him.'

'Yes, but it was a good twenty-to-thirty-year gap…'

'But, why did he pretend to be Maurice? What a funny thing to do!'

'Let me explain, as best I can,' Morton said.

'Let me get the coffee and cake first,' Winnie said, trotting out of the room talking to herself.

The explanation to Winnie had been exactly the unmitigated muddled confusion which he had feared that it would be when he had started out with his account. Morton was fairly certain that he had left the poor woman doubting her very own existence by the time he had left her flat. As he pulled up on Clarissa Duggan's pea-beach drive, he resolved not to repeat the same mistake twice.

Clarissa opened her front door just as he got out of his car. 'Morning,' she greeted flatly, appearing more haggard than ever before. 'Any news?'

Morton pulled an apologetic face. 'Not yet. How are you doing?' he asked, stepping inside the house and already fearing her answer.

She blew out her cheeks. 'I'm tearing my hair out. I'm still not sleeping. And I've had to get some pills from the doctor,' she confided, sitting on one of the sofas and directing Morton to the one opposite. 'Is it almost over?'

'Very nearly, yes,' he answered.

'I think if you can't wrap it up by the end of the week, I shall have to turn myself in to the police.'

Morton nodded, recognising her sincerity.

'You said you had some more questions about my brother, but I don't think there's too much more to say about him.'

'Well,' Morton started, taking his notebook and pen from his bag, 'it's probably a strange question, but did Maurice have any strong political views?'

Clarissa rolled her eyes and tutted. 'Yes, he did.'

Morton waited to hear what they were, but she said nothing more. So, he pushed: 'And, what were they, exactly?'

'Is it *really* relevant to your investigation?' Clarissa asked.

'Very,' he answered.

She took in a breath. 'He was fiercely *socialist*,' she answered, barely able to articulate the final word of the sentence. She stared at the floor, appearing to have been made observably uncomfortable by her disclosure. 'Which obviously went *totally* against the grain at home, you can well imagine.'

'I can imagine. And do you know anything of the political views of his two friends, William Gilmour and Hubert Spencer?'

'Same. They had their own little communist club. God only knows where they got it from. It was all very secretive. They'd spend hours debating the ins and outs of social justice and how it was that Maurice had been born into money and was expected to go off to boarding school...university and get a high-flying career, whilst poor William and Hubert were born into relative poverty and, despite being as equally intelligent as Maurice, were destined for a labouring life. All good-natured and *Boys' Own* adventure stuff at first, but then they were discovered and all hell broke loose.'

'What do you mean?' Morton asked.

'I don't suppose it matters telling you now,' she began, 'but the three of them were really into amateur radio and were members of the Radio Society of Great Britain. With the war raging they were determined that they would all be joining the Royal Signals as soon as they turned eighteen and then go on to the Diplomatic Wireless Service and then work for the Secret Intelligence Services and so on and so forth. Anyway, this one day during the early years of the war, they were approached by someone in the Radio Security Service to become VIs and—'

'Vee eyes?' Morton interjected, unsure of what she had just said.

'VIs: Voluntary Interceptors,' she explained. 'Couple of hours a night, a few nights a week, Maurice would be sitting down in the shed recording Morse signals.'

'Where were the signals coming from?'

'The Abwehr: the German Secret Service,' Clarissa answered. 'Then he'd send off his log sheets to some secret address: Hertfordshire somewhere, if I remember rightly.'

'Were all three of the boys doing this, then?'

Clarissa nodded. 'Until one day.' Again, she went silent.

'What happened?' he questioned, as gently as he could.

'Well, I was very young at the time, so I just got snippets of conversations that I eavesdropped and then what I managed to glean as an adult. I don't know how, but it was discovered that perhaps *some* of what the boys were hearing over the airwaves was ending up in the wrong hands, shall we say.'

'Do you know *which* wrong hands?'

'The Russians, I believe, which would make sense, given what William Gilmour went on to do with his life...'

'But if it was before your brother died in 1944, they would have only been...well, what...sixteen...seventeen?'

Clarissa shrugged. 'Young and impressionable minds. I can easily imagine that, had he lived, my brother would have gone down exactly the same route as William Gilmour.'

'So, what happened?'

'Well, obviously they were all dismissed as VIs. I don't know why, but the finger of blame apparently fell largely on Hubert. The investigations into my brother ended with his death and the evidence against William Gilmour was found to be circumstantial.'

Already knowing the answer to the highly complex question, Morton asked, 'What happened to Hubert Spencer?'

'I really don't know,' she answered. 'After Maurice died, I had no contact with his friends anymore and I was sent off to boarding school. I don't recall my ever seeing him again, to be honest.'

'Interesting,' Morton said, making copious quantities of notes.

'Look. Can I ask: what's all this got to do with what I've tasked you with doing? I'm the one having to pay for all this.'

'I will tell you,' he promised. 'But just not right at this very moment. Just trust me that what you've just told me is highly important and very relevant to what you've asked me to do, ok?'

Clarissa raised her eyebrows. 'I've still got Maurice's old *R.S.G.B. Bulletins*, if they're of interest?'

'What are they?' he asked.

'The monthly newsletter from the Radio Society of Great Britain.'

Morton thought for a moment, doubting that a radio magazine would be of any relevance.

'He made some notes in them,' she said, with that instantly and completely changing his mind on the matter.

'Yes, please; definitely.'

She nodded, as she stood up and shuffled from the room. 'Won't be a minute.'

Nineteen forty-four was proving to be a pivotal year in the origins of the Duggan Case. Both William Gilmour and Hubert Spencer had been recruited by the Soviets in that year; the likelihood was that Maurice Duggan had also been recruited at the same time. Morton pondered if the other two major events of that year—the doodlebug killing Hubert's parents and Maurice Duggan's drowning—were somehow connected. He suspected that they probably were.

'There you are,' Clarissa declared a few moments later, piling a ten-inch-thick stack of paper periodicals onto his lap.

The magazines were A5 in size and had bronzed slightly with age. He picked up the first one, headed THE T.&R. BULLETIN, March 1939. 'So, Maurice was into amateur radio at the age of *twelve*?' Morton asked, slightly amazed.

'Oh, yes,' she confirmed. 'He was always tinkering with electronics and gadgets and such like. I don't have an awful lot of memories of my brother, but those that I do have, are of him with his headset and Morse key, mostly shooing me away.'

'Alone or with the other two boys?'

'Both,' she replied. 'Once they'd been taken on by MI8, he had his own shack in the garden.'

'MI8?' Morton queried, having never heard of that section of British Military Intelligence before.

'Signals intelligence during the war,' she clarified.

'You know an awful lot about all this, given that you were only…four years old when war broke out,' he commented, trying his best not to sound too accusatory.

Clarissa laughed. 'Well, I actually knew next-to-nothing at the time, but after William Gilmour's arrest I became curious and questioned my father about it. He claimed to know very little, that it was all very hush-hush, but I got one or two bits and pieces from him.'

'Interesting,' Morton said, flicking through the magazines for 1939 and noticing some of the article titles: *Sunspots, Magnetic Storms and Radio*

Conditions; *The Franklin Master Oscillator in Amateur Transmission*; *A 56 Mc. Resonant Line Receiver*; *Crystal Band Pass Filters...*

In the September 1939 edition, Morton spotted the first of Maurice's annotations: a pencil circle drawn around an article, entitled *Royal Corps of Signals*. Morton read the brief story.

We have been asked by The War Office to bring to the notice of members, the advantages offered by a career in the Royal Corps of Signals. Wireless operators form about half the Corps establishment, the remainder consisting of kindred technical 'tradesmen'. A new pamphlet depicting various phases of life in the Royal Corps of Signals will shortly be available.

Morton gazed at the encircled story. From what Clarissa had just informed him about Hubert's receiving the blame for passing secrets to the Russians, he had perhaps found the reason for his adopting the life of a dead double: there was no way, with that blot on his past, that Hubert Spencer would ever have been able to join such a sensitive arm of the military or the Secret Intelligence Services under his own name.

With Clarissa watching him, Morton continued skimming through the magazines. In the December edition, he found another article where Maurice had added his own pencil additions. The story was titled *Modern 56 Mc. Receiver Designs* and included a diagram of a circuit board that Maurice had extended into the margin, adding his own electrical symbols and notes which Morton was able to read but not understand: *Eddystone Microdenser. Tuning capacity* $X_c / Z_0 = 0.50$. 'He was quite bright, then,' Morton observed.

'Oh, yes. Very,' she concurred, standing up and leaning over to see the cause of his statement. 'They're full of his diagrams and drawings. Somewhere on the back of one of them, there's a list of his friends' and acquaintances' callsigns, too.' Without letting him finish, she lifted the pile of magazines from his lap and began to thumb through them, as though they contained a flipbook animation. 'Ah, here we are,' she said, stopping and withdrawing one of them.

Morton took the proffered magazine and studied the notes written on the back. There were maybe twenty-five names and callsigns jotted down in pencil. At the top of the list, perhaps unsurprisingly, were William Gilmour and Hubert Spencer with their respective callsigns. Next on the list was *Viktor Zima*, with the callsign SU2FG.

Viktor Zima? He had been noted in the Mitrokhin Archive as being the KGB intelligence officer in charge of Nikita Sokolov, who in turn had recruited Flora Sterling. A little further down the list, his index finger struck on another familiar name: *Alexander Emmett SU6AD*.

Morton turned the magazine over to ascertain the date. He now had categorical evidence that Hubert Spencer had known of Alexander Emmett and Viktor Zima in the KGB since at least March 1944. With his finger resting underneath Alexander's name, Morton considered the implications of this discovery.

'Do you know what they talked about over the airwaves pre-war?' Morton asked Clarissa.

'Only one topic was out-of-bounds: religion. Other than that, they talked about anything and everything, I believe. The weather. Life. Friends. What they had for dinner.'

'So, these people...' Morton said, pointing to the list of names and callsigns. 'These were people he knew in real-life, or people he had encountered using his radio?'

Clarissa scrutinised the list of names. 'Well, I only know of Hubert and William on that list. So, I think it's safe to assume that the others are friends he'd met via ham radio. And look at the callsigns: less than half of them start with the letter G.'

'What does that mean?' Morton asked.

'Great Britain. So, the rest you can assume are foreigners.'

'Hmm,' Morton muttered, his suppositions now including the likelihood that Hubert had 'met' Alexander over the airwaves and had heard, there, that Alexander had died in 1944. And, with his own VI group forcibly disbanded, had taken on Alexander's identity. 'Can I borrow these, please?' Morton asked, wanting more time to examine them thoroughly.

'By all means,' she said. 'Anything that gets it all over with more quickly.'

'I'm nearly there,' he said, standing up. 'I just need to pull everything together.'

'Well, don't let me stop you,' she said. 'You get back to that funny little wall of yours and get it finished.'

Morton took the hint and packed up to leave. 'I'll be in touch very soon. Goodbye.'

'Bye,' she said, closing the front door behind him.

He got into his Mini and pulled away from Clarissa's house.

Morton drove the entire way home mulling over the investigation. He was now confident that he had everything that he needed to complete the Duggan Case. He would be able to provide Clarissa with answers to all of her questions and, as a by-product of his research, would be able to give Christopher a detailed account of certain aspects of his mother's and father's lives. Some questions still remained unanswered and would perhaps have to remain so. Morton wanted to gauge Juliette's assessment of whether or not his findings warranted a reopening of the police investigation into the suicide of the man purporting to be Maurice Duggan at Priory Flats this year. Morton's personal belief was that the man's death was highly suspicious. Given all that the man had endured and willingly put himself through during his lifetime, Morton found it incredibly unlikely that, at the age of ninety-two, he would have taken his own life. If he were correct, though, then it begged the question of why somebody would want him dead. About that, Morton had a developing theory.

He entered the house, finding it surprisingly quiet. Juliette and Grace should be at home. They were either asleep or they'd gone out. He entered the kitchen where he found a note on the table. *Gone to the playpark. Join us! x.*

And that's exactly what he would do, just as soon as he'd taken the *R.S.G.B. Bulletins* and his notepad up to his study and processed all that he had just gleaned from Clarissa.

In his study, he looked at the timeline on his investigation wall. Hubert had been living in Ardingly in December 1944. The next recorded event was his arrival in the UK in May 1946 under the name of Alexander Emmett.

Morton realised at that moment that he had overlooked something crucial: for Hubert to have arrived in the UK from Port Said in 1946, he had to have left the UK sometime between December 1944 and early 1946. What a stupid oversight.

Hastily pulling open his laptop lid, he logged in to the Ancestry website and located the *UK, Outward Passenger Lists, 1890-1960* records. He typed Hubert Spencer's name and year of birth into the search box.

Two hundred and ninety-two results.

He amended the search to a departure date of within one year of 1944.

One result.

It was for a ship, named *The City of Hong Kong*, which had departed from Liverpool in England on the 3rd April 1945, bound for Bombay. Morton clicked to view the page.

331

Port at which Passengers have contracted to land: Port Said
Name of Passengers: SPENCER, Mr Hubert J.
Age of Passengers: 18
Last address in the United Kingdom: 2 Street Lane, Ardingly, West Sussex
Profession, Occupation, or Calling of Passengers: Student
Country of Intended Future Permanent Residence: Egypt

Hubert had left the country in 1945 under his own name. To be certain that his theory, that Hubert had returned as a dead double, was correct, Morton ran a search for him in the *UK, Incoming Passenger Lists, 1878-1960* record set. As he expected, though not conclusive, there was no matching record.

Morton returned to the outward passenger page, then clicked to print it out. There was little point now in trying to squeeze it onto the investigation wall, so he collected it from the printer and placed it beside him on the desk.

As he shut his laptop, preparing to head down to the playpark to meet Juliette and Grace, he spotted something on the passenger list that made him gasp. Some*one*, to be precise.

Chapter Twenty-Nine

Ellen pulled back the lounge curtain and peered out of the window, a wide smile on her face. 'Look, Christopher, snow!' He was nestled snuggly in the crook of her arm, entirely oblivious, his wide eyes staring up at her. Pushing closer to the pane, Ellen angled him so that he might catch sight of the sizeable flakes which were tumbling silently beneath the amber streetlight. Too much to expect of a four-month-old baby, she told herself, allowing the curtain to fall and shut out the inclement weather.

She turned to face the little Christmas tree which she had just finished decorating with glass baubles and tinsel. It wasn't much to look at but it gave her a pleasing warmth inside, representing as it did, their first Christmas together as a family of three.

'What do you think of the tree, little one?' she asked Christopher, who was captivated by the strings of colourful paperchains, looping their way around the ceiling. 'I hope Daddy will like it when he gets back.'

Using just her free left hand, Ellen placed Bing Crosby's *The Voice of Christmas* on the record player. The needle turned almost silently in the outer ring of the record, then began to play *Silent Night*. Ellen gently swayed her baby to the music, closing her eyes and embracing the moment.

As she moved, her mind drifted over the raft of preparations which still needed to be done before Christmas. She pulled her thoughts back from the specifics and considered how well she had taken to domesticity. She missed her old job and most of her former colleagues but had fully accepted this new chapter of her life. Although it didn't contain the thrill of the surveillance operations, in which she had taken part, she was enjoying the unassuming pleasures of being a wife and mother, something that she was never fully convinced that she would be able to do.

The past eleven months with Alexander had been breath-taking. During that time, they hadn't spent a single day outside of each other's company. The initial energetic string of meals, walks, visits to the cinema and art galleries had gradually eased into a more quiet and comfortable existence together before Christopher had come along and centred the focus of their lives. Despite the overnight changes his arrival had brought, happiness and love still remained at the core of their family.

The barely audible *clunk* of a key turning in the front door reverted her train of thought back to all those preparations still to be completed for Christmas. 'Daddy's home,' she whispered to Christopher.

'Ellen! Christopher!' Alexander called, bursting into the lounge. 'I'm home!'

'So we can see,' Ellen said, noticing immediately that he had been drinking: she could see it and smell it, and told him as much.

'Nonsense. I've had *one* pink gin with the chaps from work. Scout's honour,' he countered, putting his arm over her shoulder and planting a toxic kiss on her cheek.

'One *glass*, perhaps,' she retorted, 'refilled five or six times.'

'That could be true,' he admitted, wrapping his arms around her midriff and knitting his fingers together on the remains of her baby-bump.

'I think it's *very* true, and you need to go and sleep it off.'

'Well, I can't do that: I've got a story to work on this evening,' he replied, rocking from side to side, totally out of time with Bing Crosby's warbling of *White Christmas*.

'Really?' she questioned. 'I'm not sure you're in the best state for writing.'

He released his grip around her and marched over to his typewriter which was on the sideboard. 'It's now, Ellen, now!' He grabbed the machine, wound in a blank piece of foolscap and sat down in an armchair with the typewriter on his lap.

'What's now?' she asked.

Alexander began to hammer the keys. 'The intercontinental ballistic missile race,' he declared. He stopped typing and stared at her. 'Ironic, isn't it, how the Allies so criticised and publicly condemned Hitler's use of the V2 rockets in the war, then, as soon as it was all over, the Americans swept in and took all the scientists and engineers involved in building them, while the Soviets took all the technology, and now they're going head-to-head to see which one of them can wipe the other from the face of the planet first, using intercontinental missiles based on the German V2 technology. I tell you...'

'It's all very worrying,' Ellen said, not liking her husband's light-hearted description.

He began typing again. 'It'll all come to espionage and covert intelligence; just like it always has. The winner will be the side with the best spy network, you mark my words.'

'Hmm,' Ellen said, carrying Christopher out of the room and into their bedroom, where she placed him down in his cot. She smiled, as his eyes began to close.

'Mark my words,' Alexander repeated, 'there'll be swallows like Flora Sterling out there this very moment, recruiting naïve scientists and persuading them to smuggle secrets out in their underpants. *Intelligence* is what it's all about, I tell you...'

Ellen froze. Alexander was still prattling on, but she was focussed on what he had just said. Pulling the bedroom door almost shut behind her, she walked into the lounge.

'...I'm sure it'll be the Americans that win the day,' he continued. 'You wait—any moment and they'll—'

'What did you say just then?' Ellen interjected, her arms folded across her chest. 'About Flora Sterling.'

Alexander paused and looked up. 'Er... I can't remember, now. What *did* I say?'

'What do you know about Flora Sterling?'

'Erm...'

He was flustered, she could tell.

'Just what you had up on the wall of your flat,' he said with a titter. 'All those jolly names involved in that surveillance operation of yours. She was one of them, wasn't she? Recruited William Gilmour?'

Ellen nodded, almost convinced. Except that she had never documented anything explicitly stating who had recruited William Gilmour because it had never been confirmed. It was a remarkably odd connection for Alexander to have made, based on the documents which, Ellen knew, he might have seen in her old flat. An uncomfortable feeling churned her thoughts, as she stared at him, heightened by the knowledge that he was clearly attempting to mask his own discomfort. His reaction told her that something was awry.

He smiled and returned to typing his story.

Uncertainty over what to say or do next rendered her unable to say or do anything at all. Should she push to encourage the unlikely scenario that he might say more? Should she dismiss her instincts and trust him, take her husband at his word?

Putting up her own mask, she asked, 'Fancy a gin?'

'Just the one,' he replied, glancing up and mirroring her smile.

Ellen left the room with what appeared to be a spring in her step. But once she was in the kitchen and out of his sight, she was consumed by complex questions competing and conflicting in her mind. As she poured two pink gins, she tried to steer her concentration back to the wall of her old spare room. She was absolutely certain that no document existed, asserting that Flora Sterling had recruited William Gilmour, but perhaps she herself had scribbled some note or other in her attempts to fathom Flora Sterling. Tomorrow, she would find the answer by looking in the box containing her case files on the Sterling Ring, which were in the loft.

Right now, she needed to exude normality. She picked up the drinks, raised the façade of ordinariness and walked into the lounge. 'Here you go,' she said, handing Alexander one of the glasses.

'Thanks,' he said, taking the glass and then chinking it with hers. 'Cheers.'

'Cheers. How's the story coming along?' She asked, sitting beside him and looking at the piece of paper protruding from the typewriter, clearly riddled with mistakes. Was that drunkenness or fear that he had just inadvertently revealed something that he wished that he hadn't?

'Just notes at this point,' he said, giving a dismissive wave.

Bing started to croon *I'll be Home for Christmas*, as Ellen sipped her gin and closed her eyes. In the darkness of her mind, she tried to untangle her thoughts. If tomorrow she could find evidence which corroborated what Alexander had just said, then the matter could be dropped. If, however, there was nothing to support it, then she would have to face the obvious question which she was refusing to address: how had Alexander come by that information? His unmentioned, presumed role in MI6?

Frustration had gnawed at her nerves all morning. The very second that Alexander had left for work, Ellen had wanted to get up into the loft and retrieve the box containing her investigations into Flora Sterling, but Christopher had refused to be put down. Until now. Ellen tiptoed away from his cot into the hallway, where she had already positioned a chair below the loft access. Reaching up, she unbolted the lock, pulled open the hatch, sending a stream of cold air down around her. She carefully lowered the ladder to the ground and then hesitated.

With one foot on the bottom rung, she peered up into the gloom above her, doubt momentarily thwarting her ascension. As her terrible night's sleep last night had shown her, if the evidence supporting

Alexander's claim could not be found, the ramifications and repercussions for them all could be unimaginable. But there was no way that she could ignore what she had heard.

Taking in a long and uneasy breath, Ellen began to climb until her upper body had entered the darkness. Her fingers fumbled on a crossbeam for a light-switch, which she knew to exist from the day when she had moved in, when the majority of her belongings were bundled up here out of sight.

She found the switch, illuminating the cold bleakness. Climbing the rest of the way into the confined space, Ellen stepped over the exposed joists onto a piece of board, upon which were stacked twenty or so boxes, neatly labelled in her own hand. She bent down and checked each in turn, not finding the one for which she was searching. It wasn't here. Ellen glanced around the loft. At the far end was one tea chest and half-a-dozen cardboard boxes: they didn't look like hers, but she still needed to check.

Holding on tightly to the beams, Ellen stepped across the joists, fully aware that if she were to slip or put one foot wrong, she would go crashing through to the room below.

Crouching down at an angle, which allowed the light to shine over her shoulder, Ellen scrutinised the cardboard boxes, despite her being able to see plainly that they definitely weren't hers. Her box, containing the Sterling Ring documents, was not here, leaving her with the unhappy conclusion that it had somehow got lost in the move.

She was on the verge of making her way back over to the hatch and the warmth of the apartment below, when curiosity compelled her into prising the lid from the tea chest. Peering inside the dim chest, she spotted a machine of some kind. An old wireless, perhaps? She reached in and lifted the heavy thing out.

An involuntary shiver ran through her when she realised that it was a radio; one identical to that which had been removed from William Gilmour's house in Burlington Avenue.

The haze of bewilderment, which had shrouded her thinking since last night, began to fade and Ellen knew what she had to do next.

Christopher was wailing. It was either the freezing weather or the roar of the passing traffic, Ellen supposed, as she stood on Curzon Street, gazing down at the ruts in the deep snow, which her unremitting drawing back and forth of the pram had created.

She looked through the grey veil to the entrance of Leconfield House. 'Come on,' she muttered to herself, as the baby continued to cry. She had wrapped him up in several layers and the pram hood was raised to protect him from the falling snow, but she knew that the bitter cold would be stinging his little exposed face.

'It's okay,' she said, leaning into the pram and stroking his red cheeks. Poor thing. She would give it five more minutes, then abandon her quest for the day and go to the nearest tearoom to warm up.

She looked at the doorway opposite, just as Angela Jones appeared under a black umbrella, darting out onto the pavement for her regular lunchtime walk to the tobacconists on Queen Street.

'Angela!' Ellen called across the street. She hadn't heard over the din of traffic. 'Angela!'

Angela looked sideways and stopped, squinting across the street until recognition dawned, then she waved. 'Ellen? Are you okay?' she shouted over.

With a gesturing wave, Ellen beckoned her over. This was neither a conversation to be shouted over the traffic, nor to be had outside Leconfield House of all places.

Angela waited for a break in the unrelenting stream of cars, then hurried over. 'What are you doing here? Has something happened?'

'I *really* need a favour,' Ellen begged.

'Go on,' Angela encouraged.

'I can't say too much. And I'm sure you'll appreciate that I wouldn't be asking if it weren't absolutely crucial—'

'Spit it out, Ellen,' Angela interrupted. 'I'm going to die from frostbite at this rate.'

'I need to know where Flora Sterling is,' Ellen said.

'Flora Sterling?' Angela checked. 'Why?'

'I can't say. Not at the moment,' Ellen answered, continuing to try to settle the baby. 'It really is crucial that I find her as soon as possible.'

Angela sighed. 'She's long gone from our surveillance, I'm afraid. I'm not even sure she's still in the UK after the all-ports alert was withdrawn. She's no longer considered an active risk in there,' she said, tilting her head towards Leconfield House.

'Would you try and find out where she is?' Ellen pushed. 'Please? It is a matter of national security.'

Angela raised her eyebrows, obviously sensing a degree of exaggeration from her former colleague.

'Please?'

'I'll see what I can do,' Angela said, 'but I'm making no promises and whatever happens is *totally* off the record.'

'Absolutely,' Ellen said. 'Thank you.'

As Angela turned to leave, Ellen grabbed her wrist. 'And don't say anything in front of my husband, will you?'

Angela shook her head. 'I think you'd better get the little one out of the cold,' she advised. 'Goodbye.'

'Thank you,' Ellen called, watching as Angela hurried back across the street. She bent over the pram and stroked Christopher's tear-stained cheeks. 'Let's go and get warmed up, shall we?'

'It's all a bit sudden, isn't it?' Alexander asked her.

Ellen frowned at his reflection, peering over her shoulder in the bathroom mirror, as she brushed her hair. 'I'm sure I told you about it before.'

Alexander shook his head. 'Not that it matters.' He kissed her on the neck and she briefly flinched. 'You deserve a night at Doris's. Christopher and I will be alright. We'll have a chaps' night in: drink some pink gin and play cards or something.'

Ellen rolled her eyes. 'You dare.'

'Is everything alright?' he asked, placing a hand on her right hip. 'You've been a bit distant these last days.'

'Just a bit tired, is all,' Ellen lied cheerfully. 'I'm not sure I'll manage to stay awake beyond nine. I expect we'll have a natter, a few glasses of wine and then go to bed.'

Alexander smiled and left the bathroom.

Ellen exhaled with relief. Since Alexander's unintentional revelation four days ago and her discovery of a radio set in the loft, identical to William Gilmour's, Ellen had found that her every waking thought was strangled with unanswerable questions which, when she actually confronted them, made her feel physically sick. She couldn't continue living in this indeterminate purgatory. Fortunately, Angela had been quick in providing her with an answer. She couldn't get an address for Flora Sterling but she had told her that a reliable source confirmed that Flora would be attending a high-society Christmas party tonight.

Ellen ran her eyes up and down her reflection: a suitably demure and sedate dress for a quiet evening at Doris's house.

As Ellen entered the lounge, she found Alexander sitting in an armchair, holding Christopher out in front of him, making peculiar baby noises. She paused at the door, smiling. But then the dark uncertainty returned, bringing with it a feeling of nausea. 'I'm off,' she said.

Alexander turned Christopher to face her, positioning him in such a way as to cover his face. 'I'll miss you, Mummy,' Alexander said in a child-like voice. 'Be a good girl and I'll see you tomorrow morning.'

Ellen kissed him on the forehead and turned to leave.

'Daddy wants a kiss, too!'

Ellen kissed Alexander. 'Look after him. Goodbye.'

'Bye!' Christopher's limp arm was waved for him.

Ellen left the apartment and headed out into the cold night. The two-day inclement-weather truce had ended and fresh snow was starting to settle on the wet pavements. Ellen pondered about taking public transport but quickly settled on the comfort and speed of taking Alexander's silver Austin Healey. She climbed in and turned the key: the ignition very reluctantly fired the car into life.

Switching on the headlamps and windscreen-wipers, Ellen used her coat-sleeve to expose a small opening through the condensation on the windscreen. She put the car into first gear and went to release the handbrake but stopped herself and looked up at the illuminated window of their apartment. She suddenly felt terribly duplicitous and disloyal. Perhaps her time working for MI5 had engrained a universal suspicion into her, even of her own husband. The thought of the evening unravelling before her, and the potential consequences of what she might find, gave rise to fresh doubt. Was this really a good idea? She could easily switch off the engine and return to the warmth of her family, saying that she had changed her mind, but she knew that the questions would never leave her alone; she had to have answers.

Ellen released the handbrake and pulled out onto the dark road, the headlights guiding a path through a thick crust of brown slush.

As she drove to Doris's house, Ellen tried to empty her mind and settle her erratic thoughts which were conjuring increasingly outlandish scenarios to explain that which she had exposed. She couldn't tell anyone but she knew that, if she could, they would find her irrational and overthinking, which maybe she was. But then her fellow Watchers had thought exactly the same thing about her theories regarding Flora Sterling, Jericho and William Gilmour.

Twenty minutes later, Ellen parked the Healey outside Doris's flat. She grabbed her bag, containing her make-up and an expensive dress which she hoped was sufficiently glamourous, and headed inside the house to transform herself for the party.

Chapter Thirty

Hyde Park Square, with its grand Georgian mansions overlooking the snow-laden trees and shrubs of the private gardens opposite, provided a beautiful backdrop to the fresh flurry settling in the amber glow of the streetlamps.

Ellen's destination was obvious from the elegant and stylish outfits worn by a steady succession of people, who were descending a flight of stairs to a basement flat in one of the mansions.

She drew closer, then glanced around her for a place to wait. She stepped under the portico entrance of number nine Hyde Park Square and waited in the shadows for an opportunity.

Moments later, it arrived in the form of an Aston Martin which drew to an abrupt halt in a parking bay right beside her. Ellen moved back further into the dimness of the covered porch and waited until the middle-aged gentleman, wearing a sharp suit and top hat, stepped from his car. As he locked the door with his back to Ellen, she emerged on the steps, as though appearing from the house behind her.

'Good evening,' she said in her plummiest of voices.

The man turned, startled, and laughed. 'Good gracious, you frightened the living daylights out of me!'

'I apologise,' Ellen said, stepping elegantly down onto the pavement. She raised her gloved hand in his direction, as though she were some exotic princess, and then instantly wondered if that was a stupid thing to have done.

Luckily for her, he smiled, took her hand and placed a kiss on her knuckles. 'Lord Mersham,' he introduced.

'Lady Eleanora,' she answered, somehow managing to keep a straight face, as she spoke those ridiculous words. 'Dare I assume that you are going to Mariella Novotny's Christmas gathering?'

'Indeed I am,' he replied, pushing out his elbow and indicating that she should thread her hand through the triangular space between his body and arm. She obliged and the pair walked towards the flat in polite conversation.

Once they had descended the stairs to the open front door, Ellen smiled up at her escort, placing a flirtatious hand upon his chest, just as they reached a young lady minding the entrance. She had a stunningly svelte figure with curled blonde hair and subtle make-up.

'Lord Mersham, darling, how lovely,' the woman greeted, air-kissing him three times.

'Mariella,' he replied.

Ellen was surprised. *This* young thing, who was at most in her early twenties, was Mariella Novotny? Ellen was expecting someone slightly older.

Mariella eyed Ellen and then Lord Mersham, awaiting an introduction, but when none was forthcoming, Ellen said, 'Lovely to see you again, Mariella,' and then pushed inside the house, as though this were a regular occurrence. As she marched into the opulent hallway, with high ceilings, chandeliers and exquisite-looking furniture, Ellen could only hope that the young host didn't call after her to check on her credentials.

Lord Mersham seemed, by the confidence in his walk, to know exactly where he was headed, leading them along the hallway to an open door on the left, from where the babble of conversation and jazz music emanated.

Ellen chanced a quick glance behind her. If Mariella had suspected her, then she wasn't showing it; she was now busy welcoming two young gentlemen, who had arrived at the party arm-in-arm.

Lord Mersham stopped just shy of the doorway and asked, 'Champagne, Lady Eleanora?'

'Marvellous,' she replied, loitering outside the party room until he had shuffled off to wherever he needed to go in order to fetch the drinks. Ellen tentatively took a step into a large, lavish lounge with mercifully over-subdued lighting. Upwards of fifty beautiful people occupied the space, chatting, mingling and some dancing rather provocatively. Her attention shifted from the people around her to the far end of the room, where her eyes settled on a most magnificent Christmas tree, covered in glass baubles and small white lights. It certainly put her pathetic effort at home to shame.

Keeping to the shadows at the edge of the room, Ellen tried, under the poor light, to ascertain whether Flora Sterling was here, yet. If she was, then Ellen couldn't find her face among the crowd. What she could see, however, was a couple draped over a chaise longue, kissing passionately. Kissing far *too* passionately for any public gathering, Ellen thought, suddenly feeling prudish. The man was now placing his hands in *very* inappropriate places and, yet, others around them seemed entirely oblivious to the spectacle.

Ellen slowly pressed further into the room, realising what it was that appeared unusual about the couple dancing closest to her: the man in the pairing was in fact a female, wearing a tuxedo and slicked-over short masculine hair.

But still no sign of Flora.

'Ah, here's my girl,' Lord Mersham said, passing her a glass of champagne. 'Here's to you, Lady Eleanora.'

She nudged her glass against his and took a drink.

'Are you going to tell me your *real* name at any point during the evening, or are you bent on staying in character, as it were?' he whispered.

She'd been detected. She looked at him, trying to maintain her composure. 'Whatever do you mean, Lord Mersham?' she asked, feigning shock.

He laughed, pushing his face close to her ear. 'I think we both know that *I* am not Lord Mersham and *you* are certainly not Lady Eleanora.' He stood up straight and winked. 'But fine, let's keep to character and play on.'

She literally had no idea what was going on here and her bemusement continued when a man, entirely naked but for a sequinned Viking mask, strolled through the party, as though it were the most normal thing to do in the whole world. Ellen glanced at Lord Mersham—or whatever he was really called—to see his reaction. Nothing but a dry smirk. She looked at other people standing nearby, who gave the naked man nothing more than the cursory glance that a swanky dress might attract.

This was a very strange party, Ellen concluded, and like none that she had ever been to before.

'So, from where do you hail, Lady Eleanora?' Lord Mersham asked.

Camden was definitely not the answer to give. 'Azerbaijan,' she said, saying the first place that came into her mind. She was still unsure of the rules and workings of this gathering, but one thing that was obvious, was that it was unnecessary to come up with an authentic provenance for her character.

Lord Mersham laughed raucously. 'Of course!'

Ellen sipped her drink, continuing to survey the room.

'Drink up, my good lady,' Lord Mersham encouraged, jiggling his own empty flute in front of her face.

She obliged, tipping the last sloshes into her mouth and handing him her glass.

'I'll just be a jiffy,' he said.

She watched the naked masked man gyrating with a woman dressed as a—what was she? A tail-less mermaid?—as an odd feeling washed over her; brought on by the fancy champagne on an empty stomach, no doubt. She looked around the room for something to eat, but her vision was becoming lazy and unfocussed. She needed to sit down for a moment. Across the room, beside the wonderous Christmas tree, were two vacant chairs. She walked over towards them, discovering a slight stagger in her gait. She sat down in one of the chairs with a sigh, looking at the people in the room but finding that they didn't make much sense to her. Concentrating hard, she managed to retrieve from her addled brain exactly what it was that she was doing there: trying to find Flora Sterling.

Ellen peered at the blurred faces moving around the room to the dulcet tones of an unseen saxophonist, not locating Flora. Perhaps she wasn't coming after all.

'Champagne, Lady Eleanora!' Lord Mersham declared.

She took the glass, resolving actually to drink no more, if this was the effect of just a single measure. 'Is there anything to eat?' she asked, forgetting her fake accent. 'I'm starving.'

Lord Mersham appeared not to have noticed the slip. 'I'll go and fetch you some canapes.'

As he trundled back towards the door, Ellen bent down with her glass and tipped the contents into the bucket of water hidden below the Christmas tree. There was something amiss with the drink; she had never had such a bad reaction to champagne before. 'Concentrate,' she told herself, taking deep breaths, needing to remind herself what exactly she was here for and not to be distracted by the blurry figures taking part in salacious embraces and provocative dancing.

'Gosh, you were a thirsty girl,' Lord Mersham exclaimed when he returned with a napkin in his open hand, upon which were two tiny squares of what looked to Ellen to be pieces of bread with a scraping of salmon and topped with a blob of something yellow. 'All I could manage, I'm afraid,' he apologised, handing her the napkin.

'Thanks,' Ellen said, stuffing them in whole, one at a time.

'More drink?' he asked.

Ellen shook her head. 'I'm feeling very tired all of a sudden.'

Lord Mersham smiled widely. 'Come with me,' he said, placing a grip under her bicep and lifting her from the chair. 'I've got just the thing you need.'

'Yes, maybe a water or a coffee will do the trick,' Ellen agreed, walking beside him out of the lounge. 'Or perhaps some fresh air.'

He led her down the hallway, past the kitchen, to three closed doors. He pulled the second one open and directed her inside. Ellen was surprised to find herself in a small bedroom. Lord Mersham closed the door behind him and grinned.

'What's this?' Ellen asked. Despite the ill effects that she was experiencing, a dawning reality hit her. 'Oh, no, you've got completely the wrong idea.' She stepped towards the door, but he blocked her way.

'Come, now, Lady Eleanora,' he said, unbuttoning his shirt.

'I'm married,' Ellen stammered.

Lord Mersham laughed. 'So am I! What a lot we have in common already.'

'Happily so,' she retorted.

Lord Mersham nodded. 'Yes, me too.'

Ellen's acute lethargy was beginning to pull on her leg muscles, compelling her to relax and sit down. But she couldn't. Not now. She had to fight against the sensations.

'Let's just talk,' Lord Mersham said, striding quickly towards her and pushing her shoulders backwards so that she fell onto the bed.

Ellen screamed, but his hand was quick to cover her mouth. She tried to struggle, but whatever had been added to her champagne had drained her energy, replacing it with an exhausted weakness.

He was on top of her now, scratching at her underwear with his free hand. 'Come on, it's what we're all here for,' he breathed into her face.

She wriggled beneath his weight and tried to wrench his hand from her mouth but failed.

She was now struggling to breathe, and panic began to set in.

Still she fought against him and against the severe fatigue.

The acoustics in the room suddenly changed. The door had been opened, Ellen realised.

Using the last scraps of her energy, she squirmed beneath him and prised his hand from her mouth. 'Help!' she just managed to say.

Then, the weight lifted, as he rolled off her. Ellen gasped for breath and sat up to see Lord Mersham cowering on the floor beside the bed.

Ellen looked up at whomever had come to her rescue, her eyes meeting with those of Flora Sterling.

Flora offered Ellen her hand and pulled her up from the bed. 'You need some air,' Flora directed, leading her by the hand out of the room and down the hallway. They marched, without speaking, through the kitchen and out of the back door to a small deserted courtyard. Flora closed the door behind them, leaving them alone in near darkness. She placed a hand on Ellen's back. 'He put something in your drink, I presume?'

Ellen, stooped over with her hands on her knees, nodded.

Flora took a packet of cigarettes from a small clutch bag, lit one for herself and then offered the packet to Ellen.

Ellen shook her head, unable to think or breathe properly.

Some time passed—how long, Ellen couldn't tell, precisely—with the silent snow falling around them and the muffled sounds of the party continuing inside. She stared at the white beneath her feet, her thoughts beginning to solidify and make some kind of sense. Flora Sterling—the person whom she had come to confront—had rescued her from goodness knows what horror and was now caring for her. It wasn't at all the conflict which she had anticipated arising from the evening. Ellen stood upright and shivered, suddenly aware of the freezing temperature. She looked earnestly at Flora. 'Thank you.'

'You're welcome,' she replied, blowing out a plume of smoke above them. 'It's the least I can do for the person who has expended *so much* energy in following me around London for months on end. I must confess to actually having enjoyed our little cat-and-mouse games, as infuriating as they could get at times.'

Ellen mirrored her smile.

'I assume it's no coincidence that you're here tonight?' Flora went on, blowing out another gust of smoke. 'I must say that I'm surprised. I thought, after my little interview with Mr Skardon, I was off the watch-list once and for all. Perhaps I need to pay him another visit…'

'You're not on the watch-list,' Ellen countered. 'And I'm not working for the section any longer.'

Flora placed the cigarette in her mouth, then promptly withdrew it. 'Oh?' she said. 'So, what are you doing here, then?'

'Jericho,' Ellen said, watching carefully for Flora's reaction.

There was no perceivable change in her bearing. 'Jericho?' she parroted.

'Yes,' Ellen said, drawing in a long breath and taking her time to pull her thoughts into coherent sentences. She spoke slowly and deliberately: 'I had to work really hard to convince the section that Jericho was the codename of a real person—a spy—passing secrets to the Soviets.' She paused, formulating the next sentence, while Flora coolly observed. 'I finally managed to convince them by retracing your steps along Burlington Avenue to the derelict property opposite William Gilmour's house. Surveillance was set up, then we watched you dropping the film cartridge off and William Gilmour retrieving it afterwards. All those state secrets to do with Operation Sawdust in Egypt, destined to be sent out to the Soviets.'

Flora raised her eyebrows and drew on the cigarette. 'Impressive detective work, I must say.'

'And everyone congratulated me that we'd finally pinned down Jericho,' Ellen added.

'Sounds like you deserved the credit,' Flora observed, still feigning ignorance of where the conversation might be headed.

'There was irrefutable evidence going back years that he had been spying for the Soviets; so, there's no doubt of his guilt in that regard.' She paused, making sure that she maintained direct eye contact with Flora. 'But you know that…because you recruited him, didn't you?'

A wry look spread over Flora's face and Ellen knew, despite the fragility of her mind, having used her husband's words, that her worst fears were confirmed. Flora needed say nothing more for Ellen to know the truth; or enough of it, at least, that he hadn't seen that information on her spare room wall at all. 'I think *recruited* is a slight over-generosity of a description,' Flora answered. '*Guided*, might be a better way of putting what actually happened.'

'Do you know what we termed the surveillance operation in the A4 section?' Ellen asked.

Flora shook her head.

'The Sterling Ring,' she revealed, fully aware that she had just taken a giant step over the strict line of confidence, demanded by the Official Secrets Act, which she had signed upon joining MI5.

Flora's face lit up, seemingly delighted by this news. 'The Sterling Ring,' she repeated. 'I like it.'

'And then everyone realised that it wasn't a ring at all. It was just a three-person chain: you took copies of state secrets from the Foreign Secretary, then passed them to William Gilmour to transmit to the Soviets. But…'

'But?'

'But it was more complicated than that, wasn't it?' Ellen suggested. 'Because somebody else was operating out in Egypt independently from you and Nikita Sokolov. A double agent, working within MI6, who relayed his own intelligence to someone higher up the command chain in the KGB: Viktor Zima. *This* double agent in MI6 was the person with the codename of Jericho, *not* Gilmour. The information you were stealing from the Foreign Secretary did, as a rule, pass along this three-person chain ending with Gilmour but, crucially, if it pertained to live operations in the Middle East, then you were instructed to contact Sokolov, who would send that information out to Jericho via Zima. To Jericho—my…husband.'

Flora tossed her cigarette to the ground, blew out a breath of smoke, then said, 'Wow, you really are quite the hot-shot detective, aren't you? Impressive, I must say.'

She turned and placed her hand on the door handle, as though about to re-enter the house.

'Aren't you going to deny any of it? Where are you going?' Ellen demanded.

'To get you a coat and a cup of water. Look at the state of you,' Flora replied.

Standing alone in the dark, Ellen saw herself, shivering and shattered. She could no longer control herself and hot, angry tears streamed down her face. How could she have been so blind? So naïve? So stupid?

Flora strode into the kitchen, where she found Mariella Novotny draped over a topless young film actor, whom Flora recognised, but whose name she couldn't bring to mind at this moment in time.

'Mariella,' Flora interrupted, 'I need to make an urgent phone call.'

Mariella waved her champagne flute in the air, sloshing the contents over the actor's torso. 'Oh dear!' she cried, running her tongue over the liquid on his bare chest. She glanced at Flora. 'Down the hall in my study.'

Flora hurried to the specified room, closed the door behind her and dialled a number. 'It's me,' she said, the moment that it was answered. 'I'm at Mariella's party in Hyde Park Square and Alexander Emmett's wife is here. She's worked everything out. No, everything. What do you want me to say to her? Deny it? Give her a false lead? What? No. No.' She reset the receiver with a slam of aggravation. She stared at the ground, replaying the very simple instruction over in her mind: 'Get rid of her'. Flora had done a lot of things for the greater good, for the cause, but killing a woman in cold blood just because she had discovered the truth about her husband was not something that Flora could reconcile herself to doing.

She'd already taken too long. She scanned around her and saw a blanket thrown over a leather sofa. Flora grabbed it and hurried from the room. In the kitchen, she ran a glass of water and then went outside. 'Here,' she said, folding the blanket around Ellen's shoulders and handing her the drink.

Ellen took the glass but looked at it suspiciously.

'It's just water,' Flora reassured her. 'Are you feeling better, yet?'

'Just really weak,' she replied.

'He must have given you a muscle-relaxant,' Flora informed her.

Ellen sipped the water, still shivering beneath the blanket.

'I think it's time you left,' Flora said. 'Go home and forget all of this'—she gestured to the party behind them—'forget what you *suspect* about your husband.'

'How can I? My God!' Ellen snapped. 'I don't even know who he is!'

'He's the man you married. He's *not* a monster; none of us are. You've fallen foul of this East versus West nonsense that you read about in the newspapers. Twelve years ago, Britain and the Soviet Union were working together to rid the world of Adolf Hitler. We're just working for something so very simple: a fair society for everyone. Is that really so bad?'

'And stealing government secrets or bringing down a plane full of nurses achieves that, does it?' Ellen spat through her tears. 'You're a traitor, William Gilmour was a traitor and my husband…is a traitor.' Ellen cast the blanket from her shoulders, sending it fluttering down into the snow. She made for the door, placed her hand on the handle and then turned. 'Before I go home and confront the traitor that I married, perhaps could you tell me how you've managed to walk away scot-free, given all the damning evidence piled up against you? Hmm? Why was the all-ports alert they put out for you suddenly retracted?'

Flora stared at her for a moment, wondering whether to tell her the truth, or not. She saw no reason not to be honest: 'Of all the intelligence that I encountered and passed on, there was one single document which I held onto. It was my get-out-of-jail-free card.'

'And what was that document, exactly?' Ellen demanded.

349

Flora grinned. 'The order which unequivocally directed MI6 to set up Operation Sawdust to assassinate President Nasser of Egypt. And it was signed by the prime minister himself, Anthony Eden.'

Ellen stared at her, seemingly comprehending the colossal political ramifications of a world leader's ordering the peace-time execution of another world leader.

'All the while I don't share my knowledge with Fleet Street, I'm a free woman,' Flora added.

'Lucky you,' Ellen said, turning away from her and opening the door to the kitchen.

'Be careful,' Flora warned her.

Ellen turned, again. 'You be careful, too. Your get-out-of-jail-free card might not be as valuable as you think, now that we have a new prime minister and a new government: you can't bring somebody down, who has already fallen.'

Flora watched her disappear inside the house, then she leant back against the wall of the house and lit another cigarette. Was the woman correct? Had her immunity diminished owing to the change at the top of the government? Her thoughts were choked, switching over to the absolute instruction that she had just been issued. As she smoked, she wondered if she had done the right thing in telling Nikita Sokolov that Alexander Emmett's wife had somehow managed to determine the detail of his double-life.

She took a long drag on the cigarette and gazed up at the falling snow. What would Nikita do next? That was the question.

The effects of the muscle-relaxant, or whatever she had been given, were lifting and so, too, the mulishness from her mind, but complete exhaustion weighed heavily on her body and every step, which Ellen took, was a physical and mental strain. She walked with the gait of a doddery old lady, her heels sliding in the snow, if she dared to walk faster, which of course made life so much simpler for the two men following her fifty yards or so behind. In an ironic reversal, Ellen was fairly sure that one of the men trailing her was none other than Nikita Sokolov. With trilby hats shielding their faces, the men kept her pace with their hands inside their long dark coats, holding a safe distance behind, as she crossed Lambeth Bridge. The two men, maintaining their statutory surveillance distance, had managed to sustain their pursuit despite Ellen's best attempts to innocuously shake them off.

Ellen ran her index fingers under her eyes, removing the cold tears which had flowed uncontrollably since leaving Mariella Novotny's extraordinary Christmas gathering, as the anxiety grew inside her about what the two men behind her wanted to do to her. She shuddered, as she looked down beneath the bridge into the freezing dark water of the River Thames.

She chanced a look behind her. Alarmingly, a small black car had drawn up alongside the two men and one of them—yes, it most certainly was Nikita Sokolov—was pointing her out to the car driver.

She had no choice but to speed up. She stopped, removed her shoes and tossed them over the iron balustrades into the water below. The freezing snow bit into her feet immediately, but now she was free to run; and she did just that.

Ellen ran to the end of the bridge, then descended the stone steps at its terminus. At the bottom, she began to head along the Embankment. Over her shoulder, she could see that the two men following her were also running and had reached the top of the steps. If she could just shake them off and get to Doris's house, then she would be safe for the time being.

Pain seared the soles of her feet, as though she were running over boiling coals. Worse, she was beginning to lose her battle against the exhaustion; the deep ache inside her calves and thighs was almost too much to bear. She could no longer breathe in sufficient oxygen to maintain her current speed.

But if she stopped, or even dared to slow her pace...

She glanced across the river at the majestic building of the Palace of Westminster, silhouetted behind the tumbling snow. The home of the British parliament, of democratic law-making. Then she thought of what Flora had just told her about the prime minister—Anthony Eden—having personally ordered Operation Sawdust, in which her own beloved husband had evidently been embroiled.

Her heart burnt with the knowledge.

She ran a finger under her wet eyes again and, as she did so, her foot snagged on something sharp, concealed beneath the carpet of snow. She yelled in pain and crashed to the floor.

She closed her eyes, clutching her bleeding foot. When she reopened them seconds later, Nikita Sokolov and his associate were looming above her.

Nikita smiled. 'We meet face-to-face...at long last,' he said, breathlessly revealing his blackened front tooth.

351

Ellen frantically looked around her, wanting to shout for help, but she was here alone with these two men.

'Look at you,' Nikita said. 'You shiver. I have car. Come.'

Nikita's silent friend reached down and wrapped his thick fingers around her right arm, hauling her up. He maintained his vice-like grip once she was upright.

'So, after such time, the face of Jericho is discovered,' Nikita said, folding his arms. 'Well done, working out what MI5 and MI6 could not and have not still.'

Ellen stared at the blood-stained snow at her feet, as the past began to make sense to her. She remembered Alexander's stiltedness the night when they had first met at Harold Austin's cocktail party, as though he were an actor who had over-rehearsed his lines about his family. Then she thought about how rushed their relationship had been in its early stages and how at that time one wall of her spare room was covered with her personal investigations into the Sterling Ring and trying to uncover Jericho's identity.

She met Nikita's cold lifeless eyes and asked the question which she would have asked Alexander, had she believed for a single moment that she would be getting out of this situation alive: 'Did he only marry me because I was getting close to finding out about his double life?'

Nikita thought for a moment. 'First, yes. But you must be something special. He fell in love and stopped his work for us and also for British Security Services.'

'And now what's going to happen?' she stammered, the freezing temperatures causing her limbs to convulse involuntarily.

'That depends on what you plan to do with what you know,' Nikita answered.

'Nothing,' she murmured. 'I love him... I love my baby... I...I won't tell...anyone...'

Nikita smiled. 'I'm sure you would not,' he replied, grabbing her left arm tightly. His associate did the same with her right arm and, sandwiched between them, Ellen was dragged through the snow towards the waiting black car.

'Where are we going?' she managed to ask.

'Wherever you want to go,' he answered.

Ellen was bundled into the back of the car, shivering, bleeding and fearing for her life.

A smouldering limp shaft of ash hung precariously from the end of Flora Sterling's cigarette which was perched between two fingers, she still holding the Bakelite telephone receiver following her phone call of moments before. An unfamiliar sensation of guilt had washed over her; something she had not felt in her entire career to that point. There was just something about that woman that had made Flora use her contacts to get a telephone number for someone inside MI5. She had told them everything, adding that she feared that Ellen's life was now in grave danger.

The ash, hanging impossibly from the unsmoked cigarette, finally gave up, dropping in an untidy grey and white heap on Mariella Novotny's polished mahogany desk.

Ellen was right: her get-out-of-jail-free card was not as valuable as she had believed. The time had come to leave. Leave the party. Leave the organisation. Leave the country.

Nikita Sokolov stepped out from the small terraced house onto the dark deserted street. He inched the front door shut, painfully slowly. He winced when the door closed with a metallic crack. He walked a few feet along the pavement to where the car was waiting for him. Except, it wasn't there. He glanced up and down the road, wondering where it had gone. His instruction to the driver couldn't have been simpler: 'wait here until I return.'

'Looking for something?' a voice said from behind, startling him. He whipped around to see a woman gazing at him. 'Nikita Sokolov,' the woman added, stepping from the shadows. She was in her early sixties, with tightly curled white hair and wearing a pair of round dark-rimmed glasses. He had no idea at all of her identity.

'Who are you?' Nikita demanded.

'I'm here to give you a choice, Mr Sokolov,' she said. 'My friends waiting in those vans just behind us can take you off to spend whatever little amount of life your emphysema permits you at Her Majesty's pleasure, or you can continue living freely as you have been, but with a new paymaster.'

Nikita made a scoffing noise. 'You want me to defect? Ha! And what is it you think I shall be going to prison for?'

'Mr Sokolov, we've followed you from the Embankment and waited while you carried Ellen Emmett inside. I'm in little doubt that, were we to open that front door, we would find Mrs Emmett deceased at your hands.'

Nikita glowered at the woman, then smirked. 'I understand, now. You had chance to save her, but instead you saw chance to bring me in. You let her die, Mrs...?'

'Mrs Strickland,' she answered.

At that moment, a group of seven or eight men in dark coats and trilby hats began to walk towards him.

'You leave no decision, Mrs Strickland,' he said.

Mrs Strickland smiled. 'Sensible choice,' she said, leading him towards the group of men along the street.

The following night, Flora Sterling parked a rental car in the short-term quayside car park at Southampton Docks and walked up the gangplank of the 3,000-ton pleasure ship, *Falaise*. She had deliberately chosen demure and sober clothing so as not to draw the attention of her fellow passengers, not that most of them were in any position to judge or to go rushing off to the authorities: this night-time excursion was popular with wealthy adulterers wishing to whisk their mistresses off on a cross-channel trip to France. She should know, she had accompanied Harold Austin on one such trip not long into their relationship. There were no passport checks or questions asked of the passengers because the three-hour docking in France was an unofficial one.

Flora headed directly to the first-class cabin, which she had booked under a false name. She planned on not leaving the room until the ship docked at St Malo at 11.15 tomorrow morning. Then, she would leave the ship alongside the other passengers for a spot of sightseeing and shopping but, unlike the other passengers, she would not be returning to the ship. Her onward journey from there was completely and wonderfully unplanned.

Perhaps a spell in Paris and then on to Switzerland: she'd always wanted to see the Alps.

Flora looked out of her cabin window at the inky water swelling and swaying around the ship, then up to the star-speckled sky. A warm, contented feeling spread through her at the prospect of the new adventure ahead of her.

Chapter Thirty-One

Morton sipped his latte, watching Christopher Emmett as he processed the news. He was staring through the window of the Ardingly Café, clearly dumbfounded. Morton had just told him that he was due a half-share of an eighty-nine-thousand-pounds legacy which someone—he had yet to reveal who, exactly—had claimed, following the death of *his* biological father.

Christopher ran his fingers through his grey hair and blew air from his flushed cheeks. 'So, this person is prepared to give me *half* of what I'm entitled to…on the proviso that I don't go to the police?' he asked incredulously. 'If I went to the police, then I'd get the whole bloody lot!'

Morton shook his head. 'This person will hand over every penny of your father's estate.'

'But…why am I to only get half, then?' Christopher stammered.

Morton set his latte down on the table and opened up one of the two reports in front of him, which he had prepared, entitled THE DUGGAN CASE. He flicked through a few pages, then turned the report around to face Christopher. 'Your closest DNA matches.'

Christopher squinted at the paper, unblinking. 'Fayez Alexander Ibrahim.' He looked at Morton. 'Close family?'

'He's your half-brother,' Morton revealed.

'What?' Christopher spluttered. 'Half-brother? Ibrahim? But he sounds foreign!'

Morton was glad that, at this moment, except for one woman sitting alone beside the window, the café was empty. 'Your father had some kind of a relationship with his mother, Nadia, in Egypt in 1956.'

"Some kind of a relationship," Christopher echoed. 'I'll say. A half-brother… Wow.'

'He's very keen to make contact,' Morton said, 'if you're willing.'

Christopher took a long breath in through his nose and then nodded. 'Yes. Yes, I suppose so. Does he know about my father's exploits? *Our* father's exploits?'

'No, I've not told him anything,' Morton replied. 'I thought I would leave that up to you.'

Christopher raised his eyebrows. 'Thanks.'

'So, are you willing to accept the inheritance money?'

'Yes,' Christopher answered. 'I won't be trotting off to the police... In fact, this person has done me a favour, haven't they? I mean, I knew nothing whatsoever about my father but I'm assuming by the thickness of this file, here, that you've uncovered quite a bit about him.'

'And about your mother,' Morton added.

'Oh, golly,' Christopher said. 'Well, are you going to tell this person to get in touch?'

Morton nodded and then turned to the woman sitting alone beside the window. 'Clarissa, come and meet Christopher.'

Clarissa stood up with a nervous smile and carried her cup of tea over to their table.

Christopher stood and offered her his hand. 'Golly, that was quick,' he quipped.

Clarissa tried to speak but was choked up with emotion.

'Take a seat,' Morton said to her.

Clarissa sat down beside Christopher, having listened to their conversation to this point.

Morton placed his hands on the two thick files in front of him. 'These are my reports,' he began. 'I'll leave you two to digest them in your own time but, knowing how baffled you probably both are, I'll give you the highlights now. Okay?'

'Yes,' they said in unison.

'So, Christopher...' Morton started. 'When I met you in St Pancras station, I believed that your father was named Alexander Emmett.'

Christopher frowned, braced for something that was about to contradict that fact. 'Yes...' he said, drawing out the word.

'I've subsequently found that Alexander Emmett was not, in fact, your father's birth name.'

Christopher slumped in his chair. 'Well, what was it, then?'

'Hubert John Spencer.'

'But why on earth did he need to change his name?' Christopher asked. 'Hang on a minute... Twice!'

'I'll come to that in a moment. So, your brother,' Morton said with a gesture to Clarissa, 'and your father'—a nod back to Christopher—'grew up in this very village together and, along with another lad, William Gilmour, were best of friends. They were all members of the Radio Society of Great Britain and were avid amateur radio operators, which meant that, in the Second World War, they were recruited by MI8 as Voluntary Interceptors, listening in to German secret service broadcasts. The three of the boys also had a shared interest in communism—'

'You're joking?' Christopher interjected.

'No,' Morton answered. 'In fact, they were very committed to the cause of communism and, at some point in early 1944, the three boys were recruited by a Soviet agent, named Flora Sterling, probably as more of an investment in the future than for the intelligence which they would have been able to provide at that time.'

'Oh, my God!' Christopher blustered. 'A commy!'

'Then,' Morton continued, 'A V1 doodlebug rocket fell on Hubert Spencer's house, killing his parents: your grandparents, Christopher.' Morton paused, aware of the chain of tragedy which he was unravelling in Christopher's family tree.

'God,' Christopher stammered. 'This is a terribly depressing story, isn't it?'

Morton felt sorry for the poor man but was compelled to continue: 'Your father then went to live with William Gilmour, four doors down from the remnants of his parents' bombed house, but, from what Clarissa here has told me, it appears that compromising material was discovered in the ruins and the boys were disallowed from continuing as VIs. Your father took most of the blame and was, therefore, unable to pursue the career path in radio and military intelligence, which he and his Soviet handlers had envisaged for him.'

'Hence the name-change,' Christopher chipped in to check that he was understanding correctly. 'Hubert—my father—needing to change his name to continue with this career path, opted for this random name in Alexander Emmett?'

'Yes,' Morton confirmed. 'Except that Alexander Emmett wasn't a random name. Alexander was another ham radio enthusiast from Port Said in Egypt, whom your father had met over the airwaves. If you look here'—he opened one of the reports to a scanned page from the Radio Society of Great Britain *Bulletin* magazine—'you can see how Hubert would likely have heard that Alexander had died and conceived of the idea.'

Christopher and Clarissa leant over the page. Christopher read the short article aloud: '*Silent Keys. We regret to announce the death of Alexander Emmett su6ad from Port Said, Egypt. Although just shy of his seventeenth birthday, he was an enthusiastic amateur and will be remembered by his many British and worldwide friends. Mr Emmett's death was brought about by a motor car accident in his hometown. Our sympathies are extended to his family and friends.'*

'So, Alexander dies,' Christopher began, 'and my father thinks, I know! I'll be him and take on his identity!'

'Yes,' Morton answered. 'And, if you turn to the next page, you'll see Hubert's disembarkation record from the UK to Port Said.'

Christopher turned the page and duly read the record with a sullen nod.

'If you look carefully at the name below his, you will see who accompanied him on that trip.'

'Flora Sterling?' Christopher read.

Morton nodded. 'There's a photo of her somewhere in here.' He flicked through the file. 'There. She's quite a key player in all of this, as you'll see.'

'Wow, my goodness,' Christopher gasped. 'She was a stunner.'

'So, then what happened?' Clarissa asked.

'Then, a few months later, having established a firm new back-story for Hubert, they return to the UK. Flora Sterling returns under her own name, but Hubert returns as his old ham radio friend, Alexander Emmett. He then gets a job as a journalist and, at some point, is picked up by MI6 to work for them, presumably *because* of his purported background in Egypt, which, at the height of the Suez Crisis, would have appeared invaluable to them. I think the spy parlance for such a person is a coat-trailer: that is to say, a spy who seeks to be recruited by the enemy in order to turn double-agent.'

'Except his background in Egypt wasn't real,' Christopher remarked.

'Quite,' Morton agreed. 'In those files, you will find evidence of his involvement in something called Operation Sawdust that was the British government's attempt to overthrow or eliminate President Nasser of Egypt.'

'What kind of involvement?' Clarissa asked.

'He was an active agent, working under the codename Jericho. What he did, precisely, I haven't been able to find out. Most of the files are closed, heavily redacted or have mysteriously vanished. The prime minister of the time, Anthony Eden issued instructions that all relevant documents be destroyed. After his resignation, two officials from the Foreign Office gathered up all the sensitive papers on Egypt, including Operation Sawdust and put them in a file, marked *SUEZ*, which has disappeared.'

'Typical,' Christopher muttered.

'It may be,' Morton said, 'that further documents are opened up to the public in the future, but, for now, the matter of one state leader trying to assassinate another in peacetime is still pretty contentious.'

'Hmm,' Clarissa agreed.

'Right, so then he returns to the UK, meets and marries my mother,' Christopher recapped. 'I'm born, my mother commits suicide, my father runs away but comes back in 1974 under another name: Maurice Duggan. Right?'

'Good gracious, this *is* complicated,' Clarissa commented. 'I'm not sure I'm keeping up...'

Morton smiled and continued regardless, as clearly as he could. 'Shortly before the first name-change to Alexander, Maurice—Clarissa's brother—had drowned whilst playing on the ice on Westwood Lake, not far from here. William and Hubert were his best friends and tried to save him but they just couldn't.'

'Oh that's sad... I'm sorry about that, Clarissa. Maybe my dad took your brother's name because he had something to do with my mum's death?' Christopher ventured, out of nowhere.

'Well,' Morton said, addressing Christopher's suggestion, 'you've missed out one or two key points.'

Christopher looked uncertainly at Clarissa, then back to Morton. 'Go on.'

'Whilst your father is busy out in Egypt, doing whatever he was doing as part of Operation Sawdust, William Gilmour was sending out state secrets to the Soviets, procured from the Foreign Secretary by his mistress, who was...' Morton suspended the sentence in mid-air, waiting.

'Flora Sterling?' Christopher accurately guessed.

'Correct. But,' Morton said, 'MI5 were on to them, employing their own agents to follow her every move. One of those agents was called Ellen Ingram.'

'What?' Christopher bellowed. 'Bloody hell! My mother worked for MI5?'

'Good grief,' Clarissa said, although Morton was unsure whether that was in reaction to his revelation or to Christopher's histrionic outburst.

'Ironically, your mother helped to bring down William Gilmour and Flora Sterling.'

'Then she topped herself...' he muttered.

Morton thought for a moment, wanting to choose his words very carefully. 'I think you need to view both of your parents' deaths with a degree of suspicion, given the lives they led.'

As he expected, Christopher shot him a look of horror. 'What are you saying?'

'I've evidence for nothing more than that,' Morton replied. '*But*, I've been through it all with my wife, who is a police officer, and she thinks that there could be something there, but that a better approach might be to get the case publicised first. I know a journalist you could try contacting.'

'If it can reveal what really happened to my parents, then yes, of course,' Christopher said. 'One thing I still don't understand, though, is why my father scarpered as soon as my mother died and why he left me as an orphan.'

'This is why I think both of their deaths hold a degree of suspiciousness: if Ellen had killed herself, then why did he need to flee and why did he need to return under a false identity? One reason could be that she didn't kill herself at all and that her death was a warning to him and a threat to you.'

'And what about his suicide in April this year? He was supposed to have fallen from his balcony. Are you saying that his death is suspicious, too?' Clarissa asked.

'More subtle than Novichok, I suppose,' Christopher murmured.

'I think that he was in the process of trying to reveal what he knew...write his memoirs,' Morton explained. 'He had a well-used book on memoir-writing and, given all those ink ribbons that came from his flat, he'd certainly been very active on his typewriter. And, yet, there wasn't a single typed sheet in his flat. Where did it all go? His neighbour in Priory Flats, Derek, said that he was always typing and another neighbour, Winnie swears she heard someone in the building just before he was supposed to have killed himself.'

'Let's hope this journalist friend of yours does a good job,' Christopher said.

'I don't know if you want these,' Morton said, bending down to remove the *Live and Let Die* book and the pair of glasses from his bag and placing them on the table. 'They belonged to your father during his stint as Maurice Duggan.'

Christopher pulled the items towards himself and smiled. 'My father the spy.'

'I've put Winnie's details in the file for you, Christopher,' Morton said. 'She's happy for you to contact her, if you wanted to know about his latter years in the village.'

'Thank you,' Christopher said. 'And thank you for all you've done. I look forward to digesting all of this in my own time but right now, I might take a walk through the village—see where he lived and visit the church. Do you fancy a walk, Clarissa?'

Clarissa smiled. 'I'd like that very much.'

The pair of them stood, picked up their respective case files, and shook Morton's hand.

'Cheerio,' Clarissa said, moving towards the café door.

'Thank you, Mortimer,' Christopher said, following her outside.

Morton watched them leave and then finished the last cold dregs of his latte.

Case closed.

Time to head home.

'Daddy!' Grace greeted, as Morton entered the house. 'Gone!' she added, thrusting a half-eaten scone towards him.

'Goodness, what flavour is it?' he asked.

'Gone!'

'S-c-one,' Morton corrected, following Grace and her trail of crumbs into the kitchen.

Juliette was standing up, rubbing her belly with a strained facial expression.

'What's up?' he asked.

'Oh, nothing. Baby Farrier is just playing football with my internal organs, is all,' she said. 'Come and feel.'

Morton went over and allowed Juliette to guide his hand to the side of her stomach. 'Oh, wow, he is active.'

'Or *she*. Want a gone?' She asked, holding up a tray of half-a-dozen scones. 'They're nice, actually.'

'So nice that they failed to sell in the shop, and so nice that you used the word 'actually' to describe them,' he said, eyeing the tray suspiciously. 'What flavour are they?'

'Chicken and fudge,' she said with a laugh.

'How horrendous.'

'Your half-aunt, Vanessa Briggs, phoned while you were out,' Juliette said.

'Oh, right. What did she have to say?'

'That you should have received an invite,' she said, sounding as though she were doubting her own words, 'to see hers and her sisters' DNA results?'

'Ooo,' Morton said, opening his emails on his mobile phone. Sure enough, he had three separate invitations from the women to become a collaborator on their DNA profiles.

'Does that mean you can find their mother, now?' Juliette asked.

'It gives me the means to *try*,' he answered, noncommittally. He closed his emails and pocketed his mobile. 'But right now, who wants to go down to Knoops and get a super, special hot chocolate and then play in the playpark?'

'Me!' Grace yelled, jumping in the air, casting scone debris all around her.

'Me,' Juliette echoed. 'Although, I think Baby Farrier would prefer a big fat milkshake, today.'

Morton picked Grace up and planted a kiss on her lips. Grace threw her arms around him and mashed the remnants of her chicken and fudge scone into the back of his hair.

Chapter Thirty-Two

6ᵗʰ August 1944, Ardingly, West Sussex

Hubert John Spencer combed a splodge of Brylcreem through his hair. He had already spent several minutes in front of the bathroom mirror, making sure that he looked his absolute best for this evening.

Pushing his face closer to the mirror, he gritted his teeth together, inspecting each tooth. All looking good. He glanced down to check that his shirt and trousers were suitably pressed, then he smiled at himself and left the bathroom, whistling a made-up tune.

'Bye,' he called into the lounge, as he opened the front door.

He just caught the murmured responses from his parents, as he shut the door. Outside, he inhaled the warm summer afternoon. The sky above him was a perfect cloudless turquoise and Hubert had a good feeling about the rest of the day to come.

Walking just a few feet along Street Lane, he opened the wooden gate to number 2 and wandered up the narrow path, past the house to the shack at the bottom of the garden.

He knocked the special tap on the door—*Marx* in Morse code—and waited for it to be unlocked from within.

'Hi, Hue,' Maurice greeted, wearing black-rimmed glasses, a Homburg hat, camel-hair coat and red suede shoes. 'Looking very dapper, I must say.'

'Thanks,' Hubert answered, stepping inside the hut and locking the door behind him. 'Nearly as fancy-looking as you for once.'

Their other friend, William Gilmour was sitting with his back to him wearing a headset. His right hand was frantically scribbling something onto a log sheet, whilst his left hand was making infinitesimal adjustments to the AR-88 radio receiver.

'Much activity?' Hubert asked Maurice.

'Yes, lots, actually,' he replied, picking up a stack of log sheets from the piece of wood balancing between two chairs which acted as a desk. He stood beside Hubert and showed him what had been transcribed today. The three of them took it in turns in pairs to listen and transcribe what they heard over the airwaves on the official Radio Security Service stationery, whilst the other of the pair made unofficial copies. The official log sheets were placed into envelopes, marked *secret* and posted to PO Box 25, Barnet, Herts. The unofficial copies were handed over to a person sympathetic to the socialism cause.

'Ah, I see the lovely Hans was back on again,' Hubert noted.

'Do you think they'll be pleased with all of this?' Maurice asked him, pointing to the copies.

Hubert nodded. It was hard to know exactly what was useful amongst what they were providing. These tiny snippets of Morse conversation between members of the German secret service were of little value in isolation but, when viewed alongside those from the past few months, helped to form a much larger picture.

William removed the headset from his ears, hanging it around his neck and then looked over his shoulder at Hubert. 'Why's it just *you* who always gets to hand them over?' he asked. 'It was the three of us, remember, at that socialism meeting in Crawley when we agreed to share what we were intercepting.'

Hubert shrugged. 'It's less of a security risk,' he answered.

William made a scoffing sound. 'Listen to the seventeen-year-old master-spy himself.'

Hubert grinned. 'Actually, I think you'll find—'

Maurice cut across him, placing his hand out in front. 'Shh!'

The three boys' silence was broken by an odd rumbling sound outside.

'It's just a plane,' William said.

Maurice shook his head. 'No. Yes. There's a plane but there's something else.'

Hubert closed his eyes, trying to separate the sounds out in his mind. Whatever was making the noise was definitely coming from the air and definitely getting much louder by the second. 'Doodlebug!' Hubert declared. '*And* a plane of some kind.'

'We need to take shelter!' William shouted, freeing the headset from his neck and diving under the desk.

'It's fine,' Hubert countered. 'The engine's still running. Keep quiet and listen.'

The combined roar from the two machines, which sounded as though they were at rooftop height, was deafening. Then, something happened. The doodlebug, without its engine cutting out was heading downwards. 'Get down!' Hubert cried, pushing Maurice to the floor.

The pair of them just managed to join William under the desk when the monstrous sound of the rocket exploding on impact nearby thundered through the ground, as though a huge earthquake had just struck with its epicentre directly below them. The shack rattled and shook, sending various items hanging from the walls crashing to the ground. The AR-88 radio receiver fell to the ground and smashed open.

'Oh, my God!' Maurice yelled, as an eerie silence fell over them.

'How did that happen?' William shouted.

Hubert knew. He had seen it happen last month. An allied aircraft had flown alongside the rocket, tipped its wing below the doodlebug wing, sending it hurtling to the ground.

'We'd better go and take a look,' Maurice said. 'It sounded really close by.'

Led by Hubert, the boys climbed out from under the table, one after the other.

'Are you alright?' William asked them both.

'Yeah, fine,' Maurice answered, looking down at himself, as if to make completely certain.

'I think I'm okay,' Hubert replied, shaken and with his ears ringing from the sound of the explosion.

'Come on,' Maurice said, opening the door.

The three boys stepped out of the shack and immediately stopped. The landing site of the doodlebug—denoted by tall flames and thick plumes of black smoke—was obvious: Hubert's parents' house.

'Were they home?' William whispered.

Hubert went to answer, but his throat was closed. He nodded.

The sun was beginning to set on Ardingly; a calm pink and orange sky juxtaposed with the destruction below. Most of the residents—or, so it seemed to Hubert—were standing in the middle of Street Lane, behind a police cordon, staring at what remained of his house. The local volunteer fire brigade had managed to get the blaze under control quickly, but what had remained of the structure had been so badly damaged that, shortly after they had left, the rest of the house had collapsed.

The group of half-a-dozen ARP wardens, in black suits and tin helmets, carefully spading at the hot debris had yet to answer the one question which nobody dared to ask: had Mr and Mrs Spencer been inside the house when the doodlebug had struck?

Hubert had heard the whispers. The muttered consensus was that they had not been seen around the village prior to the explosion, so they must, therefore, have been at home. Hubert knew the answer, of course: he had said goodbye to them only ten minutes before the doodlebug had been brought down. The best that he could have hoped for was that they had used the Morrison shelter in the dining room, but he knew from their past reluctance that that was highly unlikely.

'It was an American, thinking he were doing good,' a voice next to him said. It was Fred Taylor, an old man from the village. 'I see it coming over: a P-51 Mustang. Tipped his wing under the doodlebug's wings and down she went.'

Hubert nodded, as the anger inside him rose towards the pilot.

An audible change rippled through the crowd. Hubert looked up to see one of the wardens heading over to the policemen with something in his hands. Necks craned and people stood on tiptoe to get a better look at that which the warden was showing one of the policemen, expecting to see something confirming that Mr and Mrs Spencer had been present in the house when the doodlebug had landed.

'We need to go,' Hubert whispered to Maurice and William.

'What's the problem?' Maurice asked, shoving his glasses up to the bridge of his nose, as they pushed through the crowd.

Hubert shook his head and kept walking. When they were sufficiently far away from any other person, he said, 'That ARP warden had some of my official log sheets.'

'So?' William responded. 'They only need to make a quick—'

'On top of my copy of *From Trotsky to Tito*,' Hubert interrupted. 'Even PC Foster isn't stupid enough not to put two and two together.'

'Now what?' Maurice asked.

Hubert looked at his watch. 'You two go back and see if they find any sign of…of my parents.'

'And where are you going?' William asked.

'For advice,' he replied, running up Street Lane towards the church.

Twenty minutes later, the black Sunbeam-Talbot 90 tucked into the gateway of the field behind the church. As usual, Hubert checked around to make sure that nobody was about, then opened the passenger door and got inside.

'Hello, Hue,' she said, her perfect red lips smiling widely. 'What's wrong?'

'A doodlebug has just come down on my house,' he said, gazing through the windscreen, surprised at how calm he was feeling.

'What?' she said, with a light, disbelieving laugh. 'Are you being serious?'

Hubert nodded. 'My parents are unaccounted for…'

'Oh, my God,' she said, placing her hand on his leg. 'Why are you here, then? We can't go sneaking off to Crawley, tonight. You need to be here. My goodness!'

He nodded again. They had planned to watch *Charlie Chan in the Secret Service* at the Embassy Cinema. 'They've found some compromising material in the rubble,' he said, turning to meet her eyes for the first time. 'Log sheets and a communism book...so far.'

'Oh,' she said, facing forward and thinking hard.

He watched her, deep in concentration, as always astounded that a chance encounter at a socialism meeting in January with this stunning twenty-three-year-old had led to an ongoing affair. She had beguiled all three of them, somehow eliciting from them the fact that they were Voluntary Interceptors for MI8. They could help the cause much more than by just attending meetings and protesting against the inequitableness of capitalism, she had told them: they could actually help the Soviets to win the war, if they so desired. She had promised them a great future, suggesting that they joined the Royal Signals Corps as soon as they turned eighteen, from there to transfer to the Diplomatic Wireless Service and then into the Secret Intelligence Service. Several similar men had already followed this path, she had told them, and were now employed in the higher echelons of MI5 and MI6.

'You need to destroy everything you can,' she said, facing him. '*Anything* at all at Maurice's and William's houses—destroy it all— books, magazines, even the radio equipment.'

'Really...even the radios?'

'Everything gone,' she insisted.

Hubert nodded.

'Go now,' she said.

Hubert leant across and kissed her on the mouth.

'Good luck,' she said.

He closed the door and watched the little car drive away down the hill. He stared at the road, long after the Sunbeam-Talbot had disappeared from sight, wondering if he was in love with Flora Sterling.

Chapter Thirty-Three

Hubert was certain that he'd never been this cold before. It was saying something that he wanted to get back to the tiny room which he had been sharing with William Gilmour for the past four months. Life during that time had been unbearable for him. He'd lost his parents, his house and the single thing about which he had been obsessively passionate since the age of twelve: his radio. Hubert John Spencer's life had, to all intents and purposes, ended on the 6th August when some American idiot had decided that it was a good idea to tip a V1 rocket onto his house. Just one thing had kept him going: his relationship with Flora Sterling and the promises that she had made for his future. Plans were already afoot for Hubert John Spencer's metamorphosis into his Egyptian friend from the radio, Alexander Emmett, who, he had read in the latest edition of the Radio Society of Great Britain *Bulletin* magazine, had been killed in a motor accident.

Alexander's death would give Hubert new life. But, right now, he had a more pressing problem to deal with: to persuade his friend, Maurice Duggan not to do what he was trying to do. Maurice was striding along a narrow animal track through the woods, his suede shoes crunching on the thawing ground, as Hubert and William Gilmour struggled to keep up.

'I'm so cold,' William complained.

'Me too,' Hubert agreed, as another freezing droplet fell from the snow-laden trees above, 'but we need to stop him.'

'I *can* hear you,' Maurice said, peering through his black-rimmed glasses over his shoulder. He was wearing his usual camel-hair coat and Homburg hat. He was warm, at least. 'Just go home.'

'You need to leave the stuff where it is,' Hubert said for the umpteenth time.

Maurice stepped over a fallen tree and then stopped. 'Why?' he asked. His face was flushed and his breath, visible in the cold air, puffed out of him in quick bursts.

Hubert and William stopped short of him, both grateful for a rest.

'Because Flora said so,' Hubert answered. 'Given what they found at my house, we're still all under heavy suspicion.'

'*Your* house,' Maurice retorted. 'Not mine. The war's still on and I could be helping.' He glowered at Hubert. 'And, unlike you, I'm not under Flora Sterling's ruddy spell.'

'What's that supposed to mean?' Hubert demanded.

'It means that you do anything she tells you, without question and without running it past us two first. When did *she* suddenly become in charge? Do we even know what she does with all that we give her? I don't like it. And look at what's been happening in the last few months—Soviets, British and the Americans, all working together to defeat Hitler. We're winning by working together!'

Hubert had never seen his friend so animated before. It had all gone wrong this morning, when Hubert had passed the instruction to his two friends from Flora Sterling that they were to delay their applications to join the Diplomatic Wireless Service. 'I trust her,' Hubert said, hearing how weak he sounded, as the words came out of his mouth.

'Yes, and we know why that is, don't we?' Maurice said. 'Do you think William and I are stupid, or something?'

It was pointless to deny it. 'That has nothing to do with our work for the cause.'

'Well, what I do for the cause from now on will be my own decision. I'm going to get my stuff back and do as I please,' Maurice said, turning and marching further into the woods.

'Do you really think that after the war things will change?' William stammered. 'You think Churchill will suddenly push for a fairer society because Stalin lent a hand in fighting Nazism?'

Maurice ignored him and continued marching away from them.

'All your stuff will be ruined, anyway!' Hubert shouted after him.

Hubert went to follow, but William grabbed his wrist. 'Shall we just leave him to it?' William said.

'No,' Hubert insisted, shaking off William's grip and running after his friend.

They jogged silently through the fir trees, Maurice maintaining a lead over his two friends, until the bank began to gently decline and in front of them appeared the expanse of the frozen Westwood Lake.

Maurice rushed down to the edge of the frozen water and touched his left foot tentatively onto the ice. When it held, he placed his right foot down and stood motionlessly, presumably studying the ice for signs of fracturing. Then, he jumped up and down several times and stopped. Evidently satisfied, Maurice began to step across the lake, with Hubert and William watching on from the safety of the path which looped its perimeter.

'It was here, wasn't it?' Maurice shouted from a point around thirty feet from the edge, from where a wooden post emanated from the water, bearing a sign stating *STRICTLY NO FISHING*.

Hubert nodded. Back in June, he had tied a small rowing boat to that very post, while he had deposited the two hessian sacks into the lake.

He watched his friend get down onto his knees and begin to scrape away the dusting of fresh snow in order to reveal the ice beneath. He realised at that moment that this wasn't about Maurice's wanting to retrieve his belongings in order to use them—he couldn't, they would be ruined by now—he was trying to undermine Flora Sterling's apparent authority with his own sense of self-determination.

Maurice picked up a small rock from a selection thrown there in the failed attempts of local children to smash the solid crust sitting on the water. Returning to his knees, he began to hammer the rock down onto the frozen layer.

William whispered, 'I don't like this, Hue. We need to stop him.'

Hubert agreed. The ferocity with which Maurice was pounding the ice was idiotically dangerous. Stepping cautiously onto the ice, with William shivering close beside him, Hubert moved towards Maurice.

He paused, as his friend plucked a small triangle of glinting ice from the water, launching it into the air to the side of him. It smashed down just a few feet in front of Hubert, shattering into tiny pieces. Hubert bent down and picked up one of the larger fragments to gauge the depth of the ice upon which the three of them were now standing. It was no more than two inches thick. He held the ice splinter in front of William, who understood. They both stopped and stared at their friend.

'Maurice,' William called, without progressing further onto the lake. 'Just stop! I'll help you retrieve it when the ice has melted in a few days' time.'

But Maurice seemed not to hear. He smashed the rock repeatedly into the ice, throwing larger fragments onto the precarious surface behind him until a hole the size of a misshapen dustbin lid had been opened up.

Reaching his right arm into the water, Maurice emitted a satisfied grunt, evidently having found something. Moments later, he hauled one of the hessian sacks out onto the ice. His breathing was shallow and his coat was soaked through, but he appeared not to notice.

Hubert watched uncertainly, as Maurice untied the rope at the top of the sack. He reached inside and feverishly withdrew his personal radio set. He sat it on his lap and smiled.

Overhead, the sun peered through the trees, bathing Maurice in a mottled light and creating a scene of pure spontaneous madness in front of Hubert and William.

Maurice reached inside the sack again and pulled out something the size of a limp brick, from which water was cascading down onto the radio set.

Hubert just caught sight of the cover of the book, *The Peaceful Co-existence of Capitalism and Socialism*, as the silent air was filled with a loud snapping sound akin to a large tree cracking in half.

But Hubert knew that it wasn't a tree at all: it was the ice giving up under Maurice's weight.

Hubert watched with horror as his friend tumbled backwards through the ruptured crust. As Hubert and William rushed towards him, Maurice slid beneath the water and, for the briefest of moments, the only part of him still visible was his hand clutching the sodden copy of *The Peaceful Co-existence of Capitalism and Socialism*.

Epilogue

3rd July 2019, Ardingly, West Sussex

It was a gloriously sunny day without a cloud in the sky when Winnie Alderman ambled out of Priory Flats. It was her usual Wednesday routine: walk to the Post Office on the High Street to send off correspondence to her sister in Australia and settle any bills that needed paying, before having a cup of tea and slice of cake in the Ardingly Café with her friend, Gwen; it was the same every week.

She reached the Post Office, today, pleased to find that it was empty of customers. She approached the counter, smiled at the young assistant, whose name Winnie couldn't recall, and placed her letter to Australia on the scales.

'Six pounds ten, please,' the young lady said.

'And one more thing,' Winnie said, reaching into her jute bag and retrieving a thick parcel. She plopped it down heavily on the scales.

'That's a big one,' the assistant commented.

'Yes,' Winnie agreed. 'And it needs special delivery, signed for, guaranteed—everything.'

'Expensive,' the assistant warned.

Winnie nodded vehemently.

'For security reasons, can I ask what the contents are, please?'

'Just typed material,' Winnie answered. 'Lots and lots of paper.'

'Okay. Could you read the address to me, please?'

'Yes,' Winnie said, picking up the parcel and beginning to read. 'It's going to Christopher Emmett.' Then she carefully read out his address and paid for the postage.

Winnie walked out of the Post Office, smiling. She had done her job, as she had promised. Just as Maurice Duggan had instructed, three months to the day since his death, she had posted the parcel that he had entrusted to her. He had directed her not to tell anyone. Not the police. Not anyone in Priory Flats. Nor anybody claiming to be his family. When she had gently probed as to the contents of the parcel, Maurice had simply replied, 'My life.'

Winnie strolled in the warm morning sunshine towards the café, happy that she had fulfilled the only request made of her by her late dear friend, Maurice Duggan.

Historical information

Although this is a work of fiction and the leading characters are fictional, there are several aspects of the storyline and some key characters who really existed.

Given the nature of this book, many of the records, which Morton finds redacted or missing, are so in real life. The abstract quoted from *The Guardian* online at the very beginning of the book is genuine: thousands of politically sensitive files, containing dozens of papers have been 'mislaid' over the years, after having been borrowed from the National Archives by civil servants in Whitehall. Other files have never even made it to the National Archives in the first place, having been wilfully destroyed by the incumbent government. Anthony Eden, the prime minister during the Suez Crisis, did indeed ask his cabinet secretary to place all sensitive papers pertaining to Egypt in a file, marked SUEZ, which he then ordered be destroyed. His cabinet secretary obliged.

Operation Sawdust was a real undercover operation that received vast sums of money from 'unofficial reserves' which were held outside of the scrutiny of Parliament and most members of the government. The precise details of Operation Sawdust are not known, but it was broadly established to undermine President Nasser's government, using covert action by MI6. Not only was Nasser's Egypt against British foreign policy generally, but the country was also seen as the lynchpin of Soviet infiltration in the region. One of the leading figures involved in the organisation of covert action in the Middle East was George Kennedy Young, known as GK, who was director of SIS personnel and operations. According to Rory Cormac's book, *Disrupt and Deny*, GK informed the new chief of the Secret Intelligence Service that he had been personally selected by Anthony Eden to 'bump Nasser off', giving him what he saw as a licence to kill. Various methods of murder were considered by MI6, including using nerve gas at Nasser's headquarters, a poison dart and an exploding razor. The plots, for whatever reason, did not achieve their goal: Nasser died of natural causes in 1970.

The invasion of the Suez region of Egypt happened as described in this book. It was a highly complex plan, which involved cooperation between the British, French and Israelis and, crucially, deliberately kept the Americans in the dark. The invasion was heavily criticised around the world and, under severe pressure from the American government, Anthony Eden was forced into a humiliating cease-fire and eventual withdrawal from the region. The Suez Crisis is generally judged by historians to be the start of the decline of British influence in world affairs.

During this period of turbulence, Beirut was seen as the epicentre of Middle Eastern politics and St Georges Hotel was the trading post of information between journalists, diplomats, spies and politicians. One notable spy, who used this hotel, was Kim Philby.

Mariella Novotny was a real person, hosting elaborate society gatherings and orgies at her home of 13 Hyde Park Square, London. Attendees at her parties were the rich and elite of the day. Among their number were the key players involved in the Profumo scandal of the 1960s: Jack Profumo, Christine Keeler and Stephen Ward. There has also been much deliberation over the years about the identity of 'The Man in the Mask'—a servant at one of Mariella's parties, entirely naked but for a Viking mask—rumoured to have possibly been a Member of Parliament, a film director or even a member of the Royal Family. Mariella's diaries were stolen in a burglary following her death in 1983. MI5 files, which might well name the man, are currently redacted.

The storyline, wherein Maurice Duggan landed a Cessna at Heathrow Airport at night in 1974, was based on a real account. John William Harrison-Howe landed a small aircraft at Heathrow Airport on the 17th October 1973, having not filed a flight plan and having failed to obtain clearance from Air Traffic Control. He was sentenced on the 21st March 1974 at Uxbridge Magistrates' Court, where he was found guilty and ordered to pay a £225 fine.

The A4 Watcher section within MI5 was real. Based at Leconfield House on Curzon Street, as depicted in this story, the unit operated under the leadership of Jim Skardon. The men and women in the section were tasked with following espionage suspects and building a network of their contacts and, just as portrayed in this story, the unit only operated within the boundaries of London and only worked on weekdays. Jim Skardon was heavily involved in the investigation into the Cambridge Five, the interrogation of Klaus Fuchs and the Portland spy ring, among numerous other cases.

Many of the documents that Morton accesses from the National Archives are real, but with fictitious content. The file for William Gilmour is based on one which exists for Charles John Moody and his wife, Gerta, whom the A4 Watcher section monitored for their potential Soviet links. Phone taps, postal intercepts and interviews conducted by Jim Skardon are all featured in this document. The all-ports alert and Home Office Suspect Index for Flora Sterling is based on the KV-6 146 file, held by the National Archives for Gisela Hendrina Klein, a suspected Soviet spy.

Most of the CAB files which Morton accesses at the National Archives are real, some of which are written verbatim and include the heavy redactions, as stated in this story. The documents, letters and figures given in CAB 301/118, regarding the 'unofficial reserves' and their operational purposes, are real and parts of them have been repeated accurately in this story.

The Mitrokhin Archive is genuine and the reality of its location and accessibility at Churchill College is as portrayed in this story. The archive was described by the FBI as 'the most complete and extensive intelligence ever received from any source.' The opening up of this archive to the general public in 1999 resulted in the exposure of many people of several nationalities, who had spied for the Soviets over several decades. These included the former Scotland Yard officer, Detective Sergeant John Symonds, an MP, a journalist and Melita Norwood, dubbed 'The Spy who Came in from the Co-op'. Morton Farrier was very fortunate in this story to be able to gain access to pages which are redacted to the public in reality. For example, the cover page for MITN 1/7 reads, *pages 119-138A have been closed, removed from the binder and stored separately* and their content was fictionalised for the purposes of this book.

During the Second World War, many radio enthusiasts were employed by MI8 to work as Voluntary Interceptors, where they would record the Morse conversations between members of the German secret service. These logs were sent off to PO Box 25, Barnet, Herts, ending up at Bletchley Park for further analysis.

Granny's Scones in Rye does not exist, but it definitely should.

Among the research books, which I found useful in the writing of this book, were the following:

Aldrich, R.J., *GCHQ* (HarperPress, 2010)
Aldrich, R.J., *The Hidden Hand* (John Murray, 2001)
Andrew, C., *The Defence of the Realm* (Penguin, 2009)
Andrew, C. & Mitrokhin, V., *The Mitrokhin Archive* (Penguin, 1999)
Barratt, N., *The Forgotten Spy* (Blink, 2015)

Cormac, R., *Disrupt and Deny* (OUP, 2018)

Goodwin, N.D., *Hastings at War 1939-1945* (Phillimore, 2005)

Jeffery, K., *MI6* (Bloomsbury, 2010)

MacIntyre, B., *A Spy Among Friends* (Bloomsbury, 2014)

MacIntyre, B., *Agent Zigzag* (Bloomsbury, 2007)

MacIntyre, B., *The Spy and the Traitor* (Penguin, 2018)

McKay, S., *The Secret Listeners* (Aurum, 2012)

Pigeon, G., *The Secret Wireless War* (Arundel Books, 2008)

Twigge, S., Hampshire, E., & Macklin, G., *British Intelligence* (The National Archives, 2008)

Bulletin magazines from the Radio Society of Great Britain 1939-1949

Acknowledgements

This book, perhaps more so than any other in the series, has relied on the expert advice and knowledge of many kind people. So, my first sincere thanks must go to Peter Calver and Antony Marr for information regarding procedures in British civil registration; to Bob Bristow for enlightening me on the specifications of various light aircraft and helping me to ultimately settle on using a Cessna 150 in the story; to John Wornham for his expertise on Air Traffic Control in the 1970s; to Helen Woolven for information about policing and police procedure; to Judy Russell for her advice regarding US legal / genealogical processes; to Jonny Perl for DNA advice; to Dave Dowell for his ongoing advice and suggestions regarding US cold cases and genetic genealogy; for in-depth knowledge on ham radio usage, my gratitude goes to the three Peters: Peter Love for introducing me to the Dover Amateur Radio Club, and Peter Pennington and Peter Weatherall for providing excellent and much-needed advice on ham radio. The latter Peter also kindly loaned me copies of the Radio Society of Great Britain *Bulletin* magazines.

My grateful thanks must also go to Kirk Wennerstrom, who not only gave me invaluable technical advice regarding flying and landing a Cessna 150, but who also kindly read and edited the relevant sections to ensure accuracy. Kirk also suggested the use of the Illyushin I-14 aircraft and potential methods for its sabotage.

I am indebted to the Reverend John Crutchley, rector of Ardingly Church for assisting me with my enquiries and, at short notice, allowing me access to the parish records held at his church and also for agreeing to appear as himself in the story. Thanks also to Jens Knoops for appearing in the book as himself, once again. A visit to his hot chocolate emporium is a must for anyone visiting the town of Rye! Similarly, my gratitude to Jon Archer for permitting me to turn his young son, Alfie Archer, into an MI6 spy!

My thanks also go to Dr Rory Cormac, for allowing me to reference his book, *Disrupt and Deny*, an exceptional, authoritative and highly recommended account of spies, special forces and British foreign policy.

As always, Patrick Dengate has done a sterling job with the cover of this book, creating something much better and more evocative of the period than I could have imagined.

As most of my readers are aware, during the research stages of writing, I undertake almost everything that Morton does in the book. As part of the research for this book, I visited many record offices, where I must thank the staff for their assistance. One archive stands out far and above all others: West Sussex Record Office. Every member of staff went out of their way to help and advise, and it was a real pleasure to work there.

A very big thank you to my early readers, who gave their feedback, corrections and opinions, helping to shape the final book: Connie Parrot, Helen Smith, Jonny Perl, Cheryl Hudson Passey, Nairet Jacklin, Dr Karen Cummings, Karen Clark Cresswell, Gail Ann Pippin and Lynn Serafinn.

I owe an increasing debt of gratitude to the enthusiasts of the series, who promote my books on their influential genealogical platforms, sharing Morton's adventures with the wider world, including the following: Peter Calver at LostCousins; The Genealogy Guys (Drew Smith & George Morgan); DearMyrtle (Pat Richley-Erickson); Scott Fisher at Extreme Genes; Bobbi King and Dick Eastman; Sunny Morton; Lisa Louise Cooke at Genealogy Gems Podcast; Amy Lay and Penny Bonawitz at Genealogy Happy Hour; Andrew Chapman; Karen Clare and Helen Tovey at *Family History* magazine; Sarah Williams at *Who Do You Think You Are?* magazine; Randy Seaver; Jill Ball; Shauna Hicks; Cheryl Hudson Passey; Linda Stufflebean; Sharn White; Elizabeth O'Neal; Wendy Mathias; James Plyant; Denise Levenick; the late Eileen Furlani Souza and all of the many Family History societies around the world, too numerous to name individually, which have run such kind reviews of the series. Your support is truly appreciated.

My final thanks go to Robert Bristow for accompanying the adventure once again and undertaking tasks too innumerable to list.

Further Information

Website & Newsletter: www.nathandylangoodwin.com
Twitter: @NathanDGoodwin
Facebook: www.facebook.com/NathanDylanGoodwin
Pinterest: www.pinterest.com/NathanDylanGoodwin
Blog: theforensicgenealogist.blogspot.co.uk
LinkedIn: www.linkedin.com/in/NathanDylanGoodwin

Hiding the Past
(The Forensic Genealogist #1)

Peter Coldrick had no past; that was the conclusion drawn by years of personal and professional research. Then he employed the services of one Morton Farrier, Forensic Genealogist — a stubborn, determined man who uses whatever means necessary to uncover the past. With the Coldrick Case, Morton faces his toughest and most dangerous assignment yet, where all of his investigative and genealogical skills are put to the test. However, others are also interested in the Coldrick family, people who will stop at nothing, including murder, to hide the past. As Morton begins to unearth his client's mysterious past, he is forced to confront his own family's dark history, a history which he knows little about.

'Flicking between the present and stories and extracts from the past, the pace never lets up in an excellent addition to this unique genre of literature'
Your Family Tree

'At times amusing and shocking, this is a fast-moving modern crime mystery with genealogical twists. The blend of well fleshed-out characters, complete with flaws and foibles, will keep you guessing until the end'
Family Tree

'Once I started reading *Hiding the Past* I had great difficulty putting it down - not only did I want to know what happened next, I actually cared'
Lost Cousins

The Lost Ancestor
(The Forensic Genealogist #2)

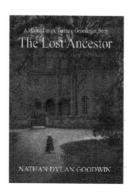

From acclaimed author, Nathan Dylan Goodwin comes this exciting new genealogical crime mystery, featuring the redoubtable forensic genealogist, Morton Farrier. When Morton is called upon by Ray Mercer to investigate the 1911 disappearance of his great aunt, a housemaid working in a large Edwardian country house, he has no idea of the perilous journey into the past that he is about to make. Morton must use his not inconsiderable genealogical skills to solve the mystery of Mary Mercer's disappearance, in the face of the dangers posed by those others who are determined to end his investigation at any cost.

'If you enjoy a novel with a keen eye for historical detail, solid writing, believable settings and a sturdy protagonist, *The Lost Ancestor* is a safe bet. Here British author Nathan Dylan Goodwin spins a riveting genealogical crime mystery with a pulsing, realistic storyline'
Your Family Tree

'Finely paced and full of realistic genealogical terms and tricks, this is an enjoyable whodunit with engaging research twists that keep you guessing until the end. If you enjoy genealogical fiction and Ruth Rendell mysteries, you'll find this a pleasing page-turner'
Family Tree

The Orange Lilies
(The Forensic Genealogist #3)

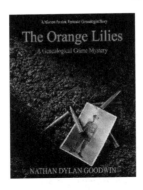

Morton Farrier has spent his entire career as a forensic genealogist solving other people's family history secrets, all the while knowing so little of his very own family's mysterious past. However, this poignant Christmastime novella sees Morton's skills put to use much closer to home, as he must confront his own past, present and future through events both present-day and one hundred years ago. It seems that not every soldier saw a truce on the Western Front that 1914 Christmas...

'The Orange Lilies sees Morton for once investigating his own tree (and about time too!). Moving smoothly between Christmas 1914 and Christmas 2014, the author weaves an intriguing tale with more than a few twists - several times I thought I'd figured it all out, but each time there was a surprise waiting in the next chapter... Thoroughly recommended - and I can't wait for the next novel'
Lost Cousins

'Morton confronts a long-standing mystery in his own family—one that leads him just a little closer to the truth about his personal origins. This Christmas-time tale flashes back to Christmas 1914, to a turning point in his relatives' lives. Don't miss it!'
Lisa Louise Cooke

The America Ground
(The Forensic Genealogist #4)

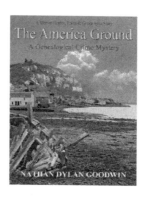

Morton Farrier, the esteemed English forensic genealogist, had cleared a space in his busy schedule to track down his own elusive father finally. But he is then presented with a case that challenges his research skills in his quest to find the killer of a woman murdered more than one hundred and eighty years ago. Thoughts of his own family history are quickly and violently pushed to one side as Morton rushes to complete his investigation before other sinister elements succeed in derailing the case.

'As in the earlier novels, each chapter slips smoothly from past to present, revealing murderous events as the likeable Morton uncovers evidence in the present, while trying to solve the mystery of his own paternity. Packed once more with glorious detail of records familiar to family historians, *The America Ground* is a delightfully pacey read'
Family Tree

'Like most genealogical mysteries this book has several threads, cleverly woven together by the author - and there are plenty of surprises for the reader as the story approaches its conclusion. A jolly good read!'
Lost Cousins

The Spyglass File
(The Forensic Genealogist #5)

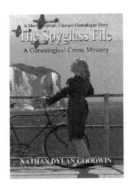

Morton Farrier was no longer at the top of his game. His forensic genealogy career was faltering and he was refusing to accept any new cases, preferring instead to concentrate on locating his own elusive biological father. Yet, when a particular case presents itself, that of finding the family of a woman abandoned in the midst of the Battle of Britain, Morton is compelled to help her to unravel her past. Using all of his genealogical skills, he soon discovers that the case is connected to The Spyglass File—a secretive document which throws up links which threaten to disturb the wrongdoings of others, who would rather its contents, as well as their actions, remain hidden forever.

'If you like a good mystery, and the detective work of genealogy, this is another mystery novel from Nathan which will have you whizzing through the pages with time slipping by unnoticed'
Your Family History

'The first page was so overwhelming that I had to stop for breath...Well, the rest of the book certainly lived up to that impressive start, with twists and turns that kept me guessing right to the end... As the story neared its conclusion I found myself conflicted, for much as I wanted to know how Morton's assignment panned out, I was enjoying it so much that I really didn't want this book to end!'
Lost Cousins

The Missing Man
(The Forensic Genealogist #6)

It was to be the most important case of Morton Farrier's career in forensic genealogy so far. A case that had eluded him for many years: finding his own father. Harley 'Jack' Jacklin disappeared just six days after a fatal fire at his Cape Cod home on Christmas Eve in 1976, leaving no trace behind. Now his son, Morton must travel to the East Coast of America to unravel the family's dark secrets in order to discover what really happened to him.

'One of the hallmarks of genealogical mystery novels is the way that they weave together multiple threads and this book is no exception, cleverly skipping across the generations - and there's also a pleasing symmetry that helps to endear us to one of the key characters...If you've read the other books in this series you won't need me to tell you to rush out and buy this one'
Lost Cousins

'Nathan Dylan Goodwin has delivered another page-turning mystery laden with forensic genealogical clues that will keep any family historian glued to the book until the mystery is solved'
Eastman's Online Genealogy Newsletter

The Wicked Trade
(The Forensic Genealogist #7)

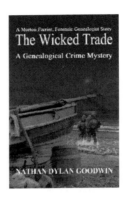

When Morton Farrier is presented with a case revolving around a mysterious letter written by disreputable criminal, Ann Fothergill in 1827, he quickly finds himself delving into a shadowy Georgian underworld of smuggling and murder on the Kent and Sussex border. Morton must use his skills as a forensic genealogist to untangle Ann's association with the notorious Aldington Gang and also with the brutal killing of Quartermaster Richard Morgan. As his research continues, Morton suspects that his client's family might have more troubling and dangerous expectations of his findings.

'Once again the author has carefully built the story around real places, real people, and historical facts - and whilst the tale itself is fictional, it's so well written that you'd be forgiven for thinking it was true'
Lost Cousins

'I can thoroughly recommend this book, which is a superior example of its genre. It is an ideal purchase for anyone with an interest in reading thrillers and in family history studies. I look forward to the next instalment of Morton Farrier's quest!'
Waltham Forest FHS

Printed in Great Britain
by Amazon